FIRE IN THE HOLE

FIRE IN THE HOLE

Cornbread Mafia Book One

NINIE HAMMON

STERLING & STONE

Chapter One

WHIPPOORWILL, whippoorwill!
   Whippoorwill!

Nathaniel and Riley Hannacker heard the bird call out in the trees and they both froze — because it wasn't in the trees and it wasn't a bird.

It wasn't even a very good imitation of one, but it was the best Joe-Joe could do. It wasn't like the little boy, the son of one of Nate's cousins, had had much practice. In all the months they'd paid him two bits a day to sit beside the lane on the bank of Possum Creek fishing, he'd only twice sounded an alarm. Both false alarms, of course, but it was his job to alert Nate and his grandson if anybody, *anybody at all* came down Stedman Lane.

And it was *their* job, their duty, to "carry the word," to let anybody else who might be out in the woods engaged in a similar activity know that "the law's in" — or at least might be — and they were about to be ambushed.

When Riley looked the question at Nate, Nate nodded and Riley lifted his chin and let out a cry. It couldn't rightly be called yelling. It was a high-pitched yodel with words in it that carried for miles. The words were unintelligible if you didn't already know what they were. Nate knew.

"Fire in the hole!"

It was a phrase adapted generations ago from their coal mining brothers, of course, where it was used to indicate that the fuse on a powder charge had been lit and it was about to explode.

In the world of moonshining, it meant the same thing that carefully spaced shotgun blasts did, but Nate had not brought his shotgun with him today. Didn't really need it the way Riley could yell. That particular skill was a source of pride among moonshiners and Riley's was the best Nate'd ever heard. He'd swear you could hear that boy's voice from Callison County all the way to the Tennessee line.

Nate glanced at the pipe on the still. There was smoke trailing up into the sky from it, but not very much. It'd be hard to see on a hazy day like today, and even harder to determine where it was coming from. It wasn't often a still was discovered by following the smoke from it anyway. If the law found a still, it was because they'd followed the moonshiner to the location and were just waiting until enough alcohol had been produced to justify a bust — enough so the case would hold up in court.

Nate certainly wasn't concerned for himself. He'd been busted before and reckoned he'd be busted again. But Riley was another thing entirely. If the alarm was a for-real this time, they both knew what to do … slip into the trees and vanish. And they would, too, but Nate did sorely hate the thought of abandoning this still. The location was perfect. The stream ran strong all year, the water in it as clear as the spring where it gushed out of the rock. The old pot still had produced thousands of gallons of good brew for — what? Six, eight years now?

They had just removed the cover and Riley was standing on a barrel above the top of the still, stirring the beer steadily with a mash-stick to prevent scorching or sticking as the beer heated. Once it was boiling vigorously, they'd fit the big copper cap over the opening and seal it, sending alcohol-rich steam into the worm — the copper coil — to condense.

"What do you think, Papa?" Riley asked.

An alarm came so seldom, you couldn't help being startled by it, even if the chances there was really anything to be worried about were almost zero. Nate dropped the dead chestnut tree branches he was feeding into the fire box and hurried as fast as he could on his gimp knee to the spot on the far side of the waiting barrels to a break in the trees where a slice of the road was visible. The spot on the stream bank where Joe-Joe was fishing was directly below them — at the bottom of the four hundred-foot rock bluff north of where Nate had placed his still. There was no access to the top of Stedman Ridge from there, unless you were a spider. Stedman Lane, a four-mile stretch of broken asphalt and potholes that nobody even lived on anymore, angled along the base of the knob.

Nate couldn't remember the last time he'd seen traffic of any kind on Stedman Lane. From the break in the trees, he'd be able to see if anybody actually turned off the lane onto the barely visible logging road that hadn't been used for that purpose in maybe fifty years. And even if they did, it'd be nigh on impossible for them to locate the little path that forked off the logging road halfway up the knob.

Drawing on a lifetime of caution, though, it was second nature. He never turned off the logging road onto the lane without stopping to use a tree branch to remove the imprint of the truck tires in the dirt. He never left the logging road and turned toward the trail from the same spot twice in a row, so the weeds wouldn't get permanently bent over. There remained a space of fifty yards of grown-up grass and weeds beyond the logging road before the shadow of the trail emerged in the undergrowth. And there existed no path of any kind from the trail where he left the truck parked to the site where his pot still sat couched under a limestone overhang.

He and his still hands — mostly just Riley as soon as he was old enough — hauled the bags of sugar, cakes of yeast and bushels of corn to the still on their backs. The kegs of finished product were strapped together and lowered by a winch to the creek, where Nate could drive out through the water in his truck and load them up, leaving no sign to mark his passage on the rocks.

A horn sounded before Nate made it to the break in the trees.

Beeeeep! Beep, beep, beep. Beeeeeep.

Then a black pickup truck drove into view, moving slowly along Stedman Lane, the horn blasting in long, then short beats, and a song Nate didn't know — something about an Eskimo named Quinn — blasting almost as loud from the rolled-down windows.

"You tell Willie Ray you'd be out here?"

"No sir!" Of course, Riley knew better than that.

Where a still was located, that was something you didn't talk about to *anybody*! But most of the shiners had a reasonably good idea where stills other than their own were located. Relationships would wear thin quick if they were all out here tripping over each other in the woods. Nate knew the Taggarts were working a couple of locations in the knobs out by the Sisters of Loretto Motherhouse.

The insistent beeping of the truck horn continued as the truck drove slowly down the potholed lane, trailing the

Eskimo song behind it through the muggy air like a lazy tail on a kite, getting fainter as the truck drew away from the creek.

"He's looking for me," Riley said. "Why else would he be out here honking his horn?"

Nate could think of no other explanation.

"Something's bad wrong or he wouldn't have come." Riley kept stirring, but his focus was on the sound of the beeping horn. "Something's happened."

Nate couldn't imagine what could be wrong enough to send Riley's best friend out looking for him, but it was important. *Had* to be. Important and bad. You didn't go out beating the bushes looking for somebody to tell them good news.

"You go on now," Nate said, crossing back behind the line of barrels. "I got this. You go find Willie Ray. Take the truck, then leave it in the trees by the falls."

Nate could see the boy wanted to argue, knowing as he did how hard it was for one man to keep the operation running at this stage, while the beer had just started to boil. But he said nothing, just climbed down off the barrel and handed his grandfather the stick.

Then the boy — *young man!* — took off through the trees at a loping gait, tall, slender and agile. Nate watched him go — a blond young man not heavy enough for football when he was in school, though he'd certainly filled out since. He'd played round-ball, though, had been a star shooting guard his senior year when the Callison County High School Wildcats were edged out by the Covington Catholic Colonels in the first round of the state championship basketball tournament.

Nate picked up the tree branches he'd dropped on the ground, shoved them into the fire box and climbed up onto the barrel where Riley had been standing to stir the beer, lost himself in the rhythmic activity, freeing his mind to worry about what had sent Willie Ray Taggart out looking for Riley.

"Something's bad wrong," Riley'd said, and the words had echoed in Nate's mind, bounced around in there like it was an empty whiskey barrel. That's what his older brother had said all those years ago, the day Mama'd poked the tiger. Wasn't anything else she could have done, of course, but that's what had started it all. She took on three federal agents — and one of them a *McClusky* — single-handed. Well, except for the mob.

Chapter Two

JESSICA MONAGHAN STOPPED, cocked her head to listen, but the sound was gone — if it had ever really been there to begin with. A kind of distant wail, carried high in the hazy sky. No, more of a yodel. She'd heard it before, or thought she had, a couple of times, and her old granny had told her it was moonshiners in the woods, calling out to one another. The same granny who'd told her that haints rise up out of their graves in the cemetery at midnight on Halloween — so "dasn't go near" — and that "the shadder of the mountain'll come fer ye when it's yore time."

Far as Jessie knew, neither one of those things had ever actually happened so it was a safe bet moonshiners weren't really out there in the woods yelling at each other, either. Probably just the squall of a loose alternator belt on somebody's truck — you could hear those things squeal ten miles away.

Scooping a dipper full of water out of the washtub in the back of the pickup truck, she closed her eyes and poured it slowly over the top of her head. It felt glorious, plastering her short blond hair down on her skull and dripping off her nose. Then she shook her head, flinging water all around like a dog getting out of the creek, turned back to the cooler of drinking water sitting on the tailgate of the truck and began filling a plastic cup. The water was still cool, but not cold as it'd been this morning when she'd packed the whole thing with ice, no water at all, because it'd melt.

She drank the whole cup down in one long gulp, and began to refill it, squinting up into the glaring sun that hadn't yet dropped down behind the knob to the west.

Knob, not mountain.

Though the real mountains of Eastern Kentucky were next-door neighbors, Callison County was not in Appalachia. It lay in a belt of almost-a-mountain hills that swung down out of Indiana and made a U-turn in central Kentucky a hundred miles or so west of the Cumberlands. The massive hills the locals called "knobs" would surely have been considered mountains but for the taller Eastern Kentucky mountains so close by for comparison. The gigantic knobs created a network of picturesque valleys, deep, secluded hollows and sheltered meadows tucked away from view, all linked together by a web of narrow, winding roads that meandered lazily among the giant hills in no particular hurry to take anybody anywhere.

The knobs that stood sentinel in Callison County set it apart from counties to the north where thoroughbred colts played tag in paddocks guarded by miles of pristine white fences. That's what the tourists came to see. The rubber-neckers drove down the interstates gawking at horse farms. But the real heart of Kentucky beat in its center, in Callison County.

She'd heard somewhere that this had been one of the hottest Augusts in Kentucky history — with no break today, which technically wasn't August but September 1st.

Of course it was good for the burley, kept the leaves from getting damp and molding, and this being her and David's very first tobacco crop, Jessie was grateful for the favorable growing conditions. Spring hadn't been too wet, summer hadn't been too dry, and hot now when they were housing. It was a bumper crop, alright, but so was everybody else's, which meant the warehouses'd be full and the buyers walking down through the stacks would pay top dollar, whatever that turned out to be since—

"I thought you were getting us some water," David called out from inside the barn.

Jessie clipped the spigot on the water cooler shut — "Hold your horses, I'm coming" — picked up the other cup she'd filled, and headed with them into the barn.

Stepping out of bright sunshine into the dark interior of the barn produced a burst of sparkles in front of her eyes, so that the forms of her husband and her brother were only shapes in a puddle of deeper darkness.

"Now that's more like it," Davie said, reaching for one of the cups. Lanny took the other and they both turned them up and drank the contents in one gulping slurp. It was at least ninety-five, maybe hotter than that outside, and she didn't want to hazard a guess at how hot it was up there in the dim top of the black barn. She was in a tank top and cut-off shorts and she was slathered in sweat. Both the men were shirtless, their bare backs shiny, jeans filthy.

They'd had the long-sleeved-shirt conversation again this morning, her Hail Mary effort, though she knew even as the words left her mouth that it was a lost cause. Davie would have stripped down buck naked if that would have kept him cool — they all would have — and given that she was certainly the only woman in the county housing tobacco with the men, that would have provided interesting conversation around supper tables from Bardstown to Danville. But David was in the most danger of getting nicotine poisoning. Jessie was working on the top rail — David was a little hinky about heights so she and Lanny took turns balancing on the beam forty feet above the barn floor. Because David was working on the middle rail, the tobacco leaves dragged over his shoulders, his sweaty back absorbing the nicotine off the leaves every time he took the stick from Lanny on the ground and handed it up to Jessie.

Nicotine poisoning was nasty. He'd gotten a big enough dose yesterday to make his head hurt, even though she'd poured water over his head and rinsed off his back on every break. Last summer, one of the hands had to be rushed to the hospital, totally out of it in the bed of the pickup truck, crazy, held down by two other men because he was trying to punch them all out. He'd puked his guts up all night, hooked up to IV solutions to replace the liquid he'd sweated and heaved. Had been unable to work for two days. And David didn't have time to lay off for two days, not now with the crop so near housed.

House is a noun, not a verb, young lady.

She recalled the English teacher when she was in junior high school — some dude from Aways From Here for sure — pointing that out the first time somebody'd told him about his daddy working in the barn.

The verb "to house" — loading tobacco sticks into the barn to dry. Might not be a verb in anybody else's world, but wasn't a farmer anywhere she knew who didn't use it as one.

She liked words, always had her nose in a book, had dreams of writing herself one day ... well, after she and David had a family and the kids were all grown and out on their own.

David extended the cup to her. "More water, woman.

Chop, chop." She merely lifted an eyebrow and looked at him and he amended, "Chop, chop, *pleeeeease*."

When she started for the door, he slapped her soundly on the butt.

"You'll pay for that!"

"Riiiiight."

She turned back to him. "Go ahead, underestimate me. That'll be fun."

"I'm sure this must be some kind of foreplay," Lanny said. "Not saying it ain't entertaining to watch, but how about you guys save it for the bedroom … or the kitchen table … or wherever you do whatever you do. I'm thirsty."

David chuckled, the sound warm and engaging. He loved to laugh, cut up and have fun. That was one of the reasons she'd married him. Thoughts of how much fun it would be tonight to make him pay for the butt-slap almost made her blush. Well, a sense of humor was *one* of the reasons she'd married him.

Then there was his jet-black hair, always in his eyes. His broad shoulders, bronzed and glistening now with sweat. Blue eyes an odd shade of blue. Certainly not University of Kentucky blue — David "bled red" for the University of Louisville Cardinals. But his eyes were a strange sky-blue, like the sky darkening before a storm. And he did have that cleft in his chin. She told him once it was deep enough to eat his morning cereal out of.

And he was *tall*. That mattered to Jessie more than to most girls because she'd spent her childhood towering over boys, painfully so in junior high school and even later in high school when the boys had *finally* started to grow. There weren't many boys secure enough that looking up at their prom date didn't take some of the fizz out of their sodas.

Still, she never lacked for dates — her father'd

complained he had to "beat the boys away from the door with a stick." Jessie was strikingly pretty — looked a lot like Grace Kelly — but she also stood six feet one in bare feet. She never owned her whole height if she could avoid it, always hedged with a vague "a fuzz over six feet." David, fortunately, was "a fuzz over six feet-*four*" and not the least bit intimidated by her height. Or by anything else about her.

"I like my women big," he'd say. "but delicate ..."

"One outta two ain't bad."

Jessica Monaghan was nobody's definition of delicate. She was big-boned and strong, loved working on the farm with her brothers and father when she was growing up, lifting hay bales, wrestling cranky calves and pulling stumps right alongside them.

"... and with hair I can spread on my toast in the morning." That hadn't come out right, but she knew what David meant. He told her sometimes that her blond hair was the color of butter. Other times, he said it was lemons. Or bananas. Or summer squash. Or Tweety Bird.

He'd also told her he hoped all their kids had hair like hers ... and he'd reach out and push a lock of it behind her ear — which never failed to send a jolt of ... what? Pure *lust!* — through her. Then he'd get that look in his eye which meant he intended to create one of those children right there on the spot.

As soon as Jessie stepped out of the barn into the sunlight she saw the plume of dust on the road. It was only a mile to the house, but somebody was in a serious hurry to get here.

Then she had an awful feeling in her gut. That happened to her sometimes and she hated it — a sudden sense of foreboding that turned the world gray. Instead of taking the empty cups to the cooler, she stood there watching as the rooster tail approached.

It was Mama!

She turned and called out into the barn.

"Davie, your mama's coming down the road like a bat outta hell."

David arrived at her side as the old green pickup slid to a stop in a fog of dust beside the barn. Mama jumped out, her hair a tangle of black and gray from the wind. And the look on her face …

Something was wrong. Bad wrong.

Chapter Three

1923

"SOMETHING'S BAD WRONG." That's what Johnny cries out when he bursts through the door, almost bowling little Nathaniel over.

He's panting, slathered with sweat, looks like he's run all the way to the house from the hollow where Pa, Uncle Pete, Pa's other brother, and various cousins operate the largest of the three Hannacker family stills.

"Ain't nobody there, Mama." Johnny leans over with his hands on his knees, trying to catch his breath. "Not nobody." Gasp! "They all musta cut and run."

Mama's face registers a flash of emotion before that mask of calm certainty settles back over her features. In that flash, Nathaniel sees it, though. Mama's afraid. He is the youngest, so maybe the others had seen it before, but in all his six years of life, Nathaniel hadn't never seen his mama scared.

But he sees the rest of it, too. Another emotion, one his mother keeps bottled up inside, like maybe she fears it'll burst out into the world and she won't ever get control of it again. Anger. Rage. Nate has never seen it on her face, but he'd heard it in her voice lots of times when she and Pa talked at night, soft so's the young'uns wouldn't hear. Of course they did hear. There were four Hannacker kids — Johnny

14

the oldest and Nate the youngest and two sisters in between — in a three-bedroom house. Wasn't no way in that house for anybody to keep secrets.

"Sheriff Landry was one thing but these new … these — they're … they're gangsters, that's what they are." Mama's voice had an edge to it even in a whisper.

"They got badges and we don't so that makes them right and us wrong," Pa always said.

Oh, they'd both admit right up front that the Hannackers broke the law — just like the Taggarts and the Jamisons, and the Mattinglys … and everybody else they knew. Law said they's supposed to pay taxes on the liquor they made and they flat out refused to do it, wouldn't hand their hard-earned money over to the government for … for what? They needed that money to feed their families. They were barely getting by as it was. They needed that alcohol to make cough syrup and all manner of other remedies. The law said they couldn't sell liquor in the counties where the folks had voted dry — which was crazy because those folks were the best customers, especially the Baptists and Methodists in Taylor County — every last one of them had a hollow leg.

And they weren't doing nothing wrong. Illegal, yes, but it wasn't wrong. There was a big difference between the two.

There was God's law and there was man's law and they wasn't breaking God's law. A thing wasn't wrong unless it broke God's law.

Father Calloway at St. Dominic's made it real clear to his parishioners what God's law was. Wasn't a single one of them who didn't know for lead pipe certain what kinda behavior God required of his people. It was serious business, obeying the laws of God. You didn't steal, or lie, or covet or do murder. Do a thing like that, break the laws of God, and you'd answer to God on Judgement Day and you'd pay for your sins in Hell.

But wasn't nowhere on that list that said you couldn't make liquor out of the corn you'd grown on the land God give you, warmed in the sun he sent to shine on you and watered by the rain he sent to make your fields fertile. Wasn't nowhere said drinking alcohol was a sin, neither — the first miracle Jesus performed was turning water into wine!

It wasn't even so much that they broke man's law. They just ignored it because it didn't apply to them. Oh, you could call them lawbreakers if you liked, they'd accept that. But they wasn't criminals. The difference might be splitting hairs to some but it was an important distinction.

Sheriff Landry'd understood the distinction. It was his job to enforce the laws of man and he was an honorable person who done his job best as he could. You could respect a man like that. If he caught you with a still, he'd arrest you on the spot. Take your still apart and pour out your good corn liquor on the ground. My, but it did hurt to see him do that.

Whoever he'd caught — Pa or one of the neighbors — would pitch in to help the sheriff most times because it was hard work to dismantle a still and they couldn't just stand around and watch him do it all by himself. Then he'd toss the pieces of it in the woods, scattered all around and give them a date they was supposed to show up in court and they'd be there for the judge to set their fine, maybe lock them up in jail for thirty and sometimes as long as ninety days, but that didn't happen very often. If the sentence fell during planting or harvest season, the judge would allow you to serve it on weekends so's you could get your crop set or out of the field. Judges understood, too. First offenders who were sentenced to prison rather than jail were almost always eligible for parole after serving a third of the sentence. The more strikes you had against you, the longer the term. In prison, the "farmer-outlaws" got better medical and dental care than they ever got at home, ate wholesome — without the damage to their livers of sampling their own brew. But most important, prison was the best place in the world to learn the craft of making liquor, with the more experienced in the group teaching the younger how to make a better product.

Truth was, the sheriff didn't make many moonshining arrests

because he didn't try very hard. Some sheriffs in other counties did —
depended mostly on whether you was in a dry county or a wet county.
Taylor County Sheriff Simon Warton was a man on a mission to
save the world from the evils of demon rum — encouraged by all the
Baptist and Methodist churches in the county. There were lots of those
— Pa knew 'cause he delivered jugs to the back porches of their elders
and deacons about once a week.

But any fool could take a look at the scar on Sheriff Warton's
arm and know he had personal knowledge of the craft of brewing
whiskey. It was a burn scar, the kind you got from a steam leak in a
still. And it might be Sheriff Landry'd made a jug or two in his time,
too. Nathaniel didn't know about things like that. But he did know the
man had got elected by people like Pa to keep the peace, and brewing
whiskey in the woods didn't hurt nobody.

But that was before Prohibition.

Nathaniel had heard the word his whole life, spoken in harsh
tones, spit out like whoever was saying it didn't like the taste of it in
his mouth.

Prohibition made it illegal to make liquor, to sell it, to drink it.
Any kind, even if you's willing to pay the taxes on it. Somebody said
they closed two hundred distilleries in one night and more'n a thousand
breweries, threw thousands of hardworking people out of their jobs.
And making whiskey was all they knew how to do, it was the reason
the families had come to this country in the first place — to brew fine
alcohol.

That wasn't all Prohibition did. It set the whole federal govern-
ment up against the moonshiners and they enforced their laws by
sending out "prohibition agents" like cockroaches all over the country,
strangers who didn't know a living soul in the communities where
they operated or some local lowlife willing to turn against his own.
The government give them rascals badges and guns and didn't care
what they did or didn't do so long as they hauled in barrels of
whiskey to pour out on the ground in front of the courthouse, stand
there and get their pictures made, showing off. And the poor fella they

beat senseless before they threw him in jail — wasn't nobody taking his picture.

They were the outlaws, the prohibition agents was, and if they'd caught Pa and Uncle Pete — they'd haul them off to Brewster and … no telling what they'd do.

Mama stands still and silence gathers around her, not a sound of any kind except Johnny gasping for breath. All the kids are scared, but none of them show it. They just stand in the kitchen, watching Mama. She stands quiet, both hands on her big belly, like maybe she's trying to soothe the little one inside. No, little ones. Least that's what Granny Thomas'd said in church on Sunday. "Why look a'here. 'Pears to me Lenora Hannacker's got more'n one bun in the oven this time."

"Hitch up, Oscar," Mama suddenly tells Johnny, and the faraway look has left her eyes. "Marianne, you help me get the kids loaded up. We're going after your pa."

Chapter Four

RILEY HANNACKER REACHED his grandfather's old truck, hidden behind a laurel bush in the trees, at a dead run. He'd been coming downhill, leaping each step and he banged his knee painfully when he slammed into the back of the truck. It was the same knee he'd hurt playing basketball, the reason why he'd had to ride the bench the first part of his senior year, and only got to play with the varsity at the end because he lied about how bad it hurt, iced it down in his room every night so Papa wouldn't see the swelling.

He gritted his teeth, squeezed his eyes and wrinkled up his face in a grimace of pain, and hopped around on his other foot, wanting to curse but bound by the silence that was second nature in the woods near a still.

Putting all his weight on his right leg, Riley limped around the truck and got in, started it, and pulled out from behind the laurel bush and through the weeds to the path which lead to the logging road that veered off Perkins Lane. Using his left foot to work the clutch hurt for a little while, but he barely noticed the pain in his knee, was so concentrated on finding out what in the world could possibly have sent Willie Ray Taggart out looking for him.

Willie Ray was Riley's best friend. They'd grown up together, Riley more or less adopted by the huge Taggart clan. Willie Ray was one of ten children, four boys and six girls, and his mother always joked that she didn't even notice when Riley ate dinner with the family, he just sort of blended in.

Riley enjoyed the loud, boisterous, rowdy Taggart crew. His own house was quiet. Just him and his grandfather. That's all there had been since Grandma Abigail had died five years ago. Just the two of them, "batching" Papa called it.

In the herd of Taggart offspring, two stuck out — Willie Ray, because of his red hair and freckles and his loud, often crude but almost always funny stream-of-consciousness babble. And Andy, a year older, because he was the polar opposite. He was blond, the Nordic kind of blond that made his eyebrows and eyelashes almost vanish, like he didn't have any. Willie Ray barely made it out of school, scooting by with C-minuses so he could play football and party with his friends. Andy had graduated the year before as the valedictorian of the class of 1966. He was studious and quiet — not shy, though. He might not even have been all that quiet, with Willie Ray around, loud, joking, cutting up and holding the spotlight squarely on himself, it was easy to forget about the quieter ones of the bunch.

Andy had a full-time job at Bourbon Cooperage, making whiskey barrels for the distilleries. He'd been saving up for college before Emily got … before he and Emily'd decided to get married.

There were six sisters, Sue Ann, Betty Jo, Lorileigh, Amy, Cora and Martha Lynn, and another brother Zeke, who was 14. They filled up a whole loud row at St. Dominic every Sunday.

Counted with LeRoy Taggart's clan were the closest Taggart cousins—the five children of Horace Taggart, LeRoy's brother — three boys and two girls and every last one of them had some shade of red hair. The whole crew lived in each other's pockets.

It was because of Willie Ray's tendency to overreact, dramatize and otherwise make mountains out of molehills that one part of Riley didn't believe anything all that terrible had happened. Willie Ray had flown off the handle about something and had to grab Riley and pull him into the center of whatever storm he was either kicking up or getting drenched by.

Still, even Willie Ray wouldn't …

It was the secret that wasn't a secret, the it's-never-talked-about thing that everybody knew without having to say it. The Taggarts had several stills — a half dozen, maybe more. Papa had once run five or six all by himself, just hired still hands, but in the past couple of years he'd gotten more involved in his "other business ventures." Now he only ran the still on the bluff above Stedman Lane and another one deep in the woods, far out behind the house, one you couldn't get to without crossing Hannacker property — so you better have a search warrant. As the moonshine market declined, the bootlegging business — providing alcohol, both taxed whiskey and untaxed moonshine to dry counties — grew. But clearly he was making more money doing what he called "odd jobs" than he'd been making on moonshine. Riley knew what those jobs were, of course, though Papa never said.

Every moonshiner knew in general terms whose stills were where, but it wasn't like you could just drop in on somebody working a still, pull up a chair and have a cigarette and a beer. Certainly, Willie Ray knew where to go looking for Riley, a general sense of the right spot. But Willie Ray was busy most afternoons, dealing cards in the back room of Bert's Tavern in the perpetual poker game that had operated non-stop for Riley's whole life. It would have taken something pretty big to have pried him away from it. Of course, this weekend was Andy Taggart's wedding at St. Martha's and maybe they were rehearsing today, and Willie Ray had taken off for that. If that was the case, though, it was even worse. If Willie Ray had bailed out of the rehearsal for his brother's wedding, actually drove down Stedman Lane blatting his horn like that trying to find Riley …

Riley bounced off the logging road back onto the lane and took off in the direction Willie Ray had gone. Stedman Lane was only four miles long, went from nowhere, to nowhere, through nowhere, as many roads in Callison County did. When Willie Ray got to the end of it, he'd turn around and come back this way.

Riley heard the honking ahead and rounded a curve to meet Willie Ray in his father's black pickup truck, poking down the road, laying on the horn — *Beeeeep! Beep, beep, beep. Beeeeeep.*

Willie Ray saw him and stopped honking, but didn't burst into a huge smile. Just pulled up until the trucks were side by side in the middle of the road, one pointed south, the other pointed north.

"What in the world—?" That was all Riley got out before Willie Ray blurted it out.

"They called up the unit."

Unit? Riley's mind stumbled. What unit? They *who* called up *what*—?

"The orders come in when I was at the armory this morning. I seen it on the sheet. I don't know if they've announced it yet, but I read it — right there, plain as day. The president called up the National Guard, the whole 151st Infantry Battalion in Bardstown and the 138th Artillery batteries in Elizabethtown and Carrolton, too."

He paused, tried a bravado smile and gave up on it halfway through.

"Pack up your sunscreen, Riley boy. They're fixin' to send our asses to Vi -et- nam."

Chapter Five

1923

LENORA HANNACKER TAKES the reins of the big gelding and slaps them on his back and he takes out at his own pace down the lane toward the road. Oscar doesn't have but one speed — plodding — but the animal could maintain that pace from sunup to sundown without faltering.

Lenora knew she could count on Oscar. He was one of the absolutes in the Hannackers' lives. He was dependable, and dependability mattered. The older Lenora got, the more hardship she had to suffer, the more she came to understand that there were glamorous virtues — and they mattered, they did. Courage. Honesty. Loyalty. She would teach those virtues to her children as her mama had taught her. But the red-headed stepchild of virtues, it seemed to Lenora, was dependability. Can somebody count on you? Will you do what you say you'll do when you say you'll do it, or do you see obligation as bendable and stretchable, pliable so that a good excuse is on the same level of virtue as doing what you said you'd do in the first place?

Lenora's children could count on her. And she could count on Samuel. Together they'd made a life for their family, carved a farm out of the wooded land, removing the trees one stump at a time with a team of mules. They'd married when she was fourteen and he was

24

sixteen, set out together to live in the little dirt-floor, one-room cabin he'd built beside Flat Rock Creek. She'd birthed her first child there in that cabin — alone because Sam had been out in the field and didn't hear her cries. The little girl was born blue, never breathed, never cried. By the time the neighbor women were summoned to help, it was all over, and the best they could do for her was get Father Calloway, and help her bundle the baby up in a soft quilt, put her in the little box Sam built to hold her, and lay her to rest in holy ground at the Saint Dominic Catholic Church Cemetery in Crawford beneath a white cross that said Martha Ann Hannacker.

Two other crosses had joined hers over the years as their family grew. Lenora didn't think about the losses — almost never — but as she drove the wagon loaded with her children into Brewster to see what had become of Samuel and Peter, she did. Her mind went there unbidden, and she was once again a teenage girl lying in sheets soaked with blood, cradling the dead baby she had just brought into the world.

She'd grown up that day. Oh, she'd thought she was an adult when she got married, carrying her first child and all. But she crossed over to adulthood from childhood alone in the cabin, rocking the cold bundle in her arms, singing a lullaby the child couldn't hear.

Now her live children are depending on her, counting on her to make things right. Because if federal agents have busted Sam and Pete with their still, they could take her husband away from her for … she didn't know how long. But she did know that the family would not survive without him. Without the meat he brought home from hunting, without his sunup to sundown slaving in the fields to grow their garden and their corn crop to use to make alcohol. When it got cold this winter, her children would go hungry unless she — Lenora Hannacker — could somehow make things right today.

Nathaniel sits beside her on the front seat, leaning into her. And she knows her youngest is desperately fighting back tears. He's the most tenderhearted of all of them, the one who looks just like his father, but for the gray eyes he'd gotten from her and the blond hair that graced her own head and those of both her daughters. She knows the child is struggling to be strong and grownup, like his older brother Johnny, who rides along beside the wagon bareback on the other draft horse, Carrot, as the old mare plods along beside her mate.

"Are they gonna … take Pa away?" Nathaniel finally asks, expressing the fear in the hearts of every one of her children.

"No, they are not, Nathaniel." Hearing the firmness in her voice helps to quell the fear in her belly. They won't. She won't let them.

When they pull into town, she can hear the crowd noises from Main Street, and she hands the reins of the horses to Johnny and instructs him to see to the animals. She takes Nathaniel and the girls with her, rushing toward the sounds.

And there they are — on the top of the steps leading up to the courthouse, Sam and Pete and three men with beards, two of them holding rifles. A crowd has gathered round and is growing bigger as Lenora shoves her way through it to the front.

She is big with the baby — maybe babies — she carries and people give way before her. It's unseemly for a woman in the family way like Lenora to be out in public like this, and her being here now makes a statement. Apparently, they've already dumped the barrels of whiskey in the street because the sweet smell of mash is in the air, and now they're hauling the two prisoners to the cars parked out front, where they'll be taken away to the regional jail in Bardstown.

Sam has been beaten. Both his eyes are black, his lips split. Pete has blood running down his face from a cut on his forehead.

And then she turns her attention to the men with the rifles and she can't catch her breath. The man giving the orders, fat and ugly, with a cigar clenched between his teeth, is Rooster McClusky!

Oh, dear God in Heaven! What she'd heard but didn't believe — it's true. The McClusky family is working both sides of the fence now. Rooster McClusky has signed on as a prohibition agent while his brother Digger McClusky is out in the woods brewing moonshine!

The generations-old loathing for the McCluskys wells up in her chest and almost gags her. It is matched by rage — and terror. She's not afraid anymore that Sam will be taken to jail. With Rooster

McClusky in charge, Sam and Pete won't make it to jail alive. They will be executed, shot "trying to escape."

If she allows her husband to be hauled away from here, she will never see him again.

"... is what happens when you break the law," Rooster says, grabs Sam by his shirt and starts to drag him across the porch to the steps. When he does, the crowd gives a low grumble and the two men with rifles bring them up, pointing at the crowd.

"Now out of our way," Rooster says. "We're taking these prisoners to—"

"They didn't do nothin'," someone calls out.

"Leave them be," someone else says.

"You ain't got no right to come in here waving them guns and—"

Rooster interrupts. "That's where you're wrong." He pulls open his coat to display his badge. "This here gives me the right to do whatever I see fit to enforce the law. And brewing whiskey is against the law."

"Your family's brewing it — why don't you go arrest them?" somebody calls out. The crowd, which is growing bigger, with people crowding in behind Lenora, grumbles in agreement.

Rooster takes the cigar out of his mouth and spits on the porch. "All of you, get out of my way."

Lenora speaks but the grumble of the crowd drowns her out. So she takes a step up onto the bottom step of the porch and speaks again, into a beat of silence that outlines her words.

"No."

The fat man looks down at her, clearly surprised that a woman, particularly one in her condition ...

"What'd you say?"

"No."

"Who are you?"

"The woman you're going to have to shoot."

He pauses for a beat before he recognizes her. "Go back home where you oughta be, you don't belong—"

Lenora speaks to the man on Rooster's left, his rifle held at the ready. He's a stranger, clearly not from Callison County.

"You come here today to kill somebody?" she asks him.

He is belligerent, wants to intimidate, but hesitates — she is a woman, after all, with child. *Then he says, "If I have to, yeah. I'll kill somebody."*

"Then you best get after it. Point that rifle at me and shoot me down like a dog in the street, kill me and my babies, *'cause that's the only way you're gonna keep me from collecting my husband and taking him home."*

She takes another step up. Four more to the top.

McClusky calls out to the crowd, "Somebody do something with this Hannacker woman before she gets hurt." He nods, and both men with rifles lift them to their shoulders and point them at her.

"You gonna have to shoot me, too," calls out a voice in the crowd. Lenora turns to see her sister-in-law, Pete's wife, Aunt Audrey, a tiny woman, not much bigger than a child, pushing her way forward.

"Fine, I'll drop you both!"

"And me!" It's a small voice from behind Lenora where she'd parked the children. It's Nathaniel.

"And me ..."

"Me ..."

"Me, too."

Before she can stop them, all four of her children have surrounded her on the steps.

Aunt Audrey's brood of five crowds up around her, too.

McClusky roars at the crowd. "You get them women and them kids out of my way, or I will shoot them down."

"How many bullets you got?" calls out Lenora's closest friend, Wilma Taggart, and she steps up onto the porch.

Suddenly, the whole crowd is moving, crowding in around them — the women first, and then the men, yelling, "You'll have to shoot me" and "I ain't moving unless you put a bullet in me."

McClusky is rattled now. The two others are clearly scared, leveling their rifles at the crowd, swinging them back and forth, trying to cover everybody who has stepped forward. Then a voice calls out from behind one of the cars parked out front.

"You shoot anybody, it'll be the last shot you ever take."

All heads turn that way.

Mose Taggart is leaned over the hood of a car, his rifle leveled at the front man on the porch.

"You ain't gonna have time to shoot nobody," cries somebody else, and suddenly weapons appear all over the crowd, pistols and rifles, aimed at the men on the porch.

"Now, you wait just a minute here," Rooster growls. "You're threatening sworn federal officers, interfering with us doing our duty. That's a crime."

Lenora turns and calls out to the crowd, "Anybody seen any federal officers here today?"

The crowd responds with a resounding, unified "No."

"I'm taking my husband home. You'll have to shoot me to stop me. And when you do, all three of you will be dead men."

"And we'll bury your bodies so far up a holler won't nobody ever find 'em," Mose Taggart calls out.

"You wasn't never here," Audrey Hannacker tells Rooster. "We got ..." she turns and looks around, "... what? Sixty, seventy witnesses who'll testify in a court of law they never seen none of the three of you."

"You think you can get away with this, that you can threaten federal officers—?"

"What federal officers?" she asks. "We don't see no federal officers."

"All we see is bottom-feeding scum who turn on their own kind." Lenora grinds the words out between clenched teeth.

"We'll come back here with fifty men, a hundred—"

"Come back with a hundred-fifty." Billy Bynam steps forward, a shotgun cradled in his arms. "It don't make no difference. Nothing happened here today." He gestures toward Sam and Pete. "These men

— they been out of town for two weeks, ain't that right?" Three or four dozen people shout support.

"There ain't no still in the woods, neither, no evidence to prove they was ever brewing whiskey," Lenora says. "At least, there won't be by the time you come back looking for it."

"You people really think you can—?"

"Here's what we think." Mose Taggart speaks in a soft voice full of menace. He walks around the car he'd been sighting behind, his rifle in the crook of his arm. "We think we got you outnumbered twenty to one, maybe thirty to one. It's your word against ours." He stops, takes his rifle in both hands but doesn't point it at them. He speaks directly to the two men on the porch who are holding rifles, the strangers. "Know this for a true fact — if either one of you ever sets foot back in this county again, you won't leave alive. Won't be no bodies for your families to claim, neither. You'll just vanish."

The two men lower their rifles slowly, point them at the ground.

Lenora walks the rest of the way up the steps, takes Sam by the arm and helps him back down, as Audrey does the same with Pete.

Rooster McClusky is fit to be tied, calls out threats as they walk away, but they are empty threats. There are easier places to enforce the prohibition laws than Callison County, Kentucky, and two of the agents here today will likely be requesting duty in one of those places first thing tomorrow morning.

Not the third, though. The third has roots deep in Callison County soil.

"You gonna be sorry," Rooster calls after them. "You gonna regret this. You're gonna pay."

"They done give a badge to a snake in the grass," Sam tells Lenora through his split lips. "McClusky ain't never gonna let it ride."

"No, he ain't. I s'pect we done poked a tiger."

Chapter Six

RILEY AND WILLIE RAY drove up in front of St. Martha's Catholic Church and pulled into the parking lot. They recognized all the cars. They'd said almost nothing on the ride into the little town of Cade's Crossing after Riley left his grandfather's truck in the spot where he could climb down to it. Didn't talk about what they ought to do now or where they ought to go. It was obvious. If the wedding rehearsal was still going on, that's where everybody'd be. The whole thing was so much like getting punched in the stomach, Riley couldn't seem to gather enough air to speak. And for once, Willie Ray had been silent, too.

"I didn't think it'd be over yet," Willie Ray said as he pulled into a space beside the little Chevy his brother Andy drove.

"You weren't supposed to be here?" Riley asks.

Willie Ray shrugged. "Yeah, but J.D.'s the best man." J.D. was the oldest of the Taggart boys. He worked for an ambulance service, was training to be an EMT. "Me and Zeke are just groomsmen and Zeke could tell me where to stand." Zeke was fourteen, the youngest boy. There were other Taggarts, of course, but they were girls.

Riley'd figured Willie Ray hadn't wanted to leave the card game.

"So you weren't going to show up at the rehearsal at all?"

Willie Ray got defensive. "I was too. But I went over to the armory this morning to see if they'd posted the training dates yet and then …" He let the rest go. "Then, I figured to come get you, that you'd … you know, you'd want to know."

Riley supposed that if he'd seen the orders first, he'd have gone looking for Willie Ray, too.

They went around the building toward the wide steps leading up to the huge oak doors.

"What are you going to say?" Riley asked. It was a given, of course, that Willie Ray'd do the talking. But even Willie Ray'd be hard pressed to think of something to say about this. How did you tell your older brother, who was getting married in two days, that his honeymoon had been officially cancelled by the U.S. government?

Inside the huge doors, it was quiet and cool. Riley's every memory of church was stepping from light into half light — flickering candles, maybe — and from sweltering hot or freezing cold — into the cool, constant temperature of a big stone building. They were all like that, all the churches in the county, the little ones like Saint Martha and the big ones like Saint Augustine in Brewster or Saint Dominic in Crawford. The cool and quiet were part of the whole experience and had rubbed a deep rut in Riley Hannacker's psyche.

But the church was too quiet, unnaturally quiet, like it was deserted. When they pushed through the double doors into the sanctuary, they found it empty.

"They're here somewhere," Riley said. There were cars in the parking lot.

They headed for the fellowship hall in the basement but heard no crowd sounds as they went down the stone steps. Didn't sound like anybody was there, but as they drew near the door, Riley could hear the sound of a voice, a single voice, like from a television. Stepping out of the hallway into the back of the room, they found a crowd of silent people standing in front of the television set in the corner.

The black and white picture was snowy, but the picture was stable, not flipping over and over like those pictures of fruit Riley'd seen in the slot machine that time they drove through Vegas. The face of the man who was speaking looked vaguely familiar, but Riley would not have recognized him if his name hadn't been printed on the bottom of the screen: Secretary of Defense Clark Clifford.

Looked like Willie Ray wasn't going to have to break the news after all.

"... morning, September 1, 1968, President Lyndon Johnson ordered to active duty the 151st Infantry Battalion, Kentucky National Guard." Riley, Willie Ray and the others were all members of one of the five platoons in the Bardstown-based Charlie Company of the battalion. "Along with the 138th artillery batteries in Elizabethtown and Carrolton."

Emily Henderson burst into tears at the words and collapsed in a folding chair. Andy stepped behind the chair and put his hands on her shoulders, patting her gently.

"... were 570 Kentucky Guardsmen and 750 Kentucky Air Guardsmen. A total of five hundred-seventy Kentucky Guardsmen and approximately seven hundred-fifty Kentucky Air Guardsman are among 24,500 men ordered to active duty in 88 units across the United States."

The man kept talking but Riley didn't catch much of the rest of what he said. He was watching the reactions of the people in the crowd in front of the television — many of them fellow guardsmen, Callison County boys who trained together at the National Guard Armory in Bardstown.

"... among twenty-four thousand, five hundred men ordered to active duty in eighty-eight units across the United States ..."

A newscaster's stern face replaced the secretary of defense on the screen then and that released the crowd from their trance. As the talking head on the television explained what the call-up meant, the people in the room began to consider the reality of what it meant in their lives.

Emily was inconsolable. Both Andy and her mother stood beside the folding chair where she sat sobbing, shaking her head, borderline hysterical.

"They *can't*. Andy can't ... we booked the cruise, we have plane tickets — we paid for plane tickets!"

The others moved away from them, gave them space. Kenny Taylor, Ronnie Benson, Ben Higgs and Randy Nickel spotted Riley and Willie Ray in the back of the room.

"Can they do that, just call the unit up like that?" asked Ben Higgs. He was a little guy with a surprising voice, deep and rumbling. Father Schwartz often asked him to read the Scripture at church. He was Andy Taggart's best friend, the only one of the groomsmen not a brother.

"They just did," Ronnie said. "What are we going to ... how's Peggy supposed to milk them cows all by herself?" The Bensons ran a large dairy farm near the Washington County line, milked over three hundred head. "She liked to worked herself to death when I was at basic." All National Guardsmen were required to attend ten weeks of basic training, the same training as the active military. The Kentucky guardsmen had trained at Fort Benning, Georgia. "My uncle and cousins tried to help, but they got their own farms to run."

The ramifications took a bit to sink in. It was harvest time. Hay. Wheat. Much of the tobacco crop was still out, bright yellow fields of burley that had yet to be housed.

Kenny Taylor was the oldest man in the unit at almost thirty. He had two little kids and his wife was expecting twins any day now. He worked at a lumber company and had joined the Guard for the extra money he could make for one day a month training and two weeks of active duty a year.

Now ... there'd be extra money, wouldn't there? Of course there would. They'd be soldiers — soldiers got paid. Riley'd heard about Active Duty Pay and Hazardous Duty Pay and Family Separation allowance — things like that. He had no idea what the amounts were — or if it would be enough to replace what Kenny was making at the lumber yard? And if it wasn't ... then what? What was Kenny supposed to do, let his family starve while he slung a rifle over his shoulder and went to ... went to *war*?

Shoot, Riley'd just bought the Ford Mustang he'd had his eye on for more than a year. Papa co-signed a bank loan for the $2,500 price tag and he made the monthly payments from his Guard check, his part-time job at Bourbon Cooperage and what he made on his tobacco crop and from what Papa called "other business endeavors."

He was instantly sorry he'd considered that. He couldn't be worried about a new car when the others had such more important problems.

Randy Nickel — they called him Five Cents —

gestured with his chin toward Andy and his bride-to-be sitting in the front of the room.

"This is sure going to throw a monkey wrench into their honeymoon plans," he said.

Five Cents was the most cheerful person Riley'd ever met, an eternal optimist. His chief claim to fame, however, was that he had an imaginary friend named Tommy. "Hey, it worked with the girls in nursery school," he'd say. Tommy went everywhere with him — sat in an empty seat next to his at the dinner table. His dates had to snuggle up really close to Five Cents when he was driving, to leave room for Tommy by the door.

Willie Ray shrugged. "My bro's not gonna be the only one. There's gonna be lots of plans with wrenches in them — screwdrivers, hammers, pliers ..."

"When do we leave?" Ben wondered. "They ain't announced—"

"I seen the orders this morning," Willie Ray said. "I's at the armory and the place was a zoo. 'Parently, we train here for three weeks and then get shipped off to ... somewhere. Fort Hood, I think."

"In Oklahoma?" Ben asked.

"Texas," Five Cents said.

"What's wrong with Ft. Knox?" Ronnie said. "Even Ft. Campbell. I could come home—"

"This is active service," Riley said. "It ain't something you come home from every night."

"They're gonna send our asses to Vietnam, ain't they?" Ben said.

That stopped all conversation.

They all knew that, of course. That's why the unit had been called up. But *avoiding* going to Vietnam was the reason most of them had joined the National Guard in the first place! Everybody understood that the possibility existed the unit could be activated. But nobody believed it would.

"Vietnam," Riley repeated the word quietly, said it out loud to make it real. Saying it didn't do the trick, but the looks on his friends' faces — that made it real.

Turning to Willie Ray, Riley said, "I need to go home. I need to … you know."

What *did* he need to do exactly? He had to tell his grandfather what was going on, but he wouldn't likely be home yet, not with what was left to do to get the run in. Shoot, he had a date tonight, was supposed to pick Sherry Lynn up at seven.

He'd have to tell her, too. Though the way word spread, by sundown probably everybody in Callison County would know. The call-up would likely throw a wrench into his own plans for easing gently out of his relationship with Sherry Lynn. She was going to be upset, probably very upset by the call-up. Not the best time in the world to break up. But he had to tell her about the guard, of course, in person — his grandfather, too.

Tell them he was … well, he was going to Vietnam.

Chapter Seven

THEY WERE EATING supper at Mama Ruth's. Of course they were.

The last thing in the world Jessie wanted right now was to sit in her mother-in-law's kitchen, not eating the fried chicken Davie's mother had whipped up for them.

Jessie would give her that. The woman could cook, no doubt about it. Which could have meant that Davie was so spoiled by her expertise that he'd spend the first five years of their married life telling Jessie how whatever she'd just made wasn't "as good as Mama's."

He'd never said that. Not one time in the fifteen months they'd been married. And she'd had some complete kitchen disasters in that time. It wasn't that she didn't know how to cook. Of course she did. She'd helped her mother feed her family, and that included two big hulking brothers who could eat two large pizzas, a gallon of ice cream and a whole chocolate cake — just for supper. Jessie knew her way around a frying pan.

But Jessie hated to cook, would rather eat paint than figure out a meal plan, the answer to the daily question of what's for supper tonight. And if there was something around the farm that needed tending to, a fence that needed mending, field that needed plowing, a cow about to calve, she always got so involved in whatever that was that she forgot all about what was occurring in her kitchen. She once helped birth a lamb while chili burned on the stove — so black she had to throw the pot away. You could smell the stink for half a mile. And there was the time she left potatoes in the pressure cooker while she helped Davie set tobacco. All the water boiled away, the pressure thing on the top blew off and the safety plug melted. Had to throw the pressure cooker away, too.

Or the time she'd got busy in the garden, flat out forgot all about making supper until she looked at her watch. She'd promised Davie a lemon pie "just like your mama makes" so she'd rushed into the house, threw the ingredients together and the pan into the over. It was ready by the time Davie got home. And when they cut into it after supper and she placed a big piece on his plate, she could almost see him salivating. The meringue had turned out perfect — for a change — and the filling was, after all, the color of Jessie's hair.

He bit into a forkful of heavenly delight, tried to swallow it, but had to leap up and spit the mouthful into the sink. She tried it, spit hers out, too. In her rush to get the pie in the oven, she'd left out a rather key ingredient, especially for a lemon pie. Sugar.

The chicken on Jessie's plate now, that she imagined was looking up at her accusingly from behind the dollop of mashed potatoes, was, of course, perfect. The inside juicy, the outside crisp and flaky. The green beans were perfect, too. Cooked all afternoon with a piece of ham hock for flavoring. The salad was made from fresh vegetables. Not "fresh vegetables," like they describe on some restaurant menu. Fresh vegetables as in the tomatoes were still warm from the sun.

Jessie had to eat, at least a bit, but she was not like her best friend in high school, Shirley. Shirley had fought a losing battle with weight gain her whole life because when she was upset about something, she ate. And it was high school, so she was always upset about something. The fact she didn't have a date for the prom added twenty pounds to her already considerable butt. And it was a vicious circle because the fact that she was overweight was a constant source of heartache … which occasioned binge eating that made matters worse.

Jessie was the opposite. She couldn't eat when she was upset. Her stomach locked up. It was like she could almost feel the door leading from her esophagus, or whatever internal organ connected the mouth to the stomach, slamming shut, could hear the click of the key in the lock.

She moved her potatoes around on her plate, arranged and re-rearranged the stack of crisp chicken. Relocation was not the same as eating, though. But just this once, nobody noticed that Jessie was not a member of the clean plate club. Davie was only nibbling at his food. Mama Ruth had hardly touched a single bite.

Oh, how Jessie wanted to go home.

They couldn't leave, of course. Not after they'd sat in Ruth's living room and watched that man, Clark Clifford, make the announcement. Jessie knew Davie wouldn't leave his mother home alone after hearing a thing like that. And Jessie couldn't ask him to. No, *wouldn't* ask. If she had even an inkling of hope he'd say yes, she'd have asked alright. But there wasn't. They had to stay. Which meant they had to eat, because it was suppertime and — even now, even at a time like this, Ruth Monaghan wasn't going to miss an opportunity to prepare a meal for her only son.

Jessie made herself believe it was just because she loved him and liked "doing for him." She wouldn't let herself — at least not for long— consider the possibility that every one of those "meals at Mama's" was Ruth's opportunity to highlight the fact that she was the better cook, that she could make things "just the way Davie liked them," and Jessie was doing well to get a meal on the table at all.

Right now, all she wanted was to be home alone with Davie. Her whole gut was tied up in a knot wrapped with a shiny red bow and she needed him to hold her gently in his arms and tell her everything was going to be all right. And it *was*. Everything was going to be all right. Really.

Jessie had never wanted to believe anything more in her whole life.

They called up the guard unit.

How could they ...?

She didn't say the words, didn't plop them out into the silence between them. They'd already done that part. The how-could-they and the why-did-they and the why-this-one-and-not-some-other-guard-unit. They had worn all the subjects totally out.

But unfortunately, *now-what?* still had some miles on it. So Mama Ruth gave it a shove and the words plopped like dead fish into the plate of fried chicken in the middle of the table.

"Now what?" the old woman asked, in that almost raspy voice that always set Jessie's teeth on edge. "What are we gonna do about the tobacco and the corn and there's still another cut left to make on the hay. And the—?"

"We'll figure it out," Davie said. He reached out and squeezed Jessie's hand under the table and it was such a loving gesture that she almost burst into tears. "It's not just us. We all got the same problems. We're all going to have to work out our lives, figure them out around this thing."

Davie wasn't just being strong for his mother and his wife — both of whom, by the way, were enormously strong women who didn't need a gesture like that. But it wasn't a gesture, a "put-on" as her granny had put it. Davie was strong. Strong in every way that mattered.

As the only boy in a family of four, and the oldest, he'd stepped into his father's shoes after he died and kept the family together — without a ripple, or at least that was how it'd looked from the outside. Jessie didn't know him that well then, and as soon as she did know him that well, it was confirmed.

He was physically strong and his character was rock solid.

Character born of a Christian home, certainly — bums on pews every Sunday at Saint Ignatius on Glen Cove Road. But character born of a strength from within that made some men lean always toward the right way, shoved them in the right direction, gave them the backbone to do the right thing, even if it was the hard thing.

She and Ruth were strong, too. If ever there was a woman anywhere who had her ducks beak-to-tail-feathers all the time it was Ruth Monaghan. And maybe Jessie had that same character strength herself, but she wasn't sure she did. Like right now. If there were any way in God's green earth, any way at all — didn't matter beans if it was legal or even moral — if there were any way to keep Davie home and not let him go to war, she'd have done it. He wouldn't have. He would never have abandoned his unit. She would have, in a heartbeat.

But there was no way.

It was ten o'clock before Davie finally said they had to go, and Jessie could have sworn Ruth almost said they'd just ought to spend the night. But she didn't.

As soon as they got into the car, Jessie started to cry. Which surprised her as much as it did Davie.

"Jessie … honey …"

She grabbed hold. Sucked it up and sucked it in and made herself stop.

"Take me home. Take me home and make love to me — please!"

That was a request you didn't have to make twice to Davie Monaghan.

Chapter Eight

RILEY PULLED into the lane leading back to Sherry Lynn's house. The dirt road wound along beside a field of corn before the woods stretched down to meet it. Her house sat back in the trees, the front yard littered with kids' riding toys in various stages of disrepair. The porch swing hung behind a trellis covered in honeysuckle. When they sat together there at night making out, listening to the eech-eech of the swing and the chorus of tree frogs and crickets, the smell of roses and honeysuckle was intoxicating. Riley didn't tell her when they'd sat there last Friday night that he got turned on now every time he smelled roses and honeysuckle.

Last Friday night. A thousand years ago.

He still couldn't get his mind around it, kept imagining a different reality, that already somebody somewhere was realizing there'd been a colossal mistake. Heads would roll somewhere when whoever was in charge found out they'd gotten hundreds of people upset for nothing. The phone lines were buzzing back and forth from the office of the secretary of defense in Washington to the 151st Infantry

Battalion, Kentucky National Guard, Charlie Company command in Bardstown right now, officers demanding to know who had done it, who'd messed up the paperwork, or transposed the orders or … or something.

Sherry Lynn's front door flew open and she raced out, calling over her shoulder, "… you didn't see me. I left before you got a chance to tell me what she said."

Sherry Lynn's younger brother, Buddy, appeared in the open doorway, shouting something. Riley missed it because Sherry Lynn flung open the passenger side door and leapt into the front seat, slamming the door behind her.

"Go!" she cried. He just stared at her.

"Go, go now, go, go, go!" She looked down the driveway to the lane. "Get out of here before Mama gets back. If she catches me, she'll ground me!"

"What are …?"

"You want to go out or not — if you do, we have to leave *right now*!"

Riley hadn't even killed the engine, so he put the car in reverse and pulled back out of the driveway and turned back down the lane.

"Hurry!" she cried, not looking at him, keeping her eye on the empty lane that led to the highway.

"I cut all my morning classes to come home early and Buddy said Mama called my dorm room right after lunch — and Kim just told her, 'oh, Mrs. Bennett … Sherry Lynn left for Brewster *hours ago*!' The moron! *Mama. Had. A. Cat!*"

Sherry Lynn was starting her sophomore year at Spencerian College in Louisville, majoring in radiology technology. She already had her one-year certificate, but she wanted an associate's, maybe even a bachelor's degree.

She suddenly looked stricken.

"Crap! There she is!"

She turned to Riley. "Don't look at her! Just smile and wave and I'll make like we're having a big, important conversation."

Sherry Lynn's mother's Pontiac came down the lane toward them.

"Don't look."

He didn't look.

Sherry Lynn turned and gave her mother a quick, absent smile as the cars passed, then continued her feigned conversation with Riley. Riley didn't know if her mother bought it or not until Sherry Lynn looked out the back window and collapsed into the seat with a sigh.

"She didn't turn around." Then she urged him on. "But go on, get out to the road and let's go before she changes her mind."

Riley did as she said, turned onto the highway and gave the little Mustang the gas. It leapt down the road in that familiar burst of power that always tightened his belly with delight. He loved that car.

Where would he leave it when …? Parked at the house? He hadn't thought about what he'd do with the car.

"She'll cool off by the time I get home, but if she doesn't, I'll be stuck at home tomorrow night — can you come over?"

Without waiting for a reply, she launched into a different subject.

"I know I said we could see whichever one you wanted, but … would you mind if we went to *Valley of the Dolls* instead of *The Graduate*? They're both playing at the Balboa." The Arco drive-in had closed. They'd been there for the last movie — watched *Mary Poppins*. "*Valley of the Dolls* starts about half an hour later, but we could just drive around, or get a shake at that new place — Charlie's. It's just … I stayed up half the night finishing the book and it

is sooooo good. If the movie's even half as good …
Okay?"

She looked at him, waiting, and he realized he ought to
say something.

"Sure, fine. Whatever."

She scooted over and popped a kiss on his cheek.

"I knew you wouldn't mind!" She snuggled next to
him, not looking at his face. She hadn't noticed that Riley
had said nothing beyond monosyllabic grunts since she got
into the car. It might be half an hour before she did. That
was Sherry Lynn — bubbly and cheerful. "Vivacious" was
the word under her picture in the yearbook. She'd always
reminded Riley of the hummingbirds that flocked to the
red water vials Papa had hung on the back porch in front
of the kitchen window. The birds flitted from one to the
next, hanging there in momentary brilliance — blue and
green — moving almost so fast you couldn't track.

Sherry Lynn could be like that, moving so fast, talking
a mile a minute. And beautiful. Oh, was she *beautiful*! Eyes
the blue of one of the hummingbird's feathers, a dark blue,
so dark it almost looked purple. You could get lost in those
blue eyes. He'd asked her for a date that first time because
she was so pretty, and kept going out with her because she
was fun to be around. Unlike Willie Ray, Riley was content
with one girlfriend at a time. None of the relationships was
going anywhere anyway. He sometimes wondered if he'd
ever be able to feel anything after Jessica. He was just going
through the motions, but you had to do that. Even if you
weren't going anywhere you had to keep treading water or
you'd drown.

Leaning forward, Sherry Lynn punched the button and
the radio came on, blasting loud out of the speakers
Riley'd worked so hard to install in the back seat.

"… *it through the grapevine* …" Marvin Gaye's voice filled

the car, and Sherry Lynn joined in, making them a duet. "*Heard it through the grapevine … ta-da, ta-da … heard it through—*"

"You haven't heard yet, have you?"

It just came out, but it was as good a way to start as any. Obviously, Sherry Lynn had not heard.

She was bobbing along with the music.

"Heard what? … *you know a man ain't supposed to cry, but these tears I can't hold inside …*"

"Turn it off."

"*And I'm about to lose my mind … honey, honey, yeah …*"

Riley reached out and flipped off the radio. Sherry Lynn pulled out of her snuggle and looked at him in surprise, really looked at him for the first time since she'd gotten into the car. There was a pleat of concern between the eyebrows in her perfect face.

"What's wrong? Something's wrong. What is it?"

There was no way to say it except to say it, straight out.

"Today they … they called up the guard unit."

"Called up? What does that—?"

"Willie Ray came and got me and we went to St. Martha's where they were rehearsing for Andy's wedding. They'd stopped the rehearsal and everybody was in the basement just standing around the TV."

"Riley, what are you talking about?"

"The guy, what's his name — Clark Clifford — he said it. Read off the names in front of the cameras, how they were calling up the whole 151st Infantry Battalion. That includes Charlie Company in Bardstown. That's *us.*"

"Active service? What does that …?"

She didn't finish. She suddenly realized what it meant.

She gasped then and her hands flew to her mouth. Her blue eyes widened and filled with tears so instantly they seemed to squirt out onto her cheeks.

She shook her head. No! Denial. Yeah, Riley'd tried sailing down that river, Denial, for a lot of the afternoon.

"Called up ... You mean they're sending you to ... *fight*? Get shot at? To *Vietnam*!"

Hearing her say it like that made it real to Riley on a whole new level. Like telling his grandfather, who hadn't said much, but his eyes ...

Riley was discovering that it might not be possible to absorb an announcement with such monumental ramifications all at one time. Too much to swallow in a single bite. It'd have to seep in, gradually, go deeper and deeper into who he was before he'd be able to recognize the truth of it. He and the others weren't just being inconvenienced, their plans interrupted, their goals postponed. They were going to *war*. To fight for their lives. Maybe to get killed.

Riley found he couldn't speak, didn't take his eyes off the road because he didn't want to look at her. He just nodded.

"But that's not ... they *can't*. You joined the guard to stay *out of* Vietnam. National Guard — N.G. — No Go."

"It wasn't a guarantee."

"Yes it was. Everybody said. You get a college deferment or join the guard. They can't just ..." He could hear it soak in as her voice changed.

"You can't go. I mean, you can't—"

"I *have to*. They're activating the unit."

She slumped back into the seat then, staring sightlessly out the windshield, tears streaming down her face.

"When?" It was a whisper. "When do you have to ... leave?"

"I'm not sure. Nobody has said yet, but Willie Ray saw the orders and they say we have to train here for a while — I don't know how long — and then I think we go to Fort Hood."

"Fort Hood?"

"Texas."

"Pull over!" Her voice was urgent.

"What—?"

"Pull over, pull over *now*."

She turned toward the door as he veered off the road into the weeds, the wheels crunching on gravel. Sherry Lynn had the passenger side door open even before the car came to a complete stop. He thought she was about to be sick, but she leapt out of the car and ran. Just ran. The woods were thick with brush and she plowed right through it and kept going. Riley jumped out of the car and ran after her. She was running as fast as she could but she was wearing heels and couldn't get any traction up the hillside. She staggered against a tree, then another, lost a shoe, stumbled, went down, got up and kept running. He merely followed along behind.

She finally reached the top of the hill and slid down the back side in the damp leaves, got to her feet and broke out of the trees on the bank of a creek. Splashing into the water — she was barefoot now — she was soon knee deep, plowing through with the bottom of her skirt soaked.

She staggered to a stop then, gasping, crying, tilted her head back and cried out.

"Nooooo!" It was a shriek of pain. "No, no, noooo."

Then she sank down to her knees in the water. The stream broke around her, flowing on both sides, soaking her to the waist. He stepped into the water and put his hands on her shoulders but she shrugged him off violently, so he backed away, left her sobbing alone on her knees in the creek.

When she finally ramped down to hiccupping sobs, he stepped back into the water and pulled her to her feet. She spun around and wrapped her arms around him, squeezing so tight he couldn't breathe.

"I love you!" It was a fierce, desperate whisper.

The words were startling. She'd never said *that* before. She was just upset, surely she didn't mean it. They were just *dating.* Having a good time. "I love you" was another thing altogether.

"You can't ... don't you *dare* ..." She pulled back out of his arms and looked into his face. Her mascara was smeared in black smudges under her eyes and trails of black streaks sliced down both cheeks. "You listen to me, Riley Hannacker. Don't you *dare* let anything happen to you." She almost growled the words. "Are you listening to me? Don't you *dare* ..."

All the air went out of her fierceness then and she sagged against him. He helped her back out of the creek and she seemed to realize for the first time that she was wet and barefoot, almost seemed confused by it. He sat her down on a rock and sat beside her with his arm around her shoulders. She was trembling.

"What's ... going to happen?" She sounded like a little girl. "The unit ... I mean. Andy and Emily are getting married day after tomorrow. How can he ... how can any of you ...?"

"I don't know." He had no idea how it could happen. Pulling her against his chest, he buried his face in hair stiff with Spray Net. Held her tight. "I don't ... I just don't know."

Chapter Nine

NATE HANNACKER SAT in the lawn chair on the front porch, smoking a cigarette and taking swigs from one of the Mason jars on the floor beside him. The lawn chair needed new webbing and he'd already got the pieces of nylon fabric to do it, planned to get Riley to help him sometime this weekend.

Now he just sat with one butt cheek hanging out the getting-bigger-every-day hole in the chair, puffing on his cigarette, watching the smoke snake up into the night sky, trying to call J.J.'s face to mind. But he couldn't. Every time he tried, the boy's features were overlaid with Riley's.

That'd been happening for a long time now. The older Riley got, the more he looked like his father had looked at his age, their images mingled in Nate's mind, particularly when he'd had something to drink. Something stronger than a beer. As soon as Riley left to pick up Sherry Lynn, Nate'd gone out to the shed and got two Mason jars filled with clear liquid, and he sat with them now, one on either side of the sagging lawn chair, watching the sun sink down behind the tree line in the western sky. The house faced west, so you could watch the sunset from the front porch. Couldn't watch sunrise, though. The sun didn't get high enough in the sky to shine until almost ten o'clock in the morning. To the east, out beyond the back yard, the land rose up to Bald Knob, which wasn't bald at all but maybe it had been a couple hundred years ago when somebody'd named it.

Riley'd asked why a knob covered with trees was called "bald." Or maybe it'd been J.J. who asked. Nate didn't know anymore.

Wasn't just their looks that done it. J.J., for Johnathan Joseph, had been named after the two who'd died on the day Nate survived, their lives stolen before they had a chance to live them. He and Riley had the same manner-isms, too. The way Riley'd wrinkle up his brow when he was concentrating, stick his tongue out between his teeth when he was playing the guitar. The almost-a-swagger walk they'd both adopted at about the same age — thir-teen or so, when they'd started getting pimples and their voices warbled up and down. They'd both been the smallest in their classes and they musta felt they needed to strut their stuff best as they could. Abby had noticed, seen J.J. start doing it and told Nate it 'peared the boy was trying to figure out how to piss on a bush.

They activated the guard unit, Papa. We're going to Vietnam. Vietnam!

Nate shook his head like to fling the words out of it, but all he managed to do was get off balance and dang near dump himself out onto the plank porch.

He lifted the jar to his lips, drank deep, felt the fire in his chest.

There was a war going on in Vietnam that didn't bother nobody but the boys fighting it and the people out in the street with signs protesting it. The rest of America didn't care. Wasn't like it'd been when he was eighteen. The whole country had cared then. Nate had *wanted* to go to shoot them bastards that had bombed Pearl Harbor. It was all Abby could do to keep him from trying to join up. Like he could have volunteered and anybody'd a'took him! Not likely, not with that gimp leg.

J.J.'d been just six years old then. His face, *J.J.s* face, flashed into Nate's mind then, not Riley — *J.J.* Abby said it'd be good for J.J. to have his pa home when most everybody else's fathers were gone, and that was right if it'd a'been true, but it wasn't. Nate'd been a lousy father to J.J.; the boy about raised himself while Nate was working harder than he'd ever worked in his life. Prohibition's repeal didn't close the market on moonshine. In fact, because of the heavy tax on alcohol sold from legitimate distilleries, moonshine sales flourished. And the end of the federal ban on alcohol meant that local governments controlled liquor sales. Some places voted wet, some dry. Bootleggers kept the dry counties stocked with alcohol, either from distilleries or moonshiners. On top of his liquor business, Nate turned his farming enterprise into a money-maker during World War II, courtesy of the government. With access to foreign fibers cut off, and with a whole navy to rebuild, the government turned to farmers to raise hemp for rope. Kentucky was chosen as the site for seed production and Nate was one of the farmers who signed up to do it. He read somewhere that in 1943 and 1944, Kentucky produced sixty million pounds of fiber.

During the war, moonshiners had a hard row to hoe because of sugar rationing and that's how Nate first became involved in his "other business venture" — fencing stolen property. It began with sugar-rationing cards. Given the ratio of ten pounds of sugar to one gallon of moonshine, you could make a tidy profit as the middleman for those who had by some means, legal or otherwise, to come by sugar-rationing cards and the moonshiners who so desperately needed them. Eventually, Nate had built a network of people in possession of all manner of stolen items and a second, equally large network of customers eager to purchase whatever he had to sell.

The years flew by, and before Nate knew it, J.J. was grown. He was seventeen, standing there in the middle of the living room holding hands with Emma Riley, saying they were going to get married. Married! Of course, he and Abby'd got married young, too, but they hadn't ... *had* to. And before Nate knew it, he was about to be a grandfather! Not even thirty-five years old. Then poor J.J. lost his Emma in childbirth, a teenager with a son of his own to raise with no mother. And Riley had just learned to walk when J.J. stood in that same spot in the living room where he'd stood with Emma ... holding out that letter saying he'd been drafted. *Drafted!* Shoot, Nate hadn't even been completely sure where Korea was on the map!

Their faces blended in his mind again, then — J.J. and Riley.

But even three sheets to the wind like he was, Nate managed to keep his mind out of the locked room where the images of the three soldiers coming across the yard were locked away. And Abby ... backing away from the screen door, the coffee cup slipping from her fingers and hitting the floor, splashing coffee everywhere, her running past him with her eyes wild, out to the chicken house.

She had to feed the chickens, didn't have time to talk to no soldiers!

She'd grabbed little Riley by the arm and took him with her — he wasn't even three years old. Had been sitting on the floor stacking up his blocks and she'd snatched him up and dragged him out the back door. Nate found her on her knees in the chicken coop, showing the boy how to grab handfuls of feed out of the bucket and toss it to the chickens — wouldn't look at Nate when he came to the fence, just kept calling out to the birds with her little chant, "Here chick, chick, chick. Here chick."

And Riley was trying, grabbing big handfuls. Then he dumped all the feed on the ground at his feet and them chickens was crowding around him, pecking, trying to get at it, scaring the kid to death and him screaming, holding his chubby arms out for his Papa, because Abby was ignoring him. Her face was blank, her eyes not seeing, just tossing that feed, keeping her back to Nate so she wouldn't have to look at him, see it on his face.

"Here chick, chick, chick. Here chick."

If Nate unlocked that door and went into that room where those images were, he wouldn't be able to find his way back out of the darkness. He was sure he wouldn't. He'd be lost there. So he didn't never talk about it, wouldn't let Abby talk about it neither. Went only once a year to put flowers on the grave — on Memorial Day, laying them on the stone that read Jonathan Joseph Hannacker, "J.J.". Born December 30, 1934. Died June 20, 1953, with that little flag insignia that meant he'd been a soldier. Lying beside his young bride, Emma Marie Riley Hannacker, her death date the same as Riley's birth date. When the boy got old enough to read he'd wanted to know why that was — why had his momma died on the day he was born? Did she fall down and hurt herself, he'd asked, his face so full of innocent concern it'd break your heart.

Now that Nate was sufficiently drunk, his mind was bouncing around, wouldn't stay on anything long, like them water spiders flitting around on the surface of the pond. He just blew by them images now, all jumbled together in the fog of his remembrance. He understood that he'd taught himself to do that over the years — to leap around. Spit on a griddle. So he wouldn't get caught there in the web of darkness.

Or drown in the sea of blood. Nightmares of blood drove Nate from sweat-soaked sheets for months … years. Wasn't J.J.'s blood, of course. He hadn't never seen J.J.'s blood, never even seen J.J.'s body, just the box they sent him home in. Nate understood even at the time that the nightmares of blood after J.J.'s death were symbolic somehow — one horror hooked to another over the passage of years.

The blood in his nightmares wasn't imagined blood. It was *real* blood. He'd seen it with his own two eyes, spreading out across the kitchen floor, with his mama shooing Nate's squealing sisters out of the room and Nate dropping to his knees and crawling under the little side table against the wall with the water pitcher and basin. Scooted back behind the long towel that draped over the table almost to the floor where he couldn't be seen. Then he peeked around the towel, looking out through the tangle of chair legs that looked like dead trees sprouting out of the wood of the kitchen floor.

Mama had taken charge, shouting orders at everybody, when moments before she'd been sitting on the edge of the girls' bed, reading to them from the Bible, totally calm and serene.

Chapter Ten

1927

LENORA HANNACKER SITS on the edge of the girls' bed, reading to them from the Bible, appearing totally calm and serene. It is an enormous act of will not to let the rising apprehension, the fear and worry, show on her face. The children see nothing but the calm assurance they know will be there whenever they look at their mother.

They need that. They are entitled to that. Children have a right to feel safe and secure even when the world is falling apart around them. When there's not enough to eat so Sam says he isn't hungry at suppertime. When she waters down the jug of milk after she milks the cow because it isn't enough to go around. Oh, they notice. Of course they do, they're not blind or stupid. They watch her patch the holes in their shoes with pieces of cardboard cut to fit, see their father squinting up into the bright, blue, cloudless sky as the ground dries out and the crops die and the garden withers.

They see, but they're not frightened by it. Their tender spirits won't be broken by the heartlessness of life unless she is. As long as their mother remains unafraid, so will they. As long as she is calm, unflappable, trusts in the care and grace of God, the children will remain unburdened by the harshness of reality living in "The Great Depression."

Lenora Hannacker's seven surviving children — there are three others under small white crosses in the Saint Dominic Catholic Church Cemetery — have a right to be unaware of the dangers swirling, the wolves circling outside the house.

Sometimes that's how Lenora sees it, she imagines wolves outside in the darkness. First one, a silver one, stands at the top of the hill, lit up until he glows in the moonlight. He howls and the cry is answered by other cries in the woods all around. From every direction, the answering cries come, surrounding the little one-room house Sam built with his bare hands — now with four rooms after his brother Pete helped him build on a room for the girls, another for the boys, and a third for her and Samuel — with a roof solid enough to keep out the rain, and a root cellar dug out of the hillside on the other side of the clothesline where she puts away jars of what she has canned out of their garden. Not enough this year. Not enough to last through winter.

In her mind, the big gray wolf lowers his head and comes down the hillside at a trot as his pack emerges from the woods all around. They're all gray wolves, every one of them, their fur made silver in the moonlight, and they form a circle around the house and begin to howl.

The cry bounces off the walls inside.

Lenora can hear it … almost believes that she does. But she smiles as she puts away the final washed dish from supper, and picks up little Becky off the floor, dislodging from her mouth the small rock she'd found there as she crawls across it as fast as a baby squirrel.

She assembles the children in the girls' room, on the edge of the big double bed where the four older girls sleep together — Marianne, Sarah and the twins Rose and Lily. Little Becky still sleeps at the foot of the bed in her parents' bedroom, in the wooden cradle Sam built years ago for Johnny.

The boys have gathered around from their room, Johnny and the little rascal Nathaniel, who has mischief in his twinkling eyes and the look of joyous rebellion on his face every moment. He has a spark the others don't, she thinks, and wonders whether that is a good thing or bad.

Seven children in thirteen years, filling the small house so that Sam wishes he'd built the rooms bigger, says he and Pete are going to add another room on when …

But there is no when.

There is work from sunup to sunset on the farm, planting and harvesting the crops and keeping the weeds out in between, tending the animals — the big draft horses, milking the cow and goats, feeding the chickens, watering the hogs. The house will never be any bigger than it is, will likely seem smaller and smaller as their family grows. More children will come, more mouths to feed. And not enough for the ones she has now.

They are fortunate to have what they have, though! So many others have nothing at all. She is grateful, reminds herself every day to be grateful. Grateful!

She opens the worn family Bible and reads to the children from it, her face set with a confident look, unafraid, even as the silver wolves encircle the house and cry out in her mind with that howl that no longer sounds lonely. Now, it sounds hungry.

Her face remains serene as she considers the real wolves outside her door. Sam and Pete were supposed to be home an hour and a half ago. She wanted to keep Sam at home, but said nothing. They are "breaking the law." And Rooster McClusky, the prohibition agent whose sneering face she sees sometimes on her imaginary wolves, is determined to arrest Sam again. Sam is more than just the fish that'd got away, of course. Sam is a Hannacker, and the McCluskys have hated the Hannackers, and vice versa, for generations.

It wasn't supposed to take long. It wasn't the only night that Sam and Pete had loaded up the back of Pete's truck and pulled in behind the trucks of three neighbor men for the trip to Lexington, where they unloaded the liquor in a dark vacant lot and men Sam didn't know came out of the shadows to claim it. If he hadn't needed the extra money so bad, Sam would have contented himself with supplying the customers he already had. But the dry throats of party-goers in the cities all around — Lexington, Louisville, Cincinnati, Nashville —

cried out for liquor, and supplying it brought in twice what it sold for locally. A group of farmers, friends, moonshiners from Callison County pooled their supplies and twice a month they hauled the brew away to the city. Tonight, it was Sam and Pete's turn to be among the transporters and the brothers were due back before supper. Supper has come and gone. The dishes washed and put away in the cupboard that should contain the overflow of jars of vegetables from the root cellar, but there is no overflow this year. Wasn't one last year, either. The shelves in the root cellar are almost bare.

Something has happened. Sam and Pete should have been back hours ago. Something has gone wrong.

She refuses to allow herself to go to the door repeatedly and look out into the darkness. Even when she hears sounds of some kind from the woods near the front yard, she stays inside, irrationally afraid that if she opens the door and looks out, she will see the silver wolf on the hillside, silhouetted against the full moon.

Howling.

Suddenly, the front door bursts open and Sam staggers in, carrying his brother over his shoulder. He drops to his knees and lays Pete out on the kitchen floor and Lenora can see he's bleeding. Bleeding bad. They're both bleeding.

Chapter Eleven

1927

NATHANIEL LOOKS across the kitchen floor from his hiding place under the wash basin table to the body of his uncle, lying there on his back, gasping for air. Blood is puddling around him, from … where? Nathaniel isn't sure. He can see the blood on the front of his shirt, can actually see what looks like a bullet hole in the fabric.

Maybe the bullet went all the way through and made a hole in his back, too, and that's where all the blood is coming from. Or maybe he has other wounds in his back that Nathaniel can't see.

Uncle Pete is a big man, five years older than Pa, with a barrel chest and a loud voice and two broken teeth in front where he was hit in the face by a still cap when the steam built too high and it exploded. He'd been burned by the hot cap, too, but he'd been a young man and the scars weren't visible anymore. He always had a full beard and maybe it was to hide them.

Nathaniel catches snatches of conversation.

"… loaded up the trucks … and when we got to Perryville …

Perryville, a little town on the road from Callison County to Lexington, was the site of the bloodiest battle fought in Kentucky during the Civil War.

"… just opened fire on us …"

62

"... *bullets flying everywhere, there musta been a dozen of them ... an ambush ... Rooster knew we were coming and he was waiting for us.*"

Pa says they'd been penned down for an hour before Pete said they'd ought to give up. They was outgunned and wasn't no sense in fighting no more.

Nathaniel hears the next words his father speaks clearly, as if all the noise in the room silenced, as if his own pounding heart stilled, as if they'd been whispered directly into his ear.

"*Pete called out he wanted to surrender. They said come out with his hands up. He threw his gun out where they could see it, stepped out with his hands high above his head. Then there was a gunshot. Rooster McClusky, I know that's who it was!* — shot Pete down like a dog.*"

Somehow, Pa had rolled Pete's body out of the glare of headlights into the darkness, "*dragged him, then ran ...*"

It must be twenty miles from their house to Perryville. How had Pa carried his brother through the woods so far?

That was impossible! He must have gotten a ride. Nathaniel never found out.

Uncle Pete is gasping for breath and there is blood in his mouth that forms bubbles on his lips when he tries to talk.

Or groans and tries to cry out.

And the puddle of blood flows out from beneath him and spreads out on the floor. A single thread of the liquid slides out toward Nathaniel, hiding under the table. He can't stop looking at it.

Inch by inch it comes, a thin stream moving across the floor, an icicle hanging from the roof that grows longer with every drip of water that slides down it and freezes there.

The blood spreads. The stream of it reaches out toward the boy trembling under the table. Like it's on purpose, reaching for him. The blood coming for Nathaniel.

There is noise, so much noise, movement, feet scuffling, Mama telling Marianne to get water and Sarah to tear up a sheet. Pa barking orders to Nathaniel's older brother, telling Johnny to move something and to hide something else in the woods.

"Sam, you're hurt, too!" Nathaniel's mother says and his father grunts, some kind of dismissive sound.

"They'll come looking for me, soon."

"Where will you hide?"

Nathaniel doesn't hear his father's answer.

He finds his hearing muffled, like he has his fingers in his ears or a pillow over his head. Thumping and bumping and voices seem soft, far away. The only thing that is real, true, not muffled or blurred is his uncle's blood on the floor, moving toward him.

Nobody steps in that trickle of blood, moving out, the surface smooth as a still pond.

It reaches the edge of the tablecloth and slides under it.

Nathaniel tries to back away from it, but there's only a wall behind him. He pulls back, flattens himself, cringes as it comes.

Then Uncle Pete arches his back and coughs violently and specks of blood splatter red raindrops on the floor.

He makes a sound, some kind of choking, gurgling sound, then his big body slumps back on the floor and is still.

Pa calls out "Pete?" Then louder, his voice full of an aching longing that is heartbreaking. "Pete!" But his uncle lies unmoving. The puddle of blood has stopped moving, too. It had spread out around him in all directions with just the one small stream of it stretching out toward Nathaniel in his hiding place, reaching for him.

When his uncle settles back into the blood on the floor the whole puddle shudders. You can see the movement on the surface of the liquid, and then the blood is as still as his uncle's body.

After that, things are out of order in Nathaniel's memory. The images are crystal clear, as visceral and real as if only a few minutes have passed since he saw them instead of decades, but the order of them no longer makes sense. At some point, Nate's mind dropped the images and they shattered into little shards of glass flying in every direction. He could never again fit them back together properly.

Uncle Pete is no longer lying on the floor. Mama and Marianne are scrubbing the floor to get the bloodstains off.

Sarah is tending to the littles in the girls' bedroom.

Pa and Johnny are ... somewhere.

They've taken Uncle Pete's body ... somewhere.

Then it is mid-morning and Nathaniel doesn't remember going to bed, doesn't think he did go to bed. He doesn't think anybody did, only the littles, and he could hear the twins playing with Becky to keep her from fussing.

Breakfast. Nobody talks. He puts food in his mouth because Mama tells him to. He chews and swallows but he can't taste it.

Mama cries out, "Marianne, wash your hands again. You didn't get all the blood——" Then she almost cries, one sob and is silent.

Johnny bursts through the door and says there's a car in the lane. Then they hear the crunch of gravel indicating that a car has pulled up in front of the house.

Doors slam. Johnny sits down on the floor Indian fashion around a washtub full of black walnuts, shelling them, though the lack of rain has made the shells leathery. Nathaniel is supposed to be helping, but he gets up when he hears car doors slam and runs to Mama, grabs her leg and won't let go.

Pa is sitting on the couch and the girls, all of them, are gathered around him. They're sitting in his lap and that's odd because the girls don't sit on Pa's lap anymore, well, Rose and Lily do sometimes, but certainly not Marianne and Sarah.

Pa is literally covered with children.

Covered up *with children.*

"You're hurt, too, Sam!" His mother'd said that.

There is a pounding on the front door and Sarah squeaks out a scream. Mama tries to peel Nathaniel off, but he won't let go, so she moves with him to the door and opens it.

Standing on the porch is Rooster McClusky. He has a dirty bandage tied around his arm, and a cigar caught tight between his teeth.

"We came for Sam Hannacker. You ain't gonna stop us this time. Where is he?"

"He's … right here," Mama says and steps back to reveal Pa sitting on the couch with the girls. Nathaniel realizes that his father has changed clothes, his hands and face are clean and he appears to be totally relaxed, just sitting there holding Becky. The baby is asleep on his shoulder, a diaper under her because she always spits up.

There are three men on the porch, but only Rooster steps into the house. Nate stares at him, remembers the look of hate he'd seen on the man's face that day when Mama went after Pa. That same look is there now — only it's uglier. Meaner.

"You're coming with me, Hannacker," he growls.

"What for?"

Pa doesn't get up in any great hurry, and Nathaniel suddenly understands that everybody's pretending Pa's been here all night, didn't go anywhere. They've cleaned up the mess … except they haven't!

The blood, the puddle of Uncle Pete's blood that was reaching out for Nathaniel. They missed it under the basin table. They'd scrubbed it away everywhere else, but it had run under the table and Nathaniel can see the edge of it from where he's sitting. No, it's just a shadow, a shadow is all. There's no blood there.

"We're looking for two men who got away from a roadblock last night, shot a federal agent! One of 'em's hit, I know I got him, figure I got 'em both. Wounded two others and captured another three."

"The men you captured — they told you Sam was with them, did they? That he was the one who got away?" Mama's voice is challenging.

He doesn't like admitting it. "You know they ain't said nothing … yet."

Of course they hadn't. And they never would.

"Then what are you doing here bothering Sam?"

"One of the trucks belonged to his brother," he snaps.

"Then might be you'd ought to go have a talk with Pete," Mama says.

"He ain't home, we done checked."

Nathaniel wonders what Pa and his brother did with his uncle's body. Was it just ... hidden out in the woods somewhere? Did Aunt Audrey know her husband wasn't never coming home?

"I can't speak for my older brother," Pa says. *Careful not to disturb the baby asleep on his shoulder, he rises slowly, gently swaying back and forth and patting her back. "But it ain't me you're looking for. I've been here all night with my family."*

Mama and all the children nod in agreement, but it's clear the man doesn't believe it. It's also clear he has no way to prove they are lying or he'd have snatched Pa up and hauled him out to his car the minute Mama opened the door. He's ... fishing.

"So ain't no reason for you to mind if I look around, then, is there?" Rooster sneers.

"Look all you want, you ain't gonna find nothing 'cause ain't nothing to find."

Except the blood on the floor! The puddle that had come for Nathaniel. If the man lifts the towel, he'll see it.

Nathaniel's heart begins to hammer and he can feel the throbbing in his temples as the man turns and goes through the doorway to Mama and Papa's bedroom, and the family hears the noise of him ransacking the room.

Nathaniel has to clean up the blood before the man sees it! But he can't. He has nothing to wipe it with and besides he'd be seen.

The man comes out of Mama and Pa's bedroom and goes into the girls' room. He grabs the blanket on the bed and pulls it off onto the floor, throws the corn husk mattress on top of it and pulls the bed out to look under and behind it. He curses and grumbles and flicks the ashes off his cigar onto the floor as he rummages around in the open chifforobe.

Finding nothing, the man goes next into the boys' room and begins to tear it apart.

Nathaniel can't take his eyes off the spot where the towel hangs about an inch off the floor. He imagines he can see the edge of the puddle of blood that's behind it, that the cloth on the table has just become as clear as a window pane and he can look through it, see what's on the other side. A puddle of blood. Blood that will prove Pa is lying and then the man will haul him away.

Nathaniel is so frightened he is sick to his stomach and his belly heaves. Clamping his mouth shut, he swallows the rising tide in the back of his throat and tries with all his might to take his eyes off the spot where the towel hides bloodstains on the floor. Surely, the man will notice that he's staring, will wonder what the little boy is looking at, what's so interesting that he can't move his eyes away? So he'll follow Nate's gaze to the table, lean over to look under it — lift up the towel and …

The man is back in the living room, looking around. Now he'll see! Nathaniel can't tell where the man is looking, what he might be examining because he can't look at the man, can't look anywhere except at the spot on the floor, his eyes locked there. He senses the man moving in that direction to the place where the blood lies pooled on the other side of the towel

A few more seconds, another step or two and the man will see.

Nathaniel suddenly can't hold onto it any longer. His stomach lurches and he staggers away from Mama's side and begins to vomit violently.

Retching and heaving, he spews the contents of his stomach every-where, watching in horror as the chunks of this morning's bacon and yellow hunks of eggs mixed in with oatmeal — green-colored for some reason — splatters all over the floor, his shoes and Mama's.

His sisters reflexively pull back. The man with the cigar twists up his face when the smell reaches him, mumbles something under his breath and turns away from the spectacle of the vomiting child and the stench of his puke.

Nathaniel isn't aware of the man leaving the room. His whole body is concentrated on the violent heaving in his belly. The man must be out on the porch, because Nathaniel can hear him yelling, directing his men to search the property.

"... check the outhouse."

Pa walks slowly to the doorway and stands watching as the prohibition agents search the chicken house and the pig pens and Nathaniel fights to get control of his retching. He has just about stopped heaving when he hears the man snarl, "We'll get you one of these days, Hannacker." He pauses. 'I'll get you. You're a marked man. Sooner or later, I will take you down."

The motor of the car starts and the tires crunch on the gravel as the car drives away.

Ma has a cloth wiping Nathaniel's face as he stands with his hands on his knees gasping, his nose full of vomit, his throat burning from the foul liquid coming out.

As soon as the sound of the car has faded, all the air whooshes out of Pa and he slumps against the door frame. Mama rushes to him and carefully picks the sleeping baby up off his shoulder and hands her to Marianne. The diaper to protect Pa's shirt from Becky's spit-up is dark with a growing bloodstain from beneath. The mask of indifference slides down off Pa's face and pain is etched deep there — emotional pain and physical pain.

Mama unbuttons Pa's shirt and pulls it off his shoulder where the bandage she had applied has soaked through. She eases him to a kitchen chair to sit while she re-bandages the wound and Nathaniel collapses trembling on the couch, his stomach still lurching.

Mama directs Sarah to clean up the mess he made, then asks Nathaniel, "You are done, right? You ain't gonna chuck again?"

"He didn't see it," Nathaniel says, shaking his head as relief spreads over him.

"See what?"

Nathaniel steps around the puddle of puke his sister is cleaning and lifts up the towel to reveal a stain just under the edge of it. A dark red stain, still sticky.

Mama gasps.

Papa burps out something that might have been a laugh, or an attempt at one. *"You sure enough kept him from looking."* His voice is breathless from the pain.

"How did blood get all the way ...?" Mama doesn't finish. Uncle Pete had been lying in the wide space in the middle of the floor. Uncle Pete, whose body had been taken ... where? Only Nathaniel had noticed that little stream of blood stretching out to the table. And at the time, he hadn't been sure it was real.

"I ... thought it was coming for me." His voice is gravelly.

"What was coming for you?" Pa asks.

"The blood." He knows it makes no sense but says it anyway. *"I thought it was coming ... to get me."*

Chapter Twelve

OVER THE YEARS AFTERWARD, that little trickle of blood sliding across the floor grew. It became buckets of blood, a river, an ocean of blood that crashed up on the shore of Nate's mind in sleep, threatening to drown him.

The nightmares lasted his whole childhood, attacked his sleep for years. But when he was no longer a boy, the day he became a man, they stopped completely. After what happened to Nate's father and brother, Nate had far worse images with which to people bad dreams, but his nights were strangely dark and silent. He remembered lying in his bed that first night, the horror still so real that closing his eyes did nothing to dispel it, the images existed on the insides of his eyelids as fresh and real as they'd appeared before his face. When his fingers had been so slick with blood he could barely hold onto the shard of glass, when the cordite stink of gunfire filled his nostrils and pain ate his world and the difference between being aware and being unconscious was no real distinction at all.

He'd closed his eyes after that and opened them again

to morning sunlight streaming through the dust motes in front of the window by his bed. There was nothing but blackness in between. He never dreamed about what had happened that night, had not dreamed at all for years. No longer a boy, he was a man who closed his eyes at night and visited a black place where no light could ever shine until he opened his eyes again the next morning.

He never dreamed of anything until after he and Abigail were married. When they lost the first child, the little girl they'd named Lenora after Nate's mother. When Abby had miscarried that first time, there had been so much blood, so much *unexpected* blood. Afterward, he'd started dreaming again of the blood sliding across the floor toward him.

After they put baby Lenora in that tiny wooden box and buried it in the ground, death always brought dreams of drowning in blood, nightmares that would waken Nate in sweat-damp sheets, holding onto a scream behind his teeth that if he loosed would eat up the world. Every time death claimed somebody he loved, even the one time life won and the tiny baby boy Abby birthed actually *breathed,* the blood dreams would stalk through his soul in the dark hours before dawn, threatening to claim him as their own and drag him down into the red liquid to drown there.

He'd even dreamed of blood when Abby died. And she'd been taken as she lay between the white sheets in a hospital, her life snatched away from her by disease, not injury. It didn't matter. She was dead and so the blood nightmares attacked Nate's sleep — for years afterward.

But eventually they'd stopped, not replaced by different dreams, normal dreams about — well, whatever it was normal people dreamed. For Nate Hannacker, night offered him two selections. Pick one — nightmares of blood, or black nothingness with no images of any kind. Not that he got to select, of course. He had no say in the matter. Those were the only offerings.

As he sat in the broken lawn chair on his front porch, sipping the liquid he'd put into Mason jars with his own hands, he felt fear pull his belly into such a tight knot he could barely breathe. He was terrified that he would go to sleep tonight and dream of blood. He only dreamed of blood after ... somebody *died*. But would he dream of blood now — as some kind of omen, some predictor of death in the future?

They activated the guard unit, Papa. We're going to Vietnam.

Riley was going to war. Walking into danger. After Nate had done everything in his power to protect the boy, the only loved one he had left! Made him wear a stupid helmet when he rode his dirt bike in the woods even if the other kids made fun of him. Seatbelts — nobody buckled those things, but he made the boy fasten his every time he rode in the car.

Nate had kept his grandson *safe*. That's why he'd signed up for the National Guard in the first place — to stay out of the crazy war on the other side of the planet that didn't matter diddly squat to anybody in America. Except the people sending a boy into the meat grinder to come back ... at least changed, maybe injured. If he came back at all.

Riley could either get a college deferment or he could join the guard. Those had been the only options for draft-age boys and Riley wasn't ready to go to college yet, didn't know what he wanted to do with his life, was ... okay, he was a little immature. But if there was one thing you could count on in life it was that you would eventually grow out of immaturity. Riley hadn't settled enough to go to college. He was just floating — farmed, made a little moonshine with Nate and bootlegged legally-made whiskey into dry counties, worked part-time making barrels at the cooperage, drove his new Mustang ... he wasn't ready to pick a career and settle down.

So Nate had urged him to join the National Guard. Charlie Company of the 151st Infantry Battalion was right there in Bardstown. Or there was the 138th Field Artillery Battery — in Elizabethtown and Carrolton. That was a much longer drive every time you had to report for duty, and Nate was afraid for a while Riley and his buddies would all decide to join the artillery battery just so they'd get to "blow things up."

None of them ever imagined that ...

Nate reached down for the Mason jar at his side, picked it up and realized it was empty. He reached for the other one and accidentally tipped it over, spilling the liquid out over the floor of the porch. He was stuck so far down in the broken chair he couldn't move fast enough to do anything to stop it, then realized there wasn't but a couple of inches of it left anyway.

He'd had enough. Didn't know what time it was, but he didn't want to be sitting on the front porch drinking himself into oblivion when Riley came home. He tried to get up. Couldn't. He was stuck down in the hole ...

Clearly he'd had too much to drink when he threw dignity to the wind and just rolled to the side, turning the chair over and dumping him out into the spilled moonshine on the porch boards. He got up onto his hands and knees, grabbed hold of the post of the porch railing and pulled himself upright.

His bad leg hurt. Ached. It did that when it was about to rain. Looking up into the black velvet of sky overhead, he realized that there were storm clouds up there, swirling around. He took a breath, trying to see if he could smell rain on the air. All he could smell was liquor.

He didn't need to smell it, though, to know. Didn't need to see it or hear its grumbling thunder. There was a storm coming. A big, black, ugly storm that could sweep away everything that mattered in the world.

Chapter Thirteen

NATE HANNACKER SHOOK his head in wonder, grateful that the motion didn't send a bowling ball banging around in his skull as it had done for most of the morning, courtesy of the white lightning he'd consumed on the porch the night before. A moonshine hangover could last for days.

"And just exactly what is it you think I'm gonna do with a tractor-trailer load of hot baseball bats?"

Fast Eddie Whitlock was nervous, not a good sign. Something was going on, but he babbled on undeterred.

"Ain't just bats. They's all kinda other baseball stuff in there, gloves and—"

"What am I supposed to do with a tractor-trailer load of bats and gloves and baseballs—?"

"Ain't no balls. Hillerich & Bradsby don't make baseballs."

"Just baseball *bats*, then, and ..." Nate waved his hand at the dark interior of the tractor-trailer, indicating whatever might be loaded up in it behind the cases of baseball bats.

"You know how much these things sell for?"

"About ten bucks each."

Fast Eddie grinned.

"Now see, that's where you're wrong, Nate. That's where you're dead wrong. These here ain't just any base-ball bat. These here is Louisville Sluggers, the best bats made in the whole country, the bats used by Babe Ruth and Hank Aaron. These here, some of them's worth two or three hundred dollars each. And have you priced a base-ball glove lately?"

Nate almost made some comment about the bats being escapees from a belfry somewhere, on the run and maybe there was a reward. Mama Whitlock's baby boy Eddie was *not* the sharpest knife in the drawer, though, and wasn't likely to get the joke. Besides, there was nothing funny about a tractor-trailer load of *stolen* baseball bats sitting next to his cornfield.

"They might be worth more than the Hope Diamond" — Eddie didn't likely get the reference — "but I can't get a buck two-ninety-eight for them if I ain't got nobody to sell them to. Why'd you bring them to *me*?"

Eddie's nervousness was plain to see now, but he popped out an answer.

"I bring you the best stuff, Nate, you know that."

And the worst stuff and a whole lot of crap in between.

"Where'd you get these?"

Fast Eddie was reluctant to say. He always was reluc-tant to reveal the sources of the stolen goods he'd been bringing to Nate at least a couple of times a week for a couple of years now. Not big-ticket items — small stuff, easy to pack, transport and fence. Stolen stereo equipment was a hot item. Nate would take every woofer and tweeter he could lay his hands on. Lawn equipment — a couple of brand new riding lawn mowers hadn't even been unloaded before Nate had a buyer, same with weed-eaters and tillers.

Stolen boat motors — Eddie once showed up with a pickup truck weighted down in the back with half a dozen Evinrude motors, still in the boxes.

But baseball bats? A *tractor-trailer load* of them! Not so much.

"I got 'em straight from the fella that lifted them."

"And the fella who lifted them got them …?" He left the question hanging out there in the air.

"From the warehouse."

"What warehouse? Come on, Eddie, don't make me drag this out of you."

Fast Eddie took his University of Louisville baseball cap off, wiped his forehead with the back of his hand and put the cap on again. He eyed Nate, obviously deciding whether he was going to tell him the truth or concoct a tale.

"Don't get a brain freeze from making up a story. What warehouse?"

Fast Eddie looked at his feet and spoke softly. "He hooked up the wrong trailer."

"The wrong trailer?"

"It was dark, and both them trailers was the same color and—"

"So your guy stole baseball bats instead of … what?"

"Cabinets."

Nate waited.

"It was supposed to be a load of cabinets for a contractor. Shower stalls, too, toilets, fixtures, all that kinda stuff. He's building a subdivision, said he'd take whatever Mama Bert could—"

"Mama Bert!"

Nate should have known.

He swore softly.

He did *not* want to get mixed up with that woman, had

managed to fly below her radar for years. She was big time, had her finger in all manner of criminal enterprises. Nate was small potatoes, a one-man band, and he was content with that. He'd long ago weighed the possibilities. The next step up the ladder from his current ventures would require a level of risk he wasn't comfortable with. What would happen to Riley if he wound up in prison? Not jail, *prison*. The rewards of a bigger operation were tantalizing and one of these days ... yeah, he'd take that plunge eventually. It was just a matter of time.

He was absolutely certain Mama Bert knew who he was and what he was doing. That woman didn't miss a thing! And she was likely aware that one day they'd butt heads. So far, though, their interests had never conflicted and apparently she was okay with that. Their business dealings had never even crossed paths. Until today, that is.

Nate held onto his temper. "Let me get this straight. You're telling me this load of baseball bats that should have been cabinets and toilets was supposed to go to Mama Bert?"

He didn't wait for an answer.

"Then what *in the Sam Hill* is this tractor-trailer doing on my farm?"

"I stopped at Rooster Run to pee, checked the cargo and seen it was bats and not cabinets, so I called my guy."

Rooster Run was a gas station between Bardstown and Interstate 65 South from Louisville.

"He was totally freaked, said they was on to her, the law. Said they was gonna come down on her with both feet, that they was just waiting for *this load* to spring the trap. So I couldn't very well deliver it! What was I supposed to do?"

"So you brought it here." Nate was incredulous.

"I had to take it *somewhere*, and—"

Whippoorwill, whippoorwill!

"— I figured you —"

Nate grabbed his arm.

"Shut up! Listen."

Whippoorwill!

That was Joe-Joe. No doubt about it. Kid sounded more like scalded chicken than he did a whippoorwill. So why was—?

There was only one explanation. Nate had been on his way to the still with Joe-Joe to shut it down, stopped by the farm to check on a sheep that'd been looking poorly. Joe-Joe'd taken his pole and gear out to the creek that ran beside the road about a quarter of a mile from the house to fish while he waited. That kid would rather fish than eat, and there was a whole lot more to catch in Flat Rock Creek than in Possum Creek on Stedman Lane.

The only possible reason for Joe-Joe to—

"Get that rig outta here!"

Nate shoved Fast Eddie toward the truck.

"What ... where—?"

"The barn." It was the only possible place to conceal the rig, but even there might not be big enough. There was already farm equipment in the barn and Nate didn't know if there'd be enough room to close the door. "Somebody's coming! Move it!"

Fast Eddie leapt up into the cab of the truck and started the engine, turned the big front wheels toward the barn and headed that way. Nate hurried back to the house, grabbed a hoe as he ran past it and stopped at the garden plot on the other side of the dirt driveway from his front door. He could see the rising dust behind the vehicle that was coming up the road.

The house blocked the view of the barn. Nate'd have to stop them here because there was a good chance the tail end of that tractor-trailer was dangling out past the barn door. He couldn't let them get any closer.

There was likely nothing to be concerned about anyway, like a week ago on Stedman Lane when Willie Ray'd come looking for Riley. Scrambling through his mind Nate couldn't imagine what the law believed they could find on his place that'd send them out here. Wasn't like he had a still hidden in the barn. Oh, they knew who Nate Hannacker was and what he was about. He didn't give a rip what they knew, long's they couldn't prove nothing. He used a tobacco barn on Round Rock Pike to store the goods he fenced and he didn't own it. They'd have a hard row to hoe to connect him to the contents. And besides, it was empty right now. Nate lived by a single guiding principle when it came to stolen property — don't hang onto nothing longer than twenty-four hours. He'd been expecting Fast Eddie to show up any time now with something.

Baseball bats!

Nate dropped to his knees and grabbed a handful of dirt, got his hands dirty and smeared it down the front of his clean coveralls.

A dark blue car turned the bend on the other side of the stand of live oak trees where Joe-Joe was sitting in the shade on the creek bank fishing. The car trailed a plume of dust behind it and riding along in that dust cloud was Callison County Sheriff Angus Gilbert.

Nate used the hoe to pull himself back up to his feet and walked out into the middle of the dirt driveway, dusting his hands off on the front of his pants. They'd either have to stop before they cleared the house or run him over.

They stopped.

Chapter Fourteen

NATE WALKED CASUALLY UP to the driver's side door of the first car that'd pulled in and the driver rolled down his window. He was in a suit and tie. Behind him, Sheriff Gil got out of his cruiser. Two deputies were riding with him and they got out, too — Skeet Burkett and Lonnie Franklin.

"I help you?" Nate asked.

"You're Nathaniel Hannacker, right?"

Nate made a point of ignoring the question, turned away and took a couple of steps toward the sheriff, who was approaching.

"Afternoon, Sheriff Gil," he said to the sheriff. The sheriff's name was Angus Gilbert, and folks either called him Gus or Sheriff Gil. "Who's your friend?" He cocked his thumb back toward the suit-and-tie dude in his car, who had now opened the door and stepped out into the dirt.

"Nate, this here is Kentucky State Police Detective Booth Graham," the sheriff said. Nate made no effort to hold out his hand to the man and the guy caught himself before he reached out to take Nate's. He smiled, the kind of smile that concealed a limitless capacity for treachery. He had an ugly face that looked like it'd been crudely chiseled out of concrete, put Nate in mind of the pictures he'd seen of gargoyles sitting on top of cathedrals in Europe. His most distinctive feature was the cratered scars on his skin from what must have been a hellacious case of acne when he was a kid.

"Well, what can I do for you gentlemen?" Nate asked, looking at the sheriff, refusing to look at the stranger because he knew it'd piss him off. Men who dressed in suits and polished black shoes to come out to talk to a farmer were either stupid or full of themselves. This guy looked like he might snare Olympic gold in both categories. Clearly, he was from Away-from-Here, that place that was the home of all people not natives of Callison County.

"We're looking for a tractor-trailer," the sheriff said.

"One of your neighbors reported seeing one coming this way," the man said and the sheriff cringed at the man's obvious faux pas. The sheriff knew there wasn't a man, woman or child between here and Brewster who'd tell a law officer if his pants was on fire. Obviously, the sheriff had no real reason to believe the truck was here — he was just fishing. "You seen it?"

"'Fraid I can't help you. I been home all morning and I ain't seen no trucks."

Nate took out a package of cigarettes, tapped one into his hand and returned the pack to his shirt pocket.

"You don't have a dog in this fight, Nate," the sheriff put in. "All we want is the truck."

The pock-faced man followed right along behind. "We're not looking to jam *you* up." His voice was as ingratiating as a used car salesman. "We got bigger fish to fry. We know where the truck was going, *who* was expecting it. Help us and we'll forget all about where we found it."

Pulling a lighter out of his overalls pocket, Nate lit the cigarette, clicked the lighter shut and put it back where he'd got it.

"Let me make sure I understand." He inhaled deeply, and spoke the smoke out of his mouth. "You ... what? *Lost* a truck? Looked high and low and can't find it anywhere. And when you *do* find it, you won't remember where it was." Nate tapped his temple. "Sounds to me like you got bigger fish to fry than a lost truck."

The man's face flushed. The sheriff's face remained expressionless. Nate could swear Skeet Burkett grinned, but he hid it quickly.

"You're saying you haven't seen a truck — is that right?" The man was snide. If there was anything Nate Hannacker hated it was snide. The man pointed down into the mud at his feet. There were deep tracks in it, plain to see. "Looks to me like a truck drove up this road sometime after last night's rain."

He smiled ... smirked, triumphant at his "gotcha."

"You know the difference between truck tracks and tractor tracks, do you?" Nate asked.

The man hadn't expected the question. Nate pushed ahead.

"Or the difference between the tracks of a John Deere and an Allis-Chalmers or an I.H.?" Nate paused for a beat. "I.H. stands for International Harvester." Another pause. "Now these tracks here, clearly they wasn't made by ag tires. Ag tires have treads that are angled at forty-five degrees." Another pause. "You did know that, right?"

Nate saw the man's jaw tighten.

"If you haven't seen a truck, surely you wouldn't mind if we had a look around — would you, Mr. Hannacker?"

"You got a search warrant?"

"You don't have anything to hide so why would you mind——?"

"I mind because I don't like you." Nate allowed no malice to color his words. He said it as casual as "because you got on pink socks." "I don't need no more reason than that. The law ain't welcome here. If you've said everything you come to say, then you can back up from here all the way to the road, 'cause you ain't going an inch farther on my land without papers."

Nate could see the man grind his teeth to hold back a response. He was one of those men who had veins in their temples that filled up and throbbed when they were upset and his were pulsing now. He'd make a lousy poker player.

Detective Graham said nothing, just turned on his heel and stalked back to his car. Maybe he'd been pulled out from under some rock because of the big fish Nate was *not* going to help them catch.

Nate didn't particularly like Sheriff Gilbert, but he did his job the best he could, and Nate knew half a dozen moonshiners and bootleggers who'd offered him bribes over the years and they hadn't got nothing for their trouble but a view of main street out through the bars of a jail cell.

Nate respected a man who stuck to his guns, lived the way he thought was right. Even if he was wrong.

Sheriff Gil hadn't wanted to bring this guy out here with him today — that was obvious. So it followed that he'd done it because he didn't have a choice. Now why would that be?

Both men started the engines of their cars. Nate made eye contact with the sheriff and nodded. The sheriff returned the nod, then shifted into reverse and began backing down the narrow lane. The state police detective would likely have driven forward into the driveway to turn around if Nate hadn't been square in the middle of the road. You could see the barn from the driveway.

The barn where the truck might or might not have its tail end hanging out the door.

The truck full of baseball bats.

What in the Sam Hill was Nate supposed to do with a truckload of stolen baseball bats?

Chapter Fifteen

"THIS IS Nate Hannacker and I believe I have something that belongs to you," Nate said when the gruff voice of Bertha Calhoun came on the line.

"That a fact?"

"It is."

"And what might it be?"

"It ain't what you was expecting." He paused. "Our mutual friend Fast Eddie managed to make off with a tractor-trailer load of the wrong thing."

"Fast Eddie." Just the way she said his name made Nate glad he wasn't ole Ed.

Bertha Calhoun was a black woman somewhere between forty-five and two hundred years old. She had a deep husky voice, sounded like a man on the phone. Nate wasn't exactly sure how she'd got to be who she was, but there was no denying that when Mama Bert said jump, criminals in a five-county area in central Kentucky asked, "How high?"

Her name began to circulate around bootlegging circles about twenty years ago when she and her husband

Earl bought the legendary watering hole called simply The Tavern. It had been there longer than most people's memories, ran full-steam serving bootleg hooch during Prohibition and "unstamped" whiskey afterward. When the distilleries paid taxes on their product, the barrels were stamped with a government seal. As the saying went: "There's them that drink stamped likker and them that drink unstamped — and them that's had both know which tastes best."

The Tavern was out on the edge of Brewster, a rough, rowdy place, nowhere you'd take a date on Saturday night. Earl kept a baseball bat behind the bar and wasn't afraid to knock heads with it to break up the fights that were just about a nightly occurrence. The couple had sixteen, maybe eighteen children before Earl died and Bertha took over running the establishment. Legend had it that a group of white guys from Taylor County gave her some lip one night and she put two of them in the hospital.

About ten years ago, Mama Bert opened up a little nightclub for black people called Club Cherry. It was on their side of the railroad tracks, a small squat building lit up like the Fourth of July every Friday and Saturday night. Weeknights, too, but there wasn't the revelry then as there was on weekends. Not Sundays, though. It was closed up tight on Sunday, and Mama Bert and whichever of her offspring happened to be around, would be sitting in their pew at Saint Joseph Catholic Church, where the black folks attended Mass.

Club Cherry sat on one side of those tracks directly across from her second nightclub, Club 88, which was for those with paler skin tones.

The thing was, the white people at Club 88 could hear the music blaring out of Club Cherry across the way and it was clear that those folks were the ones having a good time, a *real* good time. The nightclub that sweat within Club Cherry's walls was like a wild beast some nights, like you could see the walls bulging out from the rhythm of the sound inside. Nate didn't know the first thing about music, no rhythm and tone deaf, but those who did know such things marveled at how the old black woman with her gray hair cropped as short on her head as a man managed to procure for Club Cherry the talent she did. There was some kind of music circuit black performers were on and Club Cherry became one of those sites.

A black performer named Jimi Hendrix played there the summer of 1963. Black and white people alike flocked to hear him and the club got a reputation that spread all across the state. Two things kept the crowds coming back — good music and no drinking age limit. If you were old enough to plop your money down on the bar at either club, you'd be served. The Brewster City Police pretended not to see drunk teenagers who'd claim to be eighteen but clearly weren't a day over fifteen dancing in the parking lots where they could hear the music from both establishments.

Another performer named Otis Redding played in Club Cherry the next summer, and a duo called Ike and Tina Turner were regulars.

How all that had translated into a criminal empire was a mystery to Nate, but clearly it had. Mama Bert's reputation for fencing stolen property on a grand scale, tractor-trailer loads of it, had obviously been accurate. He'd also heard she dealt in farm equipment, though he couldn't figure out how in the world you could steal a combine — what, hide it under your coat when you left the showroom? Nate had no desire to do business with the woman, but he hadn't been given a choice in the matter.

"Might be the law's gonna come back here with papers

— doubt it, but it's possible. Might be they're watching the place. So what's in that trailer needs to go away quick."

"Sounds like you know a way that can happen."

"Through my cornfield. The corn's about eight feet tall now, can't see over it. About a quarter of a mile up the creek from Furman Road is the back side of it. Pull in there and come down a row of corn to the end and you'll be in front of the barn."

"I'll have somebody there inside an hour."

She certainly didn't let grass grow under her feet.

"The cab and trailer are something else. Rather the law didn't see it and only one road in and out. Well, only one they know about. Unload that trailer, and if Fast Eddy's as good as he claims, he oughta be able to wrestle that rig up the side of the knob on an old logging road. Thing is, that road don't go nowhere—"

"You get it to the end of the road, I'll take it from there."

"Works for me."

"That all you got to say?"

"Yeah."

The call clicked off without a goodbye.

"You're welcome," Nate said into the dead receiver. "Glad I could help you out. Anytime."

Forty-five minutes later, a convoy of pickup trucks smashed down three rows of Nate's corn crop and stopped in front of the barn. Nate didn't know any of the drivers. The end of the trailer was sticking out beyond the barn doors as Nate had feared. An extremely nervous Fast Eddie unlocked the trailer doors and swung them wide.

"Baseball bats?" one of the drivers asked.

"That's what I said," Nate said.

An hour later there was no sign that a tractor-trailer load of stolen baseball bats had ever been on Nate's farm

— except the smashed corn and the tracks in the mud. Nate drove his tractor back and forth across the tracks a couple of times and they were gone. Nothing left but the tracks of ag tires, the treads set at 45-degree angles, of course.

Chapter Sixteen

THE CEREMONY HAD BEEN brief and not particularly memorable, but it was the best the community could pull together on such short notice. The three weeks since the news about the guard call-up had flown by in the blink of an eye. The Brewster City Council had arranged the farewell/good luck/come-home-soon service for the boys from the Bardstown area — about forty solders in the Thunder Road Platoon and another forty in Whiskey Run. It was held in the high school auditorium at noon on their last Saturday in Callison County. On the following Monday, September 23, all 250 of the solders in Charlie Company, 151st Infantry Battalion, Kentucky National Guard would load into trucks at the armory and drive to Fort Hood in Texas for three months of further training. They'd leave Texas the first of January for ...

The boys were all on the stage, introduced one at a time to a crowd who already knew who they were by the city of Brewster's Mayor-for-Life Malcolm Murdock. Malc was all about political posturing, wet his finger and stuck it in the air every morning to see which way the wind was blowing so he'd know what it was he believed that day. He owned the county's only horse farm, Land's End, complete with thoroughbreds, white fences and barns fancier than the houses of half the county's population. Nobody ever ran against him for mayor because nobody else wanted the job. After an appropriate amount of political jawing, the boys were turned loose into the crowd.

Nate watched them connect with their friends and families. Willie Ray Taggart was greeted by his parents, no telling how many of his brothers and sisters, and assorted teenage girls, each of whom looked extremely unhappy to see the others there. It was his freckles, Riley said, that attracted the girls. An image flashed into Nate's mind and warmed him, then it was gone:

"SO THAT'S *why Willie Ray's gonna take all his clothes off, get nekkid,"* Riley *explains earnestly. He and Willie Ray are about ten years old. "Grandma won't be back for hours."*

Nate is certain the boys had decided to go on their little scientific expedition right now for that very reason — that Abby was away picking strawberries.

"It'll just be right here in the back yard. It's gotta be outside, though, 'cause I need the sunshine to see, so I don't miss none."

NATE ALWAYS SAID that if Willie Ray grew even one more freckle he'd have to hold it in his hand. The number of them had certainly been daunting when he and Riley had been ten-year-olds. Riley had not even completed counting them on one leg before they threw in the towel and ended forever Willie Ray's cherished dream of knowing how many freckles he had.

Or maybe it'd been Riley who'd wanted to know. Nate couldn't remember.

Kenny Taylor's wife, Melissa, had been expecting twins when the unit was called up and gave birth to two little girls three days later. Nate saw her now, greeting Kenny with their two other children, boys who looked to be four or five. She hadn't brought the girls — how do you even carry twin newborns? The little girls'd be walking before Kenny got back home.

Nate spotted a clot of people who'd shoved their way to the front of the crowd — McCluskys, of course. A family of uglier human beings Nate hoped he'd never see, a study in contradictions, like the family had been assembled from a random grab of humanity out of a Walmart parking lot. Some were skinny, not scrawny but what was generously called scrappy. Jackson, the son/brother/cousin they'd all come to see, fell into that category. Short, slat-thin, all bony hips and elbows and sharp shoulders, with an Adam's apple too big in his skinny neck. Jackson's father was Big-Un, who stood six-foot six and weighed every ounce of three hundred pounds.

Big-Un's grandfather had been Rooster McClusky. *He'd been sitting beside his brother, Digger, who'd been driving that night.* Nate reached down unconsciously and rubbed his knee, which had begun to throb like a rotten tooth. It usually did whenever his eyes fell on a McClusky. They made his skin crawl.

He finally spotted Riley and lifted his hand, waving. Sherry Lynn Bennett had located him first and was already wrapped around him like a scarf on a cold morning. He bit back his resentment before it could fester. She couldn't help being a McClusky — Big-Un's sister Agnes, was her mother — and she was probably a fine young woman. Yeah, fine.

Riley saw him wave and made his way through the crowd, with Sherry Lynn stuck to his side like a barnacle.

Now Nate ... he could hear Abby say.

"Hi Papa," he said and gave Nate a hug. The girl did at least let go of him long enough for the hug. Of course, afterward, she reattached.

Iron shavings to a magnet.

Nate ...

The adoration in that girl's eyes when she looked at Riley was thick enough to spread on toast. Nate cut his eyes to Riley and didn't see a commensurate level of affection. In fact, he saw Riley look away, and then the boy's eyes widened.

Nate followed the look. The scene took only seconds to play out, but Nate suspected it had been elongated in a kind of slow motion for Riley.

Jessie Monaghan was searching the crowd as Nate had been, her height making her half a head taller than the other wives and mothers. Then she spotted her husband and her face blossomed into a smile that looked like a whole box full of Fourth of July sparklers had been lit at once.

Nate cut his eyes back to Riley, whose face showed no reaction of any kind. He knew his grandson, though, could read him like the instructions on a backyard barbecue grill. It was *still* there. After what ... two, three years? Nate knew Riley had faked a sprained ankle so he wouldn't have to be a groomsman in his good friend David Monaghan's wedding, hobbled around for a week on crutches to get out of it. Feelings like that were so wrapped up in razor blades, if you got anywhere near them, you'd come away bleeding. Nate hoped it didn't turn into a problem one of these days.

Sherry Lynn was looking at Riley, too, but clearly missed the whole thing.

"I have to go now," she said, sounding devastated that she had to leave Riley even for a little while. "There's still a lot to do to get ready for tonight."

There was a going-away party and dance scheduled at the Knights of Columbus Hall.

"Pick me up at six?"

"Sharp!"

Sherry Lynn tiptoed up and pecked a kiss on his cheek, then headed off into the crowd. She didn't see Riley's eyes seek out Jessie Monaghan again, didn't see the look of longing on his face.

But Nate did.

Chapter Seventeen

SHERRY LYNN WAS HANGING up a crepe paper garland to dangle from the ceiling when she suddenly had to get away. Hopping down off the folding chair she was standing on, she rushed to the bathroom to run cold water over her wrists. She didn't really know if that helped, but that was all she knew to do.

"You okay in there?" Gloria called though the door. "You sick?"

Sherry Lynn opened the door and stood in the doorway of the closet-sized room.

"No, I'm not pregnant."

"*I know* you're not."

Gloria Mattingly was Sherry Lynn's best friend. They kept no secrets from each other and both were virgins.

"And I know *you're* not."

And it was a good thing, too, because Gloria was only the latest in the string of Willie Ray Taggart's girlfriends and he never stayed with any of them long enough to get serious.

Gloria didn't love Willie Ray Taggart — he was a bee

that flitted from one flower to another in the meadow. But Sherry Lynn *did* love Riley. They were meant to be together.

"You guys talk about it?" Gloria asked. "About getting married?"

Uh huh, they'd talked about it.

IT FEELS SO *artificial to have a conversation like this now. It's not the way it's supposed to be at all. Riley's supposed to propose to her. Save up his money and go pick out a ring and put it in a box and show up with flowers or candy or something like that and ask her to be his wife.*

But here they are, sitting in his car in the driveway of her parents' home, talking about getting married. No, talking about not *getting married.*

"Rusty and Mary Jo have decided to get married," she says, trying to make it sound casual.

"Seriously? When? We're leaving in—"

"A justice of the peace is going to perform the ceremony tomorrow. Mary Jo said they'd been talking about it but hadn't actually set a date, and then after ..."

After ...

It was like Sherry Lynn's whole life had been cleaved in two with everything that came before the call-up of the guard unit on one side in Before, *and the rest in the shadowy murk of* After.

"And I was thinking ... we should ... well, you know, at least talk about the possibility ..."

It feels so awkward, so plastic and cardboard and artificial.

Time has been telescoped, has gotten pressure cooked in the reality of the guard call-up and now nothing feels normal or natural, un-hurried or spontaneous.

"You're wondering if we ought to get married."

She lets out a huge breath.

"We have to at least talk about it. Everybody else is talking about it." She pauses but he doesn't continue. *"So ... what do you ...?"*

"I care about you, I care what happens to you, Sherry Lynn. You know I do."

Her heart fills up to bursting and her eyes fill with tears. He's so close, so close to saying the words she longs to hear. To say it out loud, speak with words the love she can see in his eyes, feel in his kisses, knows in her heart.

"I love you, too—"

"I might not come back."

He drops the words into the air between them and it feels like each is an individual stone dropped into a still pond. Each breaks the surface of the water and sends out ripples in every direction. But the ripples of the first word are not fully formed when the second word splashes in. By the time all the words have been said the pond is a turbulent water, heaving like a hurricane at sea.

"Don't say that!"

She wants to grab him, shake him, make him take the words back.

But they're true. He might not come back.

He plugs doggedly ahead.

"That's no way to start a life, hurried and frantic — desperate. It's not supposed to be that way. Just because two people care about each other — caring isn't enough. There has to be more than that. Love has to grow slow and gentle and ..."

"And ... forever."

He nodded. *"Yeah, love is supposed to mean forever. And I am absolutely not prepared to make a commitment to forever .... not right now."*

Slow. And Gentle. And forever. The words are so beautiful they steal her breath and she can't respond. She agrees. He's right. The kind of forever she wants doesn't start like this. And obviously Riley wants it to be as perfect for her as she wants it perfect for him.

. . .

WHEN THE DECORATIONS for the party were done. Sherry Lynn went home and put on the prettiest dress she owned. Did her makeup and then redid it and then did it a third time because the eye makeup kept smearing down her face.

They danced, in the hot room with only fans to move the turgid air around. They all danced, every song. Nobody sat any of them out. They danced and danced in something like an insectile frenzy.

I Say A Little Prayer For You, Aretha Franklin wailed.

Frankie Valli crooned, I Can't Take My Eyes Off You.

The Beatles cried out that "All You Need Is Love."

Was that right? Was that all you needed? If you had love, everything would work out? Sherry Lynn wanted to believe that.

The music throbbed from the speakers, seemed to make the walls of the building swell outward with the beat. Then someone shouted, "Time for the group picture."

And so they lined up. A group of about eighty young men that Jim Bingham, who owned the Callison County Tribune, was struggling to corral into a still arrangement for a picture. The women in their lives looked on.

Riley was on the end of the second row with a wistful smile, looking at her without making eye contact, almost like he was looking past her, beyond her. Willie Ray was beside him, with his arm slung nonchalantly over Riley's shoulders and his hand up behind Riley's head, making bunny rabbit ears. David Monaghan was there, staring out at Jessica, who was standing with Peggy Benson behind Sherry Lynn. Five Cents had left an open space beside him for Tommy, had his arm draped around empty air. Skinny little Ben Higgs stood in front beside Jackson McClusky, who was even smaller. Kenny Taylor, Ronnie Benson, Andy Taggart, Jude Boone, Simon Tanner, Travis

Williams, Sean Mattingly, Scooter Washington, Sam Finch, Rusty Albertson, Ricky Stephens, Billy Wilson, Caleb McAllister and all the others.

Gloria came up to stand beside her while the photographer shouted out for the group to hold still so he could get one more picture.

"They can't all come back," Sherry Lynn said, her voice soft. Not that everyone in the room wasn't thinking the same thing. "I mean, what are the odds that all of Charlie Company, all five platoons, will get called up and every one of the soldiers in them will return home unhurt?"

"Zero," Gloria said.

"So who?" Sherry Lynn looked from one earnest face to the one next to it. "Who is it? Which one of them's gonna come home in a flag-draped box?"

Chapter Eighteen

DAVIE WAS PACKING up his duffle bag. He had to leave in the morning. Jessie was picking through her underwear drawer, trying to find at least three pairs of underwear without holes. That'd be enough. She could wash them out in the sink. Would likely wash everything else in the sink, too — who knew? She and Peggy Benson, Ronnie's wife, and Andy's wife, Emily, would just have to figure it out as they went along. They wouldn't leave until Friday, take turns driving. They'd get to Texas by sometime on Sunday and hopefully the guys would be settled by then and know their schedules.

Davie had tried to talk Jessie out of going, of course, gave her a hundred reasons why it was a really bad idea to move to Texas for the three months he'd be in training there and "hang around the gate of Fort Hood hoping I'll get a pass."

"IT WON'T BE *like that and you know it. But even if it would, I'm still going.*"

"You'll have to quit your job."

She looks up from the potatoes she's peeling.

"Duh."

"They won't hold it for you while you spend three months in Texas—"

"Playing bump-and-tickle with my husband?"

"I'm serious Jessie."

"So am I. Never been more serious in my life. I am going to Texas. Period. End of discussion."

OF COURSE, it hadn't been the end of the discussion. They were still having it now, the night before he was scheduled to pull out.

Davie sat down on the side of the bed and held his hands out to her.

"Com'ere."

"We don't have time to—"

"Come here."

There was no playful tone in his voice.

"Sit." He patted the bed beside him.

"Roll over. Beg."

He just looked at her and she sat down heavily beside him.

Gratefully, he didn't hold up his hand and tick off one at a time all the reasons why moving to Texas was a bad idea.

Thumb: her job and the quitting thereof.

First finger: money, which they didn't have.

Second finger: a place to stay, which she also didn't have.

Third finger: time with him, which she might get once a week, if she was lucky.

Little finger:

She'd cut him off then and say, "… and the last little piggie said, weee, weee, weee all the way home."

He didn't hold up fingers tonight.

"I want you to stay here, Jess. I *don't want you to go*." He'd never said it quite that way before. "I mean it. I want you here, in Kentucky."

He didn't say "with your family and friends," and he didn't say "not down there fending for yourself."

She didn't bother to ask why not. She knew why not.

Or did she?

"Why not?"

There was a beat of silence she didn't like. It felt like that hanging second when a wrecking ball had swung all the way out and was hurling back to crash into the building.

"Mama needs you."

Jessie almost choked, expelled a breath of air so violently it was all she could do not to burst into a fit of coughing.

"*What?*"

"Mama needs you." He said it even quieter this time.

"I heard what you *said*. What do you *mean*?"

His shoulders slumped and he suddenly seemed very tired.

"I didn't want to say it. I've tried every way on God's green earth *not* to say it, to get you to stay here without saying it." He gave her a sideways look. "Because I knew how you'd take it. But I'm down to the end and I've run out of options." He took both her hands in his.

"My mother … needs you."

"You have lost your mind."

"I'm serious."

"Obviously you're serious. That's how I know you've lost your mind."

"Mama needs you … not one of the girls, *you*."

"Why *me*?"

He took a deep breath.

"My mother doesn't need to be alone, certainly not right now. I was okay with her rattling around in that big old house by herself when we were just down the road."

Just down the road.

Four words that had an entirely different meaning for Jessie than they did for Ruth Monaghan. And apparently, Davie had a definition of his own.

They had not moved into their dream home when they got married less than a year and a half ago. They had moved into an old double-wide trailer they'd picked up at an auction, and put it on a piece of Mama's farm by the road where a house had been long ago and burned down. There were still hookups there, water and electricity. There was a septic tank in the ground, though they almost broke a hole in the top of it with the backhoe trying to locate it, and the man who cleaned it out said he hadn't seen anything that old and stopped up in twenty years in the business.

She and Davie had talked and talked about it, didn't like putting it there, but at the time it was either take the offer of land they didn't have to pay for or not get married. One or the other.

Jessie had a job, a good job, one of the few good jobs available in Brewster and she'd been lucky to get it. Amazing as it might sound, with her large hands and big fingers, she could type one hundred words a minute over zero mistakes. The typing teacher said she'd never had another student who could type that fast except Susan Robbins, who went on to major in music at the University of Tennessee and had a career as a pianist with the Chicago Symphony Orchestra.

When the legal secretary they'd had for twenty-five years retired, the Tanner, McClusky and Fowler Law Firm needed somebody to type up court transcripts, depositions and things like that — fast and accurate. She'd had to take a typing test, along with the other job applicants, nobody from Callison County High School, thank goodness. There was one from Bardstown, the other from Springfield. She'd beat them both.

But even with that good job and the money Davie made farming, there wasn't enough to do both things, make payments on the trailer house and buy a plot of land to put it on. So they'd taken the gift from his mother, with the agreement between the two of them that they'd save every nickel they made until they had the money to buy land of their own.

Living so close to his mother was just about more than Jessie could stomach. The woman was obnoxious. She was accustomed to ordering her own daughters around and took the same tone with Jessie, made "hand me the mashed potatoes" sound like a drill instructor shouting "Attention!"

But Jessie had sucked it up, watched their little nest egg grow, always on the lookout for a piece of land they could get for what they had saved. She never found one, though she scoured the real estate pages of the newspaper every week, but she knew one would come along eventually.

To Jessie "just down the road" meant way too close. To Ruth Monaghan, it meant not close enough. Her only son farther than six inches from her elbow was not close enough. And apparently, to Davie, it had meant something else entirely all these months. It had meant close enough to keep watch over his mother.

"And you want me to stay here and … what? Move into the house with her?" Jessie almost couldn't get the words out.

"Of course not."

"What about your sisters?"

Jessie knew she was sputtering, but she felt like she was drowning and she was grasping at every log that floated down the river anywhere near her.

"What about them? You think one of them is going to take care of her? If she dropped dead on the front porch they wouldn't figure it out until the body started to stink."

True that. Ruth Monaghan had alienated her three daughters to the point that she was lucky to get a fly-by visit once every couple of months, and a call on her birthday and Mother's Day. Christmas was an uneasy truce that felt like walking tightrope atop razor wire over the Berlin Wall.

"She likes you, Jessie."

Jessie was certain she was going to choke to death on her own spit.

"*Likes* me? She tolerates me, like I was some flea-bitten dog — 'she followed me home, Mom, can I keep her?'"

"Jessie!"

"What Jessie? You know I'm right."

This was tiptoeing out there into a minefield where she and Davie had never ventured. For good reason. She didn't want to go there now, and apparently Davie didn't either since he'd waited until the night before he left to bring the subject up.

This was *not* how she wanted to spend tonight.

"You don't know Mama."

No, and I don't want to. But she didn't say that.

"She's grumpy and growls and puts people off—"

"If you say but underneath it all she has a heart of gold, I'll throw up."

"She's not a *bad* person."

Jessie could hear hurt in his voice.

"I never said she was a bad person. She's a good person, but the world is full of good people I don't want to move in with."

"I never said move in with."

"No, but that's what you meant."

"Don't tell me what I meant."

"It looks like you need somebody to tell you what you mean because it's clear you don't know."

She froze.

They were fighting. They'd never had a fight. Disagreements, sure, but they'd never had a fight.

Davie must have felt it, too, because he backed off.

"Jessie, I'm not asking you to *do* anything. I'm just asking you *not* to do something. I'm asking you *not* to move to Texas for three months just to be with me."

Three months before he shipped out for Vietnam.

Three months … and then he'd be gone for a year.

Three months … and maybe she'd never see him again.

He was willing to take that away from her. For his mother. That hurt. That hurt like being kicked in the teeth by a mule.

"Stay here," she said, numb, "and … what?"

"Nothing we don't already do."

We? That'd be the royal we. It wasn't *we* who stopped by her house before going out into the field every day. *We* didn't drop by for what David called a "howdy and shake" every evening, too. David did, and Jessie genuinely didn't mind. She'd always been proud of him that he'd taken on the head-of-the-household role when his father died, proud that he stepped up to the plate and "looked after his mama" when his sisters bailed out.

And it wasn't like he spent half the morning or evening with his mother. He'd pop in, move something she needed moved, open a jar she'd been struggling with all day, reach up to the top shelf of the cabinet to get down a spare something. Five minutes. Ten, max. She didn't know if the old woman didn't push to keep him around longer or if he wouldn't let it happen. She hoped it was the latter.

Yeah, it was "we" who took her to mass on Sundays — after David pried her car keys out of her fingers right after he and Jessie got married. Jessie stopped by Foodtown and picked up her groceries on her way home from Brewster a couple of times a week. They bagged it up and had it waiting, since Ruth Monaghan had been buying the same staple items twice a week for twenty years.

When she dropped them off, Ruth wasn't rude, barked out a grudging "thanks."

But this! Not go to Texas so she could take on the role of five-minute pop-ins morning and night and Sunday church?

"Jessie, I'm not worried about you. You can take care of yourself and the farm." That was true — there wasn't anything she couldn't handle on the farm by herself if she had to. And she was proud of that. "It's Mama I'm worried about. If something happened to her while I was gone … she fell down and hurt herself and nobody found her for days. If something like that happened, I'd never forgive myself."

Jessie couldn't seem to think.

"And you waited until now, the day before you leave, let me give my two-weeks' notice and clean out my desk and—"

"Oh, come on. You know they'll be thrilled to find out you're not leaving."

It was true that it'd been a catastrophe in the office when she'd quit. They said they couldn't get by without her.

He squeezed her hands tighter. "Look, Jess, I know I should have told you how I felt sooner, I just kept thinking I could talk you out of it — it's really a dumb thing to do for a whole bunch of very valid reasons — you know it is! I'm sorry. Do you forgive me?"

He always said that! — do you forgive me? — when he screwed something up. With those pleading puppy-dog eyes.

It wasn't fair.

"It's not fair."

"No, it's not fair. There's nothing about any of this that's fair. It just is."

Her eyes pleaded with him to take it back, to say he wanted her with him too badly to give her up, to say he was sorry he'd even suggested such a thing.

"Okay. Fine. I won't move to Texas."

She couldn't believe the words had fallen out of her mouth. She absolutely, one hundred percent didn't mean to say that, to run up the white flag and give up. Give in. But now the words were out there in the world and she couldn't take them back.

The look of relief on his face … yeah, that broke her heart, too.

"But that vacation time you've got built up — that we were saving to spend a week in the Smokies — you could use it to come … see me off before we ship out."

"I'll be standing at the gate of the base waiting for you, couldn't drag me away with that team of Clydesdales that pulled the Budweiser beer wagon in the Rose Parade when I was in the first grade. And your mother—" She stopped herself. Didn't say something caustic, wanted to but didn't. "Your mother will just have to look after herself while I'm gone."

Chapter Nineteen

RILEY'S DUFFLE bag was packed, filled with tee shirts and regulation underwear. The underwear had been a tipoff, one among many. There were still people in Callison County, family members and friends of guardsmen, who believed the unit would not be sent to Vietnam. The non-believers fell into two general categories:

Category One consisted of those who believed this was just an exercise, the unit hadn't really been called up at all, they'd be told to "stand down" before they got on the transport trucks.

The non-believers who ascribed to the Category Two philosophy believed the unit had been called up alright, but they weren't going to Vietnam. They were going to stay here in the States, or go to some non-hostile place like Germany or — somebody'd started the rumor they'd be stationed in Greenland.

The underwear was a sign. Not some mystic sign from a psychic who knew the future, just an ordinary tipoff to the nature of reality. The underwear they were issued was green. Green underwear equaled jungle assignment. Made sense, didn't it?

The trucks that would take the guardsmen to Fort Hood in Texas for three months of refresher training would leave at seven o'clock in the morning. When that training was complete, they'd ship out for ... wherever.

Papa was already seated in the lawn chair on the front porch when Riley came out and sat down on the top step of the porch in front of him. Riley was exhausted. Physically tired from all the frantic running around in the whirlwind of the past few weeks. And emotionally exhausted from ... all of it.

Tonight's farewell date with Sherry Lynn had been ... gut-wrenching. He'd held her while she sobbed, tried to be caring and sympathetic. But the clutching possessiveness was so oppressive he was suffocating. The two of them had had a lot of fun together — Sherry Lynn was bright and funny and ... at least she had been. She'd changed completely when the unit was called up and now he had to admit he wasn't sorry at all to leave her.

Riley sat still, listening to the silence that wasn't quiet when you attended to the noises. The raucous cry of the cicadas in the bushes, the crickets and tree frogs and owls. On this, his last night as a civilian, Riley tried to soak up the sounds and smells — honeysuckle and roses and violets and the sight of fireflies blinking on and off in the darkness — to haul out at some dark point later on when he needed to feel home again.

Papa didn't say anything and the cricket-warm not-silence swelled around them.

"You scared?" The question came out of the darkness behind Riley with the white puff of cigarette smoke. It wasn't a question Riley'd expected and he blurted out an answer without thinking about it.

"Yeah, I'm *scared.*"

There was a murmur of soft laughter.

"Good. You ain't stupid or crazy — you'll do just fine."

"You'd make me do it, scared or not. That's what you did with tee ball."

Riley'd signed up to play, but was ready to quit before his first game.

"Had to. Couldn't let a McClusky scare you off!"

Papa was joking. Maybe. Or maybe he was serious.

They'd gone to the baseball field the first day early, watched the older boys' games while they waited. The Little League game right before Riley's tee ball game had almost turned into a brawl.

One of the players was a McClusky — Shep was his name. The umpire called a strike on the boy, and he threw a tantrum, yelling at the umpire, swinging the baseball bat at the catcher! So the umpire threw the boy out of the game. Then the boy's father, Parker, got into the act.

"I thought he was going to kill somebody," Riley said.

Parker McClusky was the son of Ike McClusky, who'd been in the wreck that injured Papa's leg and caused his limp. There was more to the story of that wreck, a whole lot more, but Riley'd never pressed for details. Now it occurred to him that the story was one he ought to hear.

Parker McClusky roared out of the stands and yelled at the umpire, "My boy isn't out and you're not going to throw him out of the game. If you think that was a strike, you're a blind --" followed by a long string of colorful expletives.

Though he was a big, intimidating man, what Riley remembered best about him was that when Parker McClusky yelled, little flakes of white spittle formed on his lips and he blew them all over the umpire.

The umpire threw Parker out of the game and gratefully the county sheriff had been present to escort him off the field.

"I didn't want to play then. I thought if I did something wrong, there'd be a fight and the sheriff might arrest *me*. After I told Willie Ray about it, he came early for every game, hoping he'd get to see Shep's father explode."

"If he really would explode, I'd pay money to see it." There was an edge to Papa's voice. There always was when he talked about a McClusky.

They sat together in silence then. Not awkward silence, companionable silence, the silence that falls between two people who know each other so well sometimes it just messes up communication to use words.

But as the silence stretched out, a ticking clock, Riley felt a tension growing in his belly, a need to hear his grandfather speak, to memorize his voice. Like all the other things he'd been trying to memorize, to save for some dark time when he might need to haul out the memory.

"That time you sneaked into the warehouse to siphon whiskey …" Riley heard his mouth say the words and wondered what room in the sub-basement of his consciousness the thought had been dragged out of. "How'd that all go down again?"

He felt like a fool the minute he said it, sounded like a little kid begging for a story he'd already heard a dozen times. He could have asked to hear the story of what'd happened between Papa and Ike McClusky. He hadn't heard that one, but he knew it was an ugly story. Tonight wasn't a time for ugly stories.

Riley could hear the warmth of a smile in the words that came to him out of the smoke-wreathed darkness, and it occurred to him that his grandfather was probably just as glad as he was to have something to talk about that didn't have to do with fighting and dying in some jungle on the other side of the world.

"The most important thing to remember when you're siphoning whiskey is *don't crimp the hose.*"

Chapter Twenty

1925

"DON'T CRIMP THE HOSE, you hear me!" Nathaniel's father hisses in a loud whisper at Johnny, who is stretching the length of hose out onto the ground behind the truck. "Make sure it ain't got no leaks."

Nathaniel doesn't really understand the process, but clearly his father and brother know what they're doing. There is a reason why they hooked four hoses together, filled the whole thing with water and put plugs in both ends. The hose has to be full of water! It has to remain full. No leaks anywhere or the whole operation is doomed before it starts.

It has something to do with how siphoning works and Nathaniel isn't interested in that part — getting the whiskey out of the warehouse and down into the barrel in the back of the truck. All he's interested in is doing his job flawlessly. He stands off to the side watching them work and — probably for the first time in his life — he is grateful that he is so much smaller than his older brother. Small enough to fit through the opening Pa had made by moving loose boards on the side of the warehouse. It will be his job to crawl through the opening into the dark interior, carrying with him one end of the hose full of water that his brother is unloading from the back of the truck, *and the carpenter's brace his father had spent the past three afternoons showing Nathaniel how to operate.*

Pa had gotten the bung from a whiskey barrel for Nathaniel to practice on.

His older brother and cousins had been skeptical, of course. Nathaniel wouldn't be strong enough to drill a hole in the solid oak of the bung, the cork that sealed the whiskey barrel. And the first time he tried, he feared they'd been right. Pa had fit the drill bit into the brace and shown him how to hold the knob on the top as he rotated the swing arm around and around in the middle.

The first couple of times, Pa had made the beginning of a hole in the wood so Nathaniel could fit the end of the drill bit into it and it wouldn't slip. And it hadn't slipped, but the drill bit had merely spun slowly around in the hole, digging out a few splinters but not really making a hole.

They might have given up right then, but Nathaniel couldn't stand the thought of failure, not at this, the first ever time he'd been allowed to work with his father, brother, uncle and cousins. He hopped up onto the work table where the bung was lying instead of standing in the dirt beside it. After all, he would be crouched on the top of a whiskey barrel to do the job. All whiskey barrels were laid out in the warehouse with the bun facing up so they wouldn't leak.

From above, he fit the drill bit into the hole, and he didn't have to use the strength of his arms to shove the drill into the wood. He could lean on it with all his body weight.

The drill bit caught at once and with some practice, the boy was able to drill a hole big enough to insert the hose.

"I knew you could do it, son," Pa had said and Nathaniel had never been more proud in his life.

Mama, on the other hand, was not thrilled. She hadn't liked the idea from the git-go, but had perhaps not put up a proper fight about it because she thought it was a plan that would die a-borning as soon as they figured out little Nathaniel wasn't strong enough to drill a hole in a whisky barrel bung.

Once they all discovered that he could, she had dug in her heels. There was nothing wrong with making whiskey, she'd said. It was not a sin. Stealing, on the other hand, was. It was not just a violation of man's law, it was a violation of the laws of God.

"It ain't stealing," Pa had told her.

"And how do you figure that? It ain't yours and you're taking it. What would you call that if not stealing?"

"It's just sitting there, and right now it don't really belong to anybody."

That was splitting hairs, Mama'd said, and Nathaniel had no idea how Pa's plan had anything to do with hair. It was about whiskey, aged bourbon whiskey.

Since the closure of the Double Springs Distillery, there'd been disputes about the ownership, lawsuits and such that Nathaniel didn't understand. The Ballard family owned Double Springs — of course they did, they'd built the distillery from scratch, had brewed every gallon of the whiskey in every one of the 500-gallon barrels in six big warehouses on the property — warehouses that were five stories tall.

Apparently, Pa was hanging his hat on the technicality, however — that the whiskey didn't belong to anybody. And if it didn't belong to anyone, taking it was not stealing it.

And it was just sitting there, thousands of barrels of it! Golden amber whiskey that had been poured into brand new white oak barrels, charred on the inside to give the brew its distinctive taste.

After the barrels were filled, they were loaded into one of the warehouses, taken by a unique system of pulleys and ramps up to the top floor, filling up the huge racks in the darkened interior of the black warehouse with row upon row of full, freshly brewed barrels of whiskey.

The new brew was taken to the top floor because that was where it was hottest. Who knew what the temperature was in the tops of those black buildings in the heat of Kentucky summer.

When the new whiskey was taken to the top floor of the warehouses, the barrels already there were rotated down to the fourth floor to make room for them. And the barrels on the fourth floor were rotated down to the third, the ones on the third down to the second, and the ones on the second down to the first floor where they were hauled out to the bottling facility.

It took a full seven years for the barrels to make their way from the top floor of the building to the bottom, to be loaded up and bottled and shipped out — Double Springs Distillery's distinctive bourbon whiskey. The system worked flawlessly, the distilleries hummed, providing jobs for thousands of workers. Among them Nathaniel's uncle Pete, Pa's brother. He'd been what was called a ricket rider, one of the men who made certain the quarter-ton barrels were loaded properly on the aging racks, every one of them with the bung pointed upward ... or there would be more lost from the barrel than "what the angels took" — the whiskey that evaporated.

And then the country had gone mad. Prohibition had closed the distillery. And left the barrels sitting in the warehouses. There were warehouses full of whiskey at distilleries all over the country — Jim Bean, Heaven Hill, Double Springs in Kentucky and Jack Daniels in Tennessee to name a few.

It was not illegal to own the whiskey. It was, however, illegal to drink it or sell it. Or move it.

So the barrels sat, aging, growing more tasty and more valuable every day.

Of course, the federal prohibition agents sat on the distilleries like geese on dead eggs, while clever businessmen managed to convince the government they needed to use it, to squeeze it through the loophole in the law as "medicinal alcohol." Barrel by barrel, the fine aged bourbon was being gobbled up by conmen who loaded it into convoys for transport to facilities that would transform the bourbon into bunion oil, or cough syrup or any one of a dozen other remedies for what ailed a person.

But funny thing ... those convoys of whiskey ... they never actually made it to the medicinal alcohol facilities. They were hijacked —

every last one of them — by thieves who seemed to know exactly when and where the next convoy would be.

Eventually, the scoundrels would make off with every drop of that aged whiskey ... unless somebody removed it from the barrels before they got there. The glorious aged bourbon sold for an outrageous amount on the black market, to speakeasies in the city whose customers would pay a premium to have their parched throats graced by something more refined that moonshine.

Johnny has been itching to branch out, but there's no money to buy a fast car for bootlegging. He sees this small operation as a step in the right direction. Mama sees it as a step down the slippery slope to Hell itself.

Pa had finally won the argument, and now Nathaniel stands in the warm darkness behind the most remote of Double Spring's warehouses. The prohibition agents patrol the warehouses ... well, are paid to patrol them. Mostly they sit in the distillery offices playing poker, smoking cigars and getting drunk.

Uncle Pete and his boys are stationed around as lookouts — as Johnny and Pa would help out when it was Uncle Pete's truck sitting in the darkness with a hose stretching out from it to a loose board in the back of the building.

"You know what to do." Nathaniel doesn't think it's a question until his father repeats it and he realizes he needs to answer.

"Yes sir," and he recites the drill to Pa's satisfaction.

Chapter Twenty-One

EVERY SOUND SEEMS OVERLY loud in the quiet darkness. The crickets grating, the tree frogs galumphing in the woods, a barn owl somewhere questioning who, who?

Nathaniel is not scared. Not. He is not afraid!

He. Is. Not. Afraid.

And even if he is, it doesn't matter. Even if he's so frightened he wets his pants, he will do what he's been instructed to do.

And what is there to be afraid of?

Everything.

"Don't drop the drill."

"I won't." Nathaniel points to where it is tied with a bit of rope to his chest.

"Hold the hose in your teeth like I showed you so you'll have both hands free to climb."

Why is Pa telling him all this now? He's already said it—

Then it occurs to Nathaniel that Pa is frightened, too. Oh, not for the same reasons Nathaniel is, but afraid nonetheless, and he doesn't know if he's glad to know his father is concerned about him or shocked to realize his resolute, staunch, unflappable father can be rattled at all.

That's concerning, but now isn't the time to consider it.

Johnny reaches over and takes hold of the board that's loose and slides it sideways, making a hole, then looks at Pa. Pa nods and Nathaniel takes the end of the hose and gets down on his hands and knees, glad to finally be moving, doing something. His heart is pounding, making thud-thud-thud sounds in his ears that seem so loud he is sure his father and brother can hear.

He crawls through the opening into the interior of the warehouse and stands up. There is a space about five feet wide, an aisle behind the rows of barrels that march off into the distance and he stands there now in the darkness, with only the faintest light that shines in from the high windows. Pa picked a night with a full moon, so the light is enough to see what he's doing.

Nathaniel takes two steps and stops beside the barrel rack and begins pulling the hose in through the opening, coiling it on the floor beside him.

Don't crimp it.

He hears his father say that, but only in his head.

He is careful, doesn't crimp the hose, makes a looped stack of hose around and around, higher and higher. He needs to get enough hose into the building so he's not trying to pull it in from outside when he's up in the warehouse with the barrels. It needs to be coiled here, waiting.

He must climb up the lattice work of the barrel racks to the second floor. The whiskey on the bottom floor is the oldest, the best, the most valuable. But those barrels are also visible when the prohibition agents make their inspection rounds through the warehouse. A hole in the bung of one of those barrels would raise an alarm. They'd catch on. Pa and Uncle Pete intend for this to be their first, not their last foray into siphoning.

The agents don't climb up to the higher levels to inspect those barrels, so that's where Nathaniel's going. His mother put her foot down, said he could not go higher than the big oak tree he climbs at the edge of the woods near the house. Pa says that would be no higher than the second floor.

Mama would have been more upset by the prospect of her "baby son" climbing up the rack of barrels in the dark if he weren't such a monkey. Everyone has remarked on it his whole life. He's always climbing something. Out of his bed, out of the fence around the house, to the top of the barn loft, every tree he can get to in the forest. Sure-footed and agile, he has never fallen. Pa assured Mama that he wouldn't fall tonight.

And he won't. He won't fall. He won't.

When he finally has the hose coiled on the floor beside him, he bites down on the hose near the end that's plugged, like a dog on a stick, clamps down hard. The full hose is heavy, drags his head sideways. His neck instantly begins to cramp. His hands are wet with sweat. Refusing to acknowledge his fear doesn't make it go away. It seems to be growing.

It's so dark and hollow, echo-ey in the big building. So quiet.

Except it isn't.

He hears sounds and freezes before he ever takes a step. Scratching, clawing, scuttling sounds. Rats.

Nathaniel hates rats!

Why would there be rats in this warehouse? What is there for them to eat here? There must be something.

Don't think about the rats. Climb!

The barrel racks are held in place by a lattice of wood strips, forming something like a ladder on the end. Climbing it isn't difficult, even in the dark.

He climbs, feeling around for the next support post. The hose in his mouth would taste bad, rubbery, if his mouth weren't so dry. He has no spit, can't taste a thing. He reaches the top of the first-floor barrel racks. He keeps climbing.

In the darkness, there is no sense of height. He doesn't look down, has better sense than to look down, but suspects that if he did, the dark void below him would seem bottomless.

He is panting, sweating. Can feel it running down his back and chest. It is hot and stuffy in here. For all the openness, it feels close, like the air is stagnant. It is, of course, hotter as he climbs. The big building painted black, constructed to hold the heat. He can't imagine how hot it must be in the daytime.

Seeing the bottom slats of the second floor come into view, he feels such relief he only then notices that his arms and legs have started to cramp. He climbs to a point where he can step out on the floor, into the aisle between the rows of barrels on the second floor. It's dark and spooky. He stands still, panting, catching his breath. It is only then that he looks closely enough to see that the space between the top barrel on the second level and the floor of the third floor — the space where he must fit to use his drill on a barrel bung — is much smaller than he thought it'd be. His slogging heart begins to stampede in his chest.

He won't fit. Oh, he'll fit, but there has to be enough space for him to get on his knees on the barrel and use his weight to drive the drill into the bung. There's not enough room for that.

What should he do? He can't climb back down, though every fiber of his being is begging him to do just that, climb down and get out of this hot muggy building into the night air. But he can't just crawl back out and say, sorry guys, not enough room. Maybe some other day.

He looks down the rows of barrels and notices that in the center of the building where the ramps are positioned for rolling the barrels, there's open space above the last couple of barrels in the row.

But does he have enough hose to reach all the way to the center of the building? What if he gets halfway there and runs out of hose? Then what will he do?

Figure it out when you get there, he yells at himself inside his head. He takes the hose out of his mouth and drags it along behind him as he walks down between the barrels. Three barrels from the center of the building the hose pulls tight. He turns around and tugs. The hose feels heavy, only comes along with effort. He must have reached the end of the length of hose he had coiled on the floor, and now the additional hose is being fed into the building from outside. How much hose is there? He doesn't know.

Exerting steady pressure, he pulls the hose along with him as he crosses to the nearest barrel with sufficient open space above it. The hose snags, won't come any farther. He pulls, afraid to yank. Three yanks in a row is the signal for Pa to remove the plug from the other end of the hose so the water will start to run out of it ... pulling the whiskey along behind it if Nathaniel gets this end of the hose down into the barrel.

He had planned to lay the hose down on the floor, climb up onto the barrel and drill the hole, then get off the barrel and pick up the hose. He can't do that now. If he lets go of the hose, it will snake away from him, responding to the pressure of being extended too far. He will have to hold the hose between his teeth while he gets on top of the barrel and keep it there while he uses the drill.

He doesn't think his jaws are that strong.

Well, they will just have to be.

Clamping down with all his concentrated strength, he grips the hose between his teeth and climbs up on top of the barrel with the bit and brace. He stabs the bung with the sharp point of the drill bit and begins to wind. Around and around he turns it, the hose pulling at his whole head now, cramping his neck.

Suddenly, the brace falls free and he smells the sweet pungent aroma of Kentucky bourbon. Carefully, he removes the hose from his mouth. Then he gently pulls at the wax plug in the end of the hose ... careful not to allow any water to spill.

The plug comes out, he holds the hose end upright, then plunges it down through the hole he has just drilled into the whiskey below. He yanks on the hose three times as the signal to remove the plug on the other end.

"I HAD to sit there with the hose, shoving it deeper and deeper as the whiskey drained—"

Nate paused, looked closely at his grandson. Riley had leaned back against the porch post and was sound asleep. Well, that was the point of a bedtime story, wasn't it — to put the kid to sleep.

Sitting in the pale glow of moonlight, Nate studied Riley's face and tried to memorize it, to save the image for some dark time when he might need to haul out the memory.

Chapter Twenty-Two

RILEY and the rest of the soldiers had been in Texas for going on two months and Nate still hadn't gotten used to the boy being gone. The house was too quiet. He hadn't really appreciated how hard Riley worked around the farm, all the jobs he did, until he wasn't there to do them. Riley'd been the primary driver who made the rounds through the surrounding dry counties, delivering liquor, both legal and home-brewed, to convenience stores, restaurants, grocery stores, pool halls — and unlikely places like a furniture store in Springfield and the garage behind a daycare center in Campbellsville — anywhere the locals knew to go to buy what the virtuous, respectable, clean-living and in all ways holier people in their county had decided they shouldn't be drinking. Now Nate had to do it.

And feed the livestock.

And weed the garden.

And cut the final stand of hay.

And get the farm in shape for the winter months before the busy season of spring planting.

Gratefully, they'd set their tobacco crop early this

spring and it was already in the barn. He'd need to haul it to the warehouse soon to sell it. And he would. Soon's he could find a spare minute to do it, he would.

He'd shut down the only still he was operating, didn't want to hire a still hand to replace Riley and couldn't do it alone. He'd arranged with LeRoy Taggart to supply the shine he wasn't making. Demand had fallen off in the past few years anyway as the customer base changed — not many now who still had a taste for it. But the bootlegging business was still going gangbusters.

He hadn't seen Fast Eddie since the man had wrestled the empty eighteen-wheeler into the trees behind the farm and onto the logging road that snaked up the side of the knob. He knew he needed to put out the word among his other suppliers that he was in the market for merchandise, but he had just flat out been too busy.

"You doing all right, old girl?" he asked Daisy, the prize-winning cow Riley had shown at the state fair three years ago. He slapped her on the butt to urge her into the stall. "Supposed to rain tomorrow, you mind getting wet?"

He stopped, stood stock still.

I'm talking to a cow.

Oh, he'd always talked to his livestock. But he was relatively sure he'd never before tried to carry on a conversation with one.

All work and no play …

Time to go into town and have a beer. Might even get drunk.

After he showered, he drove into the edge of Brewster to The Tavern, hoped to see some of the Taggart clan there.

It was a windowless structure, had a huge bar that ran from one side of the back wall of the building to the other. Cigarette and cigar smoke hung in the air like morning haze over a creek. It smelled of manure and beer and sweat.

The Tavern featured a hodge-podge of mismatched tables and chairs, built out of sturdy oak to withstand the treatment they'd had to suffer over the years at the hands of drunks and mean men looking for a fight. There were stools in front of the bar, attached to the floor, their oak seats worn smooth by generations of Callison County backsides.

Over the bar a stuffed raccoon climbed up into the branches of a leafless tree. It had one remaining shiny marble eye and a moth-eaten coat.

He'd seated himself at the bar, ordered a beer and drank it down, lit a cigarette and squinted through the haze of smoke at familiar faces. He was about to order a second beer when the bartender, a muscular black man with a many-times-broken nose, leaned over and said:

"Mama Bert wants to see you in her office."

It didn't exactly sound like an *invitation*, and he wondered briefly what she'd do if he said "Tell her I'm busy."

He didn't, just stubbed out his cigarette in the overflowing ashtray, pulled out his wallet and placed a five-dollar bill on the bar. The bartender shoved it back at him. When he didn't pick it up, the bartender gave a nod to a fellow at the end of the bar and he motioned for Nate to follow him. There was a door in the far wall beside the hallway leading to the bathrooms. It didn't have an "employees only" sign, but he'd never seen anybody go in or out of it.

The door opened onto a short hallway with a door at the end. That door opened to a windowless "office" that wasn't an office at all. It was a small room with a loveseat, a couple of overstuffed chairs, a big coffee table and an enormous couch where Mama Bert sat drinking a beer.

She was fat, but big-boned so she carried the weight well. She wore a black Bert's Tavern tee shirt, dark pants … and plastic beach flip-flops. Pink ones, and there was a bite in the late October air.

There were big lamps on tables at both ends of the couch, but neither of them could have had more than a 25-watt bulb. The room was dim, shadowy. If you came in here straight from the bright sunshine outside — with no time in the darkened bar for your eyes to adjust — you couldn't have seen a thing.

"Have a seat." Her voice was low, full of pebbles. "I hear you put that police detective in his place the other day."

It'd been almost two months ago. Skeet Burkett had likely exaggerated the story.

Nate sat in one of the overstuffed chairs, which was more comfortable than it looked.."

"You coulda thrown me under the bus. You didn't."

Nate nodded, figured that was as close as Mama Bert ever got to a thank you.

"I'm looking to go partners in a business enterprise. You interested?"

No preamble, no explanation.

"What kind of business and why me?"

"The law's been sniffing 'round my butt lately like I's a bitch in heat. I can't fart 'thout them smelling it. Somebody put out a word on me and I ain't figured out yet who it was, but I got my suspicions. 'Til I plug up the leak, I ain't getting back in the boat. So I need to be a *silent* partner for a while. Invisible. Need me a front man who stands his ground, ain't intimidated easy."

"And the business?"

"Chop shop."

A place where stolen cars drive in one side and come out the other in marketable pieces. That was a big step up from fencing stolen stereo systems. Auto theft was a Class C felony — prison time, a pretty good-sized hunk of it.

Mama Bert went on full speed ahead like he'd already agreed.

"We don't set up until after Christmas. December is the biggest month for car sales. We swoop down the middle of January and pick up new cars with less than two thousand miles on 'em. By May, car dealerships start dumping what they didn't sell so they can stock up on the new model year, and we cherry-pick what they dumped outta auto auction lots — they's acres of 'em."

"I got a farm—"

"Most labor-intensive part is setting it up, getting the supply lines out and working, finding the right lifters, setting up the shop equipment with strippers and lining up customers. I done all that a long time ago. It operates at night so you'll be free in the daytime to plant, take care of your livestock, spring calves and the like. Once you get this hose flowing, the water mostly keeps draining right on through it."

Nate thought of siphoning whiskey out of barrels in the warehouse. She could see him hesitate.

"You need to know if you do this, you're likely gonna get crossed off the McClusky family's Christmas card list."

His jaw tensed and he knew she saw it.

"How so?"

"They was a McClusky doin' this job until I got so popular with the law. If I'd a gone down, he'd a moved in and took it over ... which makes me wonder ..." She let it go. "Now, he wasn't 'xactly *fired,* more like laid off — job just went away. Until I get things sorted out, I need somebody I ain't worried 'bout turning my back on."

"And you think that's me 'cause I put a trailer full of baseball bats in my barn?"

"More'n that. I've asked around." She paused. "Tell you what — you commit for half a year. On ... how about the Fourth of July, we renegotiate. We can go our separate ways or keep on keeping on."

He studied his shoes.

"You got a boy in that guard unit and they ain't coming home for a year. Now'd be a good time to get into something and then get back out and he ain't involved in none of it."

How did she know he'd scrupulously kept Riley out of his stolen property business? She probably knew what size his jock shorts were!

"You pay minimum wage?"

"Base of $500 a month, plus a percentage of the take — which will depend on what gets ordered, what gets delivered and what gets paid for."

That was a whole lot more money than he was making now fencing stereo equipment!

"And the job responsibilities are ...?"

"Glorified babysitter. I got the crews who know what to do, just need some oversight to keep them on the straight and narrow. This here's a job — all cash transactions — it'd be real easy to skim off the top. Might have been some of that goin' on in the past ... I ain't sayin' one way or the other. Still, it's a good idea to shake things up every now and then."

Translate that: some lowlife whose last name was McClusky had been ripping Mama Bert off, stealing a share for himself out of the take, and she knew it, just couldn't prove it. Might have been one reason she'd picked

Nate as a replacement — knew a Hannacker would never line up with a McClusky against her. If Nate took the job, he'd be putting a McClusky out of work — which would surely piss him off. Good! *Excellent.*

"What do you say?"

His voice had a hard edge to it. "Deal."

She nodded, stood up and offered her hand. He stood and took it — hard, like a farmer's hand — and shook it.

"Partners," she said. And it was possible — the light was low so he couldn't be sure — but she might have smiled.

Chapter Twenty-Three

SHERRY LYNN BENNETT had never done anything even remotely like this in her whole life and if she got caught, her parents would kill her. But she didn't care. She had to see Riley before he left for Vietnam. Nothing else mattered. So she had concocted an elaborate story, said that the family of her roommate at Spencerian, Kim Beddingfield, always spent a week snow skiing just outside of Pittsburgh during the Christmas/New Year's break and they'd invited her to go with them. The Beddingfields owned a cabin in Hidden Valley so it wouldn't be expensive ... and *surely* her parents could see that Sherry Lynn needed something to lift her spirits since Riley would be shipping out for Vietnam soon.

Her parents bought the story.

In reality, she didn't drive to the Beddingfields' house in Louisville, and then travel with them for eight hours north to the ski area in Pennsylvania. She and Gloria got into Gloria's car for a marathon drive to Texas. Two days to get there. Two days there. Two days back.

Riley had tried to talk her out of it — he was so sweet

and thoughtful, didn't want her to get in trouble — but she'd made up her mind. Several of the wives of the guardsmen had moved to Texas when the unit left at the end of September. She and Gloria would bunk in for a couple of days with Emily Taggart — so Gloria could spend time with Willie Ray, and Sherry Lynn could say goodbye to Riley.

Now she stood, checking her makeup in the mirror of the tiny bathroom in the duplex Emily shared with Peggy Benson — waiting for Riley to pick her up.

A sob escaped, a little one, but she swallowed it, and blinked rapidly to keep the tears from streaming down her face. She sniffed, squared her shoulders and peered at the girl who stared back at her. She had brown hair. It was long, came down to her shoulders in a flip made popular by Annette Funicello. It was affixed in place by half a can of Spray Net. She had big blue eyes, a small nose and full lips. She was pretty.

Okay, that was modest. She was beautiful. Riley had told her as much and so it was true. And she had to be especially beautiful tonight because it was so very, very special. Oh, not just because it was the last time she would see Riley before he shipped out, though that made it more precious and special than any other night she'd ever lived. But it was also special because tonight ... she was going to lose her virginity.

She and Riley were going to go all the way.

She'd decided it the night of the going-away party as she looked at the line of young men posing for a picture. Some of them wouldn't come back ... and she couldn't let Riley leave without giving herself to him. It wasn't supposed to be like this, under these circumstances, under the gun. But it was what it was.

As soon as she'd started dating Riley, she knew he was

the one. She would marry him someday, settle down in Callison County and have a houseful of kids. They'd never talked about that, never even got close. They'd had their whole relationship ... what was the word, "truncated" by the awful guard call-up. Now, nothing was progressing in its natural way.

She loved him! He loved her, too. He hadn't said the words, but she could tell. Boys often had trouble spitting it out, but Riley Hannacker loved her. And he certainly wanted her ... that way. They had made out at the drive-in movie in Bardstown until she'd go home with her lips chapped and her face raw from the stubble of his beard scraping against it. He'd touched her in ... those places, reached under her blouse and unfastened her bra strap and slipped his hands up to caress her breasts. In the natural order of things, it would just have happened. They'd both try not to, of course, but it would. She didn't expect to be a virgin on her wedding night but what difference did that make if she'd given herself to the man she was marrying?

None of that counted now. Life had gone off the rails and there was no way to set it right again. She stood looking at her reflection, knowing that the next time she saw her face in this mirror, she would ... what, be a woman? Oh, call it whatever you liked. She'd belong to Riley in the way only making love could cement.

She heard the doorbell and then Peggy Benson called out, "He's here." A thrill ran through her. Riley.

Tonight ... *Riley*.

He'd only been able to get leave for one day, the last day before he shipped out. Other than her time spent getting dressed up for the evening, they'd spent every minute of it together. He'd been a little distant when she first saw him, and she realized he was holding onto his own emotions, keeping himself together for her sake. She loved him so much for that. He'd borrowed a car from one of the Fort Hood soldiers and they'd had breakfast together at Waffle House, took a long walk in the park, hand in hand. It was January, but this was Texas and the afternoon was warm. He took her to a candlelit dinner at a nice restaurant. Sherry Lynn couldn't remember the name of the place and couldn't taste the food she ate. The hours flew by with wings on their feet. It seemed like the day was over almost over before it began.

Emily had told her about a beautiful lake in Belton and Sherry Lynn directed Riley there. Now they sat in the car in a secluded spot on the lakeshore … to say goodbye. In the sudden silence after he killed the engine, Sherry Lynn could hear her heart galloping in her chest, knew it must be so loud he could hear it, too. She turned to him, took his face in her hands and began to kiss him passionately. He responded as she knew he would and she gave in to his kisses, gloried in the smell of him and the feel of his touch.

The windows fogged. He began touching her and his hands set her skin on fire. She reached down to unbutton her blouse and Riley pulled away, sat up.

"Don't." His voice was husky and he was breathing hard. "I can't … I can't stop if I go any further."

"Then don't stop."

He turned and his eyes bored into hers.

She held his gaze.

"I mean it. Don't stop."

She reached out and took his hand, pried it off the steering wheel and put it on her breast.

"Don't stop!"

And he didn't.

He didn't stop.

When it was over, he lay panting on top of her.

"I'm sorry. I'm so, so sorry."

"Why are you sorry?"

"I shouldn't have. I should have stopped. I—"

"I didn't want you to stop. I'm glad you didn't. I love you!" She clung to him. "I love you!"

"Oh, Sherry Lynn … Sherry Lynn."

He repeated her name over and over. There was such love and tenderness in his voice. He didn't say "I love you" but his chanting her name said to her what she yearned to hear. She needed no words to confirm what her heart heard from his. She belonged to him now and he belonged to her.

"My love will bring you home to me," she whispered. "You'll see. And we'll be together always."

She didn't cling to him when it was time to go. She was proud of herself for that. She didn't fall apart until the next day when she and Gloria started the long trek home to Kentucky. Then she let go and began to sob. She cried for what seemed like hours, until Gloria suddenly said, "Sherry Lynn, stop crying."

"I just can't—"

"Shut up and listen."

Sherry Lynn shut up. What she heard was a knocking sound coming from the motor of the car. The sound was soft but quickly grew louder. Smoke began to boil out from under the hood. Gratefully, there was a big filling station on the road ahead and Gloria was able to coax the car into the garage there before it died.

The car could be fixed, the mechanic told her. But it would take two days!

"Two days!" Sherry Lynn cried. "I can't stay here two days. I have to get back."

Gloria had her own apartment with three other girls and it wouldn't matter if she were late getting back home. Sherry Lynn was another matter altogether. If Sherry

Lynn didn't show up on time, the whole elaborate story about the ski trip would collapse. And when her parents found out she'd lied ... found out what she'd *really* done ...

Now Sherry Lynn had something else to sob about.

It was several hours before Sherry Lynn finally cried herself out. She sat, desolate, at a picnic table under a tree where the filling station employees ate their lunch, so utterly miserable she didn't notice the car with Kentucky plates pull up to the gas pump.

Gloria noticed, though, and when she squealed "Jessie!" Sherry Lynn looked up into the face of a minor miracle. Jessica Monaghan was traveling back to Kentucky after spending a week in Texas with her husband, Davie. Actually, he'd only gotten leave for a couple of days, but now he was on a troop transport of some kind with Riley and the rest of the unit, on their way to Vietnam.

Sherry Lynn didn't know Jessie very well. They'd traveled in different circles in high school. Sherry Lynn'd been a "popular girl." Jessie'd been a farm girl who didn't care about lace and makeup and prom dresses. But they had a special empathy for each other now. They were even connected by the guys — Jessie'd dated Riley for a while and Sherry Lynn had had a couple of dates with Davie!

During the two-day drive back to Kentucky, Jessica Monaghan and Sherry Lynn Bennett bonded over their shared loss. They became friends.

Chapter Twenty-Four

THE UNIT SUFFERED ITS FIRST "CASUALTY" before the soldiers even got into the transport plane. Sean Mattingly lost his footing getting out of the back of the troop carrier, tumbled to the asphalt four feet below and broke his wrist.

"Lost his footing" was the way Sean reported it. But Jackson McClusky had been standing nearby ... and tripping people was one of Jackson's favorite contact sports.

Sean would be replaced once they arrived in Vietnam. The remainder of the company was strapped into the seats a huge C-141 transport before it hurtled down the runway at Ft. Hood, struggling to leap into the Texas sky. Riley listened to the rumble. It sounded ominous. He'd never been on any aircraft this large and neither had any of the other guardsmen but he couldn't imagine that the awful sound was *normal*.

Did every transport groan, grumble and ... growl before it took off? He didn't know, but the sound that filled his ears sounded like some caged monster, letting loose its fury on the world. Then the beast became airborne and they were on their way.

For the next twenty-two hours, as the airplane sailed above the clouds, landed and refueled in Midway, and took to the air again, Riley was haunted by the grumbling sound he'd heard at takeoff.

"Just for the record, anybody here still think we ain't shipping out to Vietnam?" Willie Ray announced to anyone within earshot, which was everyone. "'Cause if there is, we need to talk soon about some swampland in Florida I got to sell that'd make a dandy place for a second home."

Nobody spoke.

Willie Ray pulled a deck of cards out of his pocket. He never went anywhere that he wasn't prepared, at a moment's notice, to deal out a hand of five-card draw, five-card stud -- or any one of a dozen other poker games he called "Hollywood games." He didn't like to play Hollywood games. Real gamblers never did because with wild cards here and there, or some other things like "black trey's are the same as aces," things like that, there was no reasonable way to calculate the odds in your head. And a dealer who couldn't calculate odds before he played a card would not last long in a serious game.

"Who's in?" he asked, as he walked down the aisle to the area in the back where their personal duffle bags and other gear had been loaded. He grabbed one of the cargo boxes, flipped it over and sat on it like a milk crate, set another one in front of him for a table and called out to the usual suspects — Ben Higgs, Larry Bradshaw, Randy Nickel, Simon Tanner, Sam Finch, Billy Wilson and Scooter Washington — inviting them to pull up boxes of their own.

"Yo, bro," he called out to Andy. "One hand. Just one hand."

Andy leaned back in his seat and pulled his helmet down over his face.

Painted on the wallpaper of the ongoing card game, Riley sat in his own seat with his eyes closed, but he wasn't asleep. He suspected he wasn't the only person in the unit who was acting as studiedly casual as it was possible to look, so's not to look nervous.

Not to look *scared*.

He tried to busy his mind, keep it occupied, keep it distracted. He thought about Papa. That last night at home, the man had looked fragile in a way that made no sense because he was big, strong and powerful. He limped because of an old injury but otherwise could hold his own with men half his age. Had streaks of gray in his dark blond hair, but he still had a full head of it, though Riley suspected if Papa let his beard grow, it would be all white.

Riley had stopped arm-wrestling with Papa a long time ago. Because he didn't want to lose! And he didn't want to win, either.

The fragile quality Riley had sensed was more about Papa's spirit than his physical strength. His body might be a Mason Jar, but his spirit was spun glass. It'd seemed to Riley it could break apart right before his eyes. And he knew it would shatter completely if he didn't come home.

Riley thought about Sherry Lynn, and expended a considerable amount of emotional energy kicking himself for what had happened between them the night before he left. What had he been thinking! The very worst possible thing he could have done before he left was … what he had done. What *they* had done. He knew how she felt about him, knew how hard it was going to be to break up with her … and what he'd done had made it ten times harder. Well … if there was any bright side to going to Vietnam it was that he would be separated from her for a whole year.

Surely, during that amount of time a girl as beautiful as Sherry Lynn would find somebody else.

Bright side to going to Vietnam.

Riiiiight.

Riley scrambled to find something else to distract his mind, but he couldn't do it any longer — not even with regret over Sherry Lynn Bennett.

Cold truth settled around him. He could die and he wasn't even old enough to vote.

Never once in his almost twenty years of living had he ever considered ... dying. Being dead, gone. The world going on but him not in it. Riley Hannacker buried in the Saint Augustine church cemetery under a white cross while everybody he knew stood around and cried. And then ... *left*, walked out of the cemetery alive, *breathing*.

He suddenly felt like crying. Like a little kid. Felt the knot rising in his throat. How do you think about a thing like that, about dying? Where is there in your mind to consider such a thing? He could get killed in a jungle on the other side of the world and they'd ship him home in a box and—

Stop it!

Stop it right now ... no.

Not just *no it won't happen. Not just denial no. It was a bigger no than that. A more powerful no.*

This was: No, I *won't* think about that.

No, I *won't allow myself* to dwell on that.

Was that what courage was? He didn't think so. He thought courage was a thing you didn't find out you had until you were in danger. He certainly didn't feel brave. He was afraid and he could *feel* the fear. But the *no* that had welled up inside him felt ... stronger somehow. Okay, that was stupid ... but it did.

No, *I won't run,* not even in my mind.

I will fight. We *all* will — together.

He waited for that resolve, that whatever-it-was to make him feel better. It didn't. It was just there, a separate thing. He was still afraid.

When he let out the breath he hadn't realized he'd been holding, it felt like he was still holding it. He suspected the holding-his-breath sensation had taken up residence there, moved in all the furniture and changed the address labels at the post office. Riley figured he'd better get used to it, because it wasn't going anywhere.

They all heard the change in the timbre of the engine, felt the big transport begin to sink out of the sky. Riley looked out the window at a sea of black ink. There were lights on the horizon, looked like fires maybe, but the land over which they passed as they made their approach to Da Nang was the black of an empty grave.

Runway lights suddenly flared ahead, and there was a scramble for everybody to locate the gear they'd strewn about the cabin for the past twenty-two hours.

The tires landed with a bone-jarring thunk on the asphalt as everyone by a window strained to see what was out there. It was dark, nothing at all to see. Riley had practiced how to figure the time difference between Vietnam and Kentucky — made tricky by what Willie Ray called "that stupid International Dateline thingy." The time in Vietnam was eleven hours *ahead* of Kentucky, meaning sometimes it was "tomorrow" in Vietnam, or "yesterday" in Kentucky. He kept it straight in his head by imagining the world globe in his elementary school library that would only spin west to east. One day, the librarian had turned out all the lights and drawn the shades. Then she'd shined a flashlight beam on China — "this is the sun" — and began to spin the globe slowly around. The children watched the beam of the flashlight sun slowly illuminate the countries below — chasing the shadow of darkness in front of it. The light crossed India and Pakistan and Saudi Arabia and Egypt — lit up North Africa before it crossed the Atlantic Ocean and landed in North Carolina. As a third-grader, he hadn't noticed where Vietnam was on that globe. And to be perfectly honest, he wasn't exactly sure now — but he did know that if it was four o'clock in the morning here in Da Nang, it was five o'clock yesterday afternoon in Kentucky.

As soon as the bumping of the landing smoothed out, two members of the flight crew came around to each soldier, handed him two clips for his M16, and told him to load one clip in his rifle and put the other in his pocket. Then a message came over the intercom:

"When disembarking from the aircraft, move immediately to a place of cover. Do not stand around in groups. Disburse immediately. This base has just sustained a rocket attack."

Rocket attack.

The two words sent Riley's heart into overdrive.

Lining up with the other guardsmen, there was no banter, none of the normal cutting up. Even Willie Ray was silent. Riley reached up and touched his helmet. No reason. Not like he didn't think it'd be there or anything. Just … touched it, that's all.

When Riley stepped out of the aircraft onto the top of the metal stairs, the heat hit him like a fist. It had been chilly when they left Texas. Sherry Lynn had said it was freezing in Kentucky with a powdered-sugar dusting of snow on the ground.

How could you breathe *this*? How could you inhale air this wet and thick? At the bottom of the metal stairs, Riley Hannacker stepped for the first time on soil that was not American.

"I don't think we're in Kansas anymore, Dorothy," Willie Ray announced as he stepped off onto the tarmac behind him.

Riley didn't say it out loud, but thought it — as he searched for somewhere to run when they disbursed — *welcome to Vietnam.*

Chapter Twenty-Five

THERE WERE NO MORE rocket attacks while Riley and the guardsmen were at the airport. As soon as the sun dawned on their first morning in Vietnam, Riley's company was loaded up in another aircraft and flown to a place called Gia Lai, their acclimation point, where they were scheduled for a three-week stay to adjust to their new home. The weather. The heat. The bugs. The heat. The jungle. The heat. The rain. And the heat. And to the fact that this was, oh by the way, a war.

They were assembled at Gia Lai the first week of February and shipped out to their first assignment, Fire Base Eagle's Nest, where they'd join infantrymen from the 101st Airborne Division to provide perimeter security for the firebase artillery battery, the 197th Field Artillery Brigade of the New Hampshire National Guard.

The Eagle's Nest would be their base of operations when they were not out in the jungle, hunting the North Vietnamese Army. The NVA. The Viet Cong. The VC. The Cong. Or just plain Charlie.

They arrived about noon and as the choppers

descended to the landing pad they saw how "out in the bush" this fire station was. The jungle grew up to within fifteen feet of the concertina wire that enclosed the whole fire base.

"You reckon there are VC in them trees?" Ben Higgs asked, his deep, resonant voice higher-pitched than normal.

"Course not," said Ronnie Benson. "You think they'd plop a base down right in the middle of enemy territory? They done cleaned the Cong out of that jungle a long time ago."

Fire Base Eagle's Nest was in a saddle. Headquarters for the airborne unit was at the west end of the saddle, the low end. The ammo depo, supply sheds, the tent for stored generators and amenities like the shower unit were at the east end, the high end. The howitzers were in between the two. Each of the guns had its own nearby bunker. There was also a mess area and maintenance area on the north side next to the Fire Direction Center, with its big set of reinforced bunkers.

The whole base was surrounded by concertina wire with razor edges, two rows of it side by side. A third coil of wire was placed on top of the two. From the ground to the top of the wire was more than eight feet. Maggie's drawers, the red flags attached to the wire, were set every five feet. And there were two-man guard bunkers back about fifty feet from the wire, spaced about 150 feet apart.

The men spent the rest of the day getting settled, bunking in with the soldiers who operated the artillery pieces. That night in the mess hall, the Taggart brothers, Riley, David Monaghan and Ben Higgs sat together at a table.

"You see how close the jungle is to the wire when we

flew in?" The proximity had made a big impression on Ben.

"Hard to miss a thing like that," Riley said.

"Feels like the jungle's out in the back yard," Andy said. "It's farther to our chicken house than it is to those trees."

"Musta been a bitch getting Charlie out of there," Willie Ray said to the soldier who brought pitchers of water to their table.

"What planet are you from, son?" he said. "That jungle is full of VC."

Andy almost choked.

"Right there? That close?"

"Yep."

Riley didn't want to sound like a total greenhorn, but he couldn't help commenting, "That doesn't seem safe — the enemy … what … fifty yards away?"

The soldier rolled his eyes.

"Safe? No, you could say it is definitely not safe. Neither is anything else about Tweety Bird." He saw they weren't tracking. "An eagle's nest is high up in tall trees so they can look down, see everything below, hunt their prey from up there. Tweety Bird is in a cage on the ground and a cat prowls around right outside the bars just waiting for a chance to eat her alive."

He walked away from the table. The boys from Callison County didn't finish their dinner. They had lost their appetites.

Chapter Twenty-Six

THE NEXT MORNING, Willie Ray was bumming cigarettes from anybody he thought might have an extra, pontificating about getting a suntan.

"I didn't get no tan when we's in Texas but surely to goodness I'll get one here." He squinted up into the fireball in the bright sky. "What do you figure, we're about ten, maybe fifteen miles from the sun?"

"How you think I got this?" said a voice from behind them and they all turned to see a black soldier loaded with gear coming their way. He was big, broad and had a smile that took over his whole face. "When I got here" — he pointed to Andy, the Nordic blond — "me and him coulda passed for twins. This here the Thunder Road platoon of the hundred and fifty-first?"

"It is," Riley said.

"Then I've come home." He dropped his gear and his duffle bag. "I'm replacing some dude who didn't even make it onto the transport — that right?"

"Sean got himself a million-dollar broken wrist," Willie Ray said.

"Name's Butterworth, Cornelius P. Call me Ace."

"How long you think it's gonna take me to get a tan like that?" Willie Ray wondered aloud.

"Couple of days maybe, just be careful you don't burn." He licked his finger, rubbed it on his bare arm, then looked as his fingertip. "It don't come off." Glancing around, he asked, "Whoa! Ain't you got no more brothers in this outfit? This it?"

"Scooter Washington in Squad Two," Riley said. "He went off to get a couple more clips of ammo."

"Simon Tanner and Lamar Wilson," said Andy, "in the first squad of Whiskey Run."

"With Jackson McClusky." Riley's tone of voice said it all.

"And that's a bad thing because …?"

"Jackson tripped the guy you're replacing." Riley didn't know that for certain … yeah, he did, too. They all did. Nobody offered an argument.

Ace started to sit down on the ground next to Five Cents.

"Hey, watch out, you're gonna sit on Tommy!"

Ace looked around at the bare ground behind him.

"Imaginary friend," said Andy. "Just go with it."

Ace left a space between him and Randy and sat down there.

"Where you from?" Five Cents asked.

"East Harlem." Ace saw the disconnect. "New York."

"Wouldn't happen to have a smoke you ain't using?" Willie Ray asked.

Ace grinned even wider.

"Well, now that you mention it, I do indeed." He reached into the pack he'd set beside his duffle bag and pulled out a sandwich bag that looked like it was full of grass clippings. "I got some serious smoke. This here is *fine*, righteous fine, if anybody's interested."

"What is it?" Andy asked.

"You don't get out much, do you, white boy? This here's weed."

"Weed?"

"You know. Marijuana. Dope. Reefer. Pot. Grass. Mary Jane …?"

He realized that Andy was genuinely confused, wasn't pulling his leg, and he leaned his head back and bleated a big, full belly laugh.

"Son, you 'bout to make a discovery that's going to change your life."

"I doubt that."

"You fellas ain't got nowhere you supposed to be, right?"

First and second squads were waiting for the sergeant to get back from headquarters, had the afternoon to themselves.

Ace gestured to the ground around his duffle bag. "Pull up a chair, gentlemen, and get comfortable." Then he reached back into his pack and pulled out some cigarette papers. He deftly filled one with just the right amount of the green substance from the plastic bag, rolled it up and twisted both ends.

"Oh, that," Andy said. "That's what you're talking about. I've heard about that. I just didn't know what you called it."

Ace struck a match and lit one end of the joint and put the other to his lips. He took a big lungful of the smoke in, held his breath and handed the joint to Riley, who had sat down on the ground beside him.

Riley started to pass the joint along to Willie Ray on

the other side. "I don't smoke," he said. Ace spit the smoke back out of his lungs in another laugh.

"Where you boys from, did you say again?"

"Kentucky," Andy said.

"Farmers. Then you must know about hemp. This here's a kissin' cousin to hemp."

"My grandfather raised hundreds of acres during the war," Riley said. "I'd heard you could roll it up like a cigarette and smoke it — and it'd feel a little like getting drunk."

"I heard that, too," said Ronnie Benson, who had just joined the group. "You have to keep cows out of it — screws up the milk."

"But you saying didn't none of you ever *try it?*"

Riley looked at Willie Ray and winked.

"We didn't need nothing else to get high on — moonshine does the job just fine."

Ace feigned shock. "But ain't moonshine ... *illegal?*"

"Yup," Riley said.

"So's weed."

Ace took another drag off the joint and held it out to Riley again, spoke the smoke back out of his mouth. "It don't matter if you don't smoke. This ain't the same thing. You drink moonshine to get it into your blood. Well, you get the weed into your blood by smoking it."

Riley had taken an instant liking to the Harlem soldier but he had no desire to smoke the joint he'd rolled. He did, though.

Taking a big lungful of the acrid smoke into his lungs, he immediately coughed it back out. Kept coughing and coughing, his eyes watering. Ace chuckled the whole time.

"Feels like I just inhaled the burning garbage."

"Like I said, the smoking part ain't the point. It's how you feel after that matters."

The other guys gathered around, passed the joint from one to another. Riley, Andy and Willie Ray. David Monaghan, Ben Higgs, Ronnie Benson, Kenny Taylor and Randy Nickel. None of them managed to draw it in with the ease Ace did and hold their breaths like he did. Well, except Tommy. Five Cents held it out to him and he didn't cough a single time.

When the joint was burned down to ash, Ace immediately began rolling another one. He took a drag off it, held his breath and held it out to Riley, who almost refused, but didn't. Since he knew what to expect, he did better the second time around, was able to hold the smoke in his lungs for a few seconds before breathing out, and only coughed a little.

The joint went around and around the group of soldiers as Ace described his "line of work."

"This here's what I do. Correction — *did*. Sell weed on the street in Harlem. It's how I made my living before Uncle Sam issued me the cordial invitation to give up my life of easy money, drugs, booze and beautiful women to join him in a fun-filled adventure called the war in Vietnam."

The joint had gotten back around to him.

"Now, I sell it here."

He paused then, looked from one to another of them.

"How you boys feeling?"

Riley didn't feel anything. But Willie Ray definitely did.

"I feel … strange … and …"

"Mellow?" Ace suggested.

"Yeah," Willie said, and grinned a stupid grin. "Yeah, mellow."

By suppertime, every one of the guardsmen was so high the world had become a glorious place. And they couldn't wait to get in the chow line because they were famished.

Riley felt as hungry as he did when he could smell the turkey cooking in Jean Taggart's kitchen, and she had shooed him and all her offspring out on pain of death and dismemberment if any of them dared to "get under foot again" while she finished up Thanksgiving dinner.

"I was just thinking about my mama's Thanksgiving dinner," Willie Ray said, and Riley burst into uproarious laughter. Everything seemed funny.

"I was, too!" he cried. "How good it smelled."

"And she wouldn't let anybody in the kitchen—" Andy said.

"Shooed us out with the broom—" Willie Ray said.

"So we sat in the dining room waiting," Riley said.

"We didn't just wait, though, we stole biscuits," said Andy.

"Yeah … *biscuits*," Willie Ray said.

Suddenly, the thought of Willie Ray's mother's home-made biscuits slathered in home-churned butter sounded so good Riley's mouth actually watered.

Ace looked around at the group and nodded.

"It's called 'the munchies."

"What's called the munchies?" Andy asked.

"That sensation you gentlemen is feeling right now. Good weed makes you powerful hungry."

Riley and the others almost trampled each other to get to the mess hall while Ace got his gear stowed away in one of the gun bunkers.

Weed. Marijuana.

What Papa'd grown because the government had paid him to, acres and acres of it.

"If I'd known you could smoke that stuff growing

155

along the fence rows, I coulda saved a fortune on ciga-rettes," Willie Ray said.

Riley found that uproariously funny.

"It wouldn't have made you feel like this, though," he said. "Ace said what he had was really good weed."

"So how do you turn what's growing along the fence row into 'really good weed'?" Andy wondered aloud.

"You got me, bro, I couldn't tell you," Willie Ray said. "Now are you in line or ain't you? 'Cause if you don't get out of my way, I'm going to start chewing on your leg."

Chapter Twenty-Seven

JESSIE SCREAMED a lot on her way home from work. Emotion would build up through the day, as she tried not to think about where Davie was and what he was doing, which only meant she was thinking about not thinking about it, which was still thinking about it. Alone in their old pickup truck with nobody to hear, she wailed. Yelled obscenities sometimes, but mostly it was just a wordless cry of pain and longing and fear.

And that's what she was doing, on her way from Brewster one frigid late January afternoon to pay her obligatory visit to Davie's mother, when she saw a black dog that must have been hit by a car lying on the roadside. As she neared it, she could see its mangled legs, but was surprised to see it lift its head. It was still alive.

She slowed. She couldn't just leave it there to die in misery. Jessie had put down livestock before; this wouldn't be the first time. She pulled off onto the shoulder of the road. Though dressed for work, hose and heels, she pulled her winter coat close around her, got out the .45 caliber pistol she carried in the glove box and approached the dog. After releasing the safety, she leveled the pistol at the animal's head. The gunshot sounded overloud in the cold air.

As she turned to go back to the truck, the dog whimpered. It couldn't still be alive! But the sound was unmistakable! It whimpered again, and then she heard a scratching sound and a puppy poked its nose out from beneath the dead dog.

Obviously, the mother'd been hit by a car and her puppy found her, crawled under her to nurse.

Yap!

A single small bark. The puppy wiggled and pulled the rest of its body free. But it didn't come running to Jessie. It sat down and looked at her.

Yap!

It was black, with white feet — looked like it was wearing gym socks pulled up to the knee. Its nose was white, as was its chest. Its eyes were black marbles.

It yapped again. Then it cocked its head to the side as if to say, "didn't you hear me?" That did it. Jessie took a couple of steps, leaned over and extended the back of her hand to let the animal sniff it and decide if it wanted to be friends.

A tiny pink tongue darted out for a single lick. That's when she saw that the puppy was trembling — cold and scared.

There was an animal shelter where she could take it on her way to work in the morning. But right now, the shivering puppy needed to get warm.

"You're coming with me."

Jessie leaned over and picked it up and it snuggled close. When she got behind the wheel, she put the puppy on the seat beside her, returned the pistol to the glove box and cranked the heat as high as it would go.

The puppy yapped once, cocked its head to the side and crawled back into her lap.

She didn't want to drive with a shivering puppy in her lap, but all attempts to move it were futile.

She left it in the truck cab while she went to knock on her mother-in-law's door, performing what had become ritual. She'd knock three times, Mama Ruth'd holler out "I don't need nothing" or something similarly dismissive, and Jessie would leave.

When she returned to the truck, the puppy had its paws on the door, looking out the window, waiting for her. Careful not to let the puppy fall out as she opened the door, she set it on the seat and slid in beside it. Before it could move she said, "I know the drill — yap, head cock, snuggle." Then she put it back in her lap and drove home.

She gave the dog three bowls of warm milk, which it lapped up, tail thumping.

She put the dog in bed with her and woke in the middle of the night to find it sleeping on her belly.

She didn't take the dog to the animal shelter the next morning.

Jessie named him Magic. Of course she did.

JESSIE HAD it all planned out how the evening would go, her last night with Davie in the ugly little motel in Killeen, Texas, with its dingy living room/kitchenette, grungy bedroom with a lumpy bed and closet-sized bathroom. She had bought a negligee, spent a whole afternoon in Louisville looking at fancy dress stores with clothing she couldn't afford and didn't want anyway, seeking just the right thing. She found it. Given how little there was of it, some lace and see-through black netting, the price was obviously not based on the cost of the materials. It was beautifully skimpy. And she looked great in it.

Her whole plan had begun to go sideways when she walked into the bedroom as Davie was stuffing the last of his gear into his duffle bag. It hit her then, all of it, landed on her in a whole new way, which was saying something because she thought she had experienced the reality of him leaving from every possible miserable standpoint.

The image of him there, putting his shaving kit into his bag … he looked up at her, must have read her face.

"Is something wrong, Jessie?"

And that was it. She lost it, literally collapsed in the floor in tears, crying so hard she couldn't get her breath. He didn't try to get her off the floor, just sat down beside her and drew her into his arms. And the tenderness of that gesture made it even more painful.

All she could do was cry, cling to him and cry.

She never even got the negligee out of her suitcase. They just sat there on the floor while she sobbed, and then somehow, she was in bed and they were making love. And as the light faded out of the afternoon sky, that's all they did. They made love. She cried. They made love some more. It was beautiful and terrible, tender and heart-breaking. The agony of losing him had hurt so bad, holding him in her arms while he loved her felt so good. It was all things, everything and nothing, and it lasted for hours.

They didn't talk, but what could she say? *Don't go?* Or *be careful.* It was a war, people were shooting at you. *Please don't get shot?*

She felt as helpless … no, more helpless, certainly more bereft and absolutely more terrified than she'd felt sitting in the driveway of her mother-in-law's house, clutching his shirt and sobbing when she'd first learned he'd be going to Vietnam.

Jessie must have dozed off. The room was shadowy and cold. Maybe the furnace didn't work. Or maybe there wasn't one. This was Texas, after all, and maybe all they cared about was air conditioning. The only light came from the red "Vacancy" sign blinking on and off outside their window.

David was lying on his side, up on his elbow, just looking at her.

"You never have known, and that's one of the things I've loved most about you. You never understood how incredibly beautiful you are."

"David, I—"

He put his finger to her lips.

"No argument, woman, or I shall have to beat you again."

He let out a long, whooshing breath and pulled some kind of calm from somewhere inside him.

"I'm getting some blankets, and then we're making some plans."

Davie hopped out of the bed, dancing across the cold floor to the linen closet in the hallway. It was so jammed that blankets and pillows fell out when he opened the door. He wrapped several blankets around Jessie, then piled the bed high with pillows and pulled her with him to a sitting position, propped against the pillows, snuggled in the warmth of the blankets, staring out into the shadows of the room.

"When this is all over, when I get back, it will all seem like a bad dream. With it out there in front of us, though, it's hard to see anything beyond."

She sniffled.

"But we are going to look out beyond now, okay? We're

going to leap out beyond this year to next year. Are you with me? We're going to take a magic carpet ride out into tomorrow."

"Magic carpet."

"Work with me here, okay? These are *not* mere quilts you're wrapped up in. Oh, no no, no. They are magical quilts capable of transporting us forward in time. Hold onto me, as tight as when I took you for that motorcycle ride. Here we go!"

He pulled her tight to his side. "Do you feel it moving?"

She managed some sound that was affirmative, couldn't say a word.

"Okay, we're rising up, up. You're going to have to do the looking-down for both of us. You know me and heights. I'm already dizzy. Tell me what you see."

Jessie was trying. She really was, but she was so wrung out, even his joyous fantasy didn't have the power to move her.

"The top of the barn?"

"Yeah, the barn."

"Can you see that leak over the loft from here?"

"No." She choked out words. "We're too high to see it."

"We ought to be crossing over the creek, then out over the meadow on the other side."

"Yeah, I can see the cattle in Horace's field."

"Higher and higher. Now, you can't see anything because we're in the clouds. When we get on top … There, now, blue sky!"

He cried out with an enthusiasm that lifted her even though her heart was as heavy as an anvil.

"Blue sky … flying with the clouds below and the sky above and tomorrow … tomorrow ahead. What do you see coming, in tomorrow?"

She had to do this. Clearly, it mattered to David, but she felt nothing but deadness inside and saw nothing but darkness ahead.

"A house ... of our own."

"Yes, our own place. No more trailer house. No more cold showers and un-air-conditioned summers."

She didn't say, though she so desperately wanted to, "and no more just down the road from your mother."

"Jessie, we're going to farm together. I got it all planned. We're going to make enough money so you can quit your job and we can work together on the land. No more high-heeled shoes and pantyhose."

"Nothing but work boots and mud, huh?"

"We'll have a back porch, with a fenced yard."

"For the dog — I want a dog and I don't care if he sheds all over the furniture."

"And the kids."

"And the kids."

"But first we'll build a barn. And it will be on a hillside so we can look out over the crops we planted together."

She got an image, transmitted through the effort of his forced cheer, from his mind into hers. The two of them, hand in hand, looking out over their acres, their crops ready for harvest.

He paused then, and she sensed him turn to her but she couldn't see his face in the dark.

"Jessie ..."

She reached over, fumbled, found the little lamp on the bedside table and switched on the light. She wanted to see his face, memorize every line and plane of it.

"Jessie, we're going to have a good life. You'll see. We will get through this. I promise I *will* come home —

without a mark on me. And the two of us will have a long life together. Trust me, we will. Trust me."

And so she trusted. It was all she could do. She trusted that the reality of their ride out into the future would be just as he'd envisioned it.

She trusted the magic.

Chapter Twenty-Eight

MAMA BERT HAD PERSONALLY SELECTED the location of the chop shop, or so said Brodie Ray, the all-purpose, go-to guy for all information and expertise about anything and everything, the functional man in charge of the small crew of mechanics who did the actual labor. In the weeks since Nate Hannacker had taken over the chop shop, he had discovered that if there was anything to know about any automobile ever made, what it was worth, what its pieces parts were worth, and how to disassemble it in the shortest amount of time — Brodie knew it.

Brodie also knew — and would sing for you at the drop of a hat — every single popular song from the 1950's, kept his ever-present radio tuned to a Classic '50's station. The chop song reverberated with the voices of Johnny Cash, Bill Haley and Elvis Presley, the music so loud sometimes that Nate could hear it from outside the walls.

"I fell into a burning ring of fire ..."

"One, two, three o'clock, four o'clock rock ... five, six, seven o'clock, eight o'clock rock ..."

"Don't be cruel to a heart that's true ..."

Mention The Beatles, and Brodie would go into a foot-stomping fit over "those long-haired, British sissies."

Ray may have been his last name or his middle name. Nate never found out. He was probably younger than he looked. He was a wizened little man who wore overalls with no shirt under them even in the dead of winter, so that his spindly arms stuck out of them like the bony legs of a baby bird. His whole body was covered with a rug of gray-white bristly hair. His arms and shoulders, even his fingers. The only hairless place on him, at least as far as Nate had ever seen, was the top of his head. It was as hairless as, and bore a bit of a resemblance to, a baby's butt.

In a county the size of Callison County, you got to know the look of people, so you didn't very often see a stranger, and if you did, you knew him right off for what he was. Even folks you might not recognize had a kind of look to them, a family look that let you know their family tree had sprouted roots somewhere nearby.

Brodie Ray didn't look like anybody Nate had ever met, though he spouted the kind of information about a place you only knew if you'd lived there your whole life. He identified the unmarked turn-off to Barkersville by saying "You know where that big yella dawg got hit by a car about fifteen years back, lay there in the middle of the road and stunk for nigh on a week ... turn there."

Brody was proud to testify that it was Mama Bert "her own self" who had decided where to put the chop shop, in one of those spots locals would tell you "Oh ... you can't get there from here."

It was in an ancient tobacco barn. Painted black fifty years ago, the color had faded to a dull gray in the Kentucky sun. The roof was falling in on one end, the front doors hung open, with one of them dangling by a single hinge. And it was on the far side of a big creek, where only the struts and foundation remained and the bridge there that had washed away.

Nobody would have supposed that through the not-dangling-at-all inside doors flowed a steady stream of cars stolen from the streets of Louisville, Lexington, Cincinnati, maybe as far away as Bowling Green and Nashville. The creek was impassible where the bridge had washed out — with big rocks, three maybe four feet deep. But turn off the dirt road into the creek bed upstream of the not-there-anymore bridge, go about a hundred yards north and the creek was wide, flat and only a couple of inches deep.

About fifteen feet back from the falling-off-the-hinges doors was a solid wall of plywood, painted black, floor to ceiling. It formed that wall of the building, which you entered through a set of bay doors on the back side. In fact, the whole place was a building within a building. The external walls where boards had fallen away and the doors dangled sat like a mother hen on a chick on top of an inner building that was built like a bank vault and absolutely light-tight. The business enterprise conducted in the not-really-falling-down tobacco barn was a nocturnal activity, and the surrounding darkness was not disturbed by so much as a sliver of light shining out through any opening you could see.

Lots of cars were more valuable for their parts than for the blue book value, but the chop shop world revolved around one thing — who do you know? And it appeared that Mama Bert knew everybody worth knowing.

"You gotta have the lifters to get you the 'xact merchandise the buyer wants," Brodie said. "You take the order, you put it out there, and soon's a bottom feeder locates the mark, it's pop-goes-the-weasel, he's inside driving it away. He drives it right here 'thout stopping, and inside two hours, you be leaving here with the pieces parts you was wanting. Lotsa times we done chopped the car up 'fore it's even reported stolen."

"Lifters," of course, were the thieves who worked the streets of nearby cities, looking for merchandise. They were also called "bottom feeders" or "wheeler dealers."

Parked out behind the chop shop was a small fleet of junkie-monkeys, old pickup trucks held together with duct tape and Bondo that were used to deliver the pieces parts from the shop to garages that purchased the parts, used them to repair vehicles and then charge their customers the price of a right-out-of-the-factory part.

It didn't require sophisticated equipment to steal a car. A slim jim to slip down between the window and the door frame to pull up the lock mechanism, wedges to shove in between the window and the top of the door to pop the window out far enough to insert a wire with a hook on the end that fit around the lock button. A professional lifter could select a car, get inside and drive away with it in less than sixty seconds.

In truth, "chop shop" was a bit of a misnomer for the operation because as often as not, the cars lifted off the streets of nearby cities were not dismantled at all, merely "significantly changed." The VIN numbers — vehicle identification numbers — stamped on engines were all over the map, with different manufacturers adhering to their own format. Making changes in a VIN number was not impossible, if you knew what you were doing. And Brodie Ray absolutely knew what he was doing. Then apply a different color paint, wheels, maybe swap out grill work, and then you could sell it as-is to customers who ran used car lots in difference cities.

Because of Mama Bert's reputation in the world of fencing stolen property, she had accumulated a client base over the years that enabled her to match thieves to buyers for whole vehicles and not just to engine blocks.

Nate had gotten himself a copy of the Kelley Blue Book guide, a price guide that identified how much a car was worth, used mileage as one way to determine the value and in Brodie's mind, that made the book totally reliable. Nate was studying it, trying to learn as much as he could about his new occupation. He didn't know yet if he'd want the job when his six-month commitment had expired, but whenever he thought about the fact his employment had put a McClusky out of work, he couldn't imagine he'd ever want to give it up.

There was a sudden squeak of hinges and the back bay doors opened. In rolled a 1968 Dodge Charger, cherry red with a black top and red sidewall tires. Now, there was beautiful car! Nate hadn't cared about a vehicle as more than a mode of transportation since the Big Eight his father'd bought for his brother Johnny.

"This model came with either a 440 Magnum or 426 Hemi engine," Brodie said with pride, as if Nate knew what that was. "This here one's got a Hemi. It is one sweet automobile."

Nate smiled. Oh, what Johnny wouldn't have given to drive a car like this!

Chapter Twenty-Nine

1932

JOHNNY LETS OUT A CRY, a war whoop, an explosion of sound that the wind rushing through the open windows of the speeding car carries out into the bright sunshine. Nathaniel wants to yell, too, but understands that you have to earn the right to such cries, that you have to be the one taking the risks — the driver.

Someday, Nathaniel will drive. Pa said he could drive when he turned sixteen and Nate absolutely will hold him to that promise. He is fifteen now, his older brother Johnny is twenty. Two of his cousins, Mike and Ted, the sons of his father's older brother Pete, are old enough to do the job, though their brother Joe is a year younger than Nate. But only Ted is what Pa calls simply a "transporter" and others call a bootlegger, the name coming from the practice of hiding liquor in the boot. Some folks call them whiskey trippers, rumrunners or blockaders. The successful ones, the best ones, the ones who don't get caught, have a fiercely adventurous spirit.

The very best ones are left-handed, too.

When Nathaniel first heard that south-paws made the best whiskey trippers, he'd asked why that was. Johnny'd winked at him and said, "If you's left-handed, you can lean out the window and shoot and drive with the other hand."

Nathaniel is right-handed.

Even Nathaniel is not as much a "wild hare" as his brother. Johnny is cut from the same cloth as their Uncle Pete — loud and brash and utterly fearless. It's not just his job to transport the moonshine in various cars they have modified for speed, cars that look ordinary on the outside but have a souped-up engine. It is more than a job. It is his passion to drive fast and live large, and he enjoys nothing more than ripping around the winding roads of Callison County at speeds that sometimes set the car up on two wheels when he rounds sharp corners.

It was, of course, Johnny who had talked Pa into purchasing the vehicle Johnny dubbed the Big Eight.

"Henry Ford himself was the one who said it," Pa had argued in his losing battle with Johnny. "He said a car hadn't ought to have any more cylinders than a cow has teats."

They had been using Fords with V6 engines — modified, of course by Johnny, who was a master mechanic — to "transport" their liquor from the stills to the customers. And though he'd have dearly loved to go head-to-head with a prohibition agent, Johnny had never had to outrun anybody on the road. There were not so many of the agents as legend would have it and Nathaniel heard they mostly sat on their butts in their offices and didn't do anything unless they had a tip on where to find a still. And tips like that were non-existent in Callison County. Nobody talked to the feds. Nobody.

Johnny had persisted about the bigger-better-faster car until he finally wore Pa down — not by making the point that it was faster, but by arguing for its other exceptional features — extra interior room, and heavy-duty shock absorbers and he pointed out that the balanced design of the V-8 engine created more torque, more horsepower and more stability at high speeds ... when it was necessary to drive fast, of course.

Johnny swore the Big Eight handled more nimbly the faster it went. Even when nobody was in pursuit, he'd put the pedal to the metal after they'd delivered the day's goods and fly at a hundred miles an hour around the roads that wound like snakes through the valleys, knobs and hollows of Callison County.

On this particular Friday evening, Johnny is driving ridiculously, unnecessarily fast through the warm evening air, singing at the top of his lungs the tuneless song he'd made up from the age-old moonshiners' rhyme—

"Papa's in the shed, mixing up the mash, Junior's in the parlor, counting all the cash."

Nathaniel joins his voice to Johnny's. "Mama's in the kitchen, washing out the mugs, Sister's in the pantry, filling up the juuuuuugs."

"Whoooooeeeee!" Johnny shouts and the exuberance and joy make Nathaniel feel more alive than he's ever felt before. Someday he will be driving the Big Eight. Someday.

"How come you didn't come down to the train station the other night?" Nathaniel has to shout to be heard above the roar of the wind.

"I was busy!"

"Everybody was there."

"I wasn't."

Everybody meaning all the other families who made moonshine. Nathaniel didn't know how they'd found out about the train, but word of it had caught and spread like a spark spit into dry grass.

Al Capone was coming through.

Mama was among a large number of people who didn't think the occasion merited celebration. Most of the others who didn't think he deserved tribute were women, too. Nathaniel got it, though. Even his father — who had only in the years since Uncle Pete had been "murdered" fully embraced the occupation of "moonshiner" — had been among those who loaded up into cars and trucks in the middle of the night and went down to the empty train station in Brewster.

Al Capone, the man FBI Agent Eliot Ness had finally caught for tax evasion! — had been loaded up on the Dixie Flyer in Chicago and was on his way to federal prison in Atlanta.

The men stood at the station until they could hear the train coming. It was aptly named the Dixie Flyer. It was flying, wouldn't *have stopped for anything, couldn't have stopped. If the track hadn't been clear— if, as some feared, there was some attempt by Capone's men to stage an escape, whoever was involved would not survive the attempt. Those on the train wouldn't either. It would take at least a mile, maybe more, of track for a train moving that fast to stop. That screaming engine would have plowed right into and through anything that got in its way.*

It blew through the station, a streak of darkness with a single bright light cleaving the night before it like a silver hatchet. Capone couldn't possibly have seen the men who'd lined up there in the dark, with Mason jars full of moonshine, lifting them up in tribute to the man who'd fought Prohibition as hard as they had.

Mama'd been disgusted, told Pa, "That Al Capone is a criminal. He's a gangster, a murderer."

Pa'd grown quiet and gave her the kind of hard look that had only started to appear on his face in the past few years.

"Them federal agents are the ones ought to be locked up. They're the murderers."

After that, Mama had held her peace. Pa had changed since the death of Uncle Pete. His family had buried him in the church cemetery. The whole community turned out for the funeral. Nathaniel didn't know if Aunt Audrey had lied to the priest, told him what they told everybody else — Pete'd keeled over at the dinner table, musta had a heart attack or something. Pa hadn't never been the same after Uncle Pete's death. There was a hard set to his mouth, and a glint in his eye. Before, he'd been content to make a little corn liquor for his own use and to sell to friends and neighbors. After the ambush that left his brother dead, and two neighbors locked up in federal prison for killing a federal agent, he'd shifted some kind of gear. He'd built more stills, grew his business, branched out to provide alcohol to pour down the thirsty throats of a growing number of customers.

Mama doesn't like the new way of life, but there is food on the table now when there had been none before. As the years of Prohibition stacked up one on top of the other, the price of whiskey rose ten-fold, until it was selling for eighteen to twenty dollars a gallon. The littles have shoes now and winter coats, the horses new tack. Most of the money Pa makes with his expanding liquor sales is plowed back into supplies and more equipment. More stills to make more corn liquor.

And the money to replace the tired old Model A with the V8 coupe that is Johnny's pride and joy.

Today, Nathaniel's riding along with Johnny to help with the deliveries. It isn't the first time he's done that, but it is the first time he'd done it and Mama knew it. The other times, he'd sneaked off, made up excuses for where he'd been.

"What was you so busy doing you couldn't get out of bed and—"

"That's the thing, little brother," Johnny says and offers Nathaniel a wicked smile. "The key words in that sentence are "out of bed," and as you will shortly learn for yourself, the willingness to get out of bed is in direct proportion to the person who happens to be there beside you."

Mary Ann Alterman. Maybe Melody Ridgefield. Or Cora Adams. Johnny had a string of girlfriends who lived in the counties where he delivered — Callison, Washington, Taylor and Nelson Counties.

Nathan doesn't have any idea how he gets away with it, but Johnny just has a way about him. Mama keeps saying one day he'll settle down and find a steady girl. Nathaniel doubts that's on the horizon anytime soon.

Johnny slows as they enter the town limits of Brewster. Of course it is an open secret that the plain black Ford with Johnny at the wheel is not the dignified coupe it appears to be on the outside. And there are telltale signs of its real use for those with eyes to see. Johnny can't help revving the engine when he comes to the stop sign on Main Street, making the tiger under the hood growl. The Big Eight is loaded with seventy-five one-gallon containers of liquor, arranged tightly in the trunk and in the space created by the yanked-out backseats. Johnny knows how to carefully pack a load of glass jars so they didn't crack when jostled by the rutted road. Since a gallon of whiskey weighs four pounds, loading up the backseat is like driving around with four fat guys back there. Johnny has tossed one of Mama's quilts over the area so you can't see anything through the car window. He has, of course, put special shocks on the vehicle. The trouble with that is that when the car is empty of whiskey, it bounces on the heavy-duty springs. Johnny says it looks like a cat in heat.

The shipment loaded in the car now is for the middleman who takes what they brew back in the woods to ease the thirst of the patrons in one of the speakeasies in Cincinnati — The Pink Lady, the most famous one of the lot.

Johnny'd been pestering Pa for months to let him go with his friends to Cincinnati some night and go there. Mama'd says places like that are immoral, but Nathaniel can't work it out in his head why there isn't nothing wrong with making the whiskey that it's illegal to sell there, but it's immoral to go there and drink it.

Nate has only unloaded a couple of containers in the dark parking lot behind a tobacco warehouse, when Johnny storms out the door and barks.

"Load it back up!"

Nathaniel stops with a box of jars in his hand, halfway from the trunk to the ground, and he sets it on the ground beside him.

"What for?"

"I said 'Load. It. Back. Up!'" It's clear Johnny is holding onto his temper by his fingernails.

"What—?"

"They done sent off a load to The Pink Lady," Johnny hisses through clenched teeth. "Bought it this afternoon from the McCluskys."

Chapter Thirty

NATE ACTUALLY FELT bile rise up in his throat at the memory of standing in that parking lot as Johnny'd raged about the McCluskys undercutting the Hannackers' price, stealing their sale to The Pink Lady. And at the time, Nate didn't even know the fate that awaited the Cincinnati speakeasy's customers when they drank the McCluskys' brew. All he'd known then was that he and Johnny were going to have to haul their load of moonshine back to the farm.

It really shouldn't have come as a surprise. It was bound to happen eventually. The McCluskys had seen the money to be made during Prohibition in moonshine and bootlegging and they'd cashed in. Rooster McClusky had gotten a job as a prohibition agent — which said everything that needed saying about the caliber of men enforcing liquor laws. Then he used his position *working for the government* to cover for his brother, Digger, who was brewing moonshine in the hills behind his property.

Brewing *bad* moonshine!

Unlike Pa and Mose Taggart and other farmers who'd

been brewing moonshine for years, Digger didn't know what he was doing and didn't care. Hank McFarland, who'd worked as a still hand for Digger for a while before finding more suitable employment elsewhere said that the McCluseys' equipment was old, worn out and barely functioning. Digger took every shortcut there was, selling the singlings at the beginning of the run and cutting the 120-proof alcohol with creek water, *adding shoe polish* to give it an amber color. Even made horse-blanket whiskey — covered a boiling kettle of still beer with a folded horse blanket, then twisted it to squeeze out the condensed moisture into a tub.

When you sold moonshine to your neighbors and friends, there was built-in quality control. Sam Hannacker was proud of the brew he produced and maintained the same standard for the out-of-town shipments as he did for what he sold locally.

Digger worked the system, knew it was easier to get away with cutting corners when your brew was selling to a bunch of strangers you'd never bump into on the street. He made bad liquor and he sold it cheap. Which is how Nate and Johnny came to have a full load of liquor instead of an empty trunk when they pulled to a stop at the four-way stop at the corner of Main and Proctor Knott Avenue that evening and another car stopped across the street.

JOHNNY SWEARS UNDER HIS BREATH.

Rooster McClusky!

The oldest of the two McClusky brothers has risen up through the ranks to become some kind of supervisor, drives a big black car with the "Prohibition Agent" logo in gold on the door.

"Ignore him!" Johnny says and pulls away from the sign into the intersection. They pass the other vehicle and Nate's stomach clenches

into a knot. When Johnny pulls away from the sign, the car makes a U-turn in the middle of the street and follows.

"Crap!" Johnny says, not increasing his speed as he drives out of town down Miller Pike. The Big Eight should have been empty by this time of night, the load of liquor delivered and paid for. Instead, they're hauling enough moonshine to put them both behind bars for a very long time.

"We can't let him pull us over," Johnny says.

Nate watches Johnny check the rearview mirror, then the side mirror. The car remains behind them as they drive out of town onto the winding county road that leads home, not drawing up any closer, matching their speed.

Then Nate figures out what the Rooster is doing. He's waiting for the straight stretch another two miles out where he intends to pull up beside them and direct them to pull over to the side of the road.

Nate exchanges a look with Johnny. His brother's jaw is clenched, he grips the steering wheel in tight fists.

But he is smiling.

When the car in the rearview mirror begins to speed up as they round the long curve on Miller Pike, Johnny buries his foot in the floorboard and the Big Eight leaps away down the road like a scared-up rabbit.

Nathaniel looks back over his shoulder, watching the headlights of Rooster's vehicle grow smaller behind them. But then, the car begins to pull back up closer.

"Reckon he's got that thing souped up?" Nathaniel asks.

"I expect he has. Ain't gonna do him no good, though."

He flicks a look at Nathaniel. "You best find something to hold onto."

Then Johnny reaches out to the dashboard and clicks off the headlights.

The night is cloudless and a sickle moon hangs high in the black sky, but it casts scant light on the landscape below, little more than the twinkling of stars. Johnny knows this road, has driven it hundreds of times in all conditions, day and night, rain and snow, knows every turn, every curve, where the shoulder falls off on the right side and where the creek comes up right alongside it on the left.

He flies down it now by braille, concentrating on feeling his way in a landscape that is lit with bright daylight in his mind.

Fifty miles an hour.

Sixty.

Seventy.

Seventy-five.

The headlights, falling farther and farther behind now, are merely two pinpricks that only appear as the car rounds a corner and then disappear when Johnny goes around another.

But the prohibition agent is still there.

Nathaniel can't breathe. He thought he understood the nature of fear, thought he knew what it was to be utterly terrified, but he had been sorely mistaken. The fear he feels now claws at his throat and steals his breath.

Any second now ... any second they will fly off the road and go crashing off the shoulder into the woods, or a field, or a fence. They will smash headlong into a rock wall and the world will end for them both in an explosion of glass and silent screams.

He would cry out now if he had the air, but he doesn't.

"Hold on tight!" Johnny says, and Nathaniel fingers turn white, his grip on the edge of the seat strengthened to steel by desperation.

Nothing exists out in front of the car but black nothingness —and Johnny hits the accelerator! Nathaniel is almost certain they're coming up on the spot where the road makes an S curve to snake through a narrow spot between a rock wall on the south and a fifty-foot drop-off on the north side. They fly around the first curve and the car lifts up on two wheels and Nathaniel knows that this time he's gone too far, the car is about to roll over on its side and down the embankment. He closes his eyes and holds his breath.

When he feels the car crash back down on the right two tires he opens his eyes in time to feel Johnny speed up! He can't possibly intend to take the second curve faster than he took the first.

But he does.

There is a squalling sound as the tires shriek in protest and Johnny leans his weight into the steering wheel to keep the car on the road as the tires on the left side of the car begin to lift off the surface.

This time, when the car rolls, they will crash into a rock wall. Nathaniel is glad it's dark. He doesn't want to see.

Then they're through to the other side and Johnny slows, still taking corners at a ridiculous speed, slows more, is finally going fast enough to hold onto the road when he careens off the main road onto a dirt road and blasts down it, bouncing up and down to the tune of clinking bottles in the backseat.

Slamming on the brakes, the car slides to a stop in a cloud of dust that blots out the world. Johnny clicks off the ignition, and the only sounds now are the ticking of the cooling engine and Nathaniel's gasps for enough air to keep himself from passing out.

Nathaniel gets it now. Johnny's insane speed was to get the car far enough ahead so Rooster wouldn't see him turn off.

Then they hear the sound of an approaching vehicle. They wait, watch. It seems like an hour passes before Rooster McClusky blows by the side road at probably fifty miles an hour in a vain attempt to catch up to the black phantom that's no longer on the road ahead.

The sound of the vehicle fades, and Nathaniel finally gets control of his breathing. He tries to make out his brother's face in the pale glow of the moon and the faint twinkle of stars. He can see only angles and shadows, holes below his forehead where Nate knows his blue eyes are watching the road. Blue eyes sparkling.

When Johnny speaks his voice is steady.

"We need to go tell Pa about the McCluskys undercutting our price," he says. Nate only nods, doesn't trust himself to speak.

. . .

THREE DAYS LATER, a story splashed across the front page of the Cincinnati Inquirer. Seems the city's emergency rooms had filled with sick people the night before — all of them patrons of The Pink Lady speakeasy.

That lit a fire under the city's prohibitionists, who in turn, set local law enforcement ablaze. There were raids on speakeasies and more officers were assigned to locate the source and cut off the snake's head — moonshiners and bootleggers.

Pa and Mose Taggart paid a visit to the McCluskys — a bad idea all the way around but the further demonizing of Demon Run was the McCluskys' fault and somebody needed to call them on it.

Pa never talked about what'd happened that day, just spit in the dirt when the McClusky name was mentioned — "You can't reason with an animal. And that's all they are — animals."

Chapter Thirty-One

"I got a letter from Davie," Jessie told Magic, as she knelt to scratch behind his ears when she came in the back door. She told Magic everything.

Yap.

The dog's vocabulary was limited, but he managed to convey a lot of information with what he had.

"Okay, okay, I'll read it to you. Just not right now."

She hung up her coat and she was glad she was wearing a sweater underneath because the clunky old heating system in the trailer only worked in fits and spurts.

The dog was her shadow, a step behind her wherever she went. When she sat down on the edge of the bed to read Davie's letter, Magic curled up on her feet. Not *next to* her feet — *on* them.

"Carved my short-timer's stick today."

Jessie could hear the words in Davie's voice as she read them silently off the page. She carefully held the flimsy paper they all used to write letters home. It was so … insubstantial. She hated noticing that because it made the words on the page seem insubstantial, too.

She conjured up his image in the air in front of her. She supposed other people who'd just gotten a letter would picture the person saying the words to them out loud, in person.

Jessie didn't. She pictured Davie writing the letters, saying the words slowly to himself as he penned them on the page. His face would be a study in concentration because his handwriting — unlike the handwriting of most men — was beautiful. It almost looked like calligraphy. He had passed her a note in American history class their senior year, just walked past her desk and dropped it and kept walking. American history was the only class the two of them had together.

She hadn't realized what it was — a note, one of *those* notes, boy-girl notes — until she opened it and started reading and she was instantly struck by the beauty of the penmanship.

Did he get somebody, some girl to write it for him?

Nope, absolutely did not, because the first line read, "I can't stop thinking about you, Jessie, and I'm tired of just thinking."

He had asked her out. She had dated several boys after she and Riley Hannacker had split, but never more than a date or two. Riley was hard to get over, even though she had instigated the breakup. She'd sensed that he'd wanted the relationship to go further than she did, tried to put on the brakes and when that didn't work, she'd broken up with him. It'd been hard but it'd been the right decision. David Monaghan, one of Riley's friends, had never been on her radar because he'd had a steady girlfriend then, too.

That first date. She knew then, didn't even tell her best friend, of course, because it sounded so ridiculously immature and melodramatic. But she knew. In fact, she'd known when she read the note, saw the beautiful letters that danced like delicate ballerinas across the page. *That* inside David Monaghan had called out to something just like it, a mirror image of it inside Jessica Harrington.

And she had responded with her whole heart.

"A short-timer's stick is a tree limb or a branch, any piece of wood you can carve notches in. Every morning when you get up, you carve a mark on your short-timer's stick and when you have about 350 of them, you start packing your bags for home."

Davie told her about the artillery base called Eagle's Nest — that the soldiers called Tweety Bird — where the guard unit shared bunkers with the New Hampshire soldiers who fired the big guns.

"Willie Ray thinks he has died and gone to heaven being here. If he had known there was somewhere in the military where you could blow things up, he'd have broken his neck to sign up for it."

But Charlie Company were the lowly infantry. The artillery gunners shot at targets five or ten miles away, while the foot soldiers "... get to smell the VC's bad breath."

"We got in a replacement who smokes — not the stuff we hang up in a black barn but the stuff that grows wild behind it." He was being purposefully vague, but he had to mean hemp — dope. "Yes, you're hearing the voice of experience. I've tried it, liked it. But some of the others — our favorite "little guy," for instance, is a "three-packs-a-day" kinda guy, twenty-four/seven, on duty or not. We're all hoping he gets caught."

In her mind, Jessie watched Davie stop, go back and read over what he'd written so far and then put the pen down on the page and write more. She knew he was self-censoring. There were things he didn't tell her because he didn't want to worry her. But he knew better than to make it sound like tiptoeing through wildflowers chasing butter-flies, or she'd see what he was doing. It was a delicate balance, that, telling your wife "what was *really* going on" and hoping she wouldn't find out what was really, *really* going on.

Jessie could see him teetering on that high-wire, trying not to lose his balance.

Vietnam could not possibly be as ... *ordinary* and mundane as he made it appear. But they hadn't gotten to the hard part yet — infantry patrols.

She let out a breath she hadn't realized she was holding and watched the filmy paper start to shake in her trembling hands. She told herself that he was safe *right now*. That his life was not in imminent danger *right now*. That he wasn't involved in real combat *right now*.

She needed to grab that *right now* and hold on tight. Relish it, roll up warm and comfortable in it. There would come a *right now* eventually when all the Boogie Men would come out of the closet and try to eat him alive.

Chapter Thirty-Two

It wasn't as bad for Charlie Company as it could have been. Riley told himself that every day. Several times every day. They'd come to replace the battle weary 101st Airborne Division when they got back to Tweety Bird. Until they did, the guard soldiers were camped inside the fire base with the big guns and the crews who fired them — an activated New Hampshire guard unit who lived in sandbagged bunkers near their guns.

The base took mortar fire constantly. Out of nowhere somebody'd yell *incoming round* a millisecond before you heard the whizzing yourself. That gave you roughly two, maybe three seconds to find cover.

You dropped the boots you were cleaning, stopped zipping up your fly, whatever you were doing and dived for the nearest hole, piled in on whoever else had been forced to dive in, too. Unless the hole took a direct hit, the sandbags would be protection — not total but better than nothing — from the shrapnel and the jagged pieces of *whatever else* had been set to flight by the explosion.

The damage range of a mortar shell had a radius of

roughly forty meters. And, oh by the way, the instant you went boots down out of a transport you better know how to *think* in meters, because by the time you did the conversion math in your head you'd be long dead. A meter was a little over three feet, a yard. The guys who'd played football said they saw it in their heads on the grid of a field. A mortal shell in the end zone wouldn't kill you if you were standing on the fifty-yard line. Probably wouldn't kill you.

Charlie Company hadn't been at Tweety Bird three days before the first mortar shells started raining down on their heads. Riley was hunkered down in a foxhole as the rounds fell, had dived in and landed on top of some guy he didn't know, some guy with a Yankee accent.

Willie Ray had landed on top of Riley, and he'd whispered harshly in Riley's ear through the rumble of explosions, "Was you listening when they was explaining mortar shells at Ft. Benning?" They'd done their basic training at the Georgia base after they'd signed up. "Because *this* ain't that."

No, it definitely hadn't sounded this bad at the time.

"There's three ways a mortar can take you out," the training officer had said, pacing back and forth in front of the newly bald recruits. He held up one finger— "Shrapnel, little pieces of the shell casing flying out from the explosion as fast as a bullet fired from an M16. And because the pieces are moving so fast, they do more damage than just the hole they plug in you — destroy tissue all around it."

He held up a second finger.

"The blast wave. If it hits close enough, the sudden increase in pressure alone can knock down the wall of a building. So figure what it can do to the human body."

He held up a third finger.

"The heat wave from the blast can burn your skin and set your clothes on fire."

That hadn't sounded like any fun at all, but the description didn't hold a candle to the reality.

If the shells dropped straight down out of the sky, the shrapnel would hit in a perfect circle around them. But they never came straight down. They came from all angles out of the trees and hills around the base — which meant they were still tumbling from the momentum of flight when they hit the ground, still flying across the ground as much as falling toward it.

Which pretty much sprayed shrapnel every which way. Often there'd be very little damage right behind where the shell landed and devastation in front and around it.

Sometimes there was a mortar *attack*, a coordinated assault from the NVA out there in the jungle, firing shells at the artillery, trying to take out a gun, or a crew, or just blow something up, maybe hit the jackpot and land on the stored ammunition.

But even when there was no attack, the NVA would randomly lob a couple of rounds at them, didn't appear to be aiming at anything. Just wanted to keep them on their toes.

Gus Foster in Hangover had been hit by shrapnel from one a couple of days ago, sent out on a chopper to Da Nang because it'd injured his larynx. He might never be able to talk again.

One of the gunners had his left hand blown off at the wrist, nothing left, just gone.

And there was always random sniper fire, too.

Some dude they called Mr. Magoo out in the trees would send a bullet pinging off a jeep, a Howitzer barrel, or dig a hole in a sandbag three inches from your nose … stuff like that.

Ace had told them one evening as they passed around a joint, "Yeah, the brass gets a bead on a mortar and they lob a couple of tons of ordinance on their heads, blast the whole hill into dust … and they're right back out there the next day.

"I liked to killed me a grunt who actually got Mr. Magoo in his sights," Ace said. A grunt was a Marine. "Had the shot all lined up and I tackled him before he could fire. That grunt come up swinging — and I'm yelling in his face, 'Don't kill him, you idiot. They might replace him with somebody who can shoot!'"

And Riley had thought then, when they were inside the fire base with the big guns, that *this* was what fighting a war in Vietnam was like. He even said in his first letter home to Papa — *You know, it's not all that bad*.

As Rocky the Flying Squirrel so often told his sidekick, Bullwinkle the Moose — Wrongo, moose breath.

Riley and the others didn't find that out until the 101st Airborne Division got back to Tweety Bird and the hand-off was complete. Then they became infantry soldiers. No longer encamped with the artillery unit at Tweety Bird, they were dispatched on patrols into the stinking jungles — for a few days, maybe weeks at a time — on seek-and-destroy missions.

They sought. And they destroyed.

And they changed.

The caterpillar-into-a-mad-hornet transformation didn't happen all at once, of course. It began when they were sent into their first firefight. Nothing in any of their lives was ever the same after that.

Chapter Thirty-Three

Nate stood staring at the side of his pickup truck in wonder. He'd left it parked in the post office parking lot one morning in late February while he went in to buy stamps. Just stamps, that's all. He wouldn't allow himself to do what most everybody else in the whole county was doing — driving Selma stark-staring mad by showing up at the post office every day asking if they'd got any mail with *international stamps*. Folks weren't content to wait the extra day it would take after a letter arrived in Brewster to load it up in a mailman's pouch and carry it out on rural routes.

Nate had better things to do than pester the postmaster, and even if he hadn't, refusing to obsess over letters — or the lack thereof — from his grandson was a necessary exercise in discipline.

He reached out his finger to the side of his truck and traced the huge scratch. It started beside the left headlight, snaked down the side of the truck, across the driver's side door, and then extended along the whole length of the bed of the truck to the back fender.

How in the world had he scraped the paint off—? And

then he got it. He hadn't scratched anything. Somebody had keyed his truck.

It took a moment for that reality to set in. Somebody had deliberately used a car key to scrape away the paint, gouging a path from one end of his truck to the other.

He studied the scratch for a beat or two — and then burst out laughing.

Seriously?

Who in their right mind could look at his beat-up old farm pickup, with the side mirror held in place by duct tape, and believe one more scratch would matter? You keyed somebody's brand new sports car ... not their ten-year-old pickup truck.

Probably teenagers, practicing on his truck before they moved on to bigger, better things. But it'd happened while he was in the post office, and this was a school day. The county's teenage delinquents were sitting at their desks in school right now.

He looked up and down the street, saw nobody he knew. Well, he saw lots of people he knew, just nobody who'd have any interest at all in keying his truck. Random mischief, he supposed. What other explanation was there?

When he got home, he found *two* letters in his mailbox. He hadn't let himself feel disappointment that others had heard from their boys in the guard already and he hadn't. Still, knowing Riley *had* written — military mail had just botched the delivery — made him feel warm all over.

Nate carried the letters into the kitchen, sat down with them at the table, and opened the first one — mailed right after Riley got to Vietnam. The postmark on the second was just a week ago.

The first letter began in typical Riley fashion.

"Nobody has shot at me yet, so that's a plus."

It was frustrating to try to make sense out of the letter

with the censors' holes in it. It almost required the physical act of cutting and pasting, like he was putting together paper dolls. Though Nate could see that Riley was diligently trying not to reveal anything important, big hunks of his letter were slashed out, leaving thoughts dangling, descriptions incomplete.

Riley mentioned that he was having trouble adjusting to the heat. "It's winter where you are! Send me some snow." And said that Davie Monaghan was creeped out by the jungle. And that Willie Ray had gotten a poker game started as soon as they landed in [name redacted.]

He said he was fine.

He said the food was good.

He said that the insects were thick enough to walk on, that he couldn't distinguish one Vietnamese civilian from another, that in their "pajamas" they all looked the same. He hadn't needed the warning to be suspicious of everybody — even the children.

"They said kids sometimes toss grenades into jeeps."

That might have been the sentence that bothered Nate the most. Little kids tossing hand grenades into jeeps. Oh, it wasn't like that was news to anybody. It was on television all the time — which Nate found himself compelled to watch now when before he'd never had the TV on — about soldiers killed by civilians wrapped in some kind of explosive.

The second letter was shorter, but had fewer censored parts.

He said they were stationed at an artillery base — didn't bother to try to say where. It'd never have made it past the censors. He said they spent a lot of time filling up sandbags that had been destroyed by mortar fire.

Mortar fire!

And that Sean Mattingly's replacement was a soldier

named Ace. Riley liked him a lot, said he had shared with all the guys a "modified version" of what was "growing wild along the fence rows" at home.

It took Nate a moment — hemp?

Marijuana!

"I'll tell you all about it when I get home."

He said they would be moving out soon, replacing [name redacted] on patrols into the jungle.

"Don't know what mail service will be like there."

He asked about what Nate was doing, and Nate wondered if he told Riley the truth, would the censors cut that out?

Well, son, I'm in charge of an operation where we steal expensive cars off the streets in Louisville, Lexington and Cincinnati, take them to an old tobacco barn and cut them into pieces to sell for ridiculously high prices.

Did they censor incoming mail, too?

"How's Daisy?"

That struck Nate as an odd question. "I miss the old girl. I guess in my mind, she's kind of a symbol of "normal."

Nate read both letters again. And a third time. His mind was getting foggy. It might be time to start the day for the rest of the world, but he worked "the night shift." It was time for him to go to bed.

He read the letters a fourth time, tried to conjure up Riley's face but couldn't. And it wasn't because he was too tired. He just could not yet picture Riley in uniform, carrying a rifle. He could just see the kid in a tee shirt and jeans, piling hay up in the barn, or feeding Daisy, brushing her coat for the state fair, or helping him with the still, lowering the filled containers on the wench down to the river.

The Riley-the-soldier image wouldn't come, even

though he'd given Nate the standard photo of himself the Guard had taken, in his dress uniform. Appeared he was trying to look fierce but couldn't pull it off.

Nate's eyes blurred or he might have re-read the letters again. Time to get some sleep; he was expecting several important deliveries tomorrow — if the lifters could find the cars that'd been requested. That part was always a crap shoot.

The chirpy tone of Riley's letters bothered him — it seemed so artificial. Nate wanted to know the truth!

Well, Riley'd said nobody had shot at him yet. Of course, the date on the letter was February 1. Today was February 20. He probably couldn't make the same statement now.

The phone rang just as Nate was getting comfortable. The voice on the other end of the line sounded genuinely chirpy. It was LeRoy Taggart.

"I got me a baby granddaughter," LeRoy told him. Emily, Andy's wife, had delivered a healthy baby girl. "Come by sometime and I'll give you a cigar, got little pink wrappers on 'em."

"What's her name?"

"Emily's been saying all along she thought the baby'd be a boy, and she was gonna name him Andrew. Since it's a girl, she's calling her Andrea."

Chapter Thirty-Four

RILEY WONDERED what day it was, tried to pull up a calendar in his mind but couldn't. The end of February, probably. Cold back home. Riley shivered, but not from imagined cold, from the sight of the soldiers coming down the jungle trail toward them. These were the soldiers the guard soldiers were replacing, the guys *coming back* from where Charlie Company was *going to*.

He stood beside David Monaghan, watching them pass, soldiers who had been out in the jungle for ... who knew? At least a month because Company C had been waiting here at Tweety Bird that long for their return. None of them made eye contact, they all looked at the ground, with a chilling sameness that was somehow the most terrifying thing Riley had seen since he arrived.

They filed past, all of them too thin, too exhausted ... and too young. They didn't look like the seasoned soldiers who'd trained the guard unit at Fort Hood. They looked like Riley and his friends. But old eyes. Some of them. Others' eyes were dead.

When the returning soldiers had passed, he and the

rest of the platoon moved out, slowly, single file, down the winding trail into the vegetation.

Riley felt his insides begin to hum, a vibration of fear that was like a strong electric charge. With no place to discharge it grew, and grew, wound tighter and tighter in his chest until he had trouble catching his breath. They marched all afternoon, through grass taller than corn in the fields in Callison County, only the grass wasn't as user-friendly as a corn stalk. The grass was razor sharp on both sides, so it was like making your way through a field of sharpened bayonets. They marched through jungle so dense when they spread out they couldn't see the man in front or behind. You marched alone in a tunnel of green so thick Charlie could have reached out of it and grabbed you by the throat. They marched around rice patties where little people in pajamas and pointed hats were bent over ... doing something — planting it or weeding it or harvesting it. He'd never seen a full-grown rice plant so he couldn't tell.

Even though they appeared to be paying no attention to the soldiers, Riley could feel their gaze, watching. You had to keep an eye on the pajama-mamas, as Willie Ray called them. And the kids. Always had to watch the kids. One of Ace's buddies in his previous unit had stopped by a group of kids. He gave one of them a candy bar, and they gave him a satchel charge that blew both his arms off.

Hour after hour they marched. The straps of his two cotton ammunition bandoleers dug into the back of his neck, each with the weight of twenty fully loaded M16 magazines. Inside an hour, they'd rubbed him raw. His M16 got heavier with every step, and he found himself constantly checking to make sure he had the viciously sharp Bowie knife still on a scabbard at his waist. Hanging off his bandoleer straps were two M26 fragmentation hand grenades and three smoke grenades, and a compass.

When they finally stopped, he felt exhausted in a way twenty-five-mile hikes during training had not tired him. The constant tension in his muscles from fear, hour after hour, were taking a toll. Would it be this way every day until ... how many days ... he'd left his short-timer's stick in one of the bunkers at Tweety Bird. Didn't matter. He still had months to go. Months and months.

It would be dark in a couple of hours and the platoon had to set out trip flares around the perimeter, though Ace said it was his considered opinion that Charlie was so used to looking through tangled jungle vines and grasses they could spot the "hidden" trip wires a hundred yards out.

An hour later, Willie Ray, Davie, Riley, Andy, Ace, Kenny Taylor and Ronnie Benson sat around a small fire they'd have to put out before dusk, preparing to cook their K-rations — small cans the size of bars of soap full of beef or turkey loaf, ham slices and chopped ham and eggs.

Willie Ray read off the label of his can of chopped ham: "Says this here was made during World War II. We're eating food's older than we are."

There was an accessory pack that came with the K-rations. Riley dug around through it, looking for the small packets of salt and pepper that brought out what little flavor there might still be in food that'd been sealed in a container for thirty years. He found a white plastic spoon, some instant coffee, sugar and non-dairy creamer, two Chiclets — can't be out here in the jungle offending the other soldiers in your foxhole with bad breath — a small roll of toilet paper, moisture-resistant paper matches and cigarettes. He looked at a four-smoke mini-pack of Pall Malls. The Winstons, Marlboros and Lucky Strikes were better, easier to trade, but he held up what he had.

"Who's got something they wanna trade for this fine assortment of death, four Pall Mall cancer sticks for your coughing pleasure?"

Ace and Willie Ray both yelled out "I'll take them," then Ace held up a round, chocolate cookie tin and tossed it at Riley. "It's all I got except my emergency two-pack of rubbers and ain't nobody getting those."

They'd dug foxholes earlier and after they put out the fire, Riley and the others climbed into them and tried to get comfortable. The light died slowly. Fear rolled over Riley in a wave and he almost thought he could feel it as a breeze that blew across them all, chilling the backs of their necks.

They all were hyper-vigilant — not that they didn't trust the sentries, didn't believe they could actually go to sleep without fear of waking to a bayonet in the belly. Terror like Riley was feeling was too primal an emotion to turn off at will, though he supposed he'd have to learn how to do that, they all would, or they'd be stark staring crazy inside a week.

The whisper of a leaf scraping on tree bark made heads turn involuntarily and hearts gallop. Here, out in the bush, the blackness was not held back by a restraining wall of six-foot-tall loops of razor wire. It was right there off the end of their gun barrels. Riley knew he would never be able to go to sleep.

A bright light of a flare catapulted Riley from a dream about Daisy, the cow he'd gotten blue ribbons for showing in the state fair. Advancing NVA soldiers had tripped over one of the hidden wires after all, and it had sent a torch high into the black sky.

The whole world turned instantly an odd florescent white.

Thunk! Whap-whap, thunk.

Bullets flew so close by Riley's face that it felt like he could feel the air rearrange itself after their passing. He had hunkered down in his hole — like a little kid trying to hide from the Boogie Man under the covers — and now he was having trouble untangling himself from the position, struggling to sit up.

The world had changed from ink black to brilliant white between one heartbeat and the next, from silent to a cacophony of noise in a sudden explosive burst that was stunning in its intensity.

Rifles firing, the rat-tat-tat of automatic weapons, and explosions ripped through the ranks of Charlie Company. Hand grenades sounded like mortar shells or a bazooka. The foxhole three down from Riley's exploded in a cloud of dirt and white light and body parts.

Something wet slapped Riley in the side of the face. He glanced at it as it fell to his shoulder. It was a human hand. Only that, the hand.

He leveled his own rifle a full second before his mind told him to and he opened fire. The words of his training officer formed in an instant in his mind — for only an instant.

"Nobody 'rises to the occasion,' soldier. *Nobody.* Everybody defaults to the level of their training. Everybody. If you're not trained to act, you won't. You will freeze, not move, and you will die. If you are trained, you won't have to think about acting. It will just happen."

It did happen, just like the training officer had said it would.

He pulled the trigger, felt the recoil, saw one of the figures running at them in the brilliant light stumble and fall.

The light and noise and screams of the injured and dying went on for hours, days, a lifetime.

Then he pulled the trigger and there was no recoil and he heard the sickening silence of an empty magazine. The Cong soldier that would have fallen with the shot he'd intended to fire kept running at him.

Forty meters away.

Twenty.

Ten.

He could see the man's ugly face contorted in a rictus of hatred and battle rage.

It seemed to take an hour to leap to his feet and slam the butt of his rifle into the Cong soldier's weapon, knocking it aside. Momentum carried the soldier forward and he slammed into Riley, shrieking some kind of wild yell like an Indian. Riley was standing inside his foxhole, so the impact was like a Three Stooges skit.

Moe stands in front of Curly. Larry gets on his hands and knees behind Curly. Moe shoves Curly and he falls backward over Larry.

Riley fell backward out of the foxhole on his back with the Cong soldier on top of him. Both still held their rifles, but they were useless at this range, just got in the way. Riley wiggled, squirmed, tried to reach for his—

The Cong soldier had a knife. It had materialized in his hand by magic. Not there. Then there. The white glare from the florescent flares that lit the world sparkled off the razor edge of it as he plunged it down at Riley's—

The pistol shot was so close to Riley's ear that it sounded louder than a hand grenade. His face was splattered with goo. The Cong soldier dropped the knife as he collapsed away from Riley, most of the left side of his skull blown away.

Ace was suddenly beside Riley, the acrid stench of gunpowder mixed with the copper smell of blood filling his nostrils. Ace shoved the dead body the rest of the way off

Riley with the hand not holding his smoking .45 automatic.

"Keep firing." Ace spat the words at him as he yanked Riley upward and practically tossed him back into the foxhole. "There's a million of these sons of bitches."

Riley grabbed his M16, ejected the spent magazine and slammed home a new one off the bandoleer around his shoulders.

And he kept firing.

Sunrise found their camp a smoking ruin.

There were five platoons in the whole of Charlie Company — Thunder Road, Whiskey Run, Guzzlers, Likker Lovers and Hangover. They'd been named long before Riley and his friends had joined the guard, and were certainly appropriate in a county with six distilleries and no telling how many stills. Each of those platoons had four squads, ten guardsmen and ten replacement soldiers who'd been infused into the unit.

Cong bodies were everywhere. Most dead, some moaning and moving. In the pale dawn light, Ace went from one VC body to the next with his .45, putting a bullet in the skull of any one of them that moved.

Thunder Road platoon had lost four men — one dead, three wounded. None of them were guardsmen Riley knew well. But he'd met them, talked to them, traded cigarettes for cookies with them and passed a joint around to them — and now one of them would be winging it home on a Freedom Bird in a black body bag.

No one in Riley's Squad One had been wounded seriously — Ronnie Benson had jammed two fingers, maybe broken one. But they had aged, every one of them. They were twenty years older than they'd been when they were bitching about eating food older than they were and keeping their emergency rubbers safe.

Davie Monaghan knelt on the ground a few feet away from where Riley stood beside what was left of the body of the soldier who'd been in the foxhole that took a direct hit. The one whose hand ... The soldier's name was Rogers. Riley remembered. That's right, he was *Roy* Rogers, from Pasadena, California — said he'd endured a lifetime of eye-rolling whenever he introduced himself.

Now, his family would put him in a grave somewhere beneath a headstone that said Roy Rogers and everyone who passed would do a double take before they continued on their way.

Willie Ray approached Riley. They made eye contact, said nothing. What was there to say? Andy walked up beside them and Willie Ray grabbed his brother in a spontaneous hug.

"Bro ..." is all he said, then he shoved Andy away.

Riley spotted Ace. There was a desert of exploded dirt, bodies and death between them. Ace nodded. Riley nodded back. He owed that man his life.

Life and death. Permanent.

This was what the war in Vietnam was about.

Chapter Thirty-Five

"DID you understand any of that? I mean, anything at all?"

Gloria Mattingly was livid, sputtering and fuming as she drove the winding roads of Callison County home to Brewster after she, Sherry Lynn Bennett and some friends had gone to see *2001: A Space Odyssey* at a theatre in Bardstown. Sherry Lynn didn't answer. In truth, she really hadn't been paying enough attention to the movie to know what she did and didn't understand. She was grateful, in fact, that it was so strange nobody seemed to know what it meant, so Gloria and the others wouldn't figure out she'd been zoning.

Cindy Shewmaker, Marilou Donavan, and Shirley Mattingly — not related to Gloria ... well, they all were related somehow — sat in the backseat with Sherry Lynn up front beside Gloria.

"That first part. That thing, that black thing — what was that?" Cindy wanted to know.

"I thought there had to be something wrong with the sound," said Shirley. "I finally started timing it — do you know there wasn't anybody saying anything for the whole first twelve minutes of the movie?"

"The monkey and the black thing … so he gets close to it, then figures out how to use a bone to smash other bones …" Marilou began.

"And then he uses it to defeat the other tribe of apes at the water hole who have not figured out how to use bones to clobber each other …" Cindy said.

"So the black thing showed the ape how to make a weapon … and then zap, there's this big weapon out there in space," Gloria said. "So the movie was about weapons, right?"

"Why'd HAL kill everybody?" Marilou asked.

"Because they were going to unplug him," Shirley responded. "Wouldn't you kill somebody about to unplug you?"

Gloria let each of the other girls out at their houses. Sherry Lynn was last.

"How long you going to keep playing the nothing's-wrong game?" Gloria asked.

"What do you mean?"

"Oh, come on, Sherry Lynn. Who do you think you're talking to here? It's me, Gloria — yoo-hoo, I know you. You've been out to lunch for months."

"I have not—"

When Gloria started to protest, Sherry Lynn held up her hand.

"Okay, sure, I've been on a downer. Who hasn't been? I never get a letter. Why doesn't Riley write to me? Ronnie's wife, Kenny's wife, Emily Taggart — they've all gotten tons of letters. Shoot, Willie Ray has written you more often than Riley's written me and you're just one of the chicks in his chicken yard."

"You know I could go out on the street and get people

who don't claim to be my friends to say mean things to me and I wouldn't have to put up with their moodiness."

"Why doesn't he write?"

Sherry Lynn burst into unexpected tears, as surprised as Gloria was by the outburst. Her emotions were all over the map. She couldn't seem to stop crying, couldn't concentrate in class — was in danger of flunking the semester if she didn't get her act together.

Gloria pulled over to the side of the road, beneath the boughs of a sycamore tree. Tomorrow was April Fool's Day and the tree was already covered with spring buds.

Reaching past Sherry Lynn to the glovebox, she got out tissues.

"Here, blow your nose. And wipe the makeup out from under your eyes. You look like a clown." Sherry Lynn did as she was told. "So how many have you missed?"

At first, Sherry Lynn didn't get the question.

"How many what—?"

"Periods. I know you missed last month."

"I did no—"

"Yes, you did. I needed a tampon and dug around in your purse, in the side pocket, and you didn't have any. You always carry tampons when you're on your period."

"I just ran out—"

"Cut the crap! You're going to have to tell everybody eventually because it won't be long before you start to show. How about you get this off your chest with your best friend."

Sherry Lynn couldn't breathe. She hiccupped, or her diaphragm muscle tried to, but she was holding her breath and it couldn't happen, making her cough out her response, "I am not—"

"You're pregnant. I know it … and other people are

starting to wonder ... all those trips to the bathroom ... a stomach bug that lasts for months?"

"I am ... I'm not ..."

She wanted to cry again, but now she couldn't. She burst into tears when she didn't want to and she couldn't cry when she did.

Gloria put her hand on Sherry Lynn's arm.

"Tell me."

And she found the words tumbling out, as unstoppable as the hiccups.

"It's crazy. I mean, it can't be. I just can't be. We only did it once. I swear to God, swear on a stack of Bibles, only *one time* — the night before they shipped out. Everybody knows you can't get pregnant the first time you have sex. The only time you've *ever* had sex."

"We can sit here marveling at the black humor in it, but the important point is *you're pregnant*. What are you going to do about it?"

"*Do* about it?"

"You know what I mean. Are you going to have the baby ... or ..."

Sherry Lynn wanted to be outraged that Gloria would even suggest something as horrible as abortion. That was murder, killing a baby, a mortal sin. But she *had* thought about it. God help her, she had.

"Even if I wanted ..."

There was nowhere to go.

"I know a place ... if you want to."

"How on earth would you—?"

"My cousin, Ramona," she squeaked out in a singsong, "Ramona the *moan*-a. She got knocked up and she got rid of it. Some guy in Louisville did it. I could find out for you—"

"No!" She almost screamed the word. Then softer. "No, I couldn't." She stopped. Could she?

"Well, the only thing I do know for certain is you're running out of time."

"Out of … why?"

"You can't have an abortion … well, you can, but it's dangerous … after you're three months along. You're bound to be close to that."

"I … missed my third period a week ago."

"You're going to have to figure something out fast. Or … you're going to have to tell your parents and …"

Sherry Lynn was suddenly so nauseous she was afraid she was going to vomit.

"And … Riley. What about Riley, Sherry Lynn?"

Yeah, what about Riley?

207

Chapter Thirty-Six

EASTER SUNDAY ... and Saint Augustine in Brewster, the county's biggest church, had a sewage back-up. Smelled like an outhouse — which sent all the parishioners scurrying out into the hinterlands to one of the smaller churches to celebrate the holiday. Nate drove out to Saint Dominic in Crawford, the church he'd gone to as a boy. He hadn't been there in years, but it didn't matter. It'd look just like it looked the last time he saw it. Nothing ever changed there.

Getting out of his truck in the parking lot, he enjoyed the bite still in the air, the chill of a late spring morning. It'd warm up.

Daffodils were blooming, trees budding, little girls were all decked out in their Easter dresses, their mamas in Easter finery that had always put Nate in mind of how peacocks strutted right before they spread their feathers.

But the old stone building was still cold. It had no heating system. Nate stepped inside, felt the cold, looked at the familiar pews, statues and stained glass windows. And then it wasn't Easter at all anymore. It was Christmas. Midnight mass on Christmas Eve, 1933.

THE ONLY WARMTH *in the old building is the body heat from the people crowded into the sanctuary. The church is packed. It is, after all, a holy day and if any Hannacker child even considered the possibility of not going to church on a holy day, they would not be able to sit down for a week. And that's if God didn't strike them dead with a lightning bolt from heaven, which was a distinct possibility.*

The Hannackers quietly filed into their pew. Mama and Pa don't sit together. They sit at opposite ends of the pew with the children lined up in between. It's that way with all the families gathered at Saint Dominic every Sunday, parents strategically placed within ear-grabbing range of any misbehaving child.

Only the littles need correction anymore — twins Rose and Lily and Becky, the youngest. But ever since Uncle Pete's death five years ago, Pa has been a father to his brother's seven children as well. So they make room for their cousins and Aunt Audrey to squeeze into the pew as well.

None of the children makes a sound — no whispered admonishments to "move over" or declarations that someone had committed the grievous sin of encroaching on another's real estate — the allotted space for each backside in the pew. Everybody knows there are boundaries and you are absolutely not allowed to venture into the pew-space of the person sitting next to you. But it's Christmas Eve and the merest peep from any one of the children will be dealt with swiftly and painfully.

The Taggart pew is on the other side of the big aisle that goes down the middle of the church. Nate has always suspected that had been arranged to keep the children out of poking, grabbing, hair-pulling or spit-ball range of each other.

This has been a mild December. The air in the sanctuary last Christmas Eve had been foggy from the frosted breaths of the congre-

gation exhaling in unison. Children had been bundled up in whatever winter coat they had, were allowed to real-estate-invade a sibling's pew space if seeking warmth. The Hannackers were doing better than most, only because of Pa's moonshine business.

Johnny wiggles beside Nate, who wiggles in turn, and the wiggle passes down the row of children as everyone settles themselves on the solid oak pew — hand hewn. Somebody who knew their way around a chisel and mallet had made each of the pew end posts ornate works of art.

The service starts promptly at midnight.

Or would have if Mary Purdom hadn't come running in the back door just before Father John Paul started down the aisle.

"Help meeee!" she cries, hysterical. She's coatless and hatless, wearing a simple shift. Her feet are bare. Something terrible has sent her running out into the cold.

"You got to help me. It's Rudy. He's blind. He can't see."

She races to the closest person, Harvey Blinkhorn, who is seated on the end of the back row with his wife and four children. She grabs him, tries to drag him along with her.

"He's out there in the truck. You got to come now. He can't see. He can't see." Then she comes to herself, realizes where she is and what shape she's in and she collapses to her knees and begins to sob.

The whole congregation surges reflexively forward, but Father John Paul cries out for people to stay back and give her air. Folks do as directed, but don't sit back down. The children and some of the adults climb up on the pews so they can see better what's going on.

"In the truck!" She waves her arm toward the church doors. "He's in the back."

Pa, Johnny and Mose Taggart run outside to see to Rudy, and a few minutes later they carry the boy into the sanctuary and settle him on the floor in the center aisle between the last two rows of pews.

"May Ella," he cries, feeling around in the empty air as if he might find her there. The young man's voice carries through the cold air as clear as the bell on top of the building.

"She ain't breathing! Oh dear Jesus God! May Ella, wake up!"

Mary Purdom kneels beside her son and takes his hands. She looks up at the faces around her.

"He spent the afternoon at the Hargraves' house," she says. May Ella is the oldest daughter of Joe and Martha Hargrave. She and Rudy aren't engaged, not yet anyway, but everybody expected the priest to read the bans any Sunday now. "Next thing I know he's out front of the house, laying on the horn, crying out, begging for help."

Rudy keeps calling for her, crying, "May Ella, where are you, May Ella?"

"Ain't nobody else in the truck," Pa says. Then he asks Mary, "Where is May Ella?"

"I left her at the house. Wasn't no sense in bringing her. She's … gone."

Rudy starts screaming then, feels around in the air until he finds his mother, grabs her arm and yanks her toward him. "What'd you leave her behind for? She needs help."

Then he starts to cry, shaking his head back and forth, unaware of what's going on around him.

Two men in the back, Bud Oliver and Hank Gleason, volunteer to go to Mary Purdom's house, which isn't but a couple of miles away, to try to find May Ella. Mary has calmed down, at least enough to explain what happened. Only those in the back of the church can hear what she's saying.

"Rudy didn't say nothing, but … there was an open Mason jar in the truck, and I figure they … stopped somewhere to have some."

Apparently, May Ella had gotten immediately sick, and Rudy had been on his way home to get help for her when his eyesight … failed.

"He said it went away kinda gradual like. It just kept getting darker and darker as he drove, until he couldn't hardly see the headlights on the truck. I ain't got no idea how he made it home alive."

The men who'd gone to Mary's house returned then. Everyone saw them come in. Both of them just shook their heads.

Sam says quietly, trying to say it so's Rudy couldn't hear. Nate can't figure out how he did hear, hollering and carrying on like he was, but he heard.

"May Ella's dead."

Rudy screamed out, "Noooo!"

You could tell Bud didn't want to say anything but knew he had to tell the priest.

"Ain't no use in you rushing over there to give her the rights, Father. She's long gone. Her body's already cold."

Rudy stopped screaming then, clamped his hands over his mouth and shook his head back and forth.

Father John Paul asks Rudy right out if he and May Ella'd stopped to have a drink.

He nods, but can't speak.

Pa asks the next question.

"Where'd you get the liquor, son?"

The boy starts sobbing now, and it's hard to make out all his words. But one word is clear enough and it's really the only one that matters.

McClusky.

NATE FELT a hand on his arm and realized he'd been standing in the middle of the aisle, blocking it so nobody could get by.

"Excuse me," he said and moved off to the side — uncorking the bottleneck so the crowd could flow into the church.

He tried to shake away the images, but they fluttered in his head on bat wings. The McCluskys' brew had killed a teenage girl and blinded her boyfriend. Wasn't no going to the law, of course, but that wasn't a thing you could just let lie there. Trying to reason with "the animals" certainly hadn't worked.

So Pa and Johnny went out on Christmas Day, planning to burn Digger McClusky's storage barn to the ground. Hank McFarland, one of Digger's former still hands, had told Pa where it was located, an old barn back in the woods where Digger kept his moonshining supplies — sugar, blocks of yeast, equipment.

But when they opened the barn door that day, they found more than they'd bargained for. Johnny told Nate all about it.

"That barn was stacked floor to ceiling with bags of sugar, musta been hundreds of them. Enough sugar to keep making whiskey until the return of Jesus. And you know what *that* means."

Nate did. It meant that it had been the McCluskys who'd derailed a freight train coming south from Louisville about a week ago and stole the contents of the boxcars. But that wasn't all they'd done. The engineer had been killed in the crash — and so had his wife and six-year-old daughter. He'd been taking the little girl for her first train ride as a Christmas present.

Laying hands on enough sugar was always a sticking point with moonshiners. If you purchased it locally, you and the merchant had to maintain the thin fiction that your wife canned an incredible amount of fruits and berries. Nobody would have believed the McCluskys had the cunning and stones to pull off derailing a train and making off with a king's ransom in sugar, but there was the evidence, right in front of them.

Pa could have called the sheriff, shown him the barn, and the McCluskys would have gone away to the iron house for a long, long time. But there was nowhere in Pa that could do a thing like that. "Bringing the law in" went against everything Samuel Hannacker was about.

The law was crooked as a dog's hind leg. Somebody

would pay off somebody and before you knew it, the McCluskys wouldn't never see a day behind bars.

"You shoulda seen Pa's face. Don't know if I've ever seen him so mad, said 'There ain't no telling how many people the McCluskys have killed.'"

So Pa and Johnny did what they'd set out to do — they burned the barn to the ground. But instead of destroying an old barn, some moonshining supplies and equipment, they'd cost Digger McClusky a *fortune*. He could have made *thousands* of dollars selling off all that sugar.

That wasn't what started it all, of course. The bad blood between the Hannackers and the McCluskys dated back generations. But that was what had lit the fuse on the stick of dynamite that eventually blew up in their faces, left Nate's father and brother dead and him close to it. And Big Jake woulda seen to it Nate didn't see another sunrise if it hadn't been for Nate's mama.

Chapter Thirty-Seven

ONE MORNING in the middle of May, Nate came home from the chop shop and discovered that someone had splashed red paint all over the front of his house. It was just past dawn and the light wasn't terrific, so he didn't even notice until he'd parked his truck and started up the front walk.

Red paint was splattered on the door, the door frame, all over the porch and the porch steps. A whole gallon of it. He knew that because whoever had done it had left the paint can behind.

What in the world …?

Why would …?

He had no idea. The paint was dry, so it'd happened hours ago while he was at the chop shop.

At the chop shop.

Could this possibly have anything to do with …?

That was absurd.

Nate didn't know which particular member of the McClusky tribe Mama Bert had laid off to open up the position he'd filled. Rooster and Digger McClusky had populated the county with dozens of descendants, like roly-poly bugs — under every rock. But this was childish vandalism. Not even a McClusky was stupid enough to believe they could run Nate off by keying his truck and splashing paint on his house. What could anybody possibly hope to gain by …?

He sighed, stepped gingerly through the dried paint and went into the house. He'd clean up the mess tomorrow. Or get somebody else to do it, hire one of his nephews. The McCluskys weren't the only ones with a big family. Nate's two older sisters and three younger had given him ten nieces and seventeen nephews — Hannackers to the bone, though that wasn't their last name. But his Uncle Pete had left behind seven children when he died and four of them had been boys — Joe, Mike, Rufus and Ted. Only three survived to adulthood, but they'd all had children, carried the Hannacker family name to the next generation.

And there was Riley. One day, Riley would have children. He would.

Nate went to the phone and called Bobby Joe Sullivan, his sister Marianne's oldest son, and arranged for him to come by with his two brothers and a couple of gallons of white paint to clean up the mess.

That night, the chop shop was humming with activity. Lifters had brought in a red Ford Mustang that looked a lot like Riley's, a white Chevy Camaro and a dark blue Dodge Charger. The mechanics were busily disassembling the Dodge Charger, would have it reduced to pieces parts before dawn, while other workers taped off the windows and chrome on the Camaro and the Mustang, preparing to change their colors.

Brodie was everywhere at once. Nate had decided from the git-go he was not going to sit around doing nothing while the crews worked. Yeah, okay, he was the boss, but he didn't mind getting his hands dirty and was enjoying what he was learning about the automobile world and the wild beasts that inhabited it.

"They's saying they're coming out with a new model next year called the Pinto," Brodie said, watching carefully to make sure Nate left no surface on the Mustang untaped.

He'd been surprised by Nate's desire to work, had warmed up to him a bit after that.

"The fella who was here before you didn't do nuthin'," he said. That was the first and only thing Brodie'd ever said about Nate's predecessor and Nate asked no questions.

One of the workers moved Brodie's radio to get it out of the way and accidentally changed the station. When the words "Hey, Jude, don't make it bad. Take a sad song and make it better ..." came out the speakers Brodie almost had a stroke.

Unleashing a string of expletives, he cried, "Put that thing back on the right station 'fore I snatch you bald-headed."

"You know John Lennon just left his wife?" the guy asked as he fumbled with the dial, "took up with some artist named ... Yoyo or something."

"Shoulda took up with a hairy ape, they'd be a perfect match."

"My wife used to read to my grandson a story about Rumpelstiltskin," Nate said. "He got mad and drove his right foot so far into the ground it sank up to his waist, so he grabbed his left foot with both hands and tore himself in two." He paused for a beat. "I'd be careful if I's you, Brodie."

Nate took out a cigarette and fished in his pocket for a lighter as Brodie growled a response, then the static was replaced by the voices of The Crests, a group Brodie raved about.

"… sixteen candles make a lovely light …"

Brodie sighed, crooned along with them, "but not as bright as your eyes tonight."

Nate froze with the unlit cigarette in his hand when he heard the first words of the lyrics.

"I remember when I turned sixteen," Brodie said and looked at Nate. "You remember your sixteenth birthday?"

Yeah, Nate remembered his sixteenth birthday, alright. It was the worst day of his life.

NATHANIEL HANNACKER IS *certain that the day he turns sixteen will be the best day of his life.*

Mama celebrates the children's birthdays by allowing the "birthday child" to get the first, and largest, *piece of whatever sweet she has made — sometimes a cake, maybe a pie, but sometimes only cookies. Things have been better for the family in the past few years. The money generated by Pa's still — and Johnny's expert bootlegging skill — have made it possible to keep the family warm and fed. And in the spring of 1934, there are a lot of families who aren't faring nearly as well.*

But a big piece of pie isn't likely to be the high point of this special day. No sir, the high point will be when Nathaniel gets to drive the Big Eight into town to make the deliveries.

Nathaniel has wanted to drive that car ever since Pa got it for Johnny. Johnny had modified it — special shocks to hold up the weight, souped-up engine, and Nathaniel always felt fortunate just to be allowed to help Johnny on his runs.

Pa had said Nathaniel couldn't drive until he turned sixteen, which Nathaniel had taken as a promise that he'd be allowed to on his birthday. Pa probably hadn't meant it that way, but he caved in to Nate's pleading. Fine, Nathaniel could drive with Johnny as shotgun … but Pa would ride along as well. Just to keep an eye on things. Pa had been especially careful whenever they were out, knowing that the McClusky family was out for blood, payback after Pa and Johnny burned down their barn and destroyed their fortune in stolen sugar.

They'd made threats far and wide, vowed Hannacker blood would flow, but it'd been six months now and they hadn't yet made a move. Still, Pa hands Johnny a pistol as they get into the car. Pa is armed with a rifle.

When Nathaniel slides behind the wheel of the Big Eight, there isn't a thought in his mind about the McCluskys, and when he takes his foot off the clutch as he puts the other down on the accelerator, it's the most natural feeling in the world. He hadn't even driven all the way down the side of the knob to the road before it seemed like he'd been driving this car all his life.

Nathaniel won't allow himself to seem excited to be doing the driving to make deliveries. Little kids get excited about things like being allowed to drive the car. Grown men didn't get excited, took such things as a matter of course, as the way things ought to be.

He appears as casual as he is able, even leans his elbow out the window and drives with one hand ... until Pa notices.

"Two hands, son."

"Yes, sir."

They make deliveries, go to the back doors of buildings closed up and dark in the daytime and bright with lights and loud music blaring at night. A pool hall, three grocery stores, other miscellaneous businesses along with individual residences in quiet neighborhoods. At lunch time, they stop at Beans 'n Grits Diner and grab a bite to eat.

It is getting on toward evening when they finally set the last two gallons inside the back door of what appears to be an abandoned warehouse and head to Aunt Audrey's house to pick up Nate's cousin, Joe.

When Uncle Pete was killed, Pa stepped in to father his dead brother's seven children and to help the family get by. He, Nathaniel and Johnny had spent three days with Pete's boys last week sheering *the family's herd of sheep. Joe will be an extra hand to help in the morning when they start on their own herd.*

Joe is a shy fifteen-year-old boy. After his father's death, he had started to stutter.

A simple "pass the butter, please" became such a painful ordeal — "p-p-p—pass the b-b-b-butter, p-p-p-please" — that he almost never spoke at all.

Joe's eyes open wide when he gets into the back seat with Johnny and sees that Nathaniel is driving. He smiles and flashes Nathaniel a wink. Nathaniel, of course, tries to act like it's nothing out of the ordinary at all.

They are about halfway home when Johnny tells Nathaniel, "Speed up!"

Nathaniel looks in the rearview mirror and sees a car closing on them fast.

"What—?"

"Just drive faster," Johnny says, looking back.

Nathaniel keeps his eye on the road and pushes the big car up to forty … fifty … sixty miles an hour, which is stupid fast on these roads in failing light.

The car behind turns on its headlights and that's the first Nathaniel realizes how close the car is. Almost right on the back bumper. He flips on the Big Eight's headlights and the dim roadway out front leaps into clear focus.

Ping!

Nathaniel dismisses the first gunshot as his imagination.

"Get your head down!" Pa cries, and he realizes it's for real.

Nathaniel scoots as far down in the seat as he can and still see where he's going, and he concentrates on driving.

Johnny leans out the window behind him and returns fire. Pa leans out the front passenger window and does the same. Joe is curled into a ball in the back seat.

Bullets ping and plunk off metal and upholstery, and Nathaniel is so frightened he's afraid he might be sick.

It's full dark now. The sickle moon casts light and shadow behind scurrying clouds. The Big Eight is faster than the following car, but not so much faster that Nathaniel can drive off and leave them in the dust.

They round the bend at the base of Tucker's Knob and the road is straight for about half a mile.

Ahead of them, they can see the headlights of a car that has been pulled crossways across the road. A logo on the door shines, as do the bright gold letters beneath. "Prohibition Agent." Rooster McClusky's car. The moment it comes into view, the air around it begins to sparkle with the muzzle flashes of the guns that have opened fire. There must be a dozen of them.

"Fire in the hole," his father whispers.

"Get down," Nathaniel cries. "And hold on."

Johnny and Pa know what he's planning, know there's nothing else he can do. There's no time even to fire a glance at Pa beside him to get his approval. Nathaniel reaches down and flips off the headlights and sets his jaw. He's heard Johnny talk about what he's about to do, describe it, and he was never certain at the time if Johnny was just pulling his leg.

After all, Johnny did like to talk big so maybe he really hadn't ever done it himself, had only heard tell of it. What was never in doubt was Johnny's belief that the technique would work. Now, they're about to find out.

Nathaniel moves his hands on the steering wheel, away from the standard ten o'clock and two o'clock positions. He puts both hands at the bottom of the wheel, palms up, left hand at roughly 7:30, right hand at about 4:30. Johnny says that the position allows him to release his left hand and whip the steering wheel all the way around in one motion with his right. Nathaniel swallows hard, grabs a breath, prays it isn't the last one he'll ever take. He hits the brake pedal and slows to sixty, then fifty.

Releasing the brake pedal, Nathaniel spins the steering wheel in a circle of motion that is illuminated only by the sickle moon and faint starlight outside the windshield. Then he reaches down with his free hand and yanks on the emergency brake, which locks the rear wheels. The car twists violently, would have thrown Nathaniel into the windshield but for his death grip on the steering wheel.

The motion is dizzying. The temptation to give in to fear and try to straighten the trajectory is enormous, but this is all or none.

Papa's words echo in his mind. "You can't leap all the way over the Rolling Fork River in a series of small hops, son. When the situation calls for it, you got to go for broke."

The car spins 180 degrees in the darkness, switches from fifty miles an hour forward to fifty miles an hour backward, hurling up the road toward the sparkle of gunfire.

Nathaniel releases the emergency brake and jams the accelerator. The car slows its backward slide, comes to a barely perceptible stop, unleashes a screech of burning rubber on asphalt, finds a grip and shoots forward again flying at the McCluskys who'd been chasing them.

As soon as Nathaniel flips his lights back on, it will become a deadly game of chicken. Loser swerves violently one way or the other, runs off the road into the dense woods and hits a tree. Winner goes free.

He loosens his grip on the steering wheel, relaxes his fingers but tightens his jaw, piloting the black dragon away from the ambush that'd been waiting for them ahead, and back into the ambush that's waiting for them behind.

He takes a deep breath and lets it out. Then he flips on his headlights. Nathaniel will not chicken out.

Chapter Thirty-Eight

WHEN THE HANNACKERS' Big Eight Ford collided head-on
with the McCluskys' black Chrysler that night thirty-five
years ago, both cars were flying down the road at fifty miles
an hour.

Nathaniel didn't chicken out.

Neither did Digger McClusky.

Nathaniel could see the interior of Digger's car, lit by
the headlights on the Big Eight, growing brighter and
brighter. Rooster was there beside his brother in the front
seat. Two figures Nathaniel couldn't make out were in the
back. Digger's face was a mask of pure fury and pure
terror frozen in a rictus of hate.

When Nathaniel realized they were going to collide,
the world stopped spinning. That second fractured into a
million pieces; the breathless instant lasted an eternity. The
moon was gone and a light rain had begun to fall. The
raindrops froze in place, he could see them in the glow of
the combined headlights, the little diamonds trapped there,
about to be crushed between the mighty forces hurling at
them from both sides.

The rain on the roof of the car was slow. Each drop striking the metal seemed to be an individual event. The smashing of the round drop, flattening as it hit the surface and the splat sound were hours apart.

Nathaniel felt the air rush out of his lungs when his chest collided with the steering wheel and there was a give in his body, a crushing, like he could almost hear bones breaking. He turned his head to the side at the moment of impact, watched his father fly up at the windshield face first, saw the glass shatter outward, creating jagged teeth. The teeth chewed his father's face away, removed the skin from the front of his head and pushed it back up into his hair.

Nathaniel saw the razor point of the dagger of glass that sliced across his father's throat. Watched it puncture the skin, going deeper and deeper, cutting through the tissue with surgical precision so that his head remained attached to his body only by his back bone. His neck opened up and poured out his life down the front of his shirt, but it gushed slowly, some blood flung out as individual drops to mingle with the raindrops as the rest of his father's body broke through the glass.

The back end of the Big Eight rose up in the air when it struck the McCluskys' car. Knocked sideways by the impact, the car spun around, not as perfectly as Nathaniel had spun it, and then crashed down, landing on the driver's side on the road.

Then it tumbled. Nathaniel felt himself slam into the roof of the car, then sideways, rolling, rolling. The car bounced off a tree and came to rest upside down. The silence that rushed in then was a roaring not-sound. Nathaniel couldn't see. He swiped with his right hand and his vision cleared briefly before the blood pouring down his face obscured his view again.

He was lying on his back, and when he rolled over, the excruciating pain was overwhelming. Agony ate up his right leg, so stunningly intense he couldn't have breathed even if his ribs had not been broken. But he'd managed to roll over onto his belly and he could see out the broken window on the driver's side of the car.

The McCluskys' car was on the other side of the road, still upright but wrapped around a tree. Rooster had flown through the windshield and the mangled top portion of his body lay crumpled on the hood with the rest of him still inside. Digger was behind the wheel, pinned to the seat by the steering column through his chest. The engine was no longer in the vehicle but lying in the grass beside it ... on top of somebody, the head and arm beneath it were lit by the glare of the headlights on Nathaniel's car.

Nathaniel watched a man climb out of the wreckage. It was Ike, Rooster's oldest son. He was covered in blood, but Nathaniel couldn't see where he was injured. What he could see was that Ike had a pistol in his left hand.

Then the bloody figure began to stagger across the dirt on the roadside up onto the road. He held his belly now, was bent over, but he kept coming.

He was coming to kill them.

Nathaniel looked around for a weapon, but the guns his father and brother had been using were nowhere in sight. It was then that he saw Johnny, sprawled out on his belly in the middle of the road. He was trying to rise, though, had gotten to his knees when Ike reached him.

Ike stood unsteadily, then let go of his own bloody belly, grabbed Johnny's hair and lifted his face. He leaned over until he was only inches from Johnny and said something but Nathaniel couldn't hear what it was. Then Ike put the barrel of the gun to Johnny's forehead and pulled the trigger.

Johnny's head snapped back and he collapsed on his side and was still. Ike looked up, trying to see through the glare of the headlights in his eyes. He staggered forward and Nathaniel tried to think what to do. Ike had crossed the road and was approaching the car when he almost stumbled. The headlights were lighting up Ike, but Nathaniel couldn't see what was on the ground in front of him that had almost tripped him. Then Ike leaned over and grabbed something, lifted it up and pointed the pistol at it. Joe.

"Please don't kill me!" Joe's voice was so high and thin he sounded like a girl. He didn't stutter. The bang of a gunshot rang out in the stillness.

Ike kept coming. Nathaniel was lying in a pile of broken glass, huge pieces of it. He grabbed the biggest shard he could find, long and pointed. It sliced into his fingers when he picked it up but he held on and rolled over on it to conceal it. Then he lay still.

He could hear the approaching footsteps, the crackling of glass as Ike walked through it. He held his breath and lay still. When he felt Ike grab his hair and lift his head up, he opened his eyes and struck out with the shard of glass, used every bit of strength he had left. Ike made some kind of sound and Nathaniel struggled to see through the blood on his forehead. He watched Ike stumble backwards, collapse and fall on his back. The shard of glass Nathaniel had stuck into his left eye sparkled in the glaring light.

Chapter Thirty-Nine

IT TOOK three coats of white paint to cover up the red that'd been splattered on the door and front porch of Nate's house. Bobby Joe had applied the final coat right before Nate left for the chop shop three days after Nate discovered the vandalism and when he got back home about dawn, the paint was dry and the front of his house looked as good as new.

Maybe he'd ought to see if one of his nephews was interested in a part-time job helping out with the farm chores. The chop shop was an all-night gig. Farming was an all-day gig. In theory, that meant Nate could do both at the same time. In practice, that was called burning the candle at both ends. He was a strong man as fifty-one-year-old men went, but even strong men couldn't keep that up for long.

Less than a full night's sleep every night for three months had left Nate chronically irritable and snappy, and his mind foggy. That's why he had almost completed the morning's chores before he noticed Daisy … or rather, not-Daisy.

Nate's was a crop farm. He grew corn, hay, wheat, soybeans ... and, of course, burley tobacco. But even though it wasn't a dairy or a livestock-breeding operation, there was livestock on it to care for — a responsibility that had been Riley's, and now was Nate's.

For the most part, the animals belonged to Riley. They'd shown up one or two at a time over the years — first the lambs, only a couple — that were sheep now, of course, and way more than a couple of them. Then the goats, then the calves that grew into cattle, and finally the show heifers. Riley had shown each one of them in various 4-H sponsored shows, then at the county fair, and several of them made it all the way to the Kentucky State Fair.

While Riley'd been competing in livestock shows, Willie Ray had entered the horticulture and plant science competition — or what Riley called "Find the Radish" contests. It really was a whole lot more complicated than mere plant identification. Willie Ray had won a grand champion ribbon at the state fair when he was in junior high, had recognized two dozen different plants, from barley to strawberries, just by looking at a leaf, a seed or a stem. He was big into cross-pollination, too — Riley called that "Plant Sex" — was always coming up with some hybrid something. Willie Ray had once claimed he'd grown a corn plant only three feet tall so it was easy to pick. It was a joke, of course — just a small piece off the stalk of an ordinary corn plant where Willie Ray had glued pickles painted yellow to look like corn cobs.

Riley's show animals remained on the farm because ... just because. They weren't pets or anything.

They weren't pets or anything like that, though Riley did love every one of them when he was working them, grooming them every day, polishing the heifers' hooves and horns. Nate could have sold them off but didn't. They lived here same as Nate and Riley.

His small herd of cattle was very low maintenance. They slept outside in a fenced-off field at night, usually huddling together under a tree. They grazed on the grass in the field and didn't have to be watered because there was a small stream on the back side.

Other animals — sheep, lambs, goats, kids, chickens, pigs and piglets and two turkeys — required a higher level of care. Their feed was in the barn, and Nate kept their water trough full with a hose leading to a spring-fed cistern.

The big Holstein Daisy Mae came the closest to qualifying as "a pet." She was the last of Riley's show animals and he'd gotten particularly close to her, thought she was smarter than most cows and maybe she was. He'd taught her tricks — to bring him his cap, to lie down on command, things like that. The cow sometimes used her soft, velvet nose to nudge open the catch on the pen door and would be standing outside the backyard gate when Riley came out of the house in the morning.

Even though he had been gone for months, she could usually be found waiting for him there. About mid-morning, Nate noticed that Daisy was nowhere in sight. And when he thought about it, he couldn't remember the last time she had been.

He finally located her on the back side of the field. The cow was facing a tree and he approached her from behind. When he stepped around her, he saw that she had her head jammed up against the tree trunk. He hadn't never seen a cow do anything like that.

"Hey, Daisy girl, what's up?"

The cow showed no indication that she'd heard him. He put his hand on her flank and she didn't respond to his touch. That's when he noticed she was drooling. Cattle drooled sometimes, but this was a drip of saliva that hung all the way down to the ground. He hadn't thought to bring a lead, figured she'd just come right along beside him to the barn. He went back to get one, fastened it around her neck and she didn't move. He had to pull hard, turning her head before she'd follow him.

She didn't walk along behind him, though. She … *stumbled*. Her gait was odd. It almost seemed like she couldn't tell where she was going, but he wasn't sure because when he looked into her eyes they didn't focus and there was no recognition in them.

Nate called the veterinarian as soon as he got Daisy into the barn, described her symptoms. The vet was stumped, said there could be any number of reasons for behavior similar to that — some in need of immediate attention and some not, said to give it a few days and call him back if the symptoms persisted.

When Nate got home from the chop shop the following morning, Daisy wasn't in the barn stall where he'd left her. She wasn't standing with her head pressed up against a tree either. He found her shambling aimlessly around the field and as soon as he got a good look at her, he knew for sure there was something seriously wrong with the cow. Her eyelids were twitching uncontrollably, and she was yanking her head from side to side, like trying to get something off her face. He was fairly certain she couldn't see. He went back into the house and called the vet.

"I think you need to come out and take a look at her *today*, Mitch."

The vet told Nate to put the cow in a stall in the barn, that he'd be out late in the afternoon. As soon as he got her penned up, Daisy collapsed to the floor of the stall and lay there, her breathing ragged, like a cow in labor.

Shortly before sunset, the sound of a truck pulling into the driveway announced that Dr. Mitchell Garrison had arrived. He was not a man anybody would have picked to be a veterinarian. A concert pianist, maybe, with long slender fingers and delicate hands, maybe an artist. He was tall, as thin as a rail, almost gaunt, with sad, bloodhound eyes in his bony face.

When they got to her stall, Daisy was lying on her side as she had been earlier, but her breathing was no longer ragged. It was shallow and light. It didn't take a veterinarian to see that this animal was dying.

After a brief examination, the veterinarian asked Nate to show him the other livestock. Maybe it had been in evidence before, but Nate didn't think so. Surely he'd have noticed, even sleep-deprived. The other cattle had rheumy eyes and seemed lethargic. Two were standing listlessly in the middle of the field. Not grazing, just standing there.

When they returned to the barn, they found Daisy lying still in the hay, no longer breathing.

"What's going on here, Mitch? Was Daisy Mae poisoned?"

The suspicion had been growing in Nate ever since he found the cow with her head pressed against a tree. *Somebody* had keyed his pickup. *Somebody* had splashed red paint on his porch. Had somebody …?

The vet was surprised by the question.

"Well, I suppose it's possible she got into something—"

"I don't mean accidentally poisoned. I mean poisoned on purpose."

"Why would you …?" He didn't finish. "There are all kinds of things that could have killed this cow, but I'd just be blowing smoke if I said I knew exactly what happened. I'll need to take blood samples from Daisy and the other cattle to be sure."

It was late afternoon the next day before Dr. Garrison called with the preliminary results of the blood tests. He didn't mince words.

"Daisy Mae had ten times the normal level of lead in her bloodstream."

"So she *was* poisoned!"

"Not just lead, other heavy metals, too. Cadmium and zinc. Mercury levels *off the chart.*"

"Mercury? You mean like in-a-thermometer mercury?"

"I do."

Nate had steeled himself to learn that somebody was poisoning his cattle. Feeding them arsenic or strychnine, something like that. But none of this made any sense at all.

Cadmium and zinc?

Where did those come from? "Heavy metals" — what did that even mean?

"It's not totally uncommon for calves to get lead poisoning. They go around the field and barnyard, curious, like to lick and chew on things. There's lead in paint. In linoleum, too, and caulking materials. Maybe an old car battery."

"That's crazy. I've had cattle in that same field for twenty years and my Pa before me. If there'd been a car battery there, chances are one or the other of us would have noticed it."

"Lead poisoning is the usual suspect when a cow comes up suddenly blind. But the rest of it … I have no idea."

Nate was still reeling.

"The other animals, will they—?"

"Survive? I don't know for certain, but I doubt it. There's no treatment for lead poisoning. Most cattle that get it, die. And the ones that don't, the meat isn't fit for human consumption."

It was just so *wrong* … it was like the earth had gotten

cockeyed all of a sudden, had fallen out of its original orbit and gone spinning off into space. Daisy couldn't just drop over dead. With lead in her bloodstream. And *mercury*! That didn't make sense.

Four days later, Nate was coming out of the post office, searching through the envelopes in his hand for one with an international stamp, when he heard a voice from behind him.

"Afternoon, Nate."

He managed not to spin around like he'd been poked with a cattle prod.

Turning slowly, he took the measure of the man standing there. Big-Un McClusky had been aptly named. He was a mountain of a man, stood something over six feet six inches tall and weighed upwards of three hundred pounds. But he'd gotten the "Big-Un" designation from his father, Big Jake, whose size was about muscle and strength.

The man standing before Nate now was muscled, too, but he also had a beer belly that stretched his overalls tight in the middle. He had a beard that covered his whole face, not neatly trimmed, either. Looked like a bird nest knocked out of the tree by a storm.

Big-Un's scrawny son Jackson was in Charlie Company with Riley, though the two were in different squads.

"Big-Un," Nate said, tight-lipped, and nodded. He hadn't noticed Big-Un in the post office. Stepping out of his way, Nate didn't reach back to hold the door open for him. Big-Un came out of the building but didn't walk off down the street to wherever he'd parked. He stood looking at Nate.

"Heard you got some cattle acting queer."

How would Big-Un McClusky have heard a thing like that?

"I do. *Did.* One cow's already dead and there are a couple more that don't look like they're gonna make it."

That was the answer to Big-Un's question but he just kept standing there. Nate was about to turn away when Big-Un said quietly, "Stood there with they heads hanging down, did they, shaking 'em like to get a fly off they nose?"

This right here was more conversation than Nate had had with Big-Un McClusky in … he had to scramble to think of the last time he'd talked to the man and remembered it was when the North Fork River swelled up with rain and flooded over Mansfield Road. Cars had driven off into the water without realizing how deep it was, and started to float downstream. The people who came along after stopped and helped, of course. Big-Un had been one of those people. He'd been on the east side of the flooded river and Nate had been on the west. They'd hollered out, "You got any rope?" and … "tie it to my trailer hitch." Things like that, but they'd never gotten closer than the width of the rain-swollen river.

"And you know that how?"

Big-Un didn't tell him how he knew, just said, "I got me some cows been doin' the same thing."

The big man stood there for another beat, held Nate's gaze, then he lumbered off down the street.

Chapter Forty

As soon as Nate got home, he called Mitch and told him about his conversation with Big-Un McClusky.

"He called the other day and I went out to his place," the vet said. "He's got three dead cows and another half dozen sick. I took blood tests but his results were delayed. I just got them back a few minutes ago — haven't had a chance to call him, or to let you know about it." He took a breath. "It's the same thing. Whatever it is that's happening to your cattle is happening to Big-Un's cattle, too. High levels of lead, cadmium and zinc."

"But where—?"

"There is no 'where.' Those aren't naturally occurring in the environment. They'd have to be introduced. And in sufficient quantities to make a whole lot of cattle sick." Mitch paused. "You might ... want to go have a talk with Big-Un McClusky."

He said that last part carefully. Everybody knew there was bad blood between the Hannackers and the McCluskys.

Bad blood. That's what Pa'd called it, never used the

235

word "feud." Pa said *feud* drove a stake in the ground and everybody who come along afterward seen the stake stuck there. And then them folks had to decide which side of that stake they was gonna walk on, made people take sides when they didn't have no dog in the fight. Pa didn't like getting others involved in his private business.

That night at the shop, Nate tuned out Brodie's music blaring from the radio — *"westward wind is a wayward wind, a wayward wind that's prone to waaaaaander"* — as he worried the puzzle around in his head.

Something had poisoned his cattle, alright. The question was — did somebody do it on purpose? The only people who'd have any motive were the same people who'd keyed his truck and vandalized his house — McCluskys. But why would a McClusky poison Nate's cattle *and Big-Un's cattle, too*? And why lead, cadmium, zinc ... and *mercury*? Where could you even lay hands on stuff like that? And why would you bother? There were a whole lot easier ways to kill a cow than filling it up with mercury!

In a sense, Nate and Big-Un McClusky were neighbors. Sort of. As-the-crow-flies neighbors. They both lived on Bald Knob — one of the biggest knobs in the county — and their land bordered each other's somewhere out in the woods on the side it. But they had no contiguous fields or pastures, and the two families lived on opposite sides of the huge knob. It'd take half an hour to drive from Nate's house to Big-Un's. To get to the McCluskys' from Brewster, you traveled north on Cicada Station Road. To get to the Hannackers', you went south on it.

Nate watched the mechanics remove the mag wheels from a black Chrysler — all four of them, in less than a minute — as he considered the geography of Bald Knob.

On top was flat, tillable land, which wasn't the case with most of the other knobs around. It had been farmed for generations by the Lovejoy family. Big-Un's land was farther down the side of the knob; Nate's was at the base of the knob and spread out into Hickory Stump Hollow. Big-Un's was the least tillable land of the three. Not the most industrious farmers around, previous generations of the McClusky family apparently had not been out from dawn to dusk as had the Hannackers, using a team of mules to clear the land, pulling the stumps out of the ground by brute force, one at a time to enlarge the fields.

Nate wasn't completely certain how much land Big-Un owned. He did know that the Lovejoy place had hundreds of acres, open meadows where the topsoil was rich and fertile. Granny Lovejoy had died three years ago and her daughter and son-in-law had taken over the place, Oliver and Virginia Morris.

Nate shook his head. Oliver Morris was a pompous blowhard, had even *named* the Lovejoy farm "Oliver Morris Acres." Nate's farm was the Hannacker place because it was where the Hannackers lived. He couldn't imagine any further descriptor was necessary. Oliver Morris branded all his cattle with a big O and an M in the middle. Riley said the brand looked "just like an M&M." Morris had an office in the Court Square Building in Brewster for "Oliver Morris Enterprises," his other business endeavors besides the farm.

"… you listenin' to me?" Brodie asked.

Nate bluffed. "You were saying you thought Roy Orbison had a better voice than Elvis Presley."

Nate hadn't been paying attention to Brodie, but "… *pretty woman, walkin' down the street …*" was wailing from the radio and Brodie often waxed eloquent about the caliber of Roy Orbison's voice.

"No, that ain't what I said! But it is true. Orbison can hit them high notes better …"

Nate tuned him out again and went back to considering the situation of his sick cattle. When he did, he realized he'd been thinking about Oliver Morris because he was Nate's out.

Unless Nate planned to stand by and watch every animal on his farm drool, stagger and drop over dead, he would eventually have to have a conversation with Big-Un McClusky. But Morris would allow him to put off the unpleasant experience for a little while.

Nate got home shortly before dawn and called the Morris place, hoping in a spiteful way that the man would still be in bed.

He answered on the second ring.

"Oliver, this is Nate Hannacker. I called to talk to you about your livestock. Would you mind if I's to drop by sometime after lunch and ask you a couple of questions?"

"Anytime, anytime at all."

Granny Lovejoy had been a delightful soul. The last time Nate had seen her, she was in her mid-eighties, had been blind for thirty years. But her blue eyes, sunk deep in a web of smile wrinkles, were so alive and bright you'd swear she could see your face when you spoke to her.

Oliver Morris had torn down Granny's house and built something resembling a castle where hers had been. Big windows on the front paid homage to the spectacular view from the top of the knob, but it was clear Morris intended you to turn your back on the view altogether and stare slack-jawed at his palace.

Nate drove around it to the farming enterprise behind it — barns and cattle, farm equipment. The instant he got out of his pickup truck, he smelled it. The stench was *staggering*, and unmistakable — it was human excrement. The barnyard beside Morris's field smelled like it was downwind of an outhouse. The world's *biggest* outhouse.

Morris approached as Nate was still trying to contain his squinty-faced reaction to the smell.

"Yeah, I know. It stinks. But it's only for a little while in the spring, to get the beds ready for planting. Then you hit it again every few weeks — and honestly, when you get used to it you don't smell a thing.

Nate doubted that.

"What *is* it?"

"You do know, don't you, that you can buy a truckload of fertilizer from a sewage treatment plant for a fraction of what you pay for fertilizer at the feed store?"

"I did not know that."

"I'm trying it this year for the first time, buy it from a treatment plant in Louisville, but I can already tell the corn's thriving, and the soybeans are way taller than they were this time last year. I'm paying nickels on the dollar." He leaned close as if imparting a pearl of great wisdom. "That's how you make a success of agri-business, you know. Smart decisions, cutting costs and maximizing yields."

Nate sensed Morris was about to launch into a lecture on how to make money in farming so he cut him off before he could start.

"How about your livestock? How are they doing?"

"Great. I'm thinking about buying some Holsteins and milking. There's good money in that, you know."

"So ain't none of your cattle acting" — he thought of Big-Un's word and used it — "queer, then?"

"Queer?"

"Strange, odd, like something's wrong with them."

"My cattle are fine. Why do you ask?"

"I've lost some cattle in the past few weeks. All had the same odd symptoms. Mitch did tests and found high levels of lead and other heavy metals in their blood."

"Looks like you need to do a better job of policing your fields, Nate. You can't leave things laying around, you know — old paint cans, peeling wood, that kind of thing. Cows are curious creatures by nature and they'll go nosing around, lick up what they shouldn't. "

Nate ground his teeth together, kept a smile on his face that felt like it was held in place by roofing nails.

"I'm trying to figure out what's wrong so I'm out asking my neighbors if they've had similar problems."

"My livestock are prime specimens, not a puny one in the lot. I keep meticulous records — weight gain, amount of feed. That way I can compare, make informed decisions about culling the herd."

"I'm sure you do, Oliver." Nate wanted to get off the property — now. Away from the stench and away from the man. He wasn't sure which was the more distasteful. "Thanks for your help."

He turned to go and Oliver said, "Oh, I forgot to ask. Have you heard from your boy yet? Billy, isn't it?"

"Riley. And yeah, I've gotten a couple of letters."

"How's he doing over there with his friends playing soldier?"

Chapter Forty-One

"I ALMOST PUNCHED him in the face."

Riley smiled. He'd gotten a letter from Papa this morning — a chopper dropping off supplies had been carrying a mail bag.

The words, in his grandfather's big, square handwriting, swam in front of Riley's face. Out here in the bug-infested, leech-infested, Cong-infested jungle ... he'd gotten a letter from home. He had to struggle to make the reality of it fit in his head. Sometimes mail from the U.S. was delivered two months after it was written. Sometimes letters got lost and were never delivered at all. And sometimes, like today, a letter written only a week ago was in his hands as he sat under a tree in a tropical rain forest on the other side of the planet.

... over there with his friends playing soldier.

"You should have punched him in the face," Riley muttered.

"Who should have punched who in the face?" Willie Ray asked. He'd been reading his own letter — letter**s**, plural. Half the female population under the age of fifty in Callison County was writing to him.

"Check this out," Andy said, and held up a blurry picture of a baby. "Emily thinks she looks like me."

Riley took the picture. The baby looked like … a baby, coulda been anybody.

"She's definitely got your hair."

Willie Ray reached out for the picture, took it, then handed it back to Andy.

"That there is one lucky little girl," he said. "She looks like her mother, doesn't have your ugly mug hanging off the front of her head."

"My mom wants to know if the food in the mess hall has improved," Davie Monaghan said.

"What are you going to tell her?" Ben Higgs asked. For some reason, Ben never got any mail.

"That it tastes like Thanksgiving dinner."

"Right now, it *would* taste like Thanksgiving dinner," Riley said.

Charlie Company had marched out of Tweety Bird two months ago. Roughly, give or take a week. They hadn't been back since. It was probably June by now. Maybe. Hard to tell. Every day seemed just like every other day.

He thought about the letters he'd written from the fire base where he'd complained about what life was like there — how naive he'd been.

How bad the food was in the mess hall … but there *was* a mess hall.

How intimidating the black wall of jungle was only a few meters from the razor wire fence … but there *was* a fence.

He'd whined that the heat was stifling, that there were squadrons of flying, biting bugs, moaned about how the buckets of rain hammered the roofs of the bunkers so you couldn't sleep in the rumble.

But the heat in Tweety Bird fired down at you from the sun. It didn't broil you in a tangled mass of airless, steaming vegetation, with your nose full of the river stink of black mud and dead fish and the cloying stench of rotting corpses — both animals and human.

There was a roof to keep the rain out there, too. It was louder when it hammered down on your helmet.

And you could swat the mosquito that bit you, didn't have to let it suck your blood in silence for fear a slap would identify your position for the Cong in the trees.

In Tweety Bird, you didn't fall asleep standing up, jerk awake as you started to collapse, and dig at your swollen red eyes with knuckles cracked and oozing pus from jungle rot.

You didn't have to take turns examining each other for leaches that got into your shirt and down your legs no matter how tight you laced your boots.

You didn't curl up in a foxhole with your M16 clutched to your chest, your finger *inside* the trigger guard.

You didn't lose your give-a-damn, so that watching that replacement whose name you can't remember get his leg blown off by a land mine registers no emotion whatsoever.

You didn't get to the point that you couldn't conjure images of your loved ones, couldn't bring their faces up in the fog of your mind — self-preservation, because you couldn't live in two worlds, and if you let your mind dwell on that world you wouldn't last a week in this one.

"Who'd your grandfather want to punch in the face?" Willie Ray asked.

"That idiot neighbor of ours who brands his cattle. And he said Daisy died. My cow, showed her at the state fair." Riley tried to make himself care that Daisy had died but he couldn't. "He said he was going to talk to Big-Un McClusky about what killed Daisy, about sick cattle."

Willie Ray fired a look at Jackson McClusky, leaning against a tree on the other side of the clearing.

"Remind him not to turn his back or he could find a knife in it."

Here in the jungle, jammed together, depending on your buddies for your life, all that was surface fell away. You got the true measure of a man here quick. Jackson McClusky was a bottom-feeding coward who'd bail out on the whole company to save himself. Riley had already made up his mind. If somebody got hurt because of Jackson's laziness, cowardice or incompetence, Riley would kill him.

"Friendly fire," he said softly.

"Huh?" Willie Ray asked.

"Nothing. Just daydreaming, that's all."

"Dream about *snow*, then," Willie Ray said. "Not fire."

"How about a fire in the hearth and it's snowing outside the window," Ben Higgs suggested.

"And you're snuggled up under a blanket with your honey …" Willie Ray looked at Davie and winked. "Bet you could set that blanket on fire."

"I could burn the whole house down," Davie said and laughed.

Riley got up and went to where the sergeant was passing out malaria pills, blocked out the sound of laughter behind him.

Chapter Forty-Two

THE MAILBOX on the lane leading back to the house had no name on it. Just the address, a number, and a Keep Out sign. There was no marking of any kind on the dirt road that branched off the lane and meandered through the woods — presumably to Big-Un's house. Nate drove down the dirt road about half a mile and a gravel driveway branched off it. He followed the driveway through the trees and found the McClusky place at the end of it.

Nate had expected a ramshackle farm with broken fences and weeds everywhere — that's how he envisioned the McClusky place. That's not what he found. Oh, it wasn't fancy like the Morris place but neither was it off the set of *The Beverly Hillbillies*. He could see a livestock barn and a silo behind the house, and pens with small animals — lambs and baby goats that maybe were being fed with a bottle — and a chicken house off to the side of the drive-way. He thought he could smell pigs, but couldn't see any of Big-Un's livestock from here. The man had considerable acreage — way more than Nate had imagined.

A large brick house with white shutters in sore need of

a fresh coat of paint sat behind a wide porch surrounded by flowers where four rocking chairs and a porch swing sat empty. A little girl of about ten was sweeping the porch, where use had worn the paint off to bare wood. Another little girl, younger, was on her knees, doing something in the flower garden. There was a rickety fence around the yard, sagging in places, but it kept at bay the yappy little dog which had set up a cry the moment it saw Nate's truck.

A Pomeranian, maybe, a little white dog with a fox-like face and a bushy tail that curved over its back. Must have belonged to one of the kids or maybe to Dorothy McClusky, a husky woman with dark hair on her upper lip. Nate had seen her in the grocery store and in town now and then, always had a herd of children with her. He seldom saw Big-Un anywhere.

Nate pulled to a stop in front of the gate where the dog was frantically trying claw its way out, leaping up and down yapping. When Nate opened the truck door, he looked around before he got out. If Big-Un had a dog, it'd be a Doberman, a German Shepherd, a pit bull, maybe even a bull mastiff and likely not a terribly social animal.

At the Morris's house, Nate had just driven around the house to the back. Most farmers didn't spend a whole lot of time in the house. But here, he intended to go up on the porch and knock on the door. Polite. Didn't want to startle somebody and give them an excuse to shoot his head off.

The screen door opened as Nate approached the gate in the fence. Big-Un stepped out onto the porch with a shotgun cradled in his arms. Not pointed at anybody. Nate tensed.

"Precious!" Big-Un called out to the little dog. "Shut up that yapping, you hear me. Stop barking!"

The dog ignored him and Nate stood where he was, outside the gate in the fence. Big-Un came down the porch steps, hollering more instructions at the little dog that it ignored. When he got to the gate, he leaned his shotgun against the post, bent over and picked the dog up.

"Hush up, now, you hear me," he told it as he rubbed his huge hand over the dog's head and down its back. "Be a good dog and I'll give you a treat." The dog silenced like he'd taken out its batteries and Big-Un set it on the ground, reached into his overalls pocket and took out some small edible substance. He held it out toward the dog, then pulled his hand back.

"Sit."

The dog sat and he gave it the treat, which it gobbled up happily. Only then did Big-Un acknowledge Nate's presence.

"I hep you?"

There was none of the warmth in his voice that had been there when he was addressing the dog.

"I know I ain't welcome here."

"No, you ain't. But since you know you ain't welcome, you musta had a good reason for comin'. What is it?"

The man eyed him shrewdly and it occurred to Nate that he wasn't stupid. Mean as a snake, yes, but not dumb.

"I come to talk to you about what you said the other day about your cattle. How they're acting queer."

"Figured. Come on. I'll show you."

Big-Un had to fight the dog with his leg to keep it from dashing out the front gate when he opened it, then he led Nate around to the back toward the rail fence that enclosed his pasture. He pointed to several mounds of dirt on the other side of the fence.

"Used the backhoe to bury 'em — three died so far but a bunch of the others don't look good."

He gestured out toward the cattle that were visible in the field. Two were standing with their heads hanging, looked just like Daisy. Another appeared to have its head jammed into a tree, but it was too far away for Nate to tell for sure.

"Mine looked just like that. I've lost two head already, at least three more are looking sickly. That's half my herd." Big-Un raised cattle for slaughter, not just for his kids to use in 4-H projects. "You got any idea what's wrong?"

"Mitch took blood tests and said they was full of heavy metals."

"Blood tests of mine said the same thing."

"What in the Sam Hill is 'heavy metals?'"

"Lead, zinc, cadmium, mercury and some others."

"*Mercury*." Big-Un shook his head. "Like's in thermometers. That's crazy."

"That's what *I* said."

Nate took out a pack of cigarettes, lit one and inhaled deeply.

"How in the Sam Hill could a cow get ahold of thermometers? The lead ... I can kinda see that, old lead-based paint, flaking like."

Nate was surprised the man knew there was such a thing as lead-based paint.

"But they ain't been around nothin' that's painted — with lead-based or any other kind of paint. They ain't been nowhere since the day they's born but out in that field." Big-Un paused. "You think somebody's poisoning 'em?"

Nate didn't like the accusing tone he detected, but then Big-Un actually almost smiled a little. Nate expected to see a mouth full of blackened teeth, like the stumps in a forest after a fire. He was wrong. Then Nate remembered that one of the McCluskys, somebody's kid, had become a dentist. "But the onliest person I know who'd have any reason to poison my cattle is *you*."

Nate couldn't count on the fingers of both hands all

the people *he* knew who'd eagerly sign up to poison the McCluskys' cattle, but he didn't say that.

"If it's poison, why lead and mercury?" Nate said. "There's a whole lot of other poisons that'd do the trick, simpler and easier to get."

"What *is* cadmium, anyway? I don't even know what you do with it."

"Batteries."

"They's cadmium in batteries?"

Nate was tempted to let it lie and sound superior, but he didn't.

"I didn't know either so I looked it up. But unless they been licking the one in the tractor, my cows ain't been near any batteries neither."

"Paint and batteries ... that's the craziest thing I ever heard. You look up zinc?"

"No."

"Don't matter. Whatever it's used for, it ain't out there anywhere." Big-Un gestured toward the field that stretched out in front of them, empty save for some large trees, the grass and the grazing cattle.

"My cattle been eating and drinking the same thing they always have and it never made them sick before. Why now?"

Big-Un shook his head, equally bewildered.

"I went up to the top of the knob and talked to Oliver Morris about it." Nate thought about the stench. "You been up there lately? The stink will *Knock. You. Down.*"

"Me and Morris don't hang out much. What stink?"

"Crap."

"You been a farmer your whole life and you're bothered by the stink of manure?"

"Not cow crap, people crap. He's been using sewage to fertilize his fields." Big-Un gave him a disbelieving look.

"Sewage?"

"He says it's great, crops look good. More to the point, so do his cattle."

"Your cows is sick and my cows is sick, but his are fine. How you figure that?"

Nate shrugged. "You'd think that whatever they got into, they'd *all* get into it."

The two men stood side by side, their forearms resting on the top slat of the fence, looking out into the field. Nate had run out of anything to say, had found out what he'd come for. He dropped his cigarette in the dirt, ground it out with his heel and stepped back.

"You find anything, let me know." He didn't offer to shake Big-Un's hand. Big-Un didn't offer either, just nodded. "I'll do the same."

Nate got halfway across the lot toward the house, when Big-Un called after him.

"Hold up." Nate turned and Big-Un joined him in the middle of the open area in front of the barn. "What you said before — that your cattle's eating and drinking the same thing they always done."

"Yeah …"

Nate could see the big man considering. Maybe wondering if he should share his conjectures with a man he'd spent his whole life hating.

"Come on, spit it out. No use holding back now."

"I's just thinking. Ain't none of us got *pastures* that connect …"

Nate nodded. The properties bumped up against each other somewhere out there in the trees.

"They is one thing that connects all three, though — that little creek."

Nate stopped cold. A piddly little creek originated in a spring somewhere at the top of the knob and meandered aimlessly down the side, beneath a rock bluff and then dumped into the Rolling Fork River.

The creek was dry except in the spring and summer months, and even then it was so small it didn't have a name. But it did run along the back side of the pasture where Nate's cattle grazed and they drank from it, and apparently crossed Big-Un's pasture somewhere, too.

"You're thinking maybe the creek was carrying all that stuff along and the cattle drank it and they all got sick."

"Not *all*. Not Morris's."

That stopped Nate, but then it didn't.

"Whatever was in the water that made the cows sick wasn't there when it passed through Morris's land because—"

Big-Un finished the thought, "—it *started* on his land."

"The sewage!"

"That creek water was fine all these years and then all of a sudden it wasn't no more."

"But it's just human waste from a sewage treatment plant," Nate said. "Far as I know, I don't crap mercury. Do you?"

Big-Un was undeterred, had the answer he'd been looking for. "It's in that water!" And he had a mean glint in his eye that Nate would not want to be on the receiving end of.

"One way to find out for sure," Nate said. "Get me a sample of your creek water, I'll get some of mine, take them both to Mitch and get him to test 'em."

Big-Un didn't answer, just headed to the house for a Mason jar.

Chapter Forty-Three

JESSIE MONAGHAN TRIED NOT to look over at the empty seat next to her on the two-row tobacco setter. Davie'd been in that seat last spring. It was the first time the two of them had worked together on the farm and they'd discovered — to the surprise of neither of them — that they worked together like a hand in a glove.

Now, Jessie sat alone on the tobacco setter, slowly dropping the burley tobacco plants, one at a time out of the float trays, into the machine digging a trench for them. She watched them line up like West Point cadets in the ground behind the tractor.

Since tobacco seeds were so unbelievably small, they had to be planted and grown in trays until they sprouted. Then in late May and early June, the small plants with the long, dangling roots were transplanted, set in the ground to grow, dropped one at a time by hand by the two workers, sitting side by side on the tobacco setter as a third drove the tractor slowly down the row across the field. Setting tobacco was a tradition that spanned generations and had changed very little — the old tobacco setter where she sat now had been used to set tobacco by Davie's grandfather.

Her brother Lanny drove the tractor. He and her two other brothers had pitched in to help on the farm while Davie was gone. War or no war, the tobacco had to be set in the spring or there'd be none to harvest in the fall. Jessie had to take over the farm and run it herself — with help from neighbors and family. Other Callison County farmers were struggling with the same problems.

Knowing she wasn't alone did nothing to alleviate the loneliness. Other wives weren't out in the fields doing the actual work as Jessie did, so they missed their husbands in other ways, but it was Jessie's self-pitying belief that her role was harder, missing her co-worker as well as her friend, her husband, her lover—

"I think we'd ought to call it a day at the end of this row," Lanny yelled over the rumble of the tractor's motor. "If we start early, we'll be done by noon tomorrow."

There was still plenty of daylight left, no reason to quit except that Lanny had jobs on his own farm to do, couldn't spend all his time helping his sister.

"Fine — end of this row."

Jessie'd been surprised and touched by the attitude of the law firm where she worked. They gave her time off from her job to work on the farm! Oh, she always had to take work home — typing transcripts and depositions and the like far into the wee hours of the morning — with Magic keeping her feet warm while she worked, of course. The dog had a thing for her feet, and her shoes. Was likely home right now happily chewing up a pair of sandals. Folks said that chewing was a puppy thing that dogs got over as they grew older. She wasn't sure she'd have any shoes left by then.

When she had the tractor and equipment put away, she

got into the pickup truck and went to her third job, the hardest job, the one Davie thought was the most important. Davie'd told his mother that Jessie would be coming by to check on her, but in the beginning it was clear Mama Ruth hadn't understood that he'd meant Jessie'd come by *every day*! Two times every day. Halfway through the first week after he left, Mama Ruth had yanked the door open while Jessie's fist was still in the air for the second knock and barked.

"Ain't you got nothing better to do than come here pestering me all the time?"

Ruth Monaghan had once been several inches taller than she now stood. Her back had bent — osteoporosis — pointing her face toward the floor. She didn't yet have to lean her head back just to see the faces of the people in front of her but that day wasn't far off. Her hair had once been as black as Davie's, but now it was streaked with snow that reminded Jessie of comets falling across a night sky.

Davie had gotten his good looks from his *father*, who'd died when he was fourteen. His mother's features were severe — thin face, thin lips, a sharp nose and eyes that sank back into her skull so far it was impossible to tell the color. Hers was a face that even in repose seemed to be frowning — the indentions between her eyebrows were drawn constantly together, were as deep as the cleft on David's chin.

The old woman wasn't exactly fragile or frail, but she was painfully thin and it wasn't hard to imagine that a fall would surely break something. In the does-she-have-all-her-marbles department ... that depended on who you asked, and when.

Sometimes, she seemed quick and alert, in need of nobody's help to do anything, thank you very much. Other days she seemed to be in a fog, looked like she might be trying to figure out who you were and why you'd come. And on still other days, she was just a grouchy, unpleasant old lady.

That day during the first week, Jessie would have guessed she was in her Type Three persona, and it had just hit her wrong. Jessie'd been emotionally exhausted and in no frame of mind to take crap from the old woman.

"Actually, I do have better things to do. Lots of better things to do, but I am going to show up on your doorstep every day because I promised David I would. You don't have to come to the door if you don't want to but I *do* have come and knock. And I *will*."

As soon as the words had left her mouth she'd wanted to call them back, could not believe she'd talked like that to David's mother. Clearly, the old woman was having trouble believing it herself because she'd looked like Jessie'd thrown cold water in her face.

But she'd recovered quickly and launched her own volley.

"Fine, then. That's settled. You knock, and if I feel like it, I'll answer."

After that, it was a crap shoot. Some days Mama Ruth didn't even come to the door, just hollered from inside that "I don't need nothing." Other days, she said the same thing, only she did open the door and say it to Jessie's face. And other days she didn't seem to have enough oars in the water to be able to steer. Today was one of those days.

The door opened and Mama Ruth stood before her. She didn't look at Jessie, just focused on something in the air above and to the right of Jessie's head.

"I hep you?"

"I just stopped by to see how you're doing, Mama Ruth."

"How'd you know it was today?"

"How'd I know what was today?"

"The day he died. May 28, eight years ago today.

David's father had been killed in a traffic accident. The sheriff had shown up on Mama Ruth's porch with a deputy to deliver the news.

"I … *didn't* know—"

"I won't do that again. You tell David that. I ain't listenin' to strangers in uniform … ever again. You make sure he knows that."

Then she closed the door.

That was why Mama Ruth hated to hear a knock at the door. The woman lived in fear that someday it'd be an army officer sent to tell her that her only son had been killed in combat.

Jessie turned and walked across the porch and slowly down the steps. She hadn't made it to the gate in the fence when a voice from behind her called, "I got coffee. It ain't bad."

She found that the smile on her face as she turned around was real.

"Don't mind if I have a cup."

And she walked into the house, invited to enter for the first time since Davie left. Four months, three weeks, two days, eighteen hours and — she looked at her watch — thirty-seven minutes, not that she was counting or anything.

Chapter Forty-Four

NATE WAS in the Piggly Wiggly parking lot, had just settled two bags of groceries in the bed of his pickup truck when he heard a voice call out. "Hold up, Nate. I want to talk to you."

He turned around to see Parker McClusky striding toward him.

Seriously?

First Big-Un and now Parker. Was the month of May Hang Out With a Lowlife Month and Nate just hadn't noticed the holiday on the calendar?

Parker was ten years younger than Nate, tall, and looked fit. Not work-on-a-farm fit, work-out-in-a-gym fit. He wore a suit, but the tie was loose and he'd unbuttoned the top button of his white shirt. His face was square and blocky, had what Nate thought of as McClusky Neanderthal features. Ugly, but not painfully so.

He'd sprouted from Ike McClusky's limb on the family tree. The patriarch, Rooster McClusky, had had two sons, Ike and Big Jake, and three daughters. Ike had left five children behind when he ... *uh* ... *died unexpectedly* — three sons and two daughters. Parker was his oldest son. Ike's brother, Big Jake, eventually had seven children, four sons and three daughters. So the web of McClusky aunts/uncles and cousins was spread wide, some of them with the last name McClusky, some not. Nate tried to total it up once, but it was harder than counting Willie Ray Taggart's freckles.

Nate had never had a single conversation with Parker. But he'd watched the McClusky Circus during Little League games a couple of times and he couldn't imagine how a man with such an explosive temper had done so well in life. But then some of the McClusky family had prospered in spite of their lineage. And others because of it. Parker was part of a private law practice in Brewster, drove a fancy car, lived in a big house, appeared to have money to burn, though Nate had heard he was a high stakes gambler, owed money to some unsavory people you didn't want to get crossways with. Parker's boys, Shep and Jody were in their twenties, bottom-feeders to the core. Their cousins, the sons of Rooster's daughters, were about the same age and equally worthless.

Rooster's oldest daughter Annie had been appointed to the state ABC Board — Alcohol Beverage Control Board — that determined which restaurants, bars and clubs got liquor licenses and which didn't. Folks said she needed a wheelbarrow to haul all her bribery money to the bank. But his second daughter Rosalind was a dentist, apparently a pretty good one, though Nate would let every tooth he had rot in his head before he'd let Rosie touch him. His third daughter, Traci, owned several high-end dress boutiques in Louisville. Big Jake's oldest son was Big-Un, whose cattle were apparently suffering from the same malady as Nate's.

Parker smiled, and Nate thought it looked like he'd learned how from a manual. No warmth ever made it to his eyes, though his teeth were perfect, perhaps a recommendation for his Aunt Rosie's dental practice.

"I won't take but a couple of minutes of your time." He nodded toward the coffee shop next door to the grocery store. "Let me buy you a cup of coffee."

I'd rather have a migraine.

Nate didn't say that, just told him brusquely, "I got things to do," opened his truck door, got behind the wheel and closed the door in Parker's face.

Parker smiled again — well, pulled up the corners of his mouth. He stood outside the truck door and continued speaking through the open window as if Nate had been friendly and cordial. Some folks ain't got sense enough to be offended.

"My boys are a little older than your ... Billy ... *Riley.* He's in the guard unit, that right?"

Nate nodded.

"Your boy's in the same squad with David Monaghan, isn't he? David's wife Jessica works at our firm. We've tried to be as supportive as we can, let her take work home when she's got other things to do."

Jessica Harrington Monaghan. Riley's first, and so far, only love.

"My sons didn't join the guard because they weren't in danger of being drafted. Past the prime age and ..." He tried to look like he wasn't proud of himself. "I have friends in Frankfort, if you know what I mean."

A woman walked up to the car parked in the space facing Nate's truck and began to load groceries into the back seat. She was pretty, wearing a short skirt, and Parker stared at her round butt when she leaned over to get soft drinks off the rack on the bottom of the grocery cart.

He turned his eyes back to Nate without dropping a beat and continued talking.

"My oldest is Shepherd, a bit of a lost soul for a while until he settled down in a job he loved that makes him a nice chunk of change and an opportunity for advancement."

Ah, Shep, the Little Leaguer who'd tried to crack the catcher's skull with a baseball bat. Where was Parker going with all this?

"Then a couple of months ago, the promotion he was expecting was given to somebody else. And just like that he was out of a job completely, passed over for somebody who wasn't qualified to do the work." Parker paused and took off his sunglasses. "My boy had grand plans for that position, for expanding and growing it into a money machine that could have made millions. He's lost a fortune because of his boss's … oversight. He can't … he *won't* allow the error to go uncorrected. You can see the position this has put him in, can't you?"

So *that's* what this was about. It was Shep Mama Bert had been talking about when she said a McClusky had been "laid off" from the chop shop operation. It figured. He was a car nut, whipped around town in one fancy sports car and then another. Always angling to get somebody to race him so he could bury them in his dust. The handful of times Nate had seen him on the street in the past couple of years, he'd looked like he was hyped up on something, taking some kind of drug.

"But as it turns out, the person who got the job is only temporary. Only got hired until the *Fourth of July*, and then the position will come open again."

The woman in the car in front of Nate's truck backed up and pulled out of the space.

"And Shep thinks he'll get the job then, does he?" Nate raised an eyebrow.

Both men were singing from the same sheet of music now, understood what they were really talking about.

"Oh, he's *sure* he'll get it then. Why wouldn't he? The temporary person is in way over his head, doesn't know the first thing about the business."

"Well, I hope you're right and your boy isn't disappointed again." Nate turned the key in the ignition and started the truck. He should have left it at that. He didn't.

"But if I was Shep, I'd be wondering why the boss didn't keep me in the job in the first place, given that I'm so much better qualified and all. I'd be asking myself if there was something I did that made the boss reluctant to *trust* me. Maybe some ... ethical issues or emotional issues, or some medication I was taking that made me *unreliable*." He put the truck in drive. "Might be a good idea not to get his hopes up. Could be the position won't come open again for a long, long time."

Parker put a restraining hand on Nate's arm.

"Oh, it *will* come open on the Fourth of July. The temporary *won't* show up for work on July fifth."

Nate pulled his arm out of Parker's grip.

"And you know that how?"

"I know it because the person who is currently in the position isn't a fool. He's a man who understands when he's outnumbered and outgunned." Putting his hands out in front of him, palms up, Parker said, "My boy's got a temper. I'll admit it. Got it from me. I've always struggled with it — the kind of temper that when you lose it there's just no telling what you'll do."

"Childish vandalism, you mean? Scratching paint off ... or splashing paint on — *idiot*, little-kid stuff like that?"

Parker blew by the remark, intent on making his own point.

"You got a boy, too, Riley, over there in Vietnam." He

paused and said the rest slowly and with emphasis. "Your boy's no fool. He sees the *mortal* danger he's in. He understands he could get *killed* for a single wrong decision."

"The fella who's got the job now … he's outgunned and outnumbered, you say? I hear the same thing happened to him once before. He was only sixteen years old and" — Nate leaned close and said softly — "he made orphans out of five McClusky brats."

Nate put his foot on the accelerator and drove away through the vacant parking space as Parker yelled at him.

"He wouldn't have lived to seventeen if not for the Crows' Pledge."

Nate hadn't thought about the Crows' Pledge in years, didn't even find out it existed for more than a decade. The pledge that had been formed in the Saint Dominic Church sanctuary, and then kept secret for years, was the stuff of legends.

Parker was still yelling as Nate turned from the parking lot into the street.

"His mama's not around to protect him anymore!"

Nate wondered if Parker still spewed out little white speckles of spittle when he got mad.

Chapter Forty-Five

1934

MOSE TAGGART WOULDN'T LET Lenora Hannacker see her husband's body after the wreck. Said it was clear Samuel had died instantly, didn't suffer no pain, and what the wreck done to his body after he died wasn't something she needed to look at.

But he couldn't keep her away from Johnny's body. Couldn't keep her sister-in-law Audrey away from Joe's body neither. What was the point? Everybody who seen them seen they'd been shot in the head with the gun Ike McClusky had in his hand when Nathaniel killed him.

She'd had Nathaniel to focus on or she would have lost her mind. Nathaniel had been seriously injured in the wreck. His chest had been crushed against the steering wheel. He had broken three or four ribs, cracked some others. The most serious thing of all was his right leg. It had been so badly mangled the doctor in Louisville tried to get Lenora to let him cut it off but she wouldn't do it. He said Nathaniel'd never walk on it again. But that doctor didn't know her boy.

Lenora went through the motions of burying her

husband and her firstborn son, and somewhere inside she was aware of doing that. Of standing in the rain on a spring day, the black veil on her hat stuck to her face so she could barely see.

Graves. Tombstones.

Struggling every second of every day to move forward to care for the children she had left. Her girls and Nathaniel. She was all they had, and with no father to care for them, to provide for them, their survival in the world seemed to her sometimes as fragile as the filament of a spider's web carried in the breeze.

Mose Taggart and his boys took over for Sam and Johnny best as they could. But it was too much, her family and Pete's added to his own — it was too much. Lenora weighed her options. Her sister Naomi lived in Nashville. Naomi was childless and her husband had a good job with the railroad. Lenora could send some of her children — how many? *Which ones?* — to live with Naomi. She'd take them in. There was a widows' and orphans' home run by the Shriners in Louisville. If Lenora couldn't feed them, if the children were … *starving,* she could send them there.

But Nathaniel healed quickly, remarkably quickly, the doctors said. Almost miraculously so. They were amazed he was able to move around as he did with those broken and cracked ribs, and get around on that leg — though the knee didn't function properly, giving him a severe limp.

Lenora knew that it was sheer grit and nothing else that got him through. She knew he was in excruciating pain that he just refused to acknowledge. His focus was on only one thing, getting strong again so he could take care of his mother and his sisters.

He was the man of the house. They were his responsibility now.

And then came the Sunday afternoon when Mose

came by to check on them, see if they needed anything. She found out why he'd really come by when she walked him out to his car.

"Lenora, you need to know this." He took a big breath. "They's talk the McCluskys is looking to even the score, that they're gonna come after Nathaniel to make him pay for killing Ike. Now, it's probably just talk. They blow a lot of smoke when there really ain't no fire. But me and mine always keep a weapon handy — everywhere we go. You need to do the same."

Mose left. Lenora and the older girls fixed the children's supper — corn meal mush and venison. She changed the bandage on Nathaniel's healing leg. She read from the Bible to the littles — Rose and Lily were ten and Becky was six. She tucked them all into bed and when she was sure they all were asleep, she went out to the barn where they couldn't see, threw her arms around Oscar's neck and sobbed, the big gelding's horse smell comforting in some way that she couldn't have explained.

When she'd got her cry out, she wiped her eyes and blew her nose on her apron and squared her shoulders. There'd be no more crying. That part was done. Now, Lenora Wilson Hannacker had to figure out a way to protect her son.

Lenora would give her life for Nathaniel.

If her dying would ensure that Nathaniel would live, if her death would in some way protect him … she was willing to make that sacrifice.

But it wouldn't. The truth still in the husk was that she could *die* for him … and it wouldn't keep him alive. The horror of that realization stole her breath. She was willing to do anything, absolutely *anything* to protect him, but if giving up her own life wasn't enough, what *more* did she have to give?

She took a deep breath and let it out slowly. She knew what more she had. It was unthinkable, but she knew. It was her only option.

The next day, she paid a visit to her sister-in-law, Audrey, the widow of Sam's brother Pete, who'd been killed six years ago. The "prohibition agent" Rooster McClusky had shot Pete down when he tried to surrender. Now, her son, Joe, lay cold in the ground in the church cemetery with a bullet hole in his forehead, just like the one in Johnny's.

Audrey had two other sons in their twenties.

Lenora outlined what she planned to do, then sat in silence, waiting. Audrey had been horrified at first. Of course she had. Audrey was a small, delicate woman, with wispy blond hair and pale blue eyes — had been dwarfed by Pete, her big bear of a husband. Most folks didn't realize she was as strong, in all the ways that mattered, as Pete. She understood this was their only option.

"I'll stand with you," she finally whispered, took Lenora's hand and squeezed it. Then she crossed herself. "God forgive me."

Father Anthony Romano was new to the Saint Dominic parish, but he had officiated at the funerals of those killed in the crash with a tenderness and care seldom seen in someone so young. Lenora didn't tell him all of it — couldn't have told him all of it! — just that what she wanted was to "bring peace to the community." She begged him to seek out Father McSwain of the Saint Rose parish and get him to agree to help.

The meeting was held in the cold stone sanctuary of Saint Dominic where she and Audrey waited in the front pew for Maude and Thelma McClusky. They both were still dressed in black, and when the other two widows came striding down the aisle to the front, they were dressed in black, too.

"We come because the father said we *had* to come," said Maude, Rooster's widow, without looking at either of them. "He said being unwilling to" — she wrinkled her nose in disgust — "'*seek peace*' was a sin and unless we repented of it, he couldn't give us communion."

"So we said we'd come," Digger's widow, Thelma, said. "But that's all — just come, and we done that." She looked at her sister-in-law. "And now we're leaving, ain't saying one word to a Hannacker."

Maude McClusky was a big-boned woman with a man's large hands ... and dark hair on her upper lip like a man, too. She had a mouth full of crooked, blackened teeth and a single black eyebrow in a slash across her forehead.

She looked from Lenora to Audrey, glared at them.

"If this wasn't a house of God, I'd spit on you both."

She turned to march back up the aisle with her sister-in-law. Lenora got to her feet and her voice, soft but clear, followed her.

"Her name's Annie, ain't it? Your oldest girl. About four years old."

Maude's back stiffened, but she kept walking.

"With that head of blonde hair, she'll be easy to pick out." Lenora did not speak louder, but her voice seemed to fill up the whole empty church. "She'll be the first. I'll put a bullet right in the middle of them blonde curls, drop her on the school yard, or maybe outside of church, or making mud pies on your front porch."

Maude kept moving forward, taking small steps, her gait unsteady.

"Your youngest is Martha, ain't it?" Lenora asked Thelma, who'd stopped altogether, stood unmoving with her back turned toward the Hannackers. "She's gonna be harder, her being so little and all. Likely have to shoot her when somebody's a'holding her, kill them, too, I reckon. But it won't be *you* a'holdin' her. You'll be long dead 'fore I start picking off your little'uns."

Thelma McClusky whirled around. She was a short, round woman with thick strawberry blond hair caught in a bun at her neck. Her fat face was bright red and she looked like she was about to come flying back down the aisle and rip into Lenora.

"You wouldn't *dare*—"

"Oh, I absolutely *would* dare!! You need to know this for a true fact." Lenora turned slowly toward the statue of the Virgin Mary and the cross above the altar where Jesus hung, his face a study in agony. "I swear … on my *immortal soul*, on the cross of Jesus and on the Virgin Mary" — she turned and fixed a cold glare on Thelma, then on Maude — "that I will kill you and *every child in your house* … unless you leave my Nathaniel be."

Thelma was absolutely horrified. Nobody said a thing like that in church! It was *blasphemy*. She stared at Lenora wide-eyed, then crossed herself to ward off the evil. Maude crossed herself, too.

Audrey slowly got to her feet beside Lenora. "I swear the same oath. As God, Jesus and the Virgin Mary are my witnesses, I will kill—"

"You're going to Hell," Thelma screeched at them, her voice high-pitched and shrill. "Both of you, you are demons and you are going to *burn*—"

"—in a lake of fire," Maude finished for her.

"I 'spect you're right." Lenora's voice trembled slightly. "I will spend eternity in Hell for these sins." She squared her shoulders and her voice firmed. "But I will send *every one* of your children to heaven before I die."

Maude gasped, drew in a great gulp of air that sucked all the sound from the room. The church filled with silence so thick Lenora couldn't breathe. If she inhaled, she'd drown in that silence, her lungs filled with it like water.

So she could only whisper, but in the silence she might as well have been screaming.

"I know you're gunning for my boy, my Nathaniel, and I would give my life to keep him safe." She broke then, barked out a single anguished sob, and after that she was utterly real, no longer held together with determination and courage. Open, vulnerable and raw, she looked into the women's eyes, and spoke to their hearts. "But that's the thing, don't you see. It ain't enough. My life's all I got and I'd lay it down for my precious boy, but *it ain't enough*."

Her voice grew thick as she struggled to keep from bursting into tears.

"This ain't no bluff, Maude McClusky." She turned to Thelma. "It ain't something to say just to scare you. I done thought it all the way through. All I got to give, my life, ain't enough to save my boy. And if that ain't enough, ain't but one thing I got left. And it's worth more'n my life — my immortal soul."

"Your boy killed my husband and my son!" Maude raged.

"And your son killed my husband and my son!" Lenora fired back.

"They was grownups."

"So … that's it?" Lenora asked. "Long's they's … what? Old enough for they voices to change, old enough for pimples? How old they got to be to become targets?"

"My Joe was fifteen years old and Ike put a gun to his forehead and blew out the back of his head." Audrey probably didn't even realize she was crying, the tears streaming down her cheeks. "I got me two boys left and I ain't gonna put them in the ground next to their father and their brother! Ain't no other way to stop this."

She took a breath and firmed her voice. She looked Thelma McClusky dead in the eye.

"Will I … *kill* your Margaret, little Maggie with them red pigtails, her not even old enough to have lost her front teeth? *Know* that I will. I *swear* a holy oath that I will."

"Holy! *Holy?* You're talking about killing babies!"

"What *difference* does it make?" Lenora screamed. The sound echoed off the cold stone walls of the sanctuary. "Don't you see? The Hannackers got the Taggarts on our side, and you got — who? The Jamisons, maybe? This is gonna go on and on and on. You and me and Audrey and all the other mothers … we're just fattening up our boys for the slaughter, growing 'em big enough so's it's 'moral' to shoot 'em."

She stopped screaming, ground out words in a growl through clenched teeth. "*No. More.* That part's *done.*" She continued in a barely controlled rage. "The *men* ain't in charge. Not anymore. If we leave it to the men, we will spend our lives in black, burying our sons. From this moment forward, *I* will protect my son. Not some man, some Hannacker man or some Taggart man — *me*, Lenora Hannacker. I will protect him *any way I can.*" She paused before she growled, "And I ain't gonna fight *fair.*"

Maude McClusky's hands had flown up to cover her mouth and she was shaking her head slowly in denial. Thelma's eyes were huge and tears streamed down her cheeks. Both women were stunned, horrified and furious. But neither of them was disbelieving.

Audrey wiped the tears from her own cheeks.

"I am *done* crying. We're all widows." She pointed a shaking finger at the two other women. "You both have lost a husband and a son." She nodded to Lenora. "So

have we ... buried cold, dead bodies in the cemetery, sacri-
ficed on the altar of hate. The McCluskys and the
Hannackers — we're *even*. It stops here and it stops now.
We leave here in agreement or we leave here to *go to war*
and these hills will run with Hannacker and McClusky
blood — and it'll be the blood of *children*."

Silence flooded the room again.

"It ain't complicated," Lenora said. "Either *all* the children are safe ... or *none* of them is. Either they *all* grow up,
get married, have babies ... live *lives* ... or *none of them do*."

Lenora caught Audrey's gaze and hung on, nodded.
Audrey nodded back. Then the two of them looked at the
two McCluskys.

"The four of us ... we're the black crows who get to
decide."

Chapter Forty-Six

"I THOUGHT I KNEW HOT," Willie Ray said as he took his helmet off and wiped the sweat streaming down his forehead on the back of his arm. "I ain't never gonna complain about working the top rail ever again."

The soldiers had stopped in a clearing, where the radioman was busy disassembling the radio piece by piece to figure out why they couldn't make contact with Alpha One. Willie Ray and Andy sat leaned against a tree, Riley sat cross-legged beside them. The new guy everybody called Buggs, because he had buck teeth, was on the other side with Davie.

Ace was standing beside the same tree, scanning the jungle, his eyes darting back and forth in the search pattern of the combat veteran. The hillside was steep enough that they could see over the trees to the top of a dark layer of cloud that hid a valley. They'd been in that valley when they got hit yesterday. Charlie was waiting for them in the trees and they could have lost half the platoon — but it had started raining, so hard even the Cong couldn't see to shoot. Winston Peters had gotten something in his eye, a piece of shrapnel or something, and they'd had to send him out on an evacuation helicopter. But it could have been a whole lot worse.

Riley thought of the line of soldiers trailing out of the jungle the day they went out on their first patrol four months ago, four lifetimes ago.

"We'd fit right in that parade," he mumbled, not realizing he'd said the words out loud.

"What parade?" Willie Ray asked at the same time the new guy asked, "What's the top rail?"

Andy answered Buggs's question so Riley didn't have to explain what he meant. As he listened to Andy tell Ace about "raisin' bacca," he took his own helmet off and wiped at his sweat. When he did, pus from an open jungle rot sore on his hand got smeared on his forehead. He reached down and wiped his hand on his filthy trouser leg, adding a layer of new pus to the crust of old pus there. Beside the smears of dried blood — his own from smashed leeches and that VC soldier's that splattered on him when Ace gutted him with his Bowie knife. Or maybe that was just spilled spaghetti sauce from the tin that'd exploded on everybody when Andy let it get too hot over the C-4 last night ... no, the night before ... sometime.

"... guys raise tobacco?" Buggs was saying. "I didn't know they was anything in Kentucky but bourbon and race horses."

"If you smoke it, we grew it," Willie Ray said.

"Now that ain't a true fact," Ace said. "You guys ain't raising weed."

"Don't have to *raise it*," Andy said. "The stuff grows wild out behind our barn and in the fence rows. It's a *weed*."

Ace was instantly interested. "Seriously? You saying you got weed ..."

"Hemp," Andy corrected.

"Close enough. You realize you could chop that down and sell it on the street for a nickel a bag?"

"You been charging all of us more'n a nickel for what we've been smoking," Riley said.

"And I been giving you fellas my VIP discount. A nickel bag don't mean it costs a nickel. That means it costs five dollars."

"Five bucks!" Riley was incredulous. "You sell that stuff for five dollars a baggie?"

Willie Ray followed up behind him. "People pay that much for grass clippings?"

"Marijuana and hemp aren't the same," Andy pointed out.

"They're cousins—" Ace said.

"Don't you hillbillies marry your cousins, that's what I hear," Buggs said.

"… and it's illegal," Andy said.

"So's moonshine," Davie put in and looked at Riley and Willie Ray, "and that never stopped you."

"You make moonshine … seriously?" asked Buggs. "You got stills in the woods and all?" Then he got it. "*That's* why you named this platoon Thunder Road."

Riley didn't have the energy to tell him that'd been its name long before they'd joined it.

"Yeah. All the Hannackers look just like Robert Mitchum."

"Kentucky liquor isn't just moonshine," Andy said. "You never heard of Jim Bean whiskey? Heaven Hill? Maker's Mark Distillery is right down the road from my house."

"You want to know about whiskey, go talk to Caleb McAllister in Whiskey Run," Ben Higgs said. "His family owns Double Springs Distillery."

"Hey, listen to this," called out Jackson McClusky, who was seated in the shade of a different tree beside Jude Boone, whose father ran Squire Boone's Tavern in Crawford. Jackson was holding a letter and Jude was trying to take it from him.

"That's mine, give it back."

Jackson mocked him in an imitation whine — "That's mine — give it back" — holding the paper out as Jude grabbed at it. Jackson handed the letter off to Sam Finch, who handed it off to Travis Williams, who dangled it in front of Jude's nose.

Jude lunged for the letter and Travis gave it back to Jackson, who started reading …

"It's from his *Mommy*. She said she'd read in a magazine about some soldiers who were killed." Jude was trying ineffectually to grab the piece of paper back, but Jackson was as small and quick as a squirrel, danced out of his grasp and kept reading.

"Listen to this part …" He faked a high-pitched voice. "All those soldiers got killed at night …" Jackson burst out laughing, sputtering as he read the next part, "so don't you go out after dark!"

Everybody laughed then, even Riley. It was pretty funny.

Jackson collapsed to his knees, roaring. Stoned. Had to be. Weed or something more potent. McClusky was a virtual walking pharmacy. Uppers and downers. He was dangerous. Nobody wanted him on their patrol. But then, nobody'd wanted him on their baseball team in elementary school either. He was always the last kid to get picked, then he'd try to trip the batters on the other team when they went up to bat. If it was your ball, he'd spit on it before he handed it back to you.

"I'm serious here," Ace was saying when Riley tuned

back in to his voice. "You guys ever think about raising weed?"

Buggs had left during the letter-reading and Ace had gathered Willie Ray, Andy and Davie Monaghan around him.

"It's *illegal*," Andy pointed out again.

His brother gave him a baleful look. "And that's a problem because …?"

"Illegal only matters if you get caught," Ace said. "So don't."

He spoke to all of them then.

"I bet you could make a lot more money raising weed than from selling moonshine …" He stopped. "Was you serious? Do you really—?"

"Just like Thunder Road," Riley and Willie Ray said in unison, and everyone laughed again.

"Soon's I get home, I'm gonna go out behind the barn and cut that stuff down," Willie Ray said, "chop it up and put it in little baggies and peddle them on the street in Louisville—" He stopped and his grin grew wider. "Or I could cross-pollinate, grow strawberries that get you high."

Ace turned away and looked at Riley.

"I'm serious, man." He patted the pocket where he carried his bag of weed. "Somebody somewhere is growing this. I don't know who and I don't know how and I don't know where, but *somebody* is. And whoever it is is makin' a ton of money off it. I ain't no farmer. I don't know what it costs to grow something, but you can't tell me you're raising anything else you can put in a sandwich bag and sell for five, maybe ten dollars."

He had a point. Riley was too tired to consider the ramifications, but he did have a valid point. Riley could see Davie connect the dots, too, stolid Davie, who was a "citizen." Davie, who was married to Jessica … He let that go.

"I'm in!" Willie Ray cried. "We all are, ain't we?" He looked from Riley to Davie and finally to Andy, nudged him with his elbow. Then Willie Ray stuck out his hand. "Stack on it. You know, like we did in tee-ball."

You couldn't help smiling at Willie Ray.

Riley put his hand out on top of Willie Ray's.

"I get to bat first."

Davie put his hand on top of Riley's and told Willie Ray, "I'll stack on anything if it'll shut you up."

Their looks shifted to Andy, reasonable Andy, who just shook his head. Willie Ray reached out and grabbed his brother in some kind of hug around his neck, but he wiggled free.

"Tell you what, little brother," Andy said. "You raise enough weed for both of us."

"I'll do that, bro!" A broad smile split his freckled face. "For a fact. That's a promise."

Chapter Forty-Seven

Turned out getting the Mason jars full of creek water tested was a sight harder than Nate had thought it'd be. Mitch couldn't do it. The labs to which he sent various samples tested blood, not water. To test water you had to go to the Department for Natural Resources in Frankfort. The hour at Big-Un McClusky's had been a garden party compared to the three hours Nate spent hauling his lowly Mason jars from one bureaucrat to another until somebody in the Health Environmentalist's Department — he never knew there was such a thing — agreed to see what was in them. After Nate filled out and signed half a hundred-dozen forms, of course. In triplicate.

A week passed.

Two weeks.

Three weeks later, Nate went back to Frankfort determined to park his butt in the health environmentalist's office until he got the results. As soon as he thought to suspect the creek water, Nate had fenced off that pasture and fed his cattle in the barn. He only had a few head, so he could do that. There was no way for Big-Un to move all his cattle to a barn or another pasture.

Nate warmed a chair in Frankfort for most of the morning, but then he was ushered into the office where "Filmore, P. Dimwitty" was printed on the door with various initials after it indicating degrees or licenses or maybe his shoe size.

"These are the results on the water you left here to be tested." The prissy little bureaucrat held out a form in Nate's general direction, then snatched it back and began running his finger down the rows of symbols and numbers, shaking his head and clucking his tongue.

"Lead, cadmium, zinc …" The man peered over his glasses at Nate. "It's a good thing this isn't in a flowing stream."

"Excuse me?"

"You did say this was *not* water from a flowing stream, didn't you? A pond. That was your response on page …" He began to dig through the pile of documents Nate had filled out, had marked up without reading. "Because if it *was* flowing water, then I'd have to get the tank involved."

"Fish tank?"

"*Think* tank. EPA, DNR, DAM."

Nate figured out Environmental Protection Agency and Department of Natural Resources.

"DAM?"

"The Division of Abandoned Mines. You did say this was from the sludge pond of a coal mine, right? On page …"

Nate realized he'd be executing a nuclear option if he got state government involved. They might decide to bulldoze the whole knob.

He called Big-Un when he got home to give him the

news. Before he had a chance, Big-Un said, "I hear the boys was in a bad one a couple days ago."

Nate didn't have to ask "what boys?"

"How would you know …?"

"Winston Peters got wounded and they let him call home from the hospital in Germany. I seen his pa this morning."

The family members of the guard unit really ought to get together and come up with some way to share information. This was torture.

Nate didn't ask about Riley. If he'd been hurt, Big-Un woulda said.

"Winston hurt bad?"

"He got shrapnel in his eye and they flew him out of there to Germany to have it seen to by some kind of eye specialist. Ain't never gonna see outta that eye again."

Nate tried to recover his breath.

"You heard from your boy, Riley?"

"A handful of letters." Nate barked out a bleat or sardonic laughter. "He won't tell me the bad stuff. And the censors take out every third word of what he does say. To hear him tell it, he's on a tropical vacation where the natives are rude sometimes."

"Got one letter from Jack and he said his body count was fifteen VC." Now it was Big-Un's turn to bark out laughter, but it was harsh and dismissive. "Which means he's *seen* ten, shot five of 'em and maybe killed *one*." He made a *humph* sound in his throat. "I ain't got no use for a man who's all hat and no cattle."

Nate didn't want to keep talking about this. It was creepy to be having a chummy conversation with a McClusky. Big-Un wasn't slick though, like his snake-in-the-grass cousin, Parker. He was a lot of things, but he was real.

"So what'd you find out?"

When Nate gave him the full report, the big man's response was gratifyingly similar to Nate's. "We ain't gonna git the gub-mint in the middle of this. We can handle it our own selves. That creek don't run but four or five miles, then dumps into the Rolling Fork. That there's a river big enough to dilute whatever's in a piddly little creek so it don't hurt nothing."

"Okay, so it's not a public 'environmental hazard' — just your cows and mine that drink directly out of that creek. But it's going to keep making *them* sick unless—"

"We go have us a come-to-Jesus meeting with Oliver Morris."

"We don't know it's his fault."

Big-Un exploded. "Yes, we *do!*"

"No, we *don't!* It's a good *guess*, that's all, and it doesn't explain where the heavy metals came from in the first place … human sewage *doesn't have heavy metals in it.*"

"It's his doin."

"Prove it."

"How?"

"Get a sample, have it tested."

Nate was grateful he'd phoned this one in. The man didn't speak — he *roared*.

"You want me to go up there and scoop up *a Mason jar full of crap?*"

When the rumbling subsided, Nate put in. "You got a better idea?"

"Yeah, *you* go up there and scoop up a Mason jar full of crap."

"Fine. *I'll* scoop up the crap, but *you* have to take it to Frankfort to get it tested."

Big-Un let fly a string of expletives that should rightly

have melted the telephone wires, then slammed down the receiver.

Nate should have known better than to try to work with a McClusky. It was impos—

The phone rang.

"I'll send one of my boys. You come by tomorrow and pick up the jar."

Then the line went dead.

The next morning, Nate took along a plastic garbage bag when he went to pick up the Mason jar at Big-Un's so it wouldn't stink up the cab of his truck on the way to Frankfort. One of Big-Un's sons was chopping weeds by the driveway and looked up as he passed. Big-Un was in the barn with three other boys when he saw Nate.

Big-Un looked at the smallest of the three, a boy about eight years old.

"Get on out of here and feed them chickens."

"Yes sir," the boy said, and headed out. Nate got a good look at him then and did a double-take. It was the same boy—

"Twins," Big-Un said. "Got me two sets, boys and girls — so alike when they's little we had to use colored ribbons to tell who was who." He looked after the retreating boy. "They still fool us sometimes."

He turned to the smaller of the two remaining boys.

"That Rhode Island Red's taken to laying in that brush next to the hog pen. If you don't find none there, look behind the tool shed."

"Yes sir," the boy said.

Sir?

Big-Un gestured to the remaining boy, who appeared to be sixteen or seventeen.

"This here's Wade. He's the one drew the short straw and had to go scoop up the crap." He turned to the boy.

"Tell Mr. Hannacker here what you seen and what you done."

"I ain't never in my life smelt anything stunk worse than that did," he began, then responded to a hurry-up look from Big-Un and continued in a rush.

"The reason it smelled so bad was it wasn't just laying there on the ground, mixed up with the dirt and all. That Morris fella was putting it out *right then*, had it in a manure spreader that's likely gonna smell like an outhouse for the next hundred years."

Big-Un cleared his throat and the boy took the hint.

"There was a truck unloading it, said Louisville Metropolitan Sewer District on the side."

The boy paused and looked a question at his father, like wanting to know if he was saying too much. Big-Un nodded for him to go on.

"I come running back down the side of the knob and told Pa what I seen."

"And I told him to get in my truck and follow that dump truck, see where it went."

"So I followed it. You know, like in them spy movies where you follow along behind, close enough so you don't lose sight, but not so close the driver gets suspicious that he's being tailed."

It was probably a safe bet that the driver of a sewage truck didn't lose any sleep at night worrying that he was being followed.

"I seen where it turned off Interstate 65 and I kept following, like Pa said." The boy was pleased as punch with himself for being such a super sleuth. Nate, on the other hand, couldn't understand why Big-Un had sent him in the first place.

"What'd you expect to find by following the truck?"

"I'd been trying to puzzle out how human crap could

get heavy metals in it, and I had me a suspicion. Tell him, Wade. Tell him where it went."

"It went in through the gate of the South Louisville Sewage Treatment plant on Algonquin Parkway."

Big-Un smiled then, but it was only brief before the scowl recaptured his face.

"You get it? The South Louisville plant! You know what that means."

Nate tried to squirm out of his ignorance.

"What do *you* think it means?"

Big-Un wasn't fooled. He saw he'd scored points with that one and you could see him preen.

"The South Louisville treatment plant is in that industrial park. You know, where ChemMax is. Dow, DuPont and Freemont Chemicals — they're all right there in the same place, right up next to each other."

Then Nate saw where he was going, but it wouldn't work.

"Those chemical plants have specific ways they dispose of their waste products. There are all kinds of environmental safeguards. They don't just flush them down the toilet."

Big-Un sneered.

"All kinda regulations they's *supposed to* abide by — that they don't bother with unless somebody's watching. Soon as there ain't no inspectors around, they stop being careful."

Nate was skeptical, but Big-Un went on.

"My Uncle Ike's boy worked in Louisville his whole life. Jerry's a good man — the only one of Ike's git worth the price of a bullet to blow him away. He drove back and forth every day, got up before milking time, wore out an automobile ever year."

Ike. An image of Ike grabbing his cousin Joe's hair and

lifting up his head — *Please don't kill me!* — washed across Nate's mind and was gone.

"Wasn't always at Appliance Park, though." GE Appliance Park was the biggest employer in Louisville, a factory where thousands of workers turned out everything from dishwashers to double-wide refrigerators.

"He worked at the Purina Plant, too, and ChemMax. He seen what they done when they was an accident. One day at the chemical plant a forklift accidentally tipped over a barrel filled with industrial solvent. They just took a hose and washed it away down the floor drain ..." Big-Un took a breath, "... which ain't attached to the city *storm* drains. It's connected to the sanitary sewers."

Nate got it all then, leaned back against the boards on the outside of a horse stall, where a mare about to foul nickered indignantly in his ear.

"Them people up Louisville in them fancy houses, Brentwood and Forest Hills and the like — they think they crap don't stink." Big-Un barked a laugh. "It stinks alright, but it's just *plain old crap.*"

"And the sewage plant in those neighborhoods would just be treating 'plain old crap.'"

"But in the South Louisville plant ... well, it depends. What's mixed in with that crap is whatever happened to get spilled at ChemMax that day. Something that was full of lead or cadmium maybe." Big-Un grinned. "I got me a cow I'm gonna butcher, figure her blood's got enough mercury in it to fill up a hundred thermometers."

Nate actually grinned back at him.

"You and me need to go pay Mr. Oliver Morris a visit," Nate said.

"Open up a big ole can of whoop-ass and cram it down his throat."

Chapter Forty-Eight

THOUGH BIG-UN WOULD HAVE PREFERRED to break Morris's door down, Nate called and got the two of them an appointment at noon, agreed to meet Big-Un in front of the Court Square Building.

At five minutes of, the big man got out of his truck and lumbered across Main Street to where Nate stood. He wore the same oil-stained coveralls and dirty tee shirt he'd had on the day before when Nate had been at his house. Obviously, he'd been working on a piece of equipment this morning because he had grease on his hands all the way up to his elbows.

"Big-Un," he said and nodded.

"Let's get this done, my mare's fixing to foal this afternoon."

Morris's office wasn't *on* the top floor of the Court Square Building. It *was* the top floor. They stepped out of the elevator that glided up through the center of the structure and found a glass-fronted receptionist's area with Oliver Morris Enterprises, Inc. printed in raised gold lettering.

Big-Un pushed through the glass doors, leaving a greasy spot on the glass in the shape of a huge palm. Nate stepped up to the reception desk as the pretty blond receptionist managed to drag her stare away from the huge bear of a man who seemed to suck all the air out of the room. A dirty man. Not just today's dirt either. Bathing clearly was not a value in the McClusky home. The time Nate had spent with Big-Un recently had been outside and he hadn't noticed the ... aroma.

"We have an appointment with Oliver Morris at noon," Nate told her.

"Yes. Mr. Hannacker?" Nate nodded. "And Mr. McClusky?" Big-Un glared at her. "Please follow me, gentlemen. Mr. Morris is expecting you and said to show you right in."

Morris's office was expectedly huge — took up half the top floor of the building — and expectedly opulent. The floors were solid oak, quarter sawn and stained a deep cherry red. Floor-to-ceiling windows, with intricate leaded glass designs that covered three walls. There were pedestals that displayed three-foot-tall statues facing all the windows. A life-size statue of someone Nate didn't recognize stood behind Morris's desk, which was the size of a pool table, and Morris sat enthroned behind it.

He smiled when he saw them, a toothy smile under his neatly trimmed mustache, and to his credit he didn't drop a beat when he saw McClusky at Nate's side. Nate hadn't exactly put on a tux and tails for the meeting, but he was at least wearing clean jeans and a plaid button-down shirt. More important, he had taken a shower this morning.

"Come in, come in," Morris said, effusively. "I am glad to get an opportunity to spend time with my closest neighbors. I don't seem to have a spare minute, with running the farm and this business." He extended his arms expansively to include all that was in sight. It was impressive, but impersonal, reminded Nate of the interior of a bank.

He gestured at the statues. "These are signers of the Declaration of Independence — the most important of the fifty-six, anyway."

Each statue was a wearing colonial-style clothing, carrying a Bible in his left hand. Obviously, the statuary had been created for this space, which must have set Morris back more than the cost of Nate's tractor. The names were on the pedestals, and it occurred to Nate that the faces could have been anybody. Seriously, who knew what William Whipple looked like? These were probably the faces of the sculptor's neighbors.

"There is Thomas Jefferson on the end, John Hancock next to him, and Benjamin Harrison." He turned to the life-size statue behind him. "And *this* is Lewis Morris, of Westchester County, New York. Mr. Morris had ten children" — he paused dramatically — "and I am a descendent of one of those children."

Not a particularly self-aware man, Morris babbled on, oblivious to the mood of his guests, telling them that on the other side of the building was a room in which his fishing trophies were displayed on pedestals. The fish probably could have been anybody, too.

"Oh, but I'm forgetting my manners. Please do have a seat," Morris gestured to two upholstered chairs facing his desk. If Big-Un sat in one, it might collapse under his weight. At the very least they'd have to have the grease cleaned off the upholstery after he left.

Neither of them accepted the invitation to sit and Big-Un cut to the chase.

"We come to tell you to stop poisoning our creek."

"Excuse me?" Morris took an involuntary step backward from the ferocity of Big-Un's words.

"Ain't no excuse for you," Big-Un continued. "We know what you're doing and we got proof."

Morris sat down heavily in the chair he'd risen from to greet the men when they came in the door. Might be his legs wouldn't hold him up any longer.

Nate took a step forward to stand on the other side of the desk, towering over the man.

"My cattle are sick. I told you that when I came to see you in May, told you the vet says the cattle are dying because of the preposterous levels of heavy metals in their bloodstreams — cadmium, zinc, lead, mercury — things that aren't exactly naturally occurring substances on the back forty acres of my farm. Big-Un's got worse problems than I have. Twenty percent of his herd is standing around in the field, glassy-eyed and slack-mouthed — with the same blood results as mine."

The man had recovered enough to speak. After the initial shock, he was coming around. Buoyed up, as men like him always were, by his pride and his pompousness. They'd float a man tall in the water and keep him from drowning when nothing else would.

"I am sorry to hear about your livestock, but I fail to see what any of this has to do with me."

Big-Un started to speak but Nate didn't want to loose that cannon yet.

"Maybe you don't," Nate said. "I'll give you the benefit of the doubt — that you didn't know what you were doing was harmful. The reason your cattle aren't sick and mine and Big-Un's are is that your cattle aren't downstream from that field you been spreading crap on."

"What does the type of manure I chose to use—?"

"Shut up! We didn't come here to listen to you. We came here to talk. You bought that crap you're spreading on your field from the Louisville Metropolitan Sewer

District. A truck dumped a load on yesterday that came from the South Louisville Sewage Treatment plant on Algonquin Parkway."

"How could you possibly know where—?"

Nate could feel the menace of Big-Un's presence growing, like the building warmth from a grass fire headed your way.

"I said shut up. You didn't buy sewage from a plant in a residential neighborhood — where the biggest concentration comes from an elementary school. You bought sewage from a plant that treats the runoff from the biggest chemical companies in Louisville."

"I'm sure they follow strict protocols to dispose of dangerous substances."

"*Pro-to-cols!*" Big-Un roared. "I know folks has seen 'em spill 'dangerous substances' on the floor … and wash them down the drain."

"… a single industrial accident …"

"You don't have to see the spill to know there's chemicals in that sewage!" Nate said. "The chemicals are washing downstream to our farms, our livestock are drinking the creek water and the chemicals are showing up in their blood. You don't need any better proof than that!"

"Washing down the stream …?"

"We had the water tested!" Big-Un roared.

Morris sputtered and coughed. "If that's true, you need to report it to the state Department for Environmental Services so they can conduct an impartial investigation—"

"We don't need the government's help," Nate said. "We settle our own problems."

Morris had finally progressed through shock and surprise to indignation and outrage.

"Don't blame me if your cattle are sick. Obviously, neither one of you knows how to properly care for—"

That's as far as he got before Big-Un lunged. He leaned out across the desk and grabbed the man's coat lapels in one hand and lifted him up out of his chair. Then he got right in his face, which Nate was sure was not a pleasant experience.

"We're done talking," Big-Un snarled. "You listen up. You done spread your last load of sewage on that field. You hear me? You so much as drop your pants and take a dump on it, I will kick you into the middle of next week."

Big-Un shook him like a rag doll and his glasses tumbled off his face onto his desk.

Nate spoke then, his voice hard and threatening.

"As soon as we can get it figured up, we'll give you a bill for the livestock you killed."

Big-Un threw Morris back down into his chair. It was on wheels and the impact scooted it across the oak floor until it collided with the window over the street. Morris's face was white, his brow glistened with a fine sheen and Nate recognized that smell — fear sweat.

"Have we made ourselves clear?" Nate asked.

The man didn't speak, probably couldn't, just nodded.

Nate resisted the urge to put his hand on Big-Un's arm and coax him out of the room, only hoped that when he left, Big-Un would, too. Nate stepped back and without a look either at Morris or Big-Un, he strode toward the door, and gratefully, he heard Big-Un lumbering along behind him.

They got into the elevator, Nate pushed the button for the ground floor, and watched the scene in the office disappear in the closing door. It was a tableau. The secretary, her eyes huge, her mouth open ... and back behind her in his office, Morris, still sitting where Big-Un had left him.

When they stepped out onto the sidewalk in front of the building, Nate noted that Big-Un didn't appear agitated, even angry, like maybe threatening to kick the crap out of somebody was a daily occurrence in his life.

"Got to get back to my mare," Big-Un said, lumbered across the street to his truck and climbed in. The shocks on that side sagged under his weight.

Chapter Forty-Nine

THE NEXT MORNING, Nate opened the door to a knock and found Kentucky State Police Detective Booth Graham standing on his porch. There was a big, husky state trooper standing behind him. Graham was smiling.

Nate managed not to let his shock and fear show on his face. How on earth had the law connected him to—?

No, that wasn't it. This couldn't be about the chop shop. Which meant …

He *didn't!*

But clearly, he did.

Oliver Morris might not have grown up here but his wife had! *She* knew you kept the law *out* of your affairs. You didn't *invite them in.*

"Nathaniel Hannacker?" the detective asked, innocently. Oh, but he was enjoying this.

"You know good and well who I am. And you know you're not welcome on my property. So I'll thank you—"

Graham flashed a badge, like some little kid waving a sword.

"Nathaniel Hannacker, I am arresting you for terroristic threatening in the first degree and accessory to assault in the third degree." He pulled the screen door open, grabbed Nate by the upper arm and dragged him out onto the porch. "Cuff him," he told the trooper, while he went into the "you have the right to remain silent" spiel, his eyes drilling into Nate's with hateful glee.

Nate wanted to wipe the smile off his face with a shovel. Then Nate sat trussed up like a Christmas turkey in the back seat of the trooper's car while Graham in the front seat told him what he already knew.

"Oliver Morris filed formal charges against you and Big-Un McClusky for terroristic threatening, claims the two of you barged into his office yesterday and threatened to kill him. That right?"

Nate said nothing, kept his face blank even though the handcuffs were cutting off the circulation to his hands.

Graham kept talking, the snide smile never leaving his lips.

"He said Big-Un assaulted him, so he's being charged with third-degree assault."

Nate stared straight ahead, occupying his mind with random thoughts. How did they decide that what Big-Un had done — grabbing the guy by his coat and dragging him out of a chair — was third degree assault? What were the degrees of assault? Clearly there was a first and a second degree if Big-Un had been charged with third. Did that mean there was also a fifth, maybe a sixth …?

He focused on the ridiculous and preposterous to keep his face completely expressionless and his mouth shut.

"I don't mind telling you that I didn't want to be the one who arrested Big-Un. You don't strike me as a violent man, but Big-Un …"

Nate wondered what Big-Un had done when the officer

— officer*s*, surely to goodness they sent more than one — arrived. He must not have resisted arrest or they'd have tacked that charge on him, too, and Graham didn't mention it. Still, it was hard to imagine Big-Un going gently into that good night.

"You want to tell me what on earth possessed the two of you to barge into a man's office and threaten to kill him?"

Silence.

"Morris said it had something to do with sick cattle, that you blamed him because your cows had gotten sick. Is that right?"

Silence.

"Said you claimed his fertilizer was the reason your cows had died. Where would you get an idea like that?"

Silence.

Graham continued to ask questions the whole way into town and Nate didn't say a word.

In Brewster, they took him directly to the county jail, located in an old building on the far end of Main Street. They'd hold him there until he could be arraigned — maybe later today, maybe tomorrow — and then he'd be allowed to post bail.

Four judges served the four-county circuit of Callison, Washington, Nelson and Taylor Counties. Two were district judges — traffic court and misdemeanors. Two were circuit judges — felonies and, for some scary reason, divorces.

One of the circuit judges was a prune-faced man named Thacker who enjoyed nothing so much as putting people behind bars who hadn't done anything to harm anybody — and keeping them there. The other, Judge Moore, was more or less a reasonable man. Over the years, Nate had noted that often as not, he put the right people behind bars and kept them there and let the others out on bail.

He hoped he drew Judge Moore. He was too busy to sit idle in a jail cell — had crops to plant, livestock to feed, cars to steal. He'd been locked up here for three days about ten years ago, got caught with four gallons of moonshine in the back of his truck. If the law'd come along sooner, he'd have had the whole truck full, but he was finishing up his route.

Abby'd come down to post his bond right away, but Judge Thacker'd dragged his feet with the release.

Nate knew the jailer, name was Cal Mattingly. Every now and then the man would buy a quart of corn liquor when he was inviting his buddies over for a card game. He was a decent enough sort, kept the jail clean, and his wife made good meals for the prisoners.

Det. Graham grabbed Nate by the upper arm when they got to the jail and shoved him toward the door more roughly than he had to. The guy had very definitely got his panties in a wad about that trailer load of baseball bats. The trooper didn't take the cuffs off Nate until he was safely inside his cell, dangerous criminal that he was, and Graham stood outside the jail door after the jailer and closed it and locked it with Nate safely inside.

As soon as there was nobody within earshot, the snide smile dropped off Graham's face.

"Next time, Hannacker, maybe you ought to find out who you're pissing on before you lift your leg and let fly."

Nate looked at him and began to clap his hands *slowly* — Clap. Clap. Clap. — holding eye contact with the detective as he did it. The man's face flushed, his eyes squinted, and that vein in his temple, the one that'd give him away in a poker game, filled up with blood and began to throb rhythmically.

Nate kept slowly clapping while the man turned around, left the cell block and slammed the door behind him.

Then Nate sat down on the bunk in the jail and tried to think.

He'd have to call Sid Porter, he supposed. Porter was the local lawyer most of the moonshiners used when they got busted. Settling back, he leaned against the wall, sorting things out.

A single thought buzzed around in his head like a wasp shook up in a Mason jar.

Oliver Morris had called the law. Had *filed charges*. He would regret that decision. Nate would see to that.

Chapter Fifty

THEY BROUGHT Big-Un in about noon and locked him up in the cell next to Nate's. He smelled as bad, no probably worse, than he had yesterday. Nate supposed after a while he'd get used to it. What was it Riley called it — going nose blind.

Detective Graham had not accompanied Big-Un in, had gotten some other unlucky soul to serve the warrants. After the trooper closed the cellblock door behind him, Nate looked at Big-Un and shook his head.

"You b'lieve this?"

Big-Un shook his head of dirty hair, told Nate that three Kentucky State Police troopers in clean gray uniforms had shown up when he was helping a sow deliver piglets. All three had pistols pointed at him.

"I figured they was as like to shoot me as not, and I didn't want to get dead."

Then the big man's face darkened and he said two words.

"Oliver Morris."

Nate nodded understanding.

They sat together in silence, each caught up in his own thoughts. Nate doubted Big-Un had an attorney, though Nate was almost sure he'd been busted for any number of violent offenses over the years and he'd never spent any significant time locked up.

"He didn't b'lieve us," Big-Un said. "Didn't b'lieve we could — *would* — put him in a world of hurt."

"Don't know how we coulda been more clear."

"He didn't get the message, though."

"Nope."

"Might be we need to send him another one, one he can't miss this time."

The jailer came in with lunch trays, slid them through the slit at the bottom of the door. Wasn't bad. Cornbread and pinto beans. Nate'd had worse. He wasn't hungry, though he had gone nose blind to Big-Un's poor hygiene.

After the lunch trays were removed, the sun had begun to march down the western sky. Their cells were on the east side of the building and they began to cool off.

"I been puzzlin' on it and I figure the onliest way to get out of this is for Morris to drop them charges," Big-Un said.

Nate nodded.

"We got to send him a message he can't miss."

It occurred to Nate that this might not have been the first time Big-Un had reached a similar conclusion. Intimidating witnesses was likely what'd kept Big-Un out of jail before.

The big man let out a serious belch, then asked, "You been deer huntin' lately?"

Nate had no idea what to do with such a non sequitur.

"Course not. Ain't deer season." He paused. "And it'd be *breaking the law* to shoot one now."

"I hear you're a pretty good shot."

"You got the right scope, anybody's a good shot." That wasn't totally true, of course. There was a whole lot more to hunting than getting a buck in the crosshairs.

"Got me a Browning A-bolt .270, with a Diamondback HP 3-12x42 scope. Worked the rise on it and dropped a buck at six hundred yards ... last fall, you know, during deer season."

"Sooooo ... you wanna sit here and swap hunting stories or are you going somewhere with all this?"

"Them windows in Morris's office ... give a mighty fine view out onto the street, don't they?"

"Uh huh."

"Give as good a view *in* as they do *out*."

"Uh huh."

"If you's in the right spot to look, that is."

"Uh huh."

"Fourth of July's next Friday."

"What — you afraid we ain't gonna get out of here in time for the parade? What's your point?"

"That fireworks display at the park makes a whole lotta noise, and folks settin' off they own firecrackers all over town."

"So what if—?"

Big-Un looked him full in the face and said quietly, "It's gonna sound like a regular shooting gallery 'round here on the Fourth. You reckon in the middle of all that noise folks'll notice a couple of real gunshots?"

A light was beginning to come on in Nate's mind.

"Come to think of it, I don't b'lieve they would."

"Them windows in Morris's office — that fancy leaded glass. If somebody was to be in the right spot, they could take out anything in that office and wouldn't rain glass down on the street."

"The right spot. Like in the belfry of Saint Augustine

Church, say, or on the roof of the post office or the courthouse."

"We gotta make a b'liever outta Mr. Oliver Morris so's he knows for lead pipe certain there ain't *nowhere* he can hide that we can't git him."

"And you're thinking if he was to somehow be convinced we ain't bluffin'—"

"He'd drop them charges like they was setting his fingers on fire."

Nate leaned back against the concrete wall of his cell again. Sitting there inhaling Big-Un's rank body odor — and no, he'd been wrong, he hadn't gone nose blind — Nate marveled at the turn of events. He had one McClusky threatening to kill him, and here he was, plotting out a criminal enterprise with another McClusky as his "partner in crime."

Chapter Fifty-One

"Be kind to your web-footed friends, for a duck may be somebody's mother."

Jessie found herself singing the words from the childhood parody of the John Philip Sousa march as she and her mother-in-law crossed the parking lot to the Brewster City Park. An area with picnic tables under some trees on the far side had been reserved for family members of Charlie Company. The county's Fourth of July celebration had been dedicated to the unit.

"What's that you're singing?"

Jessie was walking slowly, as if she never walked any faster than this, so Ruth wouldn't get her nose all out of joint about having to walk from the far space in the parking lot where Jessie'd parked the truck.

"They's closer spaces than this," the old woman had barked.

"Yeah, a whole parking lot full, but every one of them has a car already in it."

"Something will open up. You can make another loop, somebody'll leave."

"That works in a Walmart parking lot, when people are coming and going, some people getting there to start shopping, others leaving to take their rubber tomahawks home. It doesn't work with this. All these people came here to listen to the bands and see the fireworks display. Nobody's going to decide to leave before it even starts."

"Might be somebody left the iron on at home, forgot to unplug it, so's they gotta go check. Something could open up."

Jessie got into continuous-loop conversations like this with Mama Ruth all the time. The woman wasn't senile, Jessie'd figured that out as soon as she spent some time around her. Hers was one of those steel trap minds that could snap shut on your leg in a heartbeat.

But her sense of logic was often flawed. Jessie couldn't put her finger on exactly what it was, but it didn't seem like the woman had a lick of common sense sometimes. Didn't get it about things that were so obvious you couldn't even explain them. They just *were*. This was one of those times.

"Have you never heard those words?" Jessie asked. "We sang them when I was a kid every time we heard that melody."

"I ain't never heard them words before in my whole life."

"Well, would you like to?" Without waiting for a reply, Jessie started to sing out loud. "Be kind to your web-footed friends. For a duck—"

"Shush up, you're making a spectacle of yourself."

But people around them instantly took up the tune themselves, singing along. By the time they got to the picnic tables, Jessie had a regular chorus singing with her.

"Can't take you anywhere," Mama Ruth snapped.

Jessie was getting used to that part, too. Mama Ruth's barking, constant criticism, always fault-finding. Jessie finally figured out that was just the way Ruth Monaghan reacted to life around her. Whatever she thought hopped up on her tongue and dived off the end a second after she thought it.

If everybody just blurted out whatever they were thinking, however hostile or rude it might be, the whole world would sound like Mama Ruth. In other words, the old woman wasn't much different from everybody else, from all the people she'd alienated over the years. She just spoke her mind. Jessie found she could respect it. Would never choose to be around it, of course, but she could understand and respect it. She tried not to take it personally and had just about come to terms with her dislike of the old woman.

For Ruth's part, Jessie thought the old woman was warming up to her a little, too, whether she liked it or not. Sometimes Jessie thought she fired nasty remarks out there into the air as a kind of test. To see who could take it and who couldn't. Well, Jessie Monaghan could take whatever Ruth Monaghan dealt out.

"Tell me again why you think Davie wrote you a letter you never got," Mama Ruth said and Jessie managed not to roll her eyes. Either Ruth didn't have her mental ducks beak-to-tail-feathers like Jessie'd thought and really couldn't remember the half dozen times Jessie'd already told her or she just liked hearing about it, hearing anything about "my Davie boy."

Jessie reached into her purse and pulled out David's last letter. She kept them all in her purse, took her purse everywhere she went, and kept the purse strap around her neck so she couldn't accidentally leave it somewhere. A purse-snatcher would have to strangle her to get it.

Letters were all she had of David, and she wanted

them to be as close to her as he would be if he were here. When he got home, she wouldn't let him out of her sight for a second for a month ... two months ... *three*. Mama Ruth'd said she didn't want to let him out of her sight either, which was going to prove problematic because Jessie intended to spend at least a week in bed with him. You could live on Twinkies, potato chips and bean dip, couldn't you, for a little while anyway?

Jessie extended the letter to Mama Ruth and the woman looked at it like it was a dead fish on a stick. Jessie had never offered to allow her mother-in-law to read the letters Davie sent home to her.

"You know I can't read that thing 'thout my cheaters." Her cheaters were reading glasses — the strongest prescription Jessie could find anywhere. Mama Ruth parked them on her nose and then held whatever she was reading about three inches in front of them. "You tell me what it says." Jessie had no trouble reciting it by heart. She'd read all his letters so many times she had them memorized. Besides, this was the shortest letter she'd ever gotten. "That part that makes you think he wrote a letter you never got."

Jessie pulled a couple of sentences here and there from the letter. For starters, there was the last line. He said he'd been writing the letter when the chopper came early and he wanted to get it in the mail bag, and "the last one was so long you're probably still reading it."

The last letter she'd gotten was no longer than any of the previous ones. She always stopped at the end of the road to pick up the letters in Mama Ruth's mailbox and take them to her house. He wrote her faithfully, too. Maybe because he knew Jessie wouldn't want to have to share the intimate love letters he wrote to her. But she did read to

Ruth "selected parts." The old woman seemed to understand the why of it and never asked for more. This one had been so short, there'd been no space for intimacy. It began with "My precious Baby Girl," and ended with I love you's and little hearts, but there was nothing unsharable in between.

"He told me a soldier saved Riley's life, '… a soldier named Ace, the guy I was telling you about.'"

Davie had never before mentioned anyone named Ace. He hadn't been with the activated guard unit, that's for sure. So who was he?

And there was "can't wait to hear what you think of my idea."

What idea?

In the beginning, a couple of Davie's letters had been delayed. Jessie could tell by the stamps on them when they'd been mailed. But there had never before been an occasion when she thought a letter was missing altogether.

The first pops and bangs of fireworks started before they'd even gotten to the tables. That's why Jessie hadn't brought Magic with her to the park. Well, that was one of the reasons. He was terrified of loud noises, always hid under the bed trembling during storms. And she hadn't yet gotten around to telling Mama Ruth about the dog. She was one hundred percent certain the old woman would take an instant dislike to the animal.

And there was also the fact that even though he was huge, he was still a puppy and he didn't walk obediently by her side. He dragged her behind him with the leash whenever she took him for a walk. She was determined to have him "leash trained" by the time Davie got home. He'd always made fun of people like her, would say, "Isn't it nice of that dog to take his owner out for a walk?"

Pop!

Pop-bang!

Kids all over town were already setting off firecrackers and the darkness would embolden them. In a few minutes, they'd start lighting whole strings of firecrackers at once — which was dangerous. You could lose a finger. Or worse.

Chapter Fifty-Two

THE HEAD FLEW OFF the shoulders in a spray of sparks.

After a single pop — not even a very loud one — nothing remained of the head of Mr. Lewis Morris of Westchester County, New York but settling powder. Plaster, maybe. Nate wasn't completely certain what statues were made of, but had noted that the bases on the targets in tonight's shooting gallery had seemed strong and sturdy. He didn't want to topple any if he could help it. Clean and neat. Heads gone. Everything else intact. That sent the message he and Big-Un intended Oliver Morris to receive.

But the hole the bullet had made in the leaded glass window was a bit farther to the right than Nate had been aiming. He was either pulling the shot or needed to adjust the scope. He heard a popping sound from the roof of the post office. Not loud, though. The firecrackers and bottle rockets going off all over town were a whole lot louder.

There were two elements to the gunshot sound when a weapon was fired. The first was the explosion of the gun powder in the barrel and the second was the sound of the bullet breaking the sound barrier, the familiar "crack" sound. A .308 — even if it'd had a suppressor on it — would still be so loud the sound would be immediately identifiable as a gunshot because the bullet it fired was going something like 2,600 feet per second. But Big-Un's Ruger 10/22 fired a bullet much smaller and slower. No sound. Of course, that required even greater accuracy than a larger gun. A sniper using one had to land a good, solid center shot, headshot or middle of the chest or back — otherwise the shot would only wound, not kill.

He and Big-Un McClusky weren't on the roofs of buildings in downtown Brewster tonight to "wound" any statues.

RILEY HAD HEARD that the military had chosen the M16 as the standard-issue rifle because the weapon would most likely only wound a target. It would drop a man but not necessarily kill him. The Army figured wounded soldiers drained the enemy's resources, took more time and energy than dead ones. Which meant you sometimes had to shoot one of those zipperheads two or three times. He didn't know if that was true or just scuttlebutt. Seemed to him the ones he'd dropped had stayed down.

He was one of four snipers sent out at sun-up around the camp they'd made last night next to a village called Ho Sung — a ratty village even by Vietnamese standards with only about a dozen villagers living in ramshackle huts, quietly starving to death. Settling himself behind a bush, Riley slowly poked the rifle barrel out among the branches and waited. Sitting still, he became aware of all the things he managed to ignore when he was moving. His head hurt. It always hurt, had been hurting non-stop since … he'd left his short-timer's stick in the bunker where he'd slept the last time he'd been in Eagle's Nest. He was sure the gunner had kept it. You didn't throw away another soldier's short-timer's stick.

Riley itched all over. Every inch of skin itched, in places he couldn't possibly itch, like under his fingernails. Maybe it really did itch. More likely he was imagining it, but the desperate need to scratch was the same either way. Wasn't imagining the jungle rot with running sores that was eating on his right hand. If you thought about that, it stung! His left foot tingled inside his boot, like it'd had the circulation cut off and then restored. He did *not* want immersion foot — what you got from having wet feet inside your boots twenty-four/seven. He'd heard of a guy who got it and didn't treat it and almost lost his foot.

Charlie Company had been out for — he wasn't sure how long anymore, a couple of months, but they'd be back at Eagle's Nest tonight and he could see to his foot. He couldn't remember the last time he'd had on dry socks.

A shower. He could take a *shower.*

There was movement in the tree line and two Cong soldiers emerged slowly into the clearing, rifles ready, heads on a swivel. A line of soldiers appeared behind them.

Aches, pains, itches vanished in an eye-blink and Riley was alert. And scared. Would he ever stop being scared?

NATE HAD HEARD rumors that Big-Un McClusky had some serious hardware, an arsenal of all kinds of weapons. He never believed rumors but he should have believed that one. When the man ticked off the rifles he had to choose from for tonight's job, it had been an impressive list. If it were any other man than Big-Un McClusky, he'd have been considered a "collector." That was too dainty a word to fit him, though. It wasn't like he had books of stamps or window-box cases with different kinds of insects displayed on toothpicks. Nate had helped Riley make one of those when the boy was in seventh grade. The case was a piece of cake, but the butterflies ... They were so delicate they'd fall apart if you breathed on them.

"Why couldn't you have collected something sturdy like ... oh, I don't know ... dung beetles, maybe? Now there's a bug that could withstand a pin through the belly."

Riley had just given him "that look," then went back to stabbing butterfly bellies with pins.

Riley. The boy was never more than a heartbeat away from Nate's thoughts. As he lifted the stock of his rifle to his shoulder and got it comfortable there, snug, he wondered what the boy was doing on the other side of the planet.

RILEY FIT the stock of his M16 into the crook of his shoulder and got it comfortable there. Snug. It hadn't been the firearms instructor at Fort Benning who'd taught Riley to be prepared for the recoil. It'd been Papa, who'd let him continue to grip the stock of a shotgun wrong to make a point. When Riley'd finally fired it, the recoil had jammed his finger into his eye and gave him a shiner.

Riley aimed at the head of the last soldier in the line. He'd learned that from Papa, too.

"Shoot the first turkey and the rest will scatter. Shoot the last one and sometimes they don't notice until they're all dead."

The Cong noticed, of course, but the sergeant hadn't set him on this hill to kill every soldier in the column. He just needed to get them moving in the right direction, out of the clearing and into the trees to the north — *away* from the company's camp outside Ho Sung.

He squeezed the trigger and the man's head vanished. The Cong scattered toward the tree line on the far side. Perfect.

~

NATE SQUEEZED off the final shot, watched the plaster head explode, and settled back, satisfied. He hadn't lost his touch. Though, this hadn't rightly been a test of hunting ability. Squirrels didn't line up like blackbirds on a clothesline, waiting for you to pick them off one by one. This had been considerably easier.

There'd been five statues facing the leaded glass windows on the front of the building. The statues were still standing, but Thomas Jefferson, Benjamin Harrison, Lyman Hall, John Hancock, and Lewis Morris, Oliver's great, great, great grandfather, were as headless as Ichabod Crane. The window glass hadn't shattered, either. Five holes, five headless statues.

Time to change positions now. He needed to be able to see in the windows on the south side of the building and this only showed the west view. He'd have to climb down off this roof and go up the rickety ladder to the roof of the drugstore down the street. With a gimp leg, ladders were always a challenge. But he didn't imagine Big-Un McClusky was having an easy go of it, up to and down off the roofs on the north and east sides of the building.

He wondered why Big-Un didn't send one of his boys to do the job — like he'd sent Wade to collect a Mason jar. They were probably about as good a shot as Big-Un was and carried considerably less bulk.

He suspected Big-Un had come himself because this

was *personal,* intended to send to Oliver Morris an unmis-takable message. Well, two messages, actually. One — nobody goes to the law. Nobody talks to the law. *Nobody.* And two ... you think you're safe, do you? That Big-Un McClusky and Nate Hannacker can't get at you? How's that working out for you?

Oliver Morris had kicked sand in both their faces and Big-Un likely wanted to kick sand back with his own boot.

Nate settled in on the drugstore roof, sighting in on targets visible through the east windows. Not just statues, other things. The family picture on Morris's wall, an old one because he still had all his hair. It was Oliver, his wife — who looked like a nice woman — and four little kids, two boys and two girls. And that annoying ball-bouncing thing on the side table, balls hanging off a post. You pulled back the one on either end and let it go, and it'd hit the next ball in line, and the impact would send the ball on the other end flying out. When it dropped back and hit the center ball, the original ball was knocked out to the end of its line from the impact. Over. And over. And over. Nate supposed once you started that first ball, the reaction would go on forever. It had never let up while he and Big-Un had been in the office.

Big-Un's targets on the other side of the building were more interesting. Fishing trophies from deep-sea excursions all over the walls around a gigantic swordfish, or maybe it was a marlin. Nate was not a fisherman and wasn't sure if there was a difference. There were half a dozen different trophies and Big-Un planned to take out the eyes, both eyes, on every single one.

Nate settled in on his own shots and Oliver's head vanished out of the family portrait — left a black hole where it'd been — and the ball thingy went flying off the table and crashed to the floor.

Once he was done, Nate proceeded carefully back down the ladder. He hadn't seen anybody — the whole town had been in the park watching the fireworks show that'd been dedicated to the guard unit or were home setting off their own fireworks show with firecrackers, sparklers and bottle rockets in their neighborhoods.

Nate was fitting his rifle into the rack in front of the back window of his pickup truck when he saw another truck turn off Main Street into the alley where he was parked. No headlights, but it rode low on the compressed springs on the driver's side.

Big-Un didn't stop, didn't even slow down, just made eye contact with Nate and nodded. Nate nodded back, then he drove out of the alley and went home.

After dropping the rifle off at the house, Nate headed toward the chop shop. The lighted face of his watch told him July 4th was almost over. It was already over on the other side of the planet. It was late Sunday morning there.

Chapter Fifty-Three

"Yo, Riley," said Watson, a gangly replacement from Pittsburgh who'd joined the Army right out of a steel mill and bragged in the beginning that he'd already been in hell so how bad could Vietnam be? He'd found out his first day on patrol. The guy in front of him stepped on a land mine that blew off both his legs. "You got any smokes? I'll trade you my chocolate."

Riley had been relieved of sniper duty and he'd returned to camp. They'd break camp later this afternoon for the final march to the Eagle's Nest artillery base. Two of the company's five platoons — Thunder Road and Whisky Run — would stay there overnight tonight. Those eighty soldiers would rejoin the three other platoons at a base camp somewhere tomorrow.

"Traded my last to Scooter," Riley told Watson, indicating a black soldier with a wide, flat face and pendulous lip.

Willie Ray always quickly relieved Riley of the four-smoke mini packs of Winstons, Marlboros and Lucky Strikes from his three-meals-in-one box of K-rations. But

Willie Ray didn't like Pall Malls so Riley used them for barter.

"He's got a sweet tooth, though. Bet you could trade him out of one. Willie Ray has the Winstons." He looked around until he spotted Willie Ray and gestured with his chin. "Maybe he ain't smoked all of his yet."

Willie Ray stood with a group of soldiers heating up their rations in a fire they'd started with the dregs of a gasoline can from one of the APCs — armored personnel carriers. If not for his red hair, he'd have been hard to pick out among them because they all were cookie-cutter images of each other. Black or white, officer or enlisted man, they all wore the same dirty camouflage uniforms with no insignias to designate rank — insignias made you a target.

Jackson McClusky stood out, though, because he was so much smaller than the others — no bigger than one of the NVA soldiers. He was jittery, standing first on one foot, then the other, seemed unable to be still. Who knew what he was on? He was stoned out of his mind on *something* almost all the time, had already started gulping down God-knows-what today because of the sergeant's relaxed vigilance. They'd made it through their tour in the jungle and were on their way in to the base — a cow coming into the barn at night.

Several of the soldiers were throwing the tins of peanut butter out of their K-rations into the blaze, where they'd heat up and then explode, creating "peanut butter ambushes."

Yesterday had been the Fourth of July, at least it was out there in the wide world. In his last letter, Papa had said this year's celebration at the Brewster City Park would be dedicated to the guard unit. Here in the bush, the only reminder of the holiday was the red, white, and blue wrappers on their K-rations. Well, that and the Jingle Bell Man.

Seated by the doorway of the hut in the village nearest their camp was a retarded man who had a harelip and one deformed hand. The man rocked back and forth, quietly singing melody-less songs in Vietnamese. But apparently some American soldier at Christmas had taught him to sing Jingle Bells and when he overheard somebody in Riley's unit mention the "holiday," he started singing it. Not quietly, but at the top of his lungs. The melody, such as it was, drifted in and out — sometimes it was merely a chant. But the words — even with the guy's harelip and Vietnamese accent — were easily understandable.

The first couple of times he sang it, the soldiers grinned at him. But after hearing the song over and over, non-stop, it got old. The soldiers tried everything to get him to stop singing — threatened, begged, bribed him with food. Nothing worked. All afternoon, the off-key words rang out. "ingle ells, ingle ells, ingle all a'way …" When the company was finally ready to move out, he was still singing and the soldiers couldn't get their gear packed fast enough.

The sergeant sent a three-man team out in front as scouts and designated a four-man team — Riley, Davie Monaghan, Ben Higgs and Jackson McClusky — as a rear guard, to hang back behind the rest of the unit.

The main company moved out, leaving the rear guard behind in their dismantled campsite near the village. They'd wait there for a couple of minutes before they followed.

Riley was scanning the tree line, his eyes darting back and forth in the search pattern of what he was now, a combat veteran. He heard Davie yell, "Noooo" and turned to see Jackson standing next to the Jingle Bell Man, holding the discarded gasoline can from the APC over the man's head.

"Ought to turn this little songbird into a cooked goose," Jackson cried. He was manic, and the man's singing had grated on his nerves until he was ready to snap. "Oughta *burn* him."

Chapter Fifty-Four

When Nate pulled his old pickup truck to a stop behind the not-really-a-tobacco-barn chop shop, he could hear the music even with his windows rolled up.

"One-eyed, one-horned, flying purple people eater ... "

He went inside and saw that Brodie was the only worker present and he was rocking out to the song.

"I want to know something," he said and Brodie looked up from the unidentifiable tangle of wires in front of him, some pieces parts of a car, could have been the autopsy of a robot. "Is the one-eyed, one-horned thingy trying to eat flying purple people or—"

"No, no, no. The thing is purple, the people-eater thing that can fly is purple."

"How do you know that? You can't tell from listening—"

There was a grumbling sound outside the bay doors and Brodie dropped his wrench and grinned as wide as Nate had ever seen him grin.

"You ain't gonna b'lieve what's out there," he said, gesturing to the door where the sound of a vehicle engine revving was audible even over the music. "I ain't never ... I oughta make you close your eyes like a little kid on his birthday."

Nate didn't smile at that. Birthday references never made him smile, but Brodie blew right by it.

"But seeing's how you're the boss and all, I'ma let you look at it straight up."

He went to the bay doors and pushed them open, and one of their Hispanic lifters drove the vehicle slowly into the building.

Nate couldn't help a gasp.

"That's not a ... it *couldn't* be a ..."

Brodie was grinning so broad his gums were in danger of drying out.

"Shore is! Wasn't but twenty of these babies made in '67 and they was for racing. This here is ... it's a ..." He was so awed he couldn't find the words.

Sitting before them was a cherry-red L88 Corvette Stingray.

The lifter revved the engine one more time, then killed it and got out of the car.

Nate approached the vehicle as if it were an exotic wild beast.

"They say they built two hundred of 'em after folks seen how it done when DX Motorsports ran it in Daytona. But I am here to tell ya this here is the first one I ever seen close up."

Of course, Nate had seen the order for the car. They got orders for a lot of cars they couldn't fill. He never dreamed they'd find this one.

"Where did—?" He stopped himself. "Never mind," he told the lifter. "I don't want to know."

Brodie laughed, reached up to a pegboard on the wall, found a set of keys and tossed them to the Hispanic boy, who didn't look any older than sixteen. He might have driven into the chop shop in a car worth thousands of dollars, but he'd be driving back to Louisville in one of the junkie monkey pickup trucks parked out back.

"Had to break into the garage where thees baby was parked," he said, his Spanglish accent thick. "One of my homies tole me — he knows a guy who knows a guy. Wasn't nobody home in the house. Pro'lly ain't even been reported stolen yet."

The lifter left and Nate and Brodie circled the car, their eyes gobbling it up. Then Brodie opened the driver's side door and motioned to Nate.

"G'wan, you're about to wet yourself with the wanting of it. Go take her for a spin."

Nate had never taken any of the stolen vehicles "for a spin." He was paranoid about even being in the presence of one. Receiving stolen property and altering the VIN number on a car carried the same penalties under Kentucky Law. The severity of the penalty depended on the value of the car. Unfortunately, Nate's lifters didn't steal cheap cars. Every car they brought in was valuable enough to earn the stiffest penalty — a Class C felony punishable by five to ten years in prison. Now joyriding, on the other hand, was a Class A misdemeanor and no jail time if it was a first offense. Not being an attorney, Nate wouldn't presume to offer a legal opinion, but he figured it was a pretty safe bet that you wouldn't be charged with joyriding if the car you took out for a spin was stolen.

"Drive it?" His throat was dry.

"Aw, come on, just for a little while. We so far back in the boonies here, the sun don't shine but once a week. Ain't nobody gonna see you. 'Sides, it likely ain't even a hot car ... *yet*. Law ain't on the lookout for it 'cause they don't know it's missin'."

Nate couldn't help himself. He hopped behind the wheel of the sleek wild animal on wheels — quick, before he lost his nerve. Shoot, it was way past midnight. Nobody'd be on the road. He'd just take it out for a few minutes.

He thought of Johnny.

Johnny would never forgive him if he passed up an opportunity like this.

Putting the car in reverse, he pulled out of the bay doors on the back of the building and Brodie closed them behind him. Then he traced the circuitous route across the stream to the road. He drove slowly after that, getting the feel of the machine, but he needn't have bothered. It felt like a glove on his hand, tuned to his every movement.

Then he rolled down the window and let her rip, buried his foot in the accelerator and flew down the dark country roads. And he let out a cry, like the one Johnny'd made. You couldn't holler out like that unless you'd earned it. Unless you were the driver.

The one taking all the risks.

Nate wasn't gone long. Maybe he wasn't. Shoot, he could have been gone for hours. The pure joy of speed was intoxicating.

"I could get used to this," he cried out into the wind. He wouldn't, of course. He would never in his wildest dreams have entertained the notion of owning a fancy car … until that first Chevy Camaro rolled into the shop back in January and his heart rate sped up.

He could afford a fancy car now. Oh, not a Corvette L88. That was waaaay above his pay grade. But he'd squirreled away the money he'd been making every month at the chop shop and could have dipped into that honey pot and come up with the price of a "normal" sports car easy — in cash.

He wouldn't, of course. It was a nice dream, but he was a fifty-two-year-old man who should have left such loves and pursuits far behind. And he had …

Except for tonight.

Tonight, he would dream.

He took extra care as he approached the chop shop when he brought the car back, made sure there was no other vehicle anywhere on the road, either direction. In truth, he'd only passed a couple of pickup trucks while he'd been out.

He didn't rev the engine, didn't—

When he rounded the bend, he could see light shining out the back of the old not-a-tobacco-warehouse. The bay doors were standing open. Brodie'd closed them when Nate left.

He pulled up behind the building, into *silence*. There was no music. An unfamiliar sports car with tinted windows was parked in the shadows beside his truck. Why had a lifter left an expensive sports car like that outside?

Paranoia took over, and Nate was sure that somehow they'd been busted. He turned off the engine and got quietly out of the car. He'd get closer to see what was going on … and bolt into the trees if the law was in.

"… ain't here, I tell you …" Brodie was arguing with somebody.

"That's his truck parked out back. Hannacker's here somewhere."

Who'd come here looking for—?

Shep McClusky.

Nate's mind spewed out a string of expletives he didn't say out loud.

Shep McClusky — the little piss-ant.

Parker'd made it clear that Nate had better *not* show up for work on July 5th. It was definitely July 5 and Shep had come here to claim his rightful position. Rage rolled over Nate in a red tide at such monumental arrogance. Somebody needed to beat that kid to within an inch of his life! Unfortunately … Nate wasn't the man for the job. He'd get whopped if he tried. Shep'd inherited the family body type, big, thick and muscular. And he was twenty-five years younger than Nate.

Nope, Nate would have to use brain instead of brawn. Shep couldn't possibly be the sharpest knife in the drawer if he got his jollies with juvenile vandalism. Nate'd just have to convince him there wasn't anything to fight over anymore — that he had decided to retire from the position Shep wanted. And that might even be true — Nate still hadn't made up his mind. He'd pocketed a lot of money in just six months, a sizable nest egg, and he hated to walk away from such a sweet deal. Nate wasn't a greedy man, though, and he didn't want to spend his golden years looking at the world through prison bars.

He'd figure it all out later. Right now, he needed to talk the moron off the ledge.

Taking a deep breath, Nate stepped through the bay doors, a phony smile on his face that drained away as soon as he got a look at what was going on. Brodie lay on his back on the floor. Shep was standing over him, *holding a pistol* in his left hand.

Shep spun around to face Nate, his eyes open too wide. He was *on* something, as high as the Goodyear Blimp.

"Well, well, lookie who we got here," Shep said, wagging the barrel of the pistol at Nate. "Mr. Nathaniel Hannacker in the flesh." He giggled then. Actually *giggled*! "Have fun repainting your porch, didja?" He turned back to Brodie. "You lied to me. You said he wasn't here. Tsk, tsk. Your bad."

And then *Shep shot Brodie!*

Brodie wailed and grabbed his leg and Shep let out another high-pitched giggle that wasn't a man's laugh at all. "Give you a gimp leg like your friend here," Shep told Brodie, but he'd missed the kneecap if that's what he'd been aiming for. Blood welled up around a hole in Brodie's calf.

Shep swung the pistol back toward Nate, didn't lift the barrel to point it at Nate's chest, though. His eyes were shining bright but there was no color in them because the pupils were fully dilated, forming black holes like cigarette burns in his face. "Now which one's your bad leg, Mr. Hannacker, *sir*? I'm gonna *start out* by putting a bullet in your other leg." He paused. "Then you'll limp on both of 'em ... and it'll match!"

Shep burst into another gale of hysterical giggles at his own humor. Nate used the moment of inattention to boogie! He didn't realize he was capable of moving that fast, but he made it back to the Corvette and dived behind the wheel before Shep got his wits about him.

"What the—?" he heard the young man cry. "Where you at?"

Nate spun the car around in the parking area behind the building. Shep appeared in the doorway as Nate gave the Stingray the gas, threw rocks and gravel out behind the tires.

Ping!

Nate recognized the sound, looked in the rearview mirror. Shep was standing with the pistol leveled at his car, firing one shot after another.

Ping!

Ping-ping The back windshield shattered.

Nate was a fool! He should have figured it out sooner. Shep had come here tonight expecting to take over his "rightful position." After all, his father had most certainly assured him that Nate Hannacker wouldn't *dare* show up for work on July 5th.

Then Shep had seen Nate's truck ... and he'd lost that legendary temper of his, the one that had compelled him to try to kill another ten-year-old with a baseball bat all those years ago.

Shep had said he would start out by putting a bullet in Nate's leg to make his limps match. *Start out.* Shep meant to *kill* him, wouldn't settle for anything less.

The Corvette had better be faster than whatever Shep was driving because Nate was unarmed.

Chapter Fifty-Five

"Put the gas can down," Davie Monaghan told Jackson and started toward him.

In defiance, Jackson turned the can up as if to pour out gasoline — and liquid splashed out of it into the man's hair and over his shoulders! Jackson was as surprised as the others that the can wasn't empty. He hadn't been serious; it had just been a joke.

Then the joke went south, terribly, horribly south.

The Vietnamese man leapt up as the gasoline ran down his face. He dug his fists into his burning eyes, screaming and dancing around, blind.

Jackson tried to grab him. "Gimme your canteen," he cried at Ben, and yelled at the man, "Lemme wash it off!" But the man twisted out of his grasp.

Then he tripped.

As the four soldiers watched in horror, the Vietnamese man fell into the smoldering remains of their campfire. His gasoline-soaked hair and shirt burst into flames and in seconds he became a human torch.

The shrieking was a sound unlike any Riley had ever

heard. It happened so fast, there was no stopping it. The burning man lurched to his feet, the whole top portion of his body in flames, and cavorted in a horror dance of agony. Jackson tackled the man and knocked him to the ground, burning his own left hand and arm as he rolled the man in the dirt to put out the flames. The man's cries only lasted a few moments, then he went limp and lay silent.

He was dead, his face and hair a burned ruin. He must have breathed in the flames and torched his lungs.

"Oh dear God." Jackson was horrified. "Oh dear Jesus, Mary and Joseph." He rocked back on his knees beside the body and looked at the others, who stood in shocked silence around him. "It was an accident, I never meant to *hurt* him, you know that, you saw, I didn't think there was any gas in that can. I thought it was *empty*. You did, too, you thought the can was empty just like I did, didn't you? Didn't you?"

The stink of burning flesh rose up in noxious fumes that blurred Riley's vision. Ben took a couple of steps away, leaned over and began to vomit. Davie grabbed Jackson by the arm and lifted him to his feet.

"Don't tell, please, dear God, don't tell, I didn't mean—"

"Shut up, Jackson." Davie spat the words out and Jackson fell silent.

"What *are* we going to do?" asked Ben, his voice ragged.

Good question. What were they going to do? What *should* they do?

A village woman had come forward and laid a blanket over the burned body, but the other villagers just stood by, watching. If any of them were related to the man, none of them showed it.

"We're going to tell the sergeant what happened —

exactly what happened, blow by blow — *that's* what we're going to do," Riley said.

"Copy *that*," Ben said and glared at Jackson.

"A hundred percent," Davie confirmed. "But *right now*, we're the rear guard for the company and we're not guarding."

The man was dead. Nothing to be done about that. The safety of the company had to be the priority now. They *had* to move out.

"Let's go," Riley said. "We'll report the whole thing when we get to Eagle's Nest."

Ben picked up his helmet and rifle off the ground, but when Jackson reached for his own weapon, Riley snatched it out of his hands. "I'll take that." Shock and outrage still darkened his face. "I'd just as soon not get shot in the back by 'friendly fire.' You stay *in front of me*, got it?"

Jackson said nothing, just cradled his burned left hand against his body, and the four soldiers moved out down the trail, fanning out as a rear guard, where Riley kept his eye on Jackson as he looked for Charlie in the trees. They were equally dangerous.

When they got to Tweety Bird, a medic treated Jackson, said his burns were serious enough that he needed to see a doctor, and scheduled him on the morning evacuation chopper.

As soon as Jackson's hand was bandaged, the four soldiers made their report. It was late, everybody was bone weary. The sergeant put Jackson on house arrest and he was relieved of his weapon. He wasn't confined in a brig. They didn't have one. Where was he going to run?

"At zero eight hundred hours tomorrow morning, we are going to have a sit-down with the captain and dump this whole thing in his lap," Sergeant Labronski said. "I've already requested an appointment, told him I had a 'civilian incident' to report."

The sergeant saw each of them individually. When Jackson had been dismissed, Labronski spoke again briefly to the other three.

"Jackson denied everything," the sergeant said. "Said you three had it in for him." He looked at Riley. "Something about a feud between your families back home — so you all got together and made the whole thing up."

Riley exploded. "Made it up! Surely you don't believe—"

"Calm down, hoss," the sergeant said. "You, Monaghan and Higgs … you're citizens. McClusky's a little piss-ant who's been dancing around the edges of a court-martial since he went boots-down off the transport. This ain't the Captain's first rodeo. He's been around the block a time or two."

Chapter Fifty-Six

KICKING himself for dropping his rifle off at the house before going to the chop shop, Nate flew down the dark roads, taking corners too fast, not for the fun of it anymore, though. He was making for home to get the rifle, the one he'd used earlier this evening to decapitate signers of the Declaration of Independence.

What was it his father had always said? "Don't take a knife to a gunfight." If Shep McClusky showed up at Nate's house and pointed that *pistol* at him, Nate would be armed with a *rifle*.

Headlights appeared in his rearview mirror, a car behind approaching fast.

What was Shep driving? Nate was piloting a Corvette designed as a race car and Shep was catching up. Nate wished he'd looked more closely at the sports car parked in the dark beside his truck, wished he knew what it was.

But he likely wouldn't have been able to recognize it if he had gotten a better look. He didn't have Brodie's keen eye for such things. Knowing what it was didn't matter anyway. It couldn't possibly be as fast as this Corvette. But it might be close. Which meant he'd be riding Nate's tail all the way to Nate's house, a race all the way there.

The car pulled up closer in a straightaway.

Ping!

A side mirror blew.

How could Shep be *shooting*?

You couldn't drive a car this fast and shoot a pistol out the window.

Well, you *could* ... if you were left-handed. South-paws made the best trippers because they could shoot and drive at the same time.

Plunk!

This beautiful Corvette was going to be full of bullet holes when Nate returned it to the chop shop. Brodie would be crushed that a thing of such beauty had been damaged.

Brodie.

Was he all right? Shep hadn't delivered a life-threatening wound, but it was possible Brodie could bleed to death if he didn't do some quick first aid. But this wasn't likely Brodie's first rodeo. He would bandage his wound. He would be fine. Nate, on the other hand ...

Plink ... *thunk!*

That was the sound of a slug hitting the back bumper, and another slamming into the trunk.

Shep was going for the tires.

If a tire blew at the speed Nate was driving ...

Shep would run out of bullets eventually. Nate hadn't counted the shots, hadn't noticed what kind of pistol it was, but Shep couldn't possibly have more than a few rounds left. He might be able to shoot and drive at the same time, but he couldn't *re-load* and drive, too.

But maybe he'd reloaded before he gave chase ... in which case, he had more than enough bullets to—

Thunk!

The tires.

Just one bullet in a rear tire and …

"… *outgunned* …"

Shep was armed and Nate had no weapon.

His mind stumbled over the next thought — *that wasn't entirely true.*

Nate felt the hairs on the back of his neck stand on end. A chill settled over him, a large, heavy weight plunked down in the center of his belly.

Actually, Nate *did* have a weapon. The Corvette.

Could Nate do it … do *that* again?

Plunk!

Another slug in the trunk.

Flying down dark roads at sixty, seventy, eighty miles an hour, Nate wouldn't survive a blowout. The guy chasing him was playing for keeps. That's when it happened — surprising that it took so long. *Rage* bubbled up in his chest. Not fear, pure rage. A volcanic eruption of anger from the depths of his soul swelled up and overwhelmed him.

Nate found his temper, and then lost it.

All the dead bodies through the years …

The McCluskys orchestrated an ambush and Rooster shot Nate's uncle when he tried to surrender. Uncle Pete *died.*

The McCluskys made rot-gut whisky, sold it on Christmas Eve … and May Ella Hargrave *died.*

The McCluskys had derailed a train, killed the engineer, his wife and his little girl.

Ike McClusky executed Johnny. Joe had pleaded, "Please, don't kill me!" but Ike blew out the back of his head. They *died.*

And those were just the ones Nate knew about. How many other people had the McCluskys killed, how many lives had they ruined over the years that he didn't know about?

Done.

All the doubt burned out of Nate like gunpowder ignited by a match. There was nothing left where it had been but cold rage and relentless determination.

Somebody was going to die tonight.

Might be that person's last name was Hannacker.

Might be it was McClusky.

But it was a lead-pipe certainty that not all the people flying down the dark roads of Callison County would live to see the sunrise.

Nate would roll the dice, as he had done once before. This time, he was betting his life that Shep McClusky didn't have the stones Digger McClusky'd had. Nate and Shep both would die unless Shep chickened out, because Nate never would. He hadn't at sixteen. He wouldn't now.

What little fear he still felt evaporated. He remembered how utterly terrified he'd been before. Now, he felt absolutely calm and alert and totally committed.

He needed to pick the right spot, and gratefully they were headed right for it. There was a stretch of road about three miles up that clung precariously to the side of Simmons Knob, seemed to be held in place by nothing more than a set of double guardrails. On the right side of the road beyond the guardrails was a sixty-foot drop straight down to the rocks below. On the left side of the road was a rock wall.

Nate would do it there. One hand of poker. Winner take all.

He buried his foot in the floorboard and leapt out ahead of the pursuing headlights, had to get far enough out front to be out of Shep's line of sight when he killed the headlights. And spun around.

Though he wasn't afraid, his senses seemed so heightened that he could smell the honeysuckle, Queen Anne's lace and day lilies growing on the roadside. He could hear the purring hum of the engine, feel the vibration of it in his bones. This night was not dark as the other one had been years ago. Tonight, there was a full moon, but it was already high in the sky. The stars twinkling around it looked like hunks of ice on velvet.

Headlights appeared suddenly in front of him. He blew past an old farm truck puttering along in the other lane, saw the red tail lights swerve slightly in the rearview mirror, almost like the draft of his passage had blown the truck sideways. Then the tail lights dwindled. The headlights behind dwindled, too. He glanced at the speedometer, and refused to look at it again. He was doing eighty-five, taking curves on two wheels, the glove of the car fit perfectly over the hand of his direction. Simmons Knob loomed a darker black against the night sky. He snatched a little more distance by speeding up in the straightaway leading to the curve up the side of the knob. He saw no headlights behind.

Reaching down, he flipped off his own headlights. Now he was flying through the dark warmth by braille, feeling his way along, muscle memory informing him of curves and bends.

He felt a crunch of gravel under the tires on the right side and knew he'd swerved too far. It was time to slow now. Time to remember the drill.

It had been thirty-five years since Nate had even thought about what he was about to do. He had blocked all those memories out for decades, but now he summoned them and they came running like hungry dogs.

He slowed. Eighty. Seventy-five. Seventy ... slower,

slower, slower. The headlights would appear behind him any second now, looming bigger with every heartbeat.

It was almost as if some force outside himself moved Nate's hands on the steering wheel, away from ten o'clock and two o'clock. The maneuver he'd performed only one time almost four decades ago felt as natural as falling backward into a snow drift where white fluffiness holds you, buoys you up.

Putting both hands on the bottom of the wheel, palms up, he released the brake pedal and used his right hand to spin the steering wheel in a full circle, throwing the red car into a sliding spin that slammed him against his door.

The emergency brake.

No. Oh, *no!*

He wasn't sure where it was!

It was a lever beside the seat in the Big Eight. He didn't know its location in the Corvette and he *had* to lock the back wheels. Only had milliseconds. Searching with his foot on the floorboard to the left of the brake pedal, he found a small pedal, smaller than a package of cigarettes. He jammed his foot down on the pedal with all his strength.

The pedal could activate some mechanism that opened the hood, perhaps, or the trunk?

His breathing stopped. All sensation of movement paused. Then he heard the grind of the brakes taking hold. The car twisted violently. Decades of engineering expertise had gone into enabling the little Corvette to hug the road as it did then, to hold on. A car as top heavy and cumbersome as the Big Eight was always in eminent danger of tumbling. The little Corvette spun as easily around as a record on a disc, and in milliseconds it was going backward at fifty, maybe sixty miles per hour.

Nate released the emergency brake and jammed the

accelerator. The little car responded ... the backward motion slowed, the car's momentum hung between two warring forces before the surge forward won.

The red Stingray leapt down the dark road through the smoke from the rubber of its squalling tires and flew back the direction from which it'd come.

Shep's headlights appeared. Huge. Coming fast.

Bigger. Bigger.

Nate should have been frightened but he wasn't. He had a strange sense — he knew he was imagining it, but it was comforting just the same, that he was not alone in the little red Corvette — that Pa and Johnny and Joe were riding along with him.

He waited. The headlights in front swelled, swelled.

Finally, he reached down and flipped on his own head-lights, which would momentarily blind Shep and he might swerve then in a spontaneous response.

He didn't.

Nate watched Shep's sports car hurtling down the road right at him. In a frozen moment of time, Shep had been totally aware, had refused to respond to a knee-jerk reac-tion to the sudden bright lights. Shep had made a decision at that moment. He saw Nate and *decided* to play chicken. Believed he could hold out, that he could make Nate swerve.

Nate tensed for the impact of colliding cars, took one last breath.

But Shep didn't have the stones. In a shriek of wailing tires the headlights hurtling toward Nate suddenly turned aside and the sports car leapt off the road and became airborne, flew gracefully out into the night sky above the pile of boulders far below.

Nate flew past the spot seconds after the headlights disappeared off to the right. He braked the Corvette to a stop, but the explosion ripped open the night before he had a chance to turn around. The rumble was an angry roar that bounded and rebounded off the surrounding hillsides.

Nate backed up to where bright flickering light lit up the hillside. He got out and walked to the ripped-open guard rails and looked down at the ball of flaming vehicle below. Shep McClusky was inside that inferno, burning to death, and Nate couldn't find it anywhere inside to care.

Chapter Fifty-Seven

It was coming on dawn and Nate had to get the car he was driving out of sight. A red Corvette Stingray — anybody who saw it in the daylight would remember it. But nobody ever went to the chop shop during daylight hours. Someone might pass by and see a vehicle driving up the creek bed beyond the washed-out bridge. They'd certainly be curious about where the vehicle had been going, might decide to take a little drive up that creek bed themselves and see what was up there.

Nate wanted to check on Brodie, wanted desperately to be sure the man was all right, but checking on him would put everybody in danger. Nate was close to the farm, close to home. He had to go there. He hadn't even reached his lane when he heard the wail of emergency vehicles eating up the early morning air.

He backed the Corvette into Daisy's old stall, where Riley had come every morning to brush her coat so it would shine in the show ring at the state fair. Nate covered the car with an old tarp, but that wasn't enough. He looked around for something … hay. Her stall was right below the ladder that led into the hayloft. Nate climbed up in the early morning light and used the pitchfork to shovel hay down through the opening onto the tarp covering the car. When the head of the old pitchfork broke off the handle, he tossed it on the floor, figured he'd duct tape the handle back on later in the day and pile on more hay, but it was enough for now.

When the knock came on Nate's front door a couple of hours later, he almost jumped out of his skin. He'd been determined to "act normal" when he got back to the house, and after he hid the car in the barn, he went into the house, took a shower and started to get ready for church.

Resisting the urge to peek out through the curtains to see who it was, Nate opened the front door with his tie dangling off his neck where he'd started to tie it and then couldn't find the tie pin. He was barefoot, and still had a little piece of bloody toilet paper on his chin where he'd nicked it shaving.

Standing on his front porch was Kentucky State Police Detective Booth Graham.

Nate made his face impassive.

How?

There was absolutely *no way* Nate could be linked to the burning wreck that authorities would soon determine had killed Shepherd McClusky. So how'd Graham figure it out? And why'd he come out here by himself without backup?

Was it possible he'd come here for some other reason … because now that he'd got a good look at Graham's face, it was clear this was not a man who wanted to be here.

Nate smiled, dangled it on his face between his ears like a surgeon's mask.

"You think you won, don't you, Hannacker?"

"To what do I owe the honor of your presence on this bright sunny Sunday morning?"

"Enjoy it. Roll around in it like a dog that rolls in dead animal stink—"

"I had me a dog like that once. Had to keep him on a leash or a rope all the time or he'd come home smelling like roadkill."

"Milk everything you can out of this because there won't be another one."

"Another one what, Detective Graham?" Sounded as innocent as a choir boy, voice didn't shake at all. He didn't light a cigarette, though, couldn't have pulled that off.

Graham reached into his jacket and took out some papers, handed them to Nate.

"What's this?"

"I've delivered Mr. McClusky's paperwork, this is yours — showing that the charges against you for terroristic threatening and accessory to assault in the third degree on the person of Oliver Morris have been formally dropped, the aforementioned Mr. Morris having suddenly and mysteriously decided to withdraw his criminal complaint."

"Whatever possessed Mr. Morris to do a thing like that?"

Graham didn't answer.

"Well, it was right nice of you to come all the way out here to personally deliver—"

"Wouldn't have missed it for the world, Hannacker. I wanted to look you dead in the eye when I said it."

"Said what?"

"You poked the wrong tiger, hillbilly."

Nate's voice turned to ice.

"Hillbilly ain't a term I'd toss around like I's throwing feed to chickens if I's you."

"You think you scare me … *hillbilly*?" the state police detective snarled, but his temper was in check and he was totally in control. Not good signs. A man with the self-discipline to hold his temper, and the stones to go driving up to Big-Un McClusky's farm unannounced on a Sunday morning, was a man with some grit.

"I've arrested more bad-asses in a week in one Chicago neighborhood than you could flush out of the trees in this whole godforsaken county."

"Neighbors turn their neighbors over to the police in Chicago, do they?"

Graham barked out something resembling a laugh.

"You think I'm impressed with your pathetic little 'code of silence'? I've busted ginny mobsters with 'omertà' tattooed on their chests who wouldn't snitch even when somebody busted their knuckles with a hammer."

Nate had no idea what omertà meant, but you'd have to do more than bust his knuckles to get him to admit it.

"If you're done delivering my mail and warning me about poked tigers and ginny mobsters, you need to get off my porch. Father Abernathy gives you the evil eye if you're late for Mass."

Graham produced a smile as cold as a shark in waters under the North Pole.

"My business *today* is complete. But we have other business, the two of us." He made a little contemptuous sound in his throat. "Your Neanderthal buddy Big-Un McClusky's every bit as stupid as he looks."

Now, there, Detective Graham, you have made a serious character blunder.

"So I figure last night's little shooting gallery show was *your* idea."

Wrongo, moose breath.

"Shooting gallery?"

342

"It's you who needs to be taken down a peg and you just met the man who's going to do it."

"So where is this fella? Sounds like he's a guy I need to watch out for."

"What goes around comes around, Mr. Hannacker. One day, it'll be payback time. You will regret the day you tried to make a fool of Booth Graham."

"Quivering in my boots, absolutely scared to death. Now get off my porch."

The detective gave him a final glare, turned and went down the steps. Then he turned.

"So why'd you steal his rifle?"

"Whose rifle?"

"You know whose rifle. What'd you want it for?"

"I have absolutely no idea what you're talking about."

"Morris is claiming somebody broke into his house this morning while they were at early Mass and stole his deer rifle, a 30.06 with some kind of fancy scope, took it off the rack over the mantle."

"He file a police report saying I did it?"

"He didn't file a police report."

"He's learning. But it wasn't me." Nate couldn't help smiling again. "I got my own rifle with a fancy scope, shoots just fine."

The detective made a point of turning around in a wide circle in font of Nate's house before he drove his unmarked Kentucky State Police car slowly down the driveway and out to the lane.

Nate literally sagged in relief against the door jam.

Then his phone rang. My, but Nathaniel Hannacker was a popular man today.

When he answered, Mama Bert didn't bother to identify herself. Everyone knew her voice.

"You need to watch your back, Hannacker," she said.

Did she know about the wreck? The Corvette in his barn? Brodie?

"Word's out on you and you just handed the McCluskys a get-out-of-jail-free card."

Nate was suddenly very tired.

"I appreciate the warning, but I have no idea what you're talking about."

"You and Big-Un pulled quite a stunt last night. Everybody in the county's heard about it by now. So let's say — hypothetical-like — somebody'd decided to bag themselves a Hannacker, stuff him and hang him on a plaque over their mantle. When would be a better time to do it than right now? Anything happens to you, the law ain't gonna sniff around but one tree — the one Mr. Oliver Morris is sitting in."

So why'd you steal his rifle?

Nate's thinking was muddled.

"Morris, yeah, I guess they'd blame Morris."

"You all right?"

"Long night."

"That's what I hear. You been a busy boy."

Did she know? If she did, why did she call? She knew the warning about McCluskys out to get him was a moot point now. That danger ... had been eliminated.

So why'd you steal his rifle?

Nate's head began to throb.

"You talked to Brodie? He doin' alright?"

"Brodie's fine, though he did say he'd take it outta your hide if you got so much as a scratch on that fine red Corvette you took when you ... left in such a hurry."

"There's a mark or two on it." He paused, considering what to say. Who did he think he was kidding? There wasn't nothing worth knowing that Mama Bert didn't know. Chapter and verse. "A couple of bullet holes that'll need to be plugged."

She said nothing, just made a grunting noise that sounded like, "Uh huh."

"I was going to call you today to use the get-out-of-jail-free card you gave me when we formed our silent partner-ship. It's been a good ride, but I'm done."

"Figured that's what you'd say. I ain't got nobody specific in mind for the position but I ain't sure I need to be a *silent* partner no more. There was more'n one bird got killed with one stone when Shep McClusky run through that guard rail on Hunter Lane last night." So she *did* know about the wreck. "I think maybe I done plugged the leak in my boat." She paused for a beat. "Or you plugged it for me."

Then the line went dead.

Chapter Fifty-Eight

CLEAN.

All Riley Hannacker wanted in life was to get clean. That was his soft spot, what he yearned for when they were out in the bush. Everybody had a particular itch the Hilton Hotel of the fire base scratched.

Willie Ray hungered — literally— for the mess hall at Tweety Bird. He had a hollow leg, was always mooching candy bars and cookies off the other guys along with cigarettes. And, of course, he smoked weed whenever he could get it, which kept him in a perpetual state of the munchies.

Ace wanted the barber. He kept his head shaved and when they were out on patrol kinky nubs of hair would appear on his scalp, and he'd scratch at it as if every hair itched.

Davie just wanted a roof over his head and he didn't care where it was. He was happy to go sit on a toilet in the latrine just to get out of the big empty into a world where there were walls and roofs. Of all the guardsmen, David Monaghan was the only one bothered by the jungle itself, the gigantic green beast out there beyond the campfire light. It was never quiet. Different bugs and creatures sang in the daytime than at night, but it was never silent, the low-level drone of it like a swarm of gnats flying around your face or some buzzing insect that'd climbed into your ear and was making its slow way down your ear canal to your brain.

That's the tale Willie Ray had put out there, said there were bugs in the jungle that'd crawl up on your shoulder and then into your ear, lay their eggs inside and when they hatched they'd eat your brains.

They'd been sitting round a small fire, using C-4 to heat their rations when Willie Ray had started in on it.

"Ain't no such thing," Ben Higgs had said.

Unfortunately, Willie Ray had noticed how stricken David Monaghan had looked at the story and he'd smelled blood in the water.

"You think there ain't? One of the replacements in Likker Lovers was tellin' me all about it." He'd sidled over to where David was eating and continued his story in a softer voice.

"Said they was like leeches, you couldn't feel them." The ever-present leeches exuded some kind of anesthetic so you never felt them attach to you and start sucking. Andy Taggart'd had one on his forehead and didn't even notice it.

"Onliest way you know they been there is they leave their droppings … little white specks like salt on your shoulder." He pretended to notice David for the first time, and feigned surprise. "Looks just like that!" He pointed to David's shoulder and Davie leapt to his feet dusting nonexistent white specks off his shoulder, realizing mid-swipe that he'd been had when Willie Ray brayed his donkey laugh and collapsed to his knees in hysteria.

Davie'd gotten him back a couple of days later by

opening up a couple of muffins, filling the insides with hot sauce, and setting them back among the others on the plate. They were small and Willie Ray always just popped a couple of them in his mouth whole.

Everyone at the table had been warned to avoid those two, and when Willie Ray arrived, gripped by his constant state of near starvation, he'd gobbled them down.

There was a beat of silence. His red eyebrows shot up, his eyes grew wide and he sprayed cupcake guts all over the table, knocked the sergeant out of his way as he lunged for the water pitcher, the contents of which he drank down in one long gulp.

As Riley stepped out of the dark, steamy night into the shower unit, located next to the razor wire on the high side of the saddle where the fire base had been built, he wanted a shower now more than he'd ever wanted one in his life.

He could smell the stink of burning flesh on his clothes. He was imagining it, had to be. Jack had … he shuddered at the memory … set the Jingle Bell Man on fire hours ago. It wasn't possible that the stink was still on Riley's clothes. But it was. On his skin, too.

Once they got to Tweety Bird, the squad had scattered, to collapse in exhaustion on their bunks or to scratch their particular itches. He'd seen Davie and the Taggarts headed to the mess hall at the other end of the camp and he'd join them as soon as he'd scrubbed the stink only he could smell off his skin.

He was the only man in the shower building, prayed he wasn't too late for at least a little hot water. Stripping, he went after the leeches, found two behind his right knee and one in his armpit. He snatched them off, dropped them to the floor and stomped them. Yeah, yeah, he knew you were supposed to spray them with Dapsone and kill them so they'd drop off and not leave any nasty little body parts behind. But he had brought nothing with him to the shower building but a change of uniform. He'd put antibiotic ointment on those spots when he could. Maybe Andy Taggart had some in his pack. He and Andy'd been assigned to bunk in with the crew of the Number Six gun and Riley was glad. Albert Linsley worked on that gun. An older guy, regular Army, he did a little bit of everything on Gun Number Six. He was the driver, the ammunition carrier, the outside guy, which meant that it was his responsibility to keep the enemy off the gun should they get into a tight situation. He could also fire the gun. In some totally inexplicable way, he reminded Riley of Papa. Not the same age, didn't look alike, no similar mannerisms ... but Linsley had the same kind of quiet confidence about him that Papa had, and that was a quality it felt good to get next to.

Davie Monaghan and Ben Higgs were next door in the Number Five bunker with the artilleryman whose last name was Mac-something, but everyone called him Scottie. He'd been bleeding the whole company dry in the nightly poker game. Riley was sure Willie Ray was in danger of going into nicotine withdrawal if he lost any more cigarettes. Willie Ray, Five Cents — and Tommy, of course — were another couple of bunkers down.

As Riley stepped under the water spray and turned the knob, it started to rain outside, the kind of downpour nobody back home would believe existed. A fire hose straight out of the sky. It did not produce the gentle pitter-patter of raindrops on the roof. It hit solid roofs so hard it was like being inside a kettle drum. But then the inside of a kettle drum was preferable to listening to it trying to eat a hole in the canvas of your tent or hearing it/feeling it hit your helmet.

Hot water!

Yes!

Well, warm.

Riley let it run off the top of his head all over him before he turned off the tap and began to soap up. Everywhere the soap touched stung — his whole body stung. Leach sores, the cut on his knuckle he got … somewhere. Jungle rot, all over the fingers of his right hand and down his arm. And his left foot. He hadn't examined it in good light, but it had been throbbing. Probably had trench foot, and he knew you were supposed to get on it fast.

And he would.

But the warm water sliding over his body drained all his strength and will away and washed it down the drain. He'd told the others he'd meet them in the mess hall, but he had hit such a wall, he might just pack it in. He stepped out of the shower, dried, put on clean camouflage fatigues — clean being a relative term meaning he'd washed them out in that stream by the village twenty clicks back and got some of the crud off and most of the stink out.

When he picked up the shirt he'd discarded on the floor, a whiff of burning flesh wafted up from it. He could swear … *Imagining things, Hannacker. Get a grip.*

Carrying his boots in one hand and a wad of his dirty uniform in the other, he stepped out into the night and looked out into rain so thick you couldn't see five feet. This was just about the highest point in the camp, and from it you could see the whole thing laid out before you. Even at night, you could see blobs of black bunkers, blobs of ammo stacks, bigger blobs of black artillery pieces. The rectangular blob of the water truck and all the way on the other side, there was a slight glow from shafts of light escaping under the door and around the piece of canvas over one of the front windows of the mess hall … where it was at least *possible* they were serving something hot and edible.

His stomach grumbled. He'd settle for hot. Mystery meat was better than something identifiable. He'd rather not know what the nasty-tasting stuff he was shoveling into his mouth was than know what it was supposed to taste like but didn't.

But the camp was not visible now. It had vanished in the silver downpour. Reluctant to get soaked — he'd been looking forward to sleeping in dry clothes — he stayed where he was under the overhang extending out from the door to the showers. Rain like this could last for days. It could also last for ten minutes and stop altogether. He'd wait for a little while. Hope.

Dropping his boots to the ground, he fished a dry sock out of his pocket and leaned against the building, lifted his foot and slipped it carefully on his sore toes, easing the boot on afterward. The rain let up gradually, didn't turn off like a spigot as it had turned on. It came down in torrents for maybe two more minutes, then began to ease off. When Riley straightened up to put on his right boot, the camp below him that the downpour had obliterated slowly emerged from the lessening rain.

He'd give it another couple more—

What was that?

Something was moving out there. He stopped breathing.

A whole bunch of somethings were moving!

Along the ground, crawling like maggots in the mud between the guns and the bunkers. The ground was alive with ... what could—?

Cong!

Not just Cong, *naked* Cong, slithering across the wet ground. His eye snapped to the razor wire fencing and he watched in horror as more and more slid beneath the coils. Maggie's drawers never moved. The red flags tied at five-foot intervals along the top wires could be set to dancing by the slightest movement in the coils.

The Cong soldiers had taken their clothes off so their uniforms wouldn't snag on the wire and give them away.

They were everywhere. *Inside the perimeter.*

And Riley was unarmed.

"Take your rifle to the latrine with you," the training officer at Ft. Hood had yelled at them, "or one of these days you're gonna have to defend yourself with your dick."

It was an ambush, a sneak attack. Riley had mere seconds to rouse the camp before the VC swarmed all over them in their sleep.

How could he warn them?

And then he knew.

Chapter Fifty-Nine

NATE STOOD with the receiver in his hand, staring at it, after Mama Bert hung up. His head began to throb, right in his temples, sudden-like. He'd never had a headache like that before. Maybe he was having a stroke.

He coughed out a laugh then and the throbbing immediately lessened. A stroke … riiiiiight. Not a stroke, but he was definitely running on fumes. He'd packed way too much living into the past twelve hours, with too little sleep and no food at all.

Reaching up to his neck, he pulled at the tie, loosened it and took it off. No church today. Though he was seriously sleep deprived, he didn't fear he'd doze off during Father Abernathy's homily, though that was a weekly danger he avoided only by fortifying himself before he left the house with several cups of coffee.

He passed on church because it was clear the word was out now about the wreck … the traffic accident last night that had taken the life of Shepherd McClusky, the son of Parker McClusky, the brother of … and cousin of … and uncle of … The whole McClusky clan probably knew by now. The wreck would be the only thing folks would want to talk about and Nate was not up to that. And he didn't like driving his old farm truck into town and parking it in the church lot. No sense getting people to wonder why he wasn't driving his pickup.

Trudging back into his bedroom, he changed out of church clothes into his coveralls. He'd let a lot of farm work go in the past few months. Despite Mama Bert's assurances to the contrary, his work at the chop shop had interfered with farming. He could put the rest of today to good use … if he could just un-muddy his mind.

And tonight, as soon as it got dark, he would return the red Corvette to the chop shop and retrieve the pickup he'd left there. When he'd put the car in Daisy's old stall and covered it with hay, it had been just after sunrise and the barn was shadowy. He might have left some shiny part sticking out. That'd be the first order of business and then …

He stopped. He was doing it again, recognized it for what it was. He was ping-ponging all over his mind to keep it too occupied to think about the ugly parts. A young man was dead and his death was on Nate.

Nate had a stolen car in his barn — a car so valuable that if the law found it, he'd be behind bars for all the good years he had left.

There was more, too, something else important that he was missing. The thought kept flitting out of his grasp whenever he tried to think it.

Pulling his John Deere cap off the hook by the back door, he went out without letting the screen door slam. His head still hurt. He opened one of the bay doors of the barn to let in sunlight so he could take a good look at a mound of hay in what had once been Daisy's stall, under which sat a prison sentence in a box.

Opening the stall door, he noticed something shiny on the ground and realized it was one of Daisy's state fair medals that'd been hanging on the wall of the stall. He must have knocked it off when he was pulling the car in last night. He bent down to pick it up and a bullet whizzed over his head so close he felt the air rearrange itself around it as it passed. The crack of the rifle shot was delayed a beat, but it was clear when it came.

That round had been fired from a 30.06. A deer rifle.

Chapter Sixty

THERE WERE PROBABLY thirty soldiers in the mess hall, most of them the infantry platoons that had just come in and the drivers of the armored personnel carriers that'd transported some of them.

Willie Ray sat at a table by the door with Ace and five guardsmen. Andy sat across from Willie Ray. Davie Monaghan sat next to Andy, Ben Higgs and Kenny Taylor faced each other on the other side and Ace sat at the far end.

"… and so I take the snap, looking downfield for receivers," Willie Ray was saying. He'd been the quarterback on the Callison County High School Wildcat football team that Riley hadn't played on. Ben Higgs had, though he'd ridden the bench all year, as he had every other year he'd played. It was a mystery why Coach Malone kept him on the team at all but he was a good sport about it, always said, "Yeah, I'm small, I get that. But I make up for it by being slow."

Willie Ray wasn't sitting down, just had his foot up on the chair, leaning over the table to tell his story. "… so I back up into the pocket." He demonstrated by backing up toward the door a couple of steps, "… draw back," he drew back, "… and—"

A strange sound rode the night air into the room from behind him. A cry of some kind. Everyone in the mess hall heard it and paused, but nobody could make out the words.

Except the Taggart brothers.

"Ambush!" Willie Ray screamed at the top of his lungs.

"*Cong!*" Andy cried.

Fire in the hole!

FIRE IN THE HOLE!

The words rang in Nate's head as he hunkered down in the hay in Daisy's stall, reverberated, almost sounded like the echo of a far-off cry. Nate was being ambushed. But who …?

WILLIE RAY and Andy leapt to retrieve their M16s from the spot where they'd leaned them against the wall by the door. All the other soldiers exploded in instant movement, running toward their weapons and the exits.

Andy was one step ahead, shoved Willie Ray's rifle into his hands and grabbed his own and the two of them dropped in unison behind the barrier of sandbags around the front door.

Popping up like gophers out of a hole, they peeked over the top of the sandbags.

Ben was standing in the doorway behind them. "Holy sh— ," he began, but he didn't finish. An instant later his head exploded off his shoulders and he fell backwards into the mess hall.

Ben was the first guardsman to die that night. He wasn't the last.

Willie Ray and Andy opened fire. The VC had been caught off guard out in the open, crawling across the ground. With no cover of any kind, the Taggart brothers mowed them down. But there were so many of them and … they were *naked.*

Firing opened up from all over the base then, the soldiers alerted by the gunfire from the mess hall. The night exploded from all around at the same time. Hand grenades and satchel charges — small bags of TNT about two inches by three and a half inches, weighing half a pound with five-second timers. The bigger RPGs, rocket-propelled grenades, boomed. RPGs were one-man-operated rockets with a large explosive charge in the warhead, capable of penetrating ten inches of armor. The staccato sound of the Cong's AK-47s, rat-tat-tat-tat, stitched the darkness with thumps and pings and cries of pain until a sudden rumble sounded with such a percussion it hurt the ears. One of the ammunition stacks beside one of the guns must have blown or maybe the gun itself. Over the space of maybe thirty seconds, the night had gone from dark and quiet to alive and awake and on fire, with screaming and gunfire all around.

And then it started to rain again and all the targets vanished in the downpour.

Chapter Sixty-One

NATE STAYED where he'd knelt to pick up the medallion. He dropped to his belly and crawled farther into the stall from the doorway. Who could possibly be shooting at him?

Mama Bert had said there was a word out on him, and he knew it'd been put out there by the McCluskys. But which McCluskys? And why *now*?

He'd inadvertently kicked sand in the McCluskys' faces when he took the job at the chop shop and they were pissed. Shep had come after him. And Nate had killed him.

But *nobody* knew that!

It was a car wreck, for crying out loud!

Sad, maybe even tragic, but no big surprise to anybody.

Everybody knew Shep McClusky drove like a bat outta hell, too fast, took crazy chances. Wasn't a soul in the county who'd be shocked to learn that he'd taken a header off a bluff, hit the rocks below, and his car exploded.

Nobody knew what had really happened last night on Hunter Lane but Nate and Shep. And Shep was dead.

So who was it out there with a 30.06 they'd stolen this

morning off the rack over the mantle of Oliver Morris's house?

And why did they want him dead *now*?

Was he maybe barking up the wrong McClusky tree with his suspicions? Was it Big-Un? What for? There wasn't any reason for Big-Un to come here with a stolen rifle the morning after he could have dropped Nate with a shot from his own. The two of them had turned Oliver Morris's office into a shooting gallery, and Morris was pissed — so said State Police Detective Graham.

But Oliver Morris was a wimp. A weeny. Nate and Big-Un had scared him spitless with their shooting display last night, got him to drop the charges against them. So why would the guy suddenly grow cajones and come gunning for Nate ... after claiming his rifle'd been stolen?

It made no sense—

"You're gonna die, Hannacker. You should already be dead, should have been a corpse, should have rotted in the ground thirty-five years ago for killing my daddy. But you won't get away with killing my son, my Shep ..." The voice broke. It was strong again with the next words. "You murdering bastard, I'm gonna blow your brains out the back of your head."

Parker McClusky.

How could he possibly know that Nate and Shep had played a deadly game of chicken last night — and Shep had lost?

He couldn't *know*. Nobody knew.

But he likely did know that Shep had gone to the chop shop last night to claim his "rightful position." He did know that Nate had tried to run a car loaded with McCluskys off the road three decades ago. Maybe he'd talked to Brodie, or maybe he'd just gone to the chop shop, saw Nate's pickup parked there and connected the dots.

The how didn't really matter. Parker McClusky had figured it out, knew Nate had killed his son, and there was no Crows' Pledge now to prevent him from exacting revenge.

The hinge on the other bay door of the barn squealed as it was pulled open from the outside.

Nate had three options: run, fight or hide.

No, four. He could die.

Chapter Sixty-Two

RILEY LEAPT BACKWARDS into the darkness of the shower building after his cry ignited his world with responding gunfire and bullets thunked into the walls over his head. If any of the VC came after him, he was a sitting duck here, trapped without a weapon. Scrabbling across the floor to the hallway that led to the showers, he turned the corner, jumped up and bolted for the window at the end.

He thought he heard sounds behind him but didn't turn, just flung aside the canvas window covering and dived out into the darkness. The base was alive with battle sounds now, men who'd come within seconds of being massacred in their sleep were fighting back, fighting for their lives.

Riley hit the ground and rolled, then rose and flattened himself against the wall of the building beside the window. Waited. Seconds passed. Then the canvas over the window moved back to reveal the barrel of a rifle, and Riley was ready. He grabbed the barrel and hauled the soldier out the window with it, hurling him into the mud. Riley stood above him, the Cong soldier lay on his back, refusing to release his grip on the rifle.

Then Riley lifted his foot — the one wearing a boot — and stomped it down on the man's plain-to-see private parts and he screamed and let go of the rifle. Riley yanked the weapon into his own hands, flipped it around and shot him with it, silencing his screams. The man had a pack on a strap around his neck — ammo, probably, maybe grenades and satchel charges. Riley snatched it off him and ran to the side of the building to peer around it, caught sight of fifty … no, maybe a hundred Cong soldiers racing around inside the razor-wire perimeter shooting and tossing explosives.

Gunfire from the front door of the mess hall was driving them back, but they definitely had the advantage. They were prepared, clearly organized, peeling away from the group in the center of the compound in twos and threes, running away like they knew where they were going.

The Americans were in total disarray. Most of the camp had been asleep in bunkers until the sound of gunfire catapulted them to their feet.

The barber.

Ace never did trust the little Vietnamese civilian who stood outside the guard bunkers on the edge of the barbed wire giving haircuts for fifty cents each, said he'd seen him walk back and forth like maybe he was pacing off a distance.

It started to rain again and the world dissolved away, visibility shrank to six or eight feet.

Then light.

A huge flare burst over the encampment. They'd cranked back one of the big guns and were firing off illumination. What the light revealed was chilling. The sons of bitches were everywhere.

Then Riley saw Gun Number Three take a direct hit from an RPG and explode, the back door blew off and someone came running out, engulfed in flames.

Like the Jingle Bell Man this morning that Jackson … murdered. The thought was there and then gone.

The man ran a few feet, fell and was still. The illumination went out, but it'd lit up the world for Riley to orient himself. He and Andy'd been assigned to bunk in with the crew of the Number Six gun and he'd left his gear in that bunker to go to the showers. Davie Monaghan and Ben Higgs were next door in the Number Five bunker.

Dashing furtively in the shadows from one bit of cover to another, he made his way toward the Number Six bunker. He wanted his M16 and extra clips, his .45 and an M79 grenade launcher he'd seen leaned against the wall there. It was clear Charlie wasn't intent on killing Americans. They'd come here to take out the guns, to blow up this artillery base, the one whose accuracy was applauded all over 'Nam.

With a mighty roar the mess hall went up in flames and smoke. Riley wouldn't let himself think about the others. They'd got out by now. They had. The light from the burning building backlit the Cong soldiers into black silhouettes. He didn't shoot, was reluctant to draw fire he didn't want to return. He knew how to fire an AK-47, of course, but it wasn't *his* rifle, the one Riley could disassemble and reassemble in the dark, the weapon he could *count on*. What if this moron never cleaned his AK-47 and it jammed on Riley when he needed it?

You took what you could get in a fight, but his own weapon was tantalizingly close and he ached to feel its reassuring presence in his hands.

But Riley never made it to Bunker Number Six.

Chapter Sixty-Three

RUNNING WAS NOT an option with a gimp leg. Fighting was not an option because he didn't have a weapon. And this time, he couldn't use the car as one.

Footsteps crunched on the dirt inside the barn doors. Parker was coming. Nate had only one option left — hide. And only one place to go — up.

Before Parker got far enough into the barn to see what he was doing, Nate leapt up onto the ladder leading to the hayloft and climbed it as agile as a monkey. The hayloft's outside door was swung wide, welcoming the morning sun. The light chased away all the shadows. No dim corners. Nowhere to go.

There was only hay. All Nate could do was burrow into it and … and what? Hope Parker was so stupid he wouldn't figure out that the big lump under that pile of hay was Nate.

You work with what you have. This was all he had.

The boards that formed the ceiling of Daisy's stall formed the floor of the hayloft. The seams weren't tight, there were two-inch gaps between the boards in some spots. Nate knew that movement in the loft would send dust and hay raining down through the ceiling of the stall. Any fool could see it.

Nate would have to use that knowledge to his advantage. It was all he had.

"Hannacker, I'm coming for you. You won't get away this time. There aren't any pieces of glass to use as a knife here. There's just me here with this rifle and you there with ... *nothing*." He let loose a maniacal laugh that sounded like his mind was unhinged. And maybe it was. A man with that kind of explosive temper must always be hanging onto sanity with his fingernails. But crazy or not, he could still shoot.

Nate moved purposefully in the loft, knowing that where Parker was standing now, he could see into Daisy's stall. He could see the ceiling.

"Think you can get away from me up there?" Parker cried. "Cornered like a pathetic rabbit, hiding in a hole."

Nate began to dig furiously in the hay, rearranging it, piling it up in a mound on the wall on the back side of the loft. He shoved all the hay he could in that direction, leaving the rest of the loft floor with only a foot or two lying on the boards. He knew he was sending dust and straw down through Daisy's ceiling. Knew Parker would see it, would know where the movement was coming from.

Then he slithered beneath the hay and lay still, listened to the steps as Parker climbed the ladder to the loft.

Chapter Sixty-Four

"WE NEED to blow this pop stand," Willie Ray yelled at his brother over the rumble of gunfire.

"Copy that," Andy shot back.

They were running out of ammo, and had brought with them no spare clips. They had only the minimal protection of the sandbags. The mess hall itself had not been fortified like more important buildings, such as the Fire Direction Center, the brains of the artillery unit, that was built into the side of the hill. They'd used heavy timbers on it, twelve-by-twelve-inch beams, sandbags and layers of sheet metal.

The bunkers for the gun crews varied — some were dug out four feet down with walls of sheet metal fortified with sandbags. Others were deeper or more shallow. But all of them had a better chance of withstanding an explosion than the mess hall.

"I'm in Number Two bunker," Willie Ray said, gesturing down the hillside in the rain. "Let's make for it. I got lots of clips."

Number Two was one of the best fortified of all the

bunkers. You couldn't enter directly into the doors on both sides. They faced walls of sandbags and you had to turn around the bags to get into the main portion of the bunker.

Willie Ray looked at Andy, looked out into the rain, then clapped his brother on the shoulder and shouted, "Go!" and he began to lay down a murderous barrage of bullets to keep the Cong occupied while Andy raced from the side of the mess hall through the maintenance area and toward the bunkers beyond.

There was no line of sight from where Willie Ray crouched behind the bags, so he had no idea if Andy'd made it or not before he leapt up himself and followed. Dodging from one bit of cover to another, he was knocked to the ground from the force of the explosion that totally destroyed the mess hall behind him. He staggered behind a dumpster, around a pile of batteries, made it to the bunker and dived in as a trail of gunfire laced the ground behind him.

The Number Two gunner, Randy Nickel and Ace were in the bunker. Andy wasn't.

"You seen my brother?"

Ace and Five Cents were crouched beside the doorway sandbags.

"In the mess hall," Ace said. "Ain't seen him since."

Willie Ray and Andy had taken the same route, so his brother hadn't been hit on the way, wasn't lying out there somewhere. Willie Ray would have seen. He'd gone somewhere else, changed direction. He wouldn't have done it without a really good reason, so Willie Ray just had to trust that he'd done what he had to do at the time. It wasn't like he could step out the door, bang on the dinner triangle on the back porch and holler out "Aaaannndeee."

Just then the roof of the bunker took a huge hit, had to

be a round from an RPG. More than one, maybe, a direct hit. The force of the explosion flung the men against the walls and then onto the floor. Willie Ray looked up and saw that the roof was about to fall in on them.

Chapter Sixty-Five

TIME DIDN'T PLAY crazy tricks on Nate as he faced death now as it had done thirty-five years ago. The world had cranked down into slow motion then and he had watched his father crash through the windshield, saw the glass slit his throat.

Now, time merely ticked off the remaining seconds he had left to draw breath upon the earth, one after the other.

Tick.

Tick.

Tick.

He heard Parker's feet on the ladder, heard the wood groan under his weight.

Each footstep up was a separate event. It was likely Nate would not live another five minutes, another three. He was going to die here, shot with Oliver Morris's rifle. At close range, a 30.06 would blow a hole in him big enough to drive a forklift through.

Nate's heart was hammering so loud he was sure Parker could hear the sound and would know instantly where he had burrowed into the hay.

Or smell him. He reeked of the stench of fear sweat.

Nate Hannacker didn't want to die! Neither had Joe. He had pleaded for his life and Ike had killed him anyway. Nate wouldn't plead. He wanted to live to see Riley come home, but he wouldn't plead—

"You. Are. A. *Dead man*," Parker growled.

Parker stepped off the ladder onto the floor of the loft. Hay all around. But when Parker had been in Daisy's stall, he had seen where the dust was sifting down through the ceiling. He knew where the hay in the loft had been moved.

"Come out of there and die like a man," Parker said. He took two steps away from the ladder toward the pile of hay on the far wall.

Nate couldn't see him, but could picture where he was standing, imagined him raising the rifle to his shoulder, sighting on the pile of hay.

"Die, you pathetic bastard," he said and pulled the trigger, sending a bullet ripping through the pile of hay on the floor in front of him.

Chapter Sixty-Six

RILEY DIVED through the door of Bunker Number Five and landed in Davie Monaghan's lap.

They *had* made it out of the mess hall before it blew!

"Ronnie's hurt." Davie's face said more than those two words. He motioned to the moaning figure on the bunk in the corner. "Dragged him in here. It's bad."

Davie turned his back on Riley and took up again a position at the door, crouched just inside, firing at shapes in the rain.

"Good thing you're tall," he said. In the bizarre circus of dark and light and rain outside the bunkers, the only option was to shoot the little guys and Davie had positioned himself to do just that.

"I did what I could for him, but ..." Davie spoke softly. "He's burned up, was in Number Three when it took a direct hit."

Riley couldn't see much in the dark interior of the bunker, but the face of the man on the cot was blackened and unrecognizable.

"You got another M16?" Riley asked. Davie pointed to

the far wall. Riley grabbed one of the three rifles there and joined Davie in a crouch by the door.

Shapes raced past in the rain. It seemed like everything was exploding. He saw a Cong soldier fire an RPG through the doorway of Bunker Number One and the bunker lurched upward but remained standing. The naked soldier ran toward Gun Number One, about to heave a satchel onto the Howitzer when gunfire cut him down. Maybe Davie, he'd fired. Or maybe somebody else. The satchel charge blew up in his hand and pieces of him flew in all directions.

"Don't shoooooot," cried a voice from out of the rain and a man raced through a hail of gunfire toward them.

He was way too big to be Cong, and he crashed into Davie at the door like a bowling ball hitting pins.

Andy Taggart.

Riley saw the fear stamped on his face and how pale he looked in the illumination flare that had just lit the sky.

And no eyebrows. No eyebrows at all.

Funny the things you see in such great detail before …

From this point on, Riley Hannacker's memories derailed. Like a train that hits a cow on the track, the engine bucked up and all the cars behind fell off the tracks to the left or right.

There were completely blank places. Fuzzy places. Memories that looked like exposed negatives rather than real images.

He never was able to fit them together so that scenes and images were in some kind of logical sequence.

And time slowed down. Just about stopped, then slowly began to trudge forward again, gaining speed and clarity as it moved.

Andy was still in the doorway, had just untangled himself from David Monaghan, whose helmet had been knocked off by the collision. Riley was behind the two of them in the darkness, standing with a rifle in his hand when a second illumination flare scorched the night sky.

He was looking through rain so thick anything more than a few feet away was distorted by the water. But in the sudden bright light, Riley saw clearly for an instant.

In a tiny fragment of time, he took it all in.

One of the little guys was holding an RPG launcher to his shoulder.

The barrel was aimed right at the doorway of their bunker.

The flare must have lit Riley's face, too, a chalk white face in the glare. He thought Davie saw the launcher, saw death coming at them. Andy's back was turned. Didn't matter. They all had seconds to live, way too short a time to lift the barrel of a rifle and take the little guy out.

The bright illumination paled, just a bit, just for an elongated second, and some trick of the light changed the reflections in the water falling from the sky. The distortion was gone. The world beyond was cloudy and opaque, like looking into an aquarium, but it was no longer distorted like a funhouse mirror. He could see the little guy clearly. Actually, there were two of them. One dead, lying naked in the mud, and the other straddling him holding the RPG the dead guy'd dropped.

The little guy with the RPG wasn't naked, though. He was fully dressed ... in camouflage combat fatigues.

And then the world went black.

Chapter Sixty-Seven

WHEN NATE HEARD the roar of the rifle shot, he rose up out of the thin layer of hay on the floor behind Parker, rose up like a striking rattlesnake, rose up and plunged the tines of the broken pitchfork into Parker's back, buried them all the way to the hilt.

Parker stood frozen for a moment, then the rifle fell to the floor out of his limp fingers. He dropped to his knees, looking at the four prongs of the pitchfork poking out through his shirt quizzically, unable to figure out exactly what they were and how they had gotten there.

He tried to speak, but when he opened his mouth, nothing but blood came out. One of the prongs had punctured his throat and he clawed frantically at it with both hands. He ripped open the top of his shirt, breaking a neck chain and sending buttons to ping off the walls and floor, pawed desperately at the spike sticking out of his flesh. Then he tumbled onto his side in the hay, his blood spreading out in a pool around him, dripping slowly down between the boards into Daisy's stall, splatting on the tarp covering the cherry-red Corvette.

Nate stood over the body, watching the hitching form struggle for breath. It took a minute, maybe two before the wheezing gasps ceased. Still Nate stood, with hay in his hair and all over his clothes, seemed unable to form an intent to do anything, now that the deed was done.

He had killed Parker McClusky.

Just like that.

Fifteen minutes ago, he'd been talking on the telephone to Mama Bert, her warning him that he was a marked man, and now he was … a murderer? No, not a murderer. He was a killer, though. He had been one since he was sixteen, when he took the life of Ike McClusky by plunging a piece of glass into his brain.

In the past twelve hours, he had caused the deaths of two people … both of them McCluskys. It didn't seem real, flat out seemed like some kind of nightmare where he'd wake up in sweat-damp sheets, a cry of terror on his lips.

Maybe he stood where he was for five minutes. Maybe half an hour. Maybe a lifetime.

His mind had cranked down into such a sluggish movement that it was hard to think at all. And he had to think. *Think!*

Shaking his head violently, as if to shake the images, the reality out of his mind, he dragged his hands slowly down his face, took a deep breath, then reached down and picked up the rifle that had fallen from Parker's hands.

He understood intellectually — he was a man who lived in the world and understood how it functioned — that the rational thing to do now was to call the sheriff and let the wheels of justice begin to grind. But there was nowhere in Nathaniel Hannacker's being that could countenance doing such a thing. He would deal with this. But he would need help.

He forced himself to think through what he ought to do, try to consider all the ramifications. He had to get this right the first time. There would be no do-overs.

Parker hadn't walked to Nate's farm. He had left a vehicle parked somewhere. Nate had to find it. Fast.

Given that Parker'd stolen Morris's rifle, he'd likely come to Nate's from there, so Nate got into his old farm truck and went looking. It was either the truck, Riley's red Mustang, or the stolen Corvette Stingray. He found the big Grand Prix Pontiac, black over silver, pulled back under some trees about a mile south of his house.

He'd gotten the keys out of Parker's pocket, so he drove the Pontiac back to the farm, pulled it into the barn in front of the stall where the Corvette sat beneath a tarp and a pile of hay … and where Parker's blood had likely stopped dripping on it.

He walked back to the spot where he'd found Parker's car, got his truck and brought it home, pulled it up in front of the barn below the open hayloft doors and shoved Parker's dead body off into it. Loading up a shovel and a post-hole digger, and a roll of black plastic used for hay rolls, he got into the truck and drove across the pasture to the logging road where Fast Eddie'd wrangled the eighteen-wheeler up the side of the knob. He drove up the logging road. When it disappeared into brush, he drove up an old creek bed, wound back deep into a high hollow.

It took him the rest of the afternoon to bury the body. He wrapped it in layers of black plastic. By this time, the body was stiff but Parker McClusky was a big man and Nate was exhausted by the time he'd wrapped the body and duct taped it into a solid shroud. He dug the hole deep, dumped the body into it, covered it with dirt and then piled rocks on top of the spot until it was impossible to tell the dirt had ever been disturbed.

Words from a childhood scene filled his head, Mose Taggart talking to the prohibition agents on the porch of the courthouse.

KNOW THIS FOR A TRUE FACT — *if either one of you ever sets foot back in this county again, you won't leave alive. Won't be no bodies for your families to claim, neither. You'll just vanish."*

PARKER MCCLUSKY WOULD JUST VANISH.

It was going on dusk when he got back to the house. He was filthy, exhausted and trembling. The trembling had started as he drove the truck back down the side of the knob and by the time he'd parked behind the house and got out, he was shaking so badly he could hardly stand.

It occurred to him then, that he hadn't eaten a bite of food since ... lunch before he went downtown to meet Big-Un. He made it into the house. Forced himself to eat a whole package of bologna — which was the only meat he had in the house. He ate two pieces of bread with peanut buttered slathered on them.

Then the shaking stopped.

His voice was firm when he called Mama Bert. He didn't mince words. "I got a black and silver Pontiac Grand Prix that has to go away, vanish. Little. Bitty. Pieces. "

She asked no questions, just told him to take it to the chop shop tonight, that only Brodie would be there.

As the moon rose up over Bald Knob, Nate took the 30.06 rifle apart and dropped the pieces into the septic tank.

Chapter Sixty-Eight

THERE WAS a great rumbling in Riley's head. Like Niagara Falls was pouring over the cliff between his ears. He couldn't hear because of it. Maybe. Or maybe he'd gone deaf and the rumbling didn't have anything to do with it.

Someone lifted up one of his eyelids and shined a light in it, then did the same with the other.

And from a great distance he heard a voice he didn't recognize say, "Both eyes equally responsive to light."

Then another nearby voice he didn't know said, "This guy's aren't."

"Round went all the way through, took out the back wall and exploded out there or wouldn't be anything left of any of them."

He wanted to open his own eyelids but couldn't seem to manage it, wanted to ask whoever it was who'd opened them before to do it again, but he couldn't seem to talk either.

Maybe he was dead.

No. It smelled too bad for dead. Blood and dirt and mud and feces and gunpowder.

"Whoee, lookit that, here she comes," somebody from farther away cried. "Puff's here. We're good now."

Riley had always wanted to see the legendary gunship. Puff the Magic Dragon carried an incredible amount of firepower. Four Gatling guns each with several barrels, spewed out a stream of withering fire toward the enemy and every fifth or sixth round was a tracer so you could adjust accuracy.

Riley tried to concentrate, wanted to wake up. But with the echo in his head, he couldn't seem to attend to the sounds around him, distinguish them, listen to some, ignore others. It was all just random sensory input, but he was coming around.

Then his eyes popped open.

Popped open.

Like window shades you'd been struggling to open and the cord finally comes loose. He looked around with them, didn't move his body, just his eyes. There was light on two sides, coming from the front and the back of the bunker.

He was lying on a floor. He hurt. But he couldn't distinguish exactly where the pain was coming from. Then he realized he wasn't on the floor but on a stretcher on the floor, figured that out when somebody, two somebodies picked it up and headed outside.

Into the sunlight.

The sun was shining.

It was morning.

Or afternoon, who knew, but it wasn't night.

And it was over. The rumble of horror images in his head, fighting lions locked in a cage, couldn't break free — all he had was a vague understanding there'd been a battle and it had been bad.

And he'd survived.

Then he heard Willie Ray's voice. He was yelling, "Don't touch him. Touch him and I'll cut your balls off."

"Put the knife down, son," some voice said. "We're just trying to help."

The stretcher he was riding was sailing through the air past a wall of fallen sandbags and his eyes raked over Willie Ray, sitting with his back against the sandbags, his Bowie knife in his hand, pointed at one of the medics. A gash opened up his right cheek so you could see the bone. Andy was sprawled out beside him, with his head in his brother's lap.

Willie Ray saw Riley, and cried out, "Riley, thank God! You gotta help me, man."

Andy's body had been ripped open from the chest down and his internal organs had spilled out on the ground.

"I been trying to put 'em back in but I can't do it all by myself."

Then they passed by Willie Ray, but his voice followed. "Help me put 'em back in! Riley, help!" They were moving up the hill to the sound of choppers.

Riley understood what he'd just seen. But he didn't really. It wasn't what he'd thought he'd seen. None of this was reality. Nightmare, bad dream, that's all.

They set Riley's stretcher down beside the other one they'd carried out of the same bunker. Davie Monaghan lay on it, still. He appeared to be uninjured, just unconscious. But blood was seeping out both his ears and a steady stream ran down his upper lip from his nose.

Riley closed his eyes, tried to concentrate on where he hurt, any one of all the places where he hurt. He wanted to feel the pain, needed to. But it had smeared like a kid's fingerprints into one ugly mass of hurting that started at the top of his head and went to the bottom of his feet. He looked down his body and saw one foot in a boot. His other foot was bare.

But they weren't fussing over him like they were the man on the stretcher on the other side of Davie. He didn't know the man, didn't think he did, but he was so badly burned it was hard to tell. Maybe it was Ronnie Benson. He seemed to remember Davie had said Ronnie'd been burned. He knew the man on the next stretcher, though. Ace. He didn't have both boots on either. Just one. His other leg ended just below his knee.

Riley made the mistake of looking out the open door of the chopper at the whirling blade above, going around …

… and around …

… and around. He fell down into the spinning blade and couldn't get back out again.

Chapter Sixty-Nine

"Have you heard?"

The voice on the phone was so shrill it took Jessie a moment to realize it was Mama Ruth.

She didn't ask "heard what?"

"I just got home."

"They got hit. Last night, they got attacked. They were overrun."

"How do you know?"

"Jean Taggart got a call from Emily."

"Is that all you know — overrun? What does overrun even mean?"

"Might be overrun's a polite word for massacre."

Jessica dropped the receiver of the telephone. Didn't mean to drop it, but her fingers went numb and it slipped out of them and whacked down on the floor. She could hear a voice coming from it, but she didn't pick it back up.

Count on Mama Ruth to call a spade a spade. Anybody else would have pussy-footed around and hemmed and hawed, but Mama Ruth hit the bullseye with the first shot.

Then Jessica was on the back porch, leaning over the railing, vomiting violently. She didn't remember walking there, didn't know how long she'd been there, was only aware that the pit of her stomach was missing. Gone. It had dropped right out of her body into nothingness, leaving her so empty she could hear the wind whistling mournfully through it.

A car pulled up in the driveway and somebody got out and came running toward the house without even closing the door. Jessica could see the car, see that it was Peggy Benson, wanted to call out to her that she was out here, on the back porch. But she couldn't summon enough air to call out. And in a couple of minutes, Peggy came out the back door and found her there. Jessie turned around. They stood staring at each other.

The two of them had stood together behind Sherry Lynn Bennett at the send-off party when the guys were getting their pictures made. They'd both heard what Sherry said, pretended they didn't because to admit you heard it was to admit the truth of it and neither one of them could do that.

"They can't all come back. What are the odds that all of Charlie Company, all five platoons, will get called up and every one of them will return home unhurt? Which one of them will come home in a flag-draped box?"

Then Jessie and Peggy threw themselves into each other's arms and sobbed hysterically, sobbed so loud and so long it seemed like it would go on forever. Maybe it was ten minutes, maybe two hours. Jessie didn't know, before they pulled apart.

"Do you know …?" Jessie began.

"No, nothing. Far as I know, nobody's been told anything yet. The only thing I know is they was attacked and" — she sucked in a gasp but plowed on — "and there were lots of casualties. Wounded and … dead."

And Jessie knew she had to get to David's mother. Had to.

"I gotta go, Peg. Davie's mother's old and …" She let the rest dangle. "You'll call if …"

"I'll call if I hear anything. Anything at all."

Then Jessie was in the pickup truck. Couldn't start the engine quick enough. Spit gravel out behind the back tires and almost collided with the mailbox as she fishtailed out of the driveway. The road elongated in front of her, like the funhouse mirrors where you run and run to get closer but the distance never changes.

She had to get there.

She'd promised David.

And the shock of realization was the first reasonable thought she'd had since the phone call.

Yeah, she had to get there because she'd promised David she'd look in on his mother. But that wasn't the only reason. It might not even have been the most important reason. Jessie had to get to Ruth Monaghan because they were connected, she and the old woman. Through David. The connection was as delicate as the filament of a spider's web carried on the wind and as strong as the cables holding up a bridge.

She needed Ruth Monaghan.

And Ruth Monaghan needed her.

For the first time since the first day she'd shown up on Mama Ruth's porch to ask how she was doing, Jessie burst through the door without knocking.

The house was quiet and still and a cry for Mama Ruth died in Jessie's throat. She walked through the rooms until she found the old woman right where she'd expected to. In Davie's room.

She was sitting on the edge of his bed with her back to the door, cradling something in her arms like a baby, singing a song with no words and no melody. Suddenly, Jessie felt like an intruder, like she didn't belong here, like she was treading on … holy ground. This was a place only a mother could go. Not just this room, this place, but this space of terror too great to describe where Ruth Monaghan sat rocking the bundle in her arms. Jessie saw the foot then and knew. It was David's teddy bear.

Backing out of the room without speaking, she turned and left the house, got in her truck and went home. She climbed the stairs to the old double-wide trailer house slowly, like she was going to the gallows. She went inside and closed the front door and walked into their bedroom.

Standing in the doorway, Jessie glanced around. The picture on the wall of that log cabin they'd bought in some gift shop in Gatlinburg, Tennessee. It was an ugly picture. They hadn't bought it because it was pretty. They bought it because it looked just like the cabin they'd stayed in up in the woods, a hunting lodge that David had borrowed, where they had spent their wedding night.

She walked to the closet and ran her fingers over his shirts, ironed stiff, no wrinkles.

Then she picked up their wedding picture and sat down with it on the edge of the bed. This was *her* space, her holy ground, the space where she allowed herself to experience all the terror she had thought she had cried out of her in Peggy Benson's arms. She traced the outline of his smiling face in the picture and tried not to imagine that the man in that picture was … was no more.

That he was gone.

That's when she discovered terror was a magic pitcher.

No matter how much you pour out, it's always full.

Chapter Seventy

NATE WAS up in the hayloft, moving the hay around to cover up the spot where the floorboards had been stained red, when he heard somebody pull up into his driveway. Better not be the police, that Detective Booth Graham or Sheriff Gil. He'd done told them everything he intended to say. If they'd come to arrest him, charge him with killing that boy, they'd sure took their own sweet time ...

Then he saw LeRoy Taggart's black pickup truck, how LeRoy didn't get out right away and Nate knew.

He thought of Riley that day on Stedman Ridge when Willie Ray'd come looking for him. And Johnny coming into the kitchen out of breath when the revenuers had caught his pa.

Something's bad wrong.

Nate walked slowly to the loft ladder, climbed down it just as slowly. For a ridiculous moment, he thought about *running away!* About turning and bolting through the barn and out the back and up the hill into the trees.

Running away like a little kid.

But he wasn't a man who could entertain that kind of

break with reality and he was too gimpy to go running across the field. He'd trip and break his fool neck.

He walked out in the sunshine to where LeRoy had stopped in the driveway.

"LeRoy," he said, with a nod.

"It's a bad 'un. Don't nobody know yet how bad, but they was a battle last night and …" His chin quivered just a little bit but he kept his voice level. "Our boys got smacked hard. Way I hear it, wasn't just one or two of 'em hurt. There was a bunch of casualties, wounded and" — he lost it on the last word and had to whisper it" — killed."

"You know who—?"

"Don't nobody know. They ain't officially notified any family members. They's just the word from the armory." He said the words with no emotion at all, like he was reading the ingredients label on a bottle of Pepto-Bismol. "Charlie Company of the 151st Infantry Battalion of the Kentucky National Guard is no longer a viable fighting unit."

Viable?

Nate couldn't think what to say. He needed to sit down before he fell down. His knees felt like bags of water. But LeRoy here … he had *two* boys in harm's way. Was it harder for him, to worry about them both, or easier, because if one got killed he still had—

Stop it, Nate, Abby said in his head.

He stopped.

"You want a cup of coffee?"

"How would I know?" LeRoy said. "I don't know what I want. To piss off a bridge or dance on the head of a pin or—"

He stopped abruptly. Might be Jean was talking to him in his head, too, like Nate's Abby. But he didn't think so. Jean was still alive. At home, worrying about her boys.

"Thanks for the word," Nate said. "You best get home. Jean and the littles need you."

"To do what?" he asked nobody in particular. "Ain't a thing I can do 'bout any of this. I got two boys who was in a massacre last night and I don't know if … which …?"

Nate didn't know what else to do, so he reached in the truck window and patted LeRoy on the shoulder.

"You go on now. I'll let you know if I hear …"

Wasn't no sense in saying that. Of course he would. Everybody would. Soon's somebody heard, they'd pass the word. Wasn't a thing in the world to do until then.

LeRoy nodded once.

"Nate."

Nate nodded back.

"LeRoy."

Then LeRoy made a big turn in the driveway of Nate's house. He could see the barn from that turn, which was why Nate had made the sheriff and that state police detective back out to the road.

He stood and watched the truck until LeRoy was out of sight. Then just kept standing there. And why not? Might just stand right there in this spot until—

"Nate …" Abby said in his head.

He turned around and went back into the barn.

Chapter Seventy-One

THE CITIZENS of Callison County spent the whole weekend in closer contact than any of them had ever been in their lives. The phone lines almost melted.

Nobody knew anything concrete … so they made sure everybody knew that nobody knew anything.

And by unspoken agreement they were determined to quash rumors the instant they sprouted. If some awful word was put out and it was wrong, dozens of people would be devastated.

They suspected a good many of them were going to be devastated as soon as they heard the *truth*. The numbers were released first, given out in a formal military release from the Kentucky National Guard headquarters battalion.

It began: "Ten men from Charlie Company were killed on the night of July 5, 1969 in a battle with North Vietnamese forces at Fire Base Eagle's Nest. Five of those killed were Kentucky National Guardsmen. Five regular army soldiers who had been infused into the company were also killed. There was a total of fourteen wounded. An esti-mated fifty North Vietnamese were killed."

The official release stated that the 197th Field Artillery Brigade of the New Hampshire National Guard had suffered casualties as well and that the base "withstood about 150 RPGs and satchel charges and heavy fire from AK-47s. Three howitzers were destroyed, as was an ammu-nition storage area, nine bunkers, the mess hall, the dining tent, the maintenance area, four ammunition carriers, three two-and-a-half-ton trucks, two three-quarter-ton trucks and three jeeps."

Like anybody cared how many trucks were blown up!

What people wanted to know was how seriously had the wounded been hurt and where had they been taken.

And who'd been … killed.

The release concluded "Charlie Company of the 151st Infantry Battalion of the Kentucky National Guard is no longer a viable fighting unit."

The casualties remained a mystery until Monday morning.

Peggy Benson was the first. Sheriff Gil came to her door at nine o'clock with a telegram. Peggy had never gotten a telegram in her life.

"Your husband, Ronald Albert Benson, was wounded in action in Vietnam, July 5, when the artillery base called Eagle's Nest came under attack by a hostile force. He received second and third degree burns over ninety percent of his body. He has been placed on the very seriously ill list and in the judgment of the attending physician, his condi-tion is such that there is cause for concern that he might not survive."

Word spread.

"Burned. *Burned*!"

"Over ninety percent of his body."

"Might not survive."

The phrases echoed off the hillsides from hollow to hollow all through the knobs of Callison County like the reverberation from a gong in some Hindu monastery high in the mountains of Tibet.

When the hammer blows started to fall, they came horrifyingly fast.

Kenny Taylor's wife was coming downstairs later that morning. Melissa Taylor's identical twin daughters, born three days after the guard unit was activated, had kept her up all night. Family members were staying with her, and she thought she heard someone come to the door and she went to answer it.

Two men in uniform stood there. One was a chaplain and he informed her that her husband was dead.

So were Ben Higgs and Randy Nickel. And Caleb McAllister, who was in the Whiskey Run Platoon.

Two officers came to the door of the Taggart house later that morning.

As soon as Nate heard, he went there to … what? To be with LeRoy.

The house was full of crying women. Andy's young bride Emily sat uncomprehending in the front porch swing, cradling their baby daughter, Andrea. LeRoy was in the barn building something, or so it sounded to Nate as he approached. He could hear the steady, rhythmic stokes of a carpenter's hammer on a nail. He stepped into the shadowy interior of the building that smelled of manure and sawdust and stood at the door for a moment, watching. LeRoy was standing before a ten-foot piece of two-by-four, spread across three sawhorses. And he was pounding nails down into it. Big ones, ten-penny nails. One after another after another.

Nate made a little coughing sound so he wouldn't

startle LeRoy but apparently he was already aware of Nate's presence. Without looking up, he said:

"Ain't no word on Willie Ray." He was speaking around the nails he had put in his mouth, but he was easy to understand. He'd been talking with a mouthful of nails his whole life. "Not good or bad, just no word at all."

He took a nail out of his mouth, set the point on the two-by-four, and slammed the hammer down on it. It took him only three blows to drive the huge nail into the board. He stopped hammering then, removed the two remaining nails from his mouth and tuned to face Nate. There were tears running down his cheeks.

"They took Andy, though." He spoke words full of venom, but there was no change in his tone of voice. "Them Vi-et Cong took my boy. Killed him somewhere on the other side of the world. Way I see it, it was the gubmint killed him by sending him over there where he didn't have no business being in the first place."

He took a deep, shaky breath.

"Ain't heard nothing about Willie Ray, though. You … heard about Riley?"

Nate had not.

Everyone had been doing the math. The guard said five soldiers had been killed and five families had received death notifications. That left the fourteen wounded — and nobody knew who they were or how badly they'd been injured.

Then the death toll rose to six when Ronnie Benson died on the hospital ship in the Gulf of Tonkin. And the injured toll shrank to thirteen.

It rose again to seven, when Jude Boone died in a hospital in Germany, leaving twelve wounded.

As one family after another heard from or about their

sons, the fate of the other soldiers in the unit remained a mystery.

The word changed from "If you haven't heard, that means he survived," to "If you haven't heard, that means he's hurt."

It was sporadic. Sometimes three different next of kin were notified about the injuries to a particular soldier while other families waited, hoped and heard nothing. When several families turned to the Red Cross they got results almost immediately, though Nate hadn't yet gotten word from them.

Larry Bradshaw was in Bethesda Naval Hospital in Maryland. He had lost a leg.

Sam Finch was on the same hospital ship Ronnie Benson had been on. His condition was not known.

Jackson McClusky was in a hospital in Germany. He'd been burned.

Nate thought about calling Big-Un to say he was sorry about Jack and ask if they'd heard from him — several families had gotten telephone calls.

He thought about it, but didn't.

Chapter Seventy-Two

NATE FINALLY FOUND out about Riley — from Riley himself. The phone rang on July 9 and when he answered, the voice on the other end of the line said, "Hello, Papa. I'm okay."

Nate didn't break down but he was close. He wanted to ask a thousand questions but couldn't think of a thing to say.

Sputtering, he asked, "Where are you?"

"I'm in a hospital in Japan. I know everybody's been worried, so tell them I'm fine."

Fine? They don't take you to a hospital in Japan for fine. Whatever had happened, it was way worse than Riley wanted Nate to know.

How badly had he been injured? Couldn't be a life-threatening injury. The voice on the other end of the line didn't belong to somebody who was ... dying. But it could be a life-altering injury. Had maybe been burned, so there'd be scars. He recalled the horror of hearing about Kenny Taylor, burned over ninety percent of his body. No, it wasn't that bad. Maybe had a finger or toe blown off, though. Or a foot. And the leg with it. Or an arm?

"I'll write. I promise. But other guys are waiting for the phone, there's a line of them behind me stretching all the way down the hall. I have to hang up." There was a beat of silence. "I love you, Papa."

Nate didn't know if Riley heard the "I love you, too, Riley," before the receiver in his hand went dead.

THERE WAS no line of injured soldiers. The hall was empty. Riley sat in his wheelchair — alone. Just the way he wanted it. But there were battalions of nurses who would likely tackle him if he tried to get out of the wheelchair and walk from the phone back to his room. So he just signaled one of them, and communicated with hand motions. Most of the staff spoke English, but if you just made gestures, they tended to respond in kind ... which made it less likely he'd get trapped into a conversation. He didn't want to talk, not to anybody. Certainly not to anybody *Asian*. They all were suspect, he didn't trust a single one, never turned his back on them — nurses, order-lies, doctors, none of them. Yeah, okay fine, they were *Japanese*, not *Vietnamese*. Didn't matter, the reaction was automatic and he couldn't do anything about it and didn't have the emotional wherewithal to try.

He never spoke a single word that wasn't necessary to the doctors who poked and prodded him, asking him does this hurt and does that hurt, then scolding him for being stoic. One little Asian guy looked up at him and said, "You keep pretending this doesn't hurt" — just like he'd done with that knee so he could play basketball his senior year

— "you're going to get released before you're properly healed."

He would never be *healed*. Ever. But he surely did *not* want them to send him home while he was still bleeding!

Shrapnel had scraped all the skin off Riley's back. He overheard a doctor compare it to "ground beef." It had taken hours for surgeons to remove the fragments and they told him they hadn't gotten them all, that he'd be "picking pieces of metal" out of his back for months. Maybe for years. He's also suffered a severe laceration down his left thigh, from his groin to his knee. He hadn't asked how many stitches it'd taken to close it. He didn't care.

Those were the "*flesh* wounds," of course. The other wounds were far, far more serious. "Life-threatening." He'd heard that term tossed around a lot and thought "yeah, that." And he couldn't, absolutely could *not* go back to the world with *those* still bleeding, either.

Right now, he didn't want anything but to be left alone. He didn't want to talk. Didn't even want to think. Certainly didn't want to *remember*.

But when Albert Linsley, the older guy, regular Army, the driver on Gun Number Six came to visit — he was changing planes in Tokyo and had a layover — Riley found that he did, too, want to talk. Only to Al, though, just Al. Because Al reminded him of Papa. They talked about absolutely nothing — football and the carburetor on Riley's Ford Mustang, and whether those huge jugs hanging off Dolly Parton's chest were real or silicone. Al stayed for two hours and when he was gone, Riley couldn't have told you a thing the man said. But as Riley formed words and they came out to the end of his tongue and hopped out of his mouth, something began to loosen inside him.

After Al left, Riley took a firm hold on his own shoulders and gave himself a good shake. Not a snap-out-of-it shake. There was no such thing. But a get-on-with-it shake. He'd come to understand something during that conversation, something the two battle-weary soldiers never said a word about. And yet they did. With their eyes. *That* night, *that* battle, *that* horror was *all* they talked about with their eyes. And in that wordless conversation, Albert Linsley confirmed for Riley Hannacker a hard, immutable truth. Riley would *never* get over what happened, what he'd seen and lived through. It was impossible. Al hadn't and he didn't have a scratch on him anywhere ... anywhere you could see. All Riley *could* do now, what he *had to* do was put one foot in front of the other. He had to keep on keeping on.

When Riley had first come to, he'd scrambled to untangle it all, to figure it out, to fit the broken pieces of the puzzle together so there was a complete picture of what happened before the nothingness took him. Riley's concussion certainly wasn't the worst of his injuries, but the little Asian doctor said that a concussive blow could, and very often did, wipe out the memories of what had happened right before the injury and for a time after it. Sometimes those memories came back in a week, a month, a year. Sometimes they never did.

He and Al did talk about what happened earlier that day, before the battle, when Riley, Ben Higgs and Davie Monaghan had watched Jackson McClusky kill a civilian — okay, it was an accident, but it had still been his fault the man had been burned alive. The story had spread across Eagle's Nest before the battle faster than a grass fire. No one had any trouble believing Jackson had done such a thing.

"He knows he skated on that one." Al shook his head in disgust. "That Higgs boy and Sergeant Labronski are dead and your head injury makes 'them crazy charges' you 'made up' about him suspect. Comes down to your word against his."

Riley's word and the word of David Monaghan.

But Davie had no words. Davie lay pale against the white sheets, perfectly still. His room was up on the fifth floor in a ward with ... others lying perfectly still. Riley'd only visited once and couldn't make himself go back. What was the point?

Chapter Seventy-Three

Nate was so anxious to see Riley that he couldn't keep his foot off the accelerator. He'd be going the speed limit and then look down and he was doing eighty.

At the same time, he was so reluctant to face Riley — what could he say? — that he'd find himself driving slower and slower. He'd notice that then, and speed up.

He didn't have any idea how fast he'd been traveling when he saw the revolving blue lights appear in the rearview mirror.

Abby would have covered her ears at the obscenities he spit out. He didn't have *time* right now to get a ticket. He considered making a break for it — this guy wouldn't be the first law enforcement officer a Hannacker had outrun. Unfortunately, this pickup wouldn't win a race with a one-legged chicken.

He pulled over to the side of the road and stopped in a cloud of dust.

It wasn't a gray-uniformed Kentucky State Policeman with the ridiculous pointy hat. It was a county mounty —

uniform two ugly shades of brown but at least the hat was reasonable. A sheriff's deputy from Nelson County.

"I just clocked your vehicle going 77 miles per hour in a 55-mile-per-hour zone and you sped up after I pulled out." The officer's eyes were flicking over the front seat and floorboard while he stood there. Nate kept his hands on the steering wheel. "I need to see your license, title and registration slip."

Nate yanked his wallet out of his pocket, pulled out the license and shoved it at the officer.

"What's your hurry Mister" — the officer read off the license — "Mr. Hannacker?"

Nate found himself babbling.

"I'm going to Ft. Knox. To the hospital there. My boy, my grandson, he was injured in Vietnam" — the officer's head snapped up — "and he's been in a hospital in Japan. They just brought him home today."

"He with the guard unit that got called up, the one that …?"

Nobody wanted to use the word massacred, but what else fit?

"Yes. Riley Hannacker. Please, just give me the ticket so I can—"

"You wait here, Mr. Hannacker."

He strode with purpose back to his cruiser — taking Nate's driver's license with him! He opened the door, but didn't get in, just leaned in and picked up something — the microphone on his radio. He looked at Nate's driver's license as he spoke and then came immediately back to Nate's car.

He handed Nate his driver's license and tipped his hat.

"If you'll please pull in behind me, Mr. Hannacker, sir, I'll give you an escort to the base."

Nate was so stupefied he just sat holding his driver's license while the deputy sheriff's car pulled out onto the road in front of him. Then he dropped his license into his shirt pocket and pulled in behind it.

The blue flashing lights came on. Then the siren.

And away they went. Oh, they weren't flying, weren't blowing nobody's doors off, but they weren't going the speed limit either.

A few minutes later, Nate looked into his rearview mirror and saw a car approaching fast behind him. He didn't even know what it was until a second deputy sheriff turned on his lights as he pulled in behind Nate. Then he flipped on his siren.

A third sheriff's deputy car pulled off a side road when they passed and fell in behind that one, lights flashing. Siren wailing.

Nate could only see the three deputies' vehicles behind him, nothing farther back, so he didn't see it coming when a gray Kentucky State Police cruiser suddenly appeared out of nowhere and blew by them like they were standing still. It slowed and pulled over in front of the first deputy's car in front.

Turned on the lights and the siren.

There were cars pulled off on both sides of the road when they passed, people sitting in them watching as the little parade flew by. All them sirens, you coulda heard them ten miles out.

The two police cars in front drove past the front entrance of the military base and pulled off the road just beyond it.

Nate waved as he turned in but he didn't know if they saw.

"State your name and your business, sir," said the

starched and pressed young soldier at the gate. They weren't fooling around. Two soldiers stood at attention in front of the gate, and when it opened, two others appeared behind. They all had rifles in their hands.

Nate had his driver's license handy, right there in his shirt pocket. He pulled it out and handed it to the soldier. "My name is Nathaniel Hannacker and I'm here to see my grandson, Riley Hannacker." He realized he should have identified Riley in proper, military terms … that PFC first class thing … He couldn't remember it. "He's in the hospital. They just flew him in from Japan. I called ahead. My name oughta be on some kind of list somewhere. They said it would be. The lady I talked to said you'd give me a pass."

The officer stepped into the guard shack and ran his finger down the paper on a clipboard hanging from a nail by the door. He reached to the counter inside and picked up the top one off a stack of laminated signs. There were two stacks. Blue ones and red ones. There were only a couple of red ones, and the officer handed one of them to Nate — "Visitor Pass. VIP." — and told him it would allow him to park in any lot on the base, to put it on the dashboard of the truck where it could be seen from the outside. When the soldier handed back Nathaniel's driver's license, he cocked his chin toward the road.

"What's all that about?"

Nate turned to look.

Nine law enforcement vehicles were lined up beside the road on both sides of the front gate. There were five deputy sheriff cars, three from Nelson County, one from Hardin County and one from Bullitt County — Nate didn't know when they had shown up, or when the second Kentucky State Police cruiser, the Bardstown City Police and the Shepherdsville City Police cars had joined the parade. All the vehicles had their blue or red lights flashing. Officers stood in a line beside the cars. Some of the cars musta had more than one officer because it looked like there were more than a dozen of them. They all were facing Nate's pickup, standing ramrod straight. And they had their hats off.

Chapter Seventy-Four

Nate walked into Riley's hospital room and thought he might burst into tears. The young man lying in the bed there looked so pale and thin. And so young. He'd wondered in the elevator what he would say. What did you say to somebody who'd been to hell and barely managed to crawl out alive, leaving a lot of buddies behind who didn't make it out?

He needn't have worried. When Riley looked up and saw him, his gaunt, haggard face lit up with a smile and he opened his arms and cried "Papa!"

Nate hugged him tight, held the hug overlong.

That was all the ice that needed to be broken between them. Of course, there were things Nate was careful not to say, was sure there were a ton of things Riley was careful not to say, too. Was likely learning how to tamp them permanently down somewhere deep, things he'd never say to anybody.

Nate understood that. He would never tell the boy about the battle he'd fought on their own farm while Riley was fighting for his life on the other side of the world. Some secrets needed to stay buried with the dead.

But he did tell him what had happened to him on his way to the hospital that morning and Riley listened with growing astonishment.

"*Seriously?*" The boy was incredulous. "For a Hannacker!"

Nate made an X sign over his heart. "If I'm lyin' I'm dyin'." He paused. "But I have had a couple of brushes with the law in the past few weeks that weren't so cordial as that, even spent the night as a guest of Callison County in one of their choicest suites, had a terrific view of Main Street … well, except for the bars."

"You were in jail?"

"Yup."

"What for?"

"Terroristic threatening and accomplice to assault in the second degree … or maybe the third. 'Parently there are degrees of beating the crap out of somebody but I can't keep them straight."

"Who'd you beat up? And why?"

"I wasn't the one doing the beating. Doesn't matter, though, because the guy changed his mind and dropped the charges. Mighty thoughtful of him, that was."

"Aw, come on, tell me."

"It's a long story — some night on the porch I'll tell you the whole thing, blow by blow. The man we locked horns with was none other than the M&M guy from the top of the knob."

"Oliver Morris?"

"The same."

"Who's 'we'?"

"Me and my partner in crime, my cellmate … Big-Un McClusky."

Nate expected Riley to be surprised, to disapprove. He didn't expect him to be horrified — and furious.

"Jackson's daddy."

He said the name Jackson as if it tasted like vomit on his tongue.

"I'd be careful about partnering up with a McClusky if I were you. You could get … *burned* bad."

Clearly Nate had stepped on a landmine.

"Had a run-in with Jackson, did you?"

"You could call it that."

Nate was quiet for half a minute, then said softly, "I'm sure you ain't heard, but Parker McClusky disappeared. His boy Shep was killed in a car wreck, you know, and after that, Parker was just … gone. They've looked and looked but can't nobody find him anywhere." He caught Riley's gaze and held it. "He just …" — Nate whispered the last word — "… *vanished*."

Understanding passed between them. There was a hardness in Riley's voice when he spoke again that Nate had never heard there before. "Them folks need to be real careful or the same thing's gonna happen to Jackson one of these days."

Silence swelled between them.

Finally, Nate spoke, hauled sunlight and cheer back into the room in heavy sacks on his back.

"When can I spring you out of here, take you home and put some meat on those bones?"

"What, did you learn to cook while I was gone?"

"Pizza Hut delivers."

The cute little nurse with the turned-up nose stuck her head into the room and said, "Time to go, Mr. Hannacker." Nate must have looked like she'd kicked him in the belly, because she added, "But you can come back tomorrow. Won't be long before we kick him out of here and you can take him home with you."

He hugged Riley, felt how bony his neck was, and went to the door of his room, then turned back.

"Want some doughnuts?" Riley loved doughnuts.

"Sure!"

"I'll bring a dozen when I come back tomorrow and you can eat every one in the box." He stood in the doorway for a heartbeat. "I love you, Riley," then turned and left.

Chapter Seventy-Five

JESSIE KNEW she needed to get the doctor to write it all down. Then she could take it somewhere, to a library or somewhere like that, and get a book and look up all the words she didn't understand. Why did doctors always talk in medical-speak, using big words normal people couldn't pronounce without practicing in front of a mirror? Like their patients had been sitting right alongside them in those medical school classes, taking notes.

She looked down at Davie, lying on a hospital bed with her and Mama Ruth on one side and the two doctors on the other. She was seized by an almost uncontrollable urge to lean over and whisper in his ear, "Did you understand a word that man just said?" And Davie would whisper back, "Nope, not a single one." Then he'd wink at her.

But you had to open your eyes to wink. Davie's eyes were closed. He hadn't opened them. Yet. Davie hadn't opened his eyes *yet.*

Jessie just wanted them all to go away and leave her and Davie alone. So she could talk to him, really concentrate on what she was saying instead of babbling and crying and sounding like the kind of hysterical woman that made Davie cringe. Oh, he had sympathy for people who were hurting, crying because their hearts had been broken. He cared. But right now, she didn't want him to *have to* care, to have to *do* anything. She didn't want him to have to give sympathy. Or *open his eyes* because they all wanted him to. Or *wake up*. Jessie wanted to do *for* Davie, to give *to* Davie. Not take *from* him.

Might be right now Davie was down inside himself somewhere, the place he'd gone to escape the awful, waiting for them all to stop pestering him. To let him be. He'd open his eyes, he'd wake up when he was good and ready to, and all their demands on him were just wearing him out.

He needed the time and space and love to recover at his own rate. That's what the first doctor had said, the one who'd explained what "closed-head" injury actually meant.

"The brain isn't squeezed tight into the skull, jammed in there like a fat woman into a corset."

Jessie'd liked him when he said that. She figured a man who'd say a thing like that at a time like that was someone who could be trusted to tell you the truth.

The parade of other doctors had said variations of the same thing. She had lost track of exactly how many there had been since she'd stood frozen in a doorway sometime in July, she didn't know anymore exactly when it had been. It was a doorway in … some hospital, somewhere. It was when she'd seen for herself that it was true — David had kept his promise. He really didn't have a mark on him. No wounds at all except the one you couldn't see. But all the doctors had said the injury to his brain that you couldn't see was severe. David's brain had been hurt very badly.

They said the injury had been caused by a concussive

force, an explosion of some kind in a small space, that had literally banged his brain into the sides of his own skull.

The banging around itself had caused damage.

The bleeding afterward had caused more damage. The subsequent swelling had caused more damage still.

That doctor was the one who'd first told her, "Don't believe anybody who tells you they are certain that your husband will never come out of this coma. That his brain has been so badly injured it won't ever function properly again. Don't believe that. Nobody knows *for certain*. The human body is an amazing thing, capable of healing itself in ways we don't understand."

That had been Doctor Rik. He'd said to call him that, explained that with a last name like Deadrik, he'd rather be called Doctor Rik than Doctor Dead.

He'd passed through David's room several times, one of the horses on the merry-go-round of medical people, but he wasn't like the two doctors speaking now — Tweedledum and Tweedledee. He had used words you could understand. Made it simple. Didn't sugar-coat reality, but didn't slam the door on all hope, either.

"Is it *likely* that your husband will recover?" he'd said. "No, I'm sorry, but it's not. A complete and full recovery from a brain injured this bad almost never happens. But is it *possible* your husband will recover? Yes, Mrs. Monaghan, it is possible."

One of the doctors on the other side of the bed — the short, bald one with the ridiculous Hitler mustache stuck under his nose like a postage stamp — was looking at her strangely. She realized he must have said something specifically to her or asked a question or something and she had not responded appropriately. She'd been doing a lot of inappropriate responding lately.

"I'm sorry, what did you say again?"

"I said there is nothing further we can do for him. His condition is stable. Beyond that, there is no treatment."

"I can recommend nursing care facilities in your area that care for PVS patients," the other doctor said and Jessie cringed. PVS stood for Persistent *Vegetative* State. Jessie had never in her life heard a term more demeaning, but most of these doctors tossed the term around like a big red ball at the beach. Dr. Rik had patiently explained the difference between PVS, a coma, and brain death.

"PVS and coma are about duration, but otherwise they are essentially the same thing — a deep state of unconsciousness. A coma rarely lasts more than two to four weeks." When the doctor had said that, David had not gone beyond the "about a month" definition of a coma. He'd passed that now, though. "PVS can last for years." Which was the good news, as much as anything could be good, because "brain *death* was permanent, absolute and irreversible." Davie's brain was *not* dead.

"Would you like for me to give you a list?" the doctor asked.

"A list of what?"

"Of nursing care facilities in your area that offer care for ..."

Like they could afford a "private nursing care facility!" There was only one option open to them for a nursing care facility — the VA Hospital. She'd been there once years ago. It was an indescribable horror.

It finally occurred to Jessie where this conversation was going. They were being kicked out. The we-can't-do-anything-for-your-husband was medical-speak for "he's taking up bed space here we need for patients we *can* do something for."

Mama Ruth had been quicker on the uptake than Jessie. The old woman seldom said anything anymore to the medical personnel, just stood, listened and nodded. She wasn't speaking to the doctors now, though. She touched Jessie's arm and when Jessie turned to her she said, "It's time now. You and me need to take our boy home."

Jessie moved into Mama Ruth's house so the two of them could look after Davie. They put a hospital bed and other medical equipment for him in the "parlor" of the old house and made it into Davie's room.

Jessie *and* Magic moved in.

The dog could have been a problem, but Jessie wouldn't let it be. Mama Ruth hadn't even known Jessie had a dog until the day they brought Davie home. His mother had ridden with him in the ambulance from the hospital in Ft. Campbell, and when it pulled up in front of her house, Jessie and Magic met her at the door.

"What's that dog doin' in my house?"

"His name's Magic. He's my dog."

Magic had grown far bigger than Jessie ever thought he would. No way to know, he was just a mutt, but as she recalled, the black dog she'd shot that day on the side of the road had been a fairly small dog.

Magic was huge. Had to have a German Shepherd heritage, maybe mixed with some kind of mastiff. Or might be Great Dane, though he was dense and compact, not leggy. He weighed 150 pounds if he weighed an ounce. And without her "Magic" Jessie might not have made it through those first days, the time it was all settling in.

Seemed like the dog quit being a puppy then, though he wasn't even a year old. Over the course of less than a week, he stopped being playful, clumsy, knocking things over and chewing up her shoes. Just stopped doing it. He never left Jessie's side, was there when she'd suddenly collapse on the floor in tears and she'd cling to him and sob into his black fur.

He'd stood beside her while Mama Ruth yelled, looking from Jessie to the screaming woman and back to Jessie like he was watching a tennis match.

"You get that mongrel outta here right now. Animals b'long outside — not leaving fur all over my furniture. Ain't gonna have no wolf in my house ... looks like he could bite your leg plum off in one gulp—"

"No," Jessie said. Quiet. Firm. Uncompromising. "Magic stays. He's my dog ... and Davie's."

While Mama Ruth stood on the front porch yelling at Jessie, the two soldier orderlies had unloaded the gurney from the back of the ambulance, rolled it into the house and settled Davie in the bed. They went back out to the ambulance and the EMT came in behind them to check Davie's vital signs, to make sure he was stable before they left.

"Uh ma'am," the EMT called out. "The dog ..."

Jessie and Mama Ruth rushed into the living room to find Magic beside Davie's bed — *between* Davie and the EMT. His teeth were bared and he was growling softly.

"You wanna call him off?" the EMT said. "He won't let me get near the bed. Every time I try, he looks like he's about to bite off my leg."

"... in one gulp," Mama Ruth said.

She left the room then and never said another word about Magic. The dog slept under Davie's bed. Sometimes, when Jessie came into the room, she'd find the dog licking Davie's limp hand.

Chapter Seventy-Six

RILEY THOUGHT he caught a whiff of Shangri-La, the perfume Sherry Lynn always—

He opened his eyes and she was standing in the doorway.

A flash of irritation washed over him. Riley wished she'd called before she came. Looking up and seeing her was … jarring. Okay, admit it — not altogether pleasant. He realized that she hadn't been going through the stuff he had in the seven months since he'd last seen her. Oh, not the war, internal stuff. The withdrawing you do as you let go of someone. Before you break up. Sherry Lynn was obviously right where she'd been when he shipped out, like one of those monkeys banging cymbals together and you take the battery out. Soon as you put it back in, the monkey takes up right where it left off.

He really ought to try to get back there emotionally, too, the best he could. That's where he needed to be. At that time, he hadn't made the decision to break up … oh, yes, he had, he just hadn't told himself about it yet. He'd been coasting, comfortable in a pleasant, fun relationship that was just cruising along, going nowhere in particular, costing him nothing.

Note to self: get the nurses to refuse visitors unless they've called in advance.

"Riley?"

There was so much emotion packed into that single word, it must have weighed a ton.

Care/concern/sympathy.

Anxiety/relief/joy.

Uncertainty/awkwardness/uneasiness.

With fear dripping down the sides like hot chocolate on a melting sundae.

What was she afraid of — that he'd found somebody else? In the jungle?

She didn't even know what a boom-boom girl was and he only had the vaguest of notions.

He didn't call out her name, didn't want the greeting to be like some movie where the heroine rushes into the hero's arms and he kisses her passionately.

So he pointed to the chair beside the bed. "Sit down … don't just stand there. It's so good to see you."

So much for not sounding like a movie. He sounded like he'd read the whole thing off a cue card.

She rushed into the room and perched on the edge of the chair like a bird on a telephone wire. She didn't look good. She'd put on weight, looked like a lot, but it was hard to tell in that lacy blouse that flowed around her. It wasn't just that, though. Her face was drawn and worn, her skin sallow. Her hair didn't even have its normal shine.

"Tell me how you've been." Best he could do.

"Why didn't you write?" She bleated out the words like a little kid about to cry.

"I did write!"

"Three letters! *Three* letters in *seven* months!"

He didn't need somebody on his case right now, flat out did not.

"Sorry. I'll do better the next time I go to war."

That had sounded harsh, had come out more unkind than he'd meant.

He smiled and reached out to her and she leapt up — probably to kiss him but she settled for taking his offered hand.

"What's going on around here? I haven't had much news about home."

"That's something you say to your cousin who comes back from summer camp. Didn't you *miss* me?"

"Of course I missed you."

"Then act like it!"

"I'm sorry." What did he have to apologize for? He'd been *busy*!

He wasn't expecting her to grab him in a hug but she did, a strangle-hold. It pulled at the wounds on his back — not as bad as Papa's hug, but he hadn't minded that. He did mind this, and gave a grunt of more pain than he felt.

She let go, stepped back, and the floodgates opened. She poured out a stream-of-consciousness babble that only barely made sense.

"I didn't mean to hurt you. I'd never hurt you. I don't ever want to cause you pain because I know what it's been like for you, fighting in the jungle."

Probably not.

"And then coming home and the others — some of them didn't."

He felt the doors of his soul begin to slam shut. Bang! Bang! Bang! She wasn't self-aware enough to see it, though, was too caught up in her own emotion to pay any attention to his. That made him mad.

"But it's all over now, you're home, everything will be wonderful now, I'll make you so happy you'll forget all about the war."

Maybe she saw then. Or maybe she just finally ran into her own wall. She stepped back, literally as well as figuratively, and took a breath.

"What an incredibly shallow thing to say. Somebody needs to slap me."

And *that* sounded like his Sherry Lynn, a good, loving person — with a sense of humor. Not some hysterical teenager.

"Can I have a do-over?"

He smiled.

"I won't need long to get my foot out of my mouth; you got a tire iron I could borrow?"

The smile he gave her then was warm and genuine.

"If I could make a movie of seeing you for the first time after all that's happened, what you just saw is everything that would wind up on the cutting room floor."

"Hey, it's okay," he said and meant it. "We're all nuts. Some of us way nuts, some not so much. But there's going to be a lot of readjustment going on."

He took her hand and didn't mind the physical contact now. Sherry Lynn had left the building, but now she was back. His girl *friend* had returned.

"We'll just take it slow and easy and—"

"Easy works. I'm in for easy. But slow … not so much. Slow's not an option."

She looked into his eyes and he saw such desolation in hers it broke his heart. She blinked and tears streamed down her cheeks. She kept her eyes squeezed tight shut as she spoke and her words were measured and deliberate. She sounded so very, very sad.

"Riley, I'm pregnant. It's yours. That last night in the car when we … the baby is due in September. You *have to* marry me. Now. *Right now.*"

Chapter Seventy-Seven

A COMMUNITY-WIDE MEMORIAL service for the Callison County soldiers who'd been killed in the Eagle's Nest battle was conducted in August at Saint Augustine Catholic Church in Brewster. White crosses stood sentinel in the area in front of the altar. Each had a name printed on the crossbar, a helmet on top and dog tags dangling.

Andrew Taggart

Ben Higgs

Kenny Taylor

Ronnie Benson

Jude Boone

Caleb McAllister

Randy Nickel

Randy's mother'd had a small piece of metal, a miniature dog tag engraved with the name *Tommy* and it hung on Randy's cross.

There had been individual funerals, of course, staged one after another on a schedule reminiscent of the weddings less than a year before.

Willie Ray Taggart had returned for his brother Andy's

funeral, uninjured except for a jagged gash across his cheek that extended from the corner of his right eye to his chin. He should have returned to the unit to serve the remainder of his enlistment, but he was in no emotional condition to serve out the rest of his enlistment and certainly not to rejoin the fighting in Vietnam.

He received a medical discharge after he spent three months in the Bethesda Naval Hospital in Washington D.C., in the psychiatric ward.

Riley Hannacker and Sherry Lynn Bennett got married while he was still in the hospital at Ft. Knox. The circumstances didn't matter. Any kind of festive celebration of life would have been unthinkable. Their son was born the last week in September, small but perfect. They named him Nathaniel Andrew Hannacker, planned to call him Drew. When Riley was released from the hospital, he moved his little family into the house with his grandfather.

The Christmas of 1969 was grim. The families who'd lost sons/brothers/husbands and fathers were still shell-shocked. The families whose loved ones had survived could not celebrate their good fortune, not when so many others were hurting. The families with injured loved ones concentrated on getting by, one day at a time, while their boys' damaged bodies and ravaged minds struggled to mend.

The Hannackers put up their traditional tree on Christmas Eve, after Riley spent the afternoon untangling the Christmas lights, and they decorated it with all the family ornaments — with one addition. Nate got Drew a Baby's First Christmas ornament at the Hallmark Store in Bardstown.

Sherry Lynn took the baby to the big Christmas gathering of her mother's family — the McCluskys — alone. Riley stayed home. Jackson would be there and Riley refused to be in the same room with him.

In early January, 1970, the remaining members of Charlie Company of the 151st Infantry Battalion, Kentucky National Guard returned to the United States. The guard members were trucked to the armory in Bardstown and dismissed on 30-day leaves. With their year of active service complete, they would all cycle out to put their lives back together.

That January was the coldest in Kentucky history. Snow fell the week the unit was deactivated, white drifting down from a dead gray sky onto the quiet crowd of people who'd gathered at the armory to welcome the boys home.

Spring wrestled winter the whole month of April and didn't win until the first week of May, when the trees seemed to bud overnight and the crocuses pushed their determined noses up out of the cold ground.

May was planting time on the farms of Callison County.

~

NATE AND RILEY sat together on the front porch the evening before the Kentucky Derby. The Run for the Roses had been conducted the first Saturday in May for the past ninety-six years.

Today had been a beautiful day for a different horse race at Churchill Downs — the Kentucky Oaks. The traditional race for fillies was always held every year on the Friday before the Derby. The thoroughbreds had run beneath a bright blue sky with the smell of azaleas on the breeze. Tomorrow promised to be just as inviting.

Riley cocked his ear, and listened. The only sound was the crickets in the grass and the tree frogs out in the darkness. Drew had been fussy all day, but it appeared Sherry Lynn had finally gotten the baby quieted.

"I've been thinking about that piece of bottom land," he said.

Nate was lighting his cigarette and he looked up, surprised. "You have? What have you been thinking about it?"

Riley and his grandfather had talked a lot about the future. It was a whole lot easier to talk about than the past. They talked about the Hannacker farm, planned to put all their efforts into it, intended to work hard to grow the business.

Nate hadn't talked much about the venture he'd been involved in with a silent partner while Riley was away, just said the money he'd made was five times what he'd been making with moonshine and bootlegging, "a boatload of cash." It was enough to pay for new equipment to expand, to buy livestock to replace what'd been lost — enlarge the herd.

Riley hadn't gone back to his job at the cooperage and didn't intend to. He had a wife and child to support now, and he needed full-time employment. Farming was what he knew. And he had plans. Big plans.

"That field is the perfect place," he said.

His grandfather barked out a laugh.

"That field ain't the perfect place for nothing."

That's why Nate had given it to Riley, a piece of land where he could try his hand at his own burley crop last year. The field was down on the back of the farm, hemmed in by woods on three sides and no proper road leading to it. It had been nearly impossible to get the tractor and tobacco-setter back there.

Riley looked out into the cricket-warm darkness, watched the fireflies blinking on and off. And remembered.

"Actually, it *is* the perfect place for what I plan to grow there."

"And what's that?"

Riley turned to his grandfather and said the word quietly.

"Marijuana."

❧

IT WAS DARK. Willie Ray Taggart was drunk. He stayed drunk a considerable amount of the time now, but today he'd had the excuse of celebrating the Kentucky Oaks. And tomorrow he'd have the excuse of the Kentucky Derby.

He shouldn't have gone home, though, seen his little brother Zeke on the tractor, getting that field behind the barn ready for planting. That's where Willie Ray had planned to grow it, in that field. Watching Zeke plow up the dirt had got him to thinking …

Thinking was not a good thing, oh my no. Willie Ray reached up and touched the silver line of scar that slashed across his face. Not a good thing at all.

And he shouldn't have come here. But he couldn't help it. He had to talk to Andy and where else could he go?

He put his arm around the white cross he was leaned against, like putting his arm around a buddy. Around his brother. Like he'd done that day when they'd stacked hands.

That was the last time he'd ever hugged Andy.

His spinning mind slowed, the blurred images cleared. He could see Andy. As he had looked *that* day, not later, after …

He saw Andy's blond hair — the tropical sun would have bleached it out totally white if he'd ever taken his helmet off. Riley'd put his hand on top of Willie Ray's, said he'd stack on it if he got to bat first, but Andy'd wiggled out of Willie Ray's hug, didn't join in the pledge.

"Tell you what, little brother, you raise enough weed for both of us."

That's what Andy'd said. And Willie Ray had said he would. He had promised he would.

He reached up and wiped the wet off his cheeks. He straightened and patted the cross.

"I promised, bro." Willie Ray's words were slurred, but his voice was firm. His voice was *strong.* "I promised and a promise is a promise."

Chapter Seventy-Eight

JESSIE HAD TAKEN to spending time in the tobacco barn. Whenever she could grab a few spare minutes, she'd get in the truck and go there. She didn't really have time today. Tomorrow was Derby Day and most Kentucky businesses were closed the Friday before it for the running of the Kentucky Oaks. A day off meant Jessie had to jam into it all the things she couldn't do while working full-time at Tanner, McClusky and Fowler Law firm and looking after Davie at night.

And farming. It was springtime, and Jessie had a farm to run. *Three* full-time jobs. Jessie didn't care. She'd happily have worked a dozen full-time jobs to earn enough money to get Davie the care he needed. Physical therapy for his muscles that were shrinking, atrophying before her eyes and around-the-clock nursing care to save his mother's life. Mama Ruth was working herself to death. Jessie was young and strong. Mama Ruth wasn't. At the pace the old woman was going now, Ruth Monaghan wouldn't last a year. She looked worse every day. The old woman had lost weight, was pale and drawn. Jessie knew that there were times during the day when Mama Ruth wasn't tracking, maybe didn't quite know what was going on, where she was or what she was doing. No telling what she might do, or *not* do, during those times. And Davie's life was in her hands.

Jessie had to provide some other daytime care for her husband. Had to find the money somewhere.

Her "shift" caring for Davie started after she cooked supper for her and Mama Ruth. Yeah, she cooked for Mama Ruth. Black humor. She'd gotten downright domesticated, as a matter of fact — had taken up *knitting.* There was a recliner in the parlor they'd made into Davie's room, in arm's reach of the bed. Jessie could "sit with him," but still doze, get a few hours of sleep at night. When she was awake, she needed something to do with her hands, so Mama Ruth had shown her how to knit. She wasn't making anything, just knitted a single long strand of yarn, though Mama Ruth said she was going to take the strand, stitch it together into a quilt or something. Jessie didn't care.

She preferred nights to days. At night, there was no danger that she'd be interrupted by one of Davie's sisters, stopping by — to see *him,* not their mother — or one of a small band of conscientious, loyal souls who helped Ruth Monaghan care for her wounded son. Jessie didn't want anyone to find her sobbing hysterically. At night, she could stare at David, talk to him nonstop, babble as if he could hear her. And maybe he could. *Maybe he could.* Tell him how much she loved him, say the intimate things you couldn't say in the daylight.

Today was special, though. She had said nothing about it to Mama Ruth, but she'd asked Davie's oldest sister, Sharon, to fix dinner for her mother. Then, she had rushed around doing all the tasks on her monstrous to-do list, struggling to finish so she could have time to herself in the tobacco barn. Time for her and Davie.

Yesterday, when she'd gone to the mailbox she'd found a letter from Davie. It was a good thing she was on her way to work and didn't have to face Mama Ruth for a while. She saw the letter and totally lost it. When she got herself together again, she went to the little convenience store at the bottom of the hill, called in and said she'd be late for work, then sat in her car and read the letter over and over and over. The missing letter, the one she knew was out there somewhere, had finally arrived. More than ten months late, but it *had* arrived. Jessica Monaghan would have sworn she didn't have a tear left anywhere in her to cry, but she had sobbed.

Now, she parked the pickup truck in front of the tobacco barn, got out and walked slowly toward the open doors.

Ghostly images flitted around in the shadows beyond, voices whispered on the wind.

DAVID EXTENDS *the cup to her. "More water, woman. Chop, chop." She merely lifts an eyebrow and looks at him and he amends, "Chop, chop, pleeeeease."*

When she starts for the door, he slaps her soundly on the butt.

"You'll pay for that!"

"Riiiight."

She turns back to him. "Go ahead, underestimate me. That'll be fun."

SHE STEPPED into the empty barn that smelled of burley and machinery, wandered around, touching things and remembering. Then she went back out to the truck and climbed up into the bed of it. That gave her a view over the huge field that was waiting for the seedlings to be put into a tobacco setter and placed one by one in the dark earth. She leaned back on the top of the cab and thought about the magic carpet that had carried the two of them out into the future.

"I promise I will come home — without a mark on me. And the two of us will have a long life together. Trust me, we will. Trust me."

She pulled the fully memorized letter out of her shirt pocket and held it in front of her in the fading sunlight.

In his perfect handwriting Davie told her about the evening he had sat around a campfire in the middle of a jungle, dreaming of the future.

"... somebody somewhere is growing the marijuana Ace is selling. Some farmer. Riley's grandfather grew hundreds of acres of hemp during the war — it's the same thing."

It was illegal, he said. And he didn't care. It was a mindset Jessie understood — had never agreed with, but understood.

"What else could we grow that sells for five bucks, maybe ten for a sandwich bag full? I think this is it, honey, our ticket to a house of our own, a farm of our own, a place to raise our kids."

Her eyes blurred with tears.

"... truth is, I have to do this. I stacked hands with Riley and Willie Ray and they'll kick me off the tee ball team if I renege."

Looking out over the barren field, she wiped the tears away. Jessica Monaghan had no idea how to grow marijuana, had never even seen any. But she'd figure it out.

That night, she sat beside Davie's bed, her mind occupied and spinning as her fingers worked the strand of yarn.

"Woof!"

Jessie looked up from her knitting. Magic had been asleep under Davie's bed, but now he was sitting beside it. He almost never barked.

"Woof!"

Then he cocked his head to the side.

"Oh, no, no, no you don't," she told the big black dog, laughing. "I know the drill — yap, head cock, snuggle. You're too big to sit in my lap now."

But he didn't try to climb up into her lap. Instead, he turned, rose up on his hind legs and put his big paws on the side of the bed. He leaned his head down and licked Davie's hand.

Jessie looked past the dog to Davie's face.

She froze, stopped breathing.

Davie's eyes were *open*.

THE END

The Hannackers and the McCluskys have been enemies for generations. Now that the cash crop of choice for both is marijuana, the stakes have risen – and Riley Hannacker joins other Vietnam vets from Callison County to form a marijuana-growing co-op called the Cornbread Mafia.

Get Blowin' Up A Storm today.

A Note from the Author

Thank you for reading *Fire In The Hole*.

If you enjoyed this book, please consider writing a review on your favorite bookselling site so other readers might enjoy it too. Just a couple of sentences would mean a lot to me.

Thank you!

Ninie Hammon

About the Author

Ninie Hammon (rhymes with shiny, not skinny) grew up in Muleshoe, Texas, got a BA in English and theatre from Texas Tech University and snagged a job as a newspaper reporter. She didn't know a thing about journalism, but her editor said if she could write he could teach her the rest of it and if she couldn't write the rest of it didn't matter. She hung in there for a 25-year career as a journalist. As soon as she figured out that making up the facts was a whole lot more fun than reporting them, she turned to fiction and never looked back.

Ninie now writes suspense--every flavor except pistachio: psychological suspense, inspirational suspense, suspense thrillers, paranormal suspense, suspense mysteries.

In every book she keeps this promise to her Loyal Reader: "I will tell you a story in a distinctive voice you'll always recognize, about people as ordinary as you are--people who have been slammed by something they didn't sign on for, and now they must fight for their lives. Then smack in the middle of their everyday worlds, those people encounter the unexplainable--and it's always the game-changer."

Also By Ninie Hammon

The Saved

The Unexplainable Collection

Five Days in May

Black Sunshine

The Based on True Stories Collection

Home Grown

Sudan

When Butterflies Cry

The Knowing Series

The Knowing

The Deceiving

The Reckoning

The Fault

Stand-alone Psychological Thrillers

The Memory Closet

The Last Safe Place